NEED YOU NOW

MIKA JOLIE

NEED YOU NOW
Copyright © 2014 Mika Jolie
Publisher
My Happy Chaos Publishing
www.mikajolie.com

Copyright © 2015 Mika Jolie

Cover design by Okay Creations

Edited by Theresa Stillwagon

Proofread by PK Designs

ALL RIGHTS RESERVED: This literary work may not be reproduced or transmitted in any form or by any means, including electronic or photographic reproduction, in whole or in part, without express written permission.

All characters and events in this book are fictitious. Any resemblance to actual persons living or dead is strictly coincidental.

PUBLISHER

My Happy Chaos Publishing

www.mikajolie.com

1

"Sex is the consolation you have when you can't have love."
Gabriel García Márquez

*A*t the age of twenty-eight there were things Lily should be immune to or come to expect, like colds and cheating boyfriends. Correction—cheating lovers. Really, she had no clear definition of what role Adam played in her life, and that was part of the problem. Of course, after she caught her fiancé sexting another woman, you'd think she'd be more guarded. Nope. Instead she went to Martha's Vineyard for a weekend. Hooked up with the sexy Italian, gave him the benefit of the doubt and agreed to their long distance, no strings attached, no dating or exchanging any bodily fluid with anyone else relationship.

Ha! Once again, she found herself to be the butt of the joke.

Lily fought back a sneeze, and the terrible need to close her heavy eyelids and drift into a sweet, mindless sleep. Except she already knew such sweet relief would be impossible to achieve for several reasons.

First reason, it appeared she'd managed to catch a cold in the middle of September—the wonderful month when summer said its final farewell to autumn, when one could start saying goodbye to the stifling heat, welcome the cool, crisp air of fall, and go for long jogs against the backdrop of colorful leaves.

Nope. Not her.

Instead, she spent most of the day cuddling with her new BFFs—a box of tissues and antibiotics. How she managed to get out of bed and wiggle her way into her sexy, come-get-me little black dress was still a mystery.

"We could have rescheduled," the strong, masculine voice said from across the table.

She flashed her date a smile and tried her best to show some interest, because the second reason for sleep deprivation was why she had agreed to this blind date. Adam Aquilani, the lethally gorgeous, unflappable Formula One racer. The reason behind her superhuman strength. She needed to forget him and say *arrivederci* to her lover for the past year.

"No, I'm okay. Just a little cold." In reality, she was b-o-r-e-d out of her brain and every muscle in her body ached. She needed her bed. She was angry at Adam. He needed to stop occupying all of her functioning brain cells. Just the knowledge that he possessed the ability to penetrate her thoughts during this hour was irritating.

She was done with him. Wasn't she?

Well, of course she was. She just needed to tell him. And she would do that first thing in the morning and interrupt his beauty sleep at wherever the hell he was at the moment. Morocco. No, Italy. He should be there now with his parents for a few days before flying back to Boston. Possibly jet-lagged. She smiled as she considered his displeasure when she'd interrupt his sleep.

Yes, the time difference suited her just fine, although she would have preferred to catch him while he was in Morocco for his race. After a year of sleeping with him, she knew his days never started before nine in the morning, North America, Eastern Time zone, regardless of the continent.

She would call and tell him to go to hell. That was sure to bruise his inflated ego. She'd bet her beloved 1997 SL320 convertible Benz that no female had ever given the great Adonis his walking papers. This would be a first.

A sudden, grating sound interrupted her thoughts as her phone chirped inside her tiny green purse on the table. She glanced at the thin watch around her wrist; probably one of her overly protective brothers checking up on her. She decided to ignore the call. Time to show some interest in…oh…what was his name again? *Shit!* She couldn't remember her date's name. She just knew it wasn't Adam. And thank goodness for that. What's-his-name was sexy in his own way—tall, dark, and handsome. As a matter of fact, he even resembled the dark, brooding Italian she was getting ready to dump.

Wait, could one dump a fuck buddy?

She needed to check the etiquette on that. But not now. She needed to focus and enjoy what's-his-name…Paul. There, she remembered.

She smiled in relief. Paul smiled back before ordering a bottle of wine. Okay, the wine would help.

"So, Paul, you must enjoy working with children." Small talk always lightened awkward situations.

Her date's handsome face frowned a little, only to be replaced quickly with a smile. "Of course, they're fun."

See, she could do it. Her phone chirped again.

"Should you check to make sure all is well?"

Lily dismissed the suggestion with a slight wave. "That's one of my overly protective brothers."

Paul's face knitted in agreement. "Oh…how many are there?"

"Three," she answered as casually as possible. No need to tell him her brothers had threatened to break the legs of her last boyfriend. Correction—ex-cheating scumbag fiancé.

Paul choked on his water and flagged the waiter. It was obvious the thought of three protective brothers scared the guy a little bit. Lily didn't blame him. She wondered how Adam would react to her brothers. He'd most likely go toe-to-toe with them.

Did he even know she had siblings? She searched her mind and tried to remember if they ever talked about anything other than what are you wearing? Another round? Let's fuck.

Nope. Nothing.

She leaned forward and tried her best to appear more inviting. "They can be a bit much, but nice guys."

"I'm sure," Paul replied, his voice, deceptively calm.

"Tell me all about your life as a pediatrician," she quickly suggested, hoping to shift gears and focus back on handsome doctor Paul. Her friend responsible for this set up had told her he was reliable and a one-woman-at-a-time type of guy. Not the type who would be caught on camera kissing scantily-clad women with fake, perky breasts after a victory race.

"Actually, I'm a chiropractor," Paul corrected.

Oh. Damn. Her mistake. Embarrassed, she fanned her warm cheeks. "I'm so sorry." She made a mental note to get all the facts straight next time she agreed to a blind date.

Her phone beeped again. Damn it! It wasn't like her brothers to bother her that much…unless something was actually wrong. "I'm sorry, but I need to check my messages. Something may be wrong." She offered the apology while reaching for her phone.

The text read—

Liliana

Her heart hitched. Oh Lord, only one man ever called her by her full name.

The second text read—

Where are you?
I've been trying to reach you for two days.

Her breath caught. She'd been ignoring his calls and text messages the last two days. She needed to focus and figure out how to dump his ass. Even the fact that her best friend, Minka, had defended him and advised her to give him a chance to explain had set her off. She couldn't blame her friend, though. Her mind was clouded and she was high on love. In about eight weeks, Minka was going to marry one of

Adam's best friends. Except Jason had been a model fiancé and never felt the need to kiss any other but his lovely soon-to-be wife. She couldn't say that about Adam Aquilani.

I'm imagining you naked in my bed.

Oh, God. The room became sweltering hot. She sat in the broiling heat Adam generated even miles away.

I'm horny and I want to make you come.
Phone sex?

Her breath rose to her chest and that little spot between her thighs throbbed with need. She didn't need to read further. She knew the messages would get more explicit. That was Adam's way and somehow he'd managed to entangle her in his dirty little games, including phone sex.

As if the metallic device burned her skin, she dropped the phone in her purse and turned her attention to Paul.

"Is everything okay?" he asked, his eyes on her.

"Ummm, yes. Sorry about that."

"You look flushed."

Flushed was an understatement. More like completely turned on and would jump Adam if he were the one sitting across from her. Except it was good old pop-your-back Paul. And thank God for that.

"I'm okay." But her voice came out a little shaky, rough.

Paul continued to stare at her, confusion evident. Lily flashed him a perky smile, leaned toward him and tried to appear interested.

Her date smiled pleasantly as he reached for her hands. "Lily, there's someone else." It was more a statement than a question, his voice calm with no hint of anger.

Damn you, Adam!

Stricken with guilt, she pulled her gaze from his. It was one thing to want revenge on her lover, but it was another to bring an innocent party into her mess. "Yes," she confirmed in a soft whisper. It made her angry that someone could have such a hold on her even miles away. Hell, right now he was on another continent altogether. "No...I mean, kind of, but not really." Damn it, she was rambling. Lily let out a frustrated sigh and looked into Paul's friendly eyes. "He's not a boyfriend."

Paul chuckled, probably over how ridiculous she sounded. He released her hand and leaned back in his chair. "Well, whatever he is, he's pretty persistent. Is he going to show up here?" he asked with genuine concern.

"Oh, God no. He's in Italy."

Paul brows went up. "You're dating a man who lives in Italy? That's almost an impossible relationship unless he's some globe-hopping superstar."

She almost laughed in agreement but instead said, "We're not dating."

Her date nodded, seeming to finally understand the status of her relationship. "How about we continue to enjoy dinner with no expectations? Maybe I can even convince you to drop him and go for something steadier and closer to home. You don't seem like the casual type."

Paul was right on one thing, she'd never done the casual thing until she threw caution to the wind and threw herself at Adam. As for convincing her to go for something steadier and closer to home, she doubted that very much but decided to continue their date anyway. Although the more she tried to brush Adam out of her mind, the more he penetrated.

Stubborn was his middle name.

---

*L*ily stepped out of the elevator while fumbling in her purse for the keys to her apartment. Once she and Paul managed to get the whole Adam thing out of the way, they had a good time. Oh, the chemistry was zilch, zero, all because of the man she'd been casually sleeping with the past year.

A whole freaking year of great, mindless sex, wherever and whenever. A low groan escaped her throat as she opened the apartment door.

As soon as Lily stepped inside her condo she knew she had company, and it wasn't one of her brothers. She didn't need to see him to know who it was either. His presence filled her condo. The smell of nature, similar to the wilderness–rugged, undiscovered, and comforting even in silence only belonged to one man.

Her body tingled, betraying her. *Traitor.* It was definitely time for a tête-à-tête with her body. It should not be so weak while in a state of indignation.

Since her lover was obviously inside, Lily did what any sane woman who was about to dump someone would do. She slowly removed her jacket and escaped into the powder room to ensure she looked like she was coming back from an awesome date. She reapplied the red lipstick and tousled her dark brown pixie hair to give it the appearance that someone's fingers had already been there, and then pulled the little strapless black dress an inch or two above her thighs.

Well, her eyes were on the puffy side. And she looked a little dazed from her cold, but those attributes could work to her advantage.

There, Mr. Italian-sex-god.

She found him on her sofa. All six foot plus of perfect lean muscles fast asleep. She didn't approach him. Not out of concern of waking him up. Nope. She learned long ago, one should not seek out a predator. He could and would eat her alive. Instead, she stood a few inches away, mesmerized. Even asleep, the man managed to look sexy as hell.

She scanned the body she'd become familiar with. He appeared as if he threw whatever was within reach on, and oh my, how beautiful he looked in casual attire. His jeans sat low on his lean hips, the Captain America cotton V-neck tee stretched across his broad shoulders and his rock-hard abs. She knew that because she'd kissed every part of him on many occasions.

A smile tugged the corner of her lips. Such a conundrum he was. Born American, raised in Italy, and now splitting his time between the two countries. A man without a home, who belonged everywhere and nowhere.

She took in his large frame. He was too big for her sofa; his worn New Balance hung over the armrest. He'd gotten a haircut since she last saw him. Although now shorter, his jet-black hair was still unruly with strands wildly tousled in his face. Lily fought the urge to reach out, brush the curls aside and touch the scar on his left eyebrow. For a fleeting moment she wondered how he got it.

Lily quickly dismissed the desire to know everything about the man on her sofa and continued to survey him. His jaw was firm and strong, even in sleep stood with pride. His arrogant masculine nose was slightly crooked, like it had been broken and left to its imperfections. His lips full, well-defined and inviting; even in a relaxed state they looked sinfully delicious. She fought the need to surrender to her desires and suck on his lower lip.

Memories of the many times they brought her to ecstasy flashed in her mind. Even the thin crease on the corners of his mouth, not from age but of laughter, was downright sexy. Every piece of him was molded to perfection, a thing of beauty and he knew it.

Oh, God. She should not be thinking about ecstasy or how perfectly sculpted he was. She needed to dump him, not jump him. Lily blew out a breath and started to walk past him into the living room to make her way down the hall to her bedroom. She could dump his ass in the morning. She paused inches away from him and stole one last glance, noticing for the first time the fatigue on his face.

Well, what did you expect, Lily? The man looked like he'd flown straight from Morocco when he was supposed to be in Italy relaxing.

Why would he do that?

"Because you refused to answer your phone," he muttered, his eyes still closed as he reached and caught her arm. "I never made it to Italy."

His voice and the realization she'd spoken out loud startled her. Oh, well, at least she didn't voice all the crazy thoughts of what she'd like to do to his body. "You didn't go see your parents?"

Eyes still closed, he shook his head. "I came straight here."

This meant he'd been in her condo during those text messages.

Puzzled, she stared at his handsome face. The question she wanted to ask but didn't dare. Why?

"It's late," he continued in a calm but steely voice, eyes still closed. "Where were you? Although I have a feeling I already know. You're all dressed up."

"How do you know that? Your eyes are closed."

He chuckled, that cocky, confident chuckle that used to irritate her when they first met. No, she corrected. It still irritated the hell out of her.

"How long have we been together now? A little over a year."

So he was keeping track. A year, three months and two weeks, but who was counting? "We are not together."

He smiled that sweet, sexy smile that always made her want to devour him. Tonight was no exception.

"You were checking me out," he continued, his voice filled with humor, though Lily also traced fatigue underneath.

She stared at him. Long, thick eyelashes no man should have swept over his hard and handsome face. "I wasn't," she lied. "You look tired, so I was concerned." Naturally she cared, even if they were fuck-buddies.

Eyes the color of the earth—rich and fertile—opened, captured her gaze, and held. Lily loved his eyes. They were expressive and changed based on the time of day. At sunset, they'd have golden flecks in them which would fade as night settled in. They had the power to captivate her, hold her hostage.

She always found herself gazing into them a little longer than she probably should. They held warmth and knowledge in them. Secrets as well. Secrets that sparked her curiosity but never felt close enough to him to ask. Even after a year of sleeping together, they were still strangers.

"So you actually care," he teased, bringing her back to the reality of the state of their relationship. They didn't do feelings, sentiments or any of that mushy stuff. No, those were for Keely and Blake and now Minka and Jason.

Still holding her hand, he came to his feet and circled his arms around her waist. His lips touched the corner of hers. The same lips that had been kissing another woman only forty-eight hours ago. Peeved, she brought her free hand against his muscular chest and pushed out of his grip.

"What are you doing here?"

He raised an eyebrow. "I missed you."

"You flew from Morocco to see me. I didn't realize I was that good." She walked past him into her small kitchen to turn on the stove and retrieved a tea kettle. She needed a hot toddy, tea with a nice shot of whiskey to take care of this darn cold.

Of course he followed, every piece of her sensed his presence in the tight space of her kitchen. God, he radiated sex. Pure, unadulterated, raw, wonderful sex. And good-looking, she reminded herself. Too freaking good-looking for his own good. Good looks and sex appeal were a lethal combination. Her body went damp, responding to his closeness.

She went about setting the kettle in an attempt to show his presence didn't affect her. That was a complete lie, of course. She felt his gaze warm on her back as he leaned against her bench top inspecting her every move, her black fitted dress and her four-inch heels elongating her legs. She glanced at him as she walked over the pantry to retrieve the raw honey. His lips twisted into a snarl; obviously the realization she'd been out on a date had settled.

"What happened to our not sleeping with anyone else rule?" His voice was controlled and tight. She knew him well enough to know he was livid.

Good. That makes two of us.

"I was on a date, Adam. That doesn't necessarily mean I was screwing someone's brains out." She crossed her arms over her chest and smiled at him. "Something you wouldn't be familiar with."

"We had an agreement."

Lily squared her shoulders and forced herself to face what she was trying to postpone until the morning. No time like the present, her mother always said. And the images of Adam lip-locking with that woman still seared anger through her. She reached for her phone on the counter, flipped through her pictures until she landed on a particular one and tossed it across the room at him. He caught the device just as it hit his chest.

"Our agreement is now void." Take that. Two can play this game.

She watched his eyes focus on the picture, the one of him kissing that floozy. His brows creased and then the unexpected happened. He smiled.

He actually smiled and looked amused. Why was he smiling? Feeling her anger rising, Lily glared at him, but he seemed unfazed and took three easy steps to close the gap between them. She cursed her kitchen for being so small. Her only reaction was to take a step back, away from him and ended pinned against the wall. Literally.

"You stayed up and watched my race." A smug smile tugged the corners of his mouth, satisfaction radiating off of him. As much as she hated his profession, she actually watched him win the last Formula One. He was missing the point.

"I couldn't sleep."

He grinned. "You're lying."

So what? Everyone who knew her could detect when she was lying. "Whatever."

One long, tanned finger stroked her bottom lip. "She kissed me," he explained. His voice low and husky. "The camera chose not to show the part where I broke it off. Do you know why I did that?"

She knew. They had an agreement. Nonetheless, she waited, wanting to hear it once more.

"Because of you. Because of us." His lips were dangerously close to hers now. "I only want to kiss you, touch you, fuck you."

"There is no us," she managed to argue, but even in her own ears, the argument lacked strength and conviction.

2

"In a perfect world, you could fuck people without giving them a piece of your heart. And every glittering kiss and every touch of flesh is another shard of heart you'll never see again."
Neil Gaiman

"*A*m I forgiven?" he whispered.

Oh, so close, she could easily slip her tongue into that delicious mouth of his and take over.

No. At least that's what common sense told her to say. Instead her lips parted for him, wanting and need to feel his mouth on hers. But she held back, savoring the sweet torture. "I don't want to forgive you."

His eyes gleamed with amusement. "We can't kiss until you do. It's important to me that you believe I would never break a promise." The beguilement was now replaced by an intense look of determination. The heat of his breath caressed her face, making her shiver with need.

She closed her eyes and blocked the seriousness in his. Not too long ago, similar words were spoken and broken by another man. Only the funny thing was, she believed Adam. He'd kept their promise for the last year. Sex and fun, but only with each other. At least, until the kiss. With his lips so close she couldn't think straight.

"Liliana?"

The sound of her name in that seductive accent slid over her and pooled in her belly. Did he really need to say her name? That was pure sexual torture. No man should have the power to make a woman's name sound so sensuous.

"I'm thinking."

His finger trailed along her cheek to her jaw then her bottom lip.

"You're not playing fair," she breathed softly.

He threaded his fingers through her hair, yanked her head back and skimmed his lips over her neck, almost but not quite kissing her. "I never intended to play fair. So say you believe me."

She did. But something else nagged her. Fear that she might be a bit too inexperienced for the game they were playing. Fear, sooner or later her heart would be affected and want more.

Liar. You already want more, the little voice inside her taunted.

Lily quickly shut it down. Wanting Adam was one thing, allowing her heart to get involved was another matter. Her goal had always been to keep a firm grip on her emotions, live on the wild side a bit and be reckless. But somewhere along the way, her heart had gone bonkers and changed direction. The nonchalant, unconcerned was all an illusion.

The truth was she cared. More than she'd like to admit.

Even after the disaster of her engagement, she still believed in the HEA–Happily Ever After. Just not with Adam. Behind that calm, cool demeanor, lay a force she'd only seen during moments of passion, but she guessed it ran deeper than he'd allowed her to see.

A *bête noire*, that was Adam. Too dark, too intense, and too impulsive. A part of her feared him, fear of being consumed by him, driven over and flattened to nothing, burned to a crisp by his intensity. Nope, she wanted none of that. The last thing she wanted to do was lose herself in loving him.

"I believe you, Adam."

He tilted her chin. "But there's more. Tell me what's bothering you."

The fact they expected nothing from each other helped and made it easier for Lily to voice any concern. Finally she opened her eyes. "When will we know this is too much?"

Rich cocoa eyes penetrated hers, giving her once again a glimpse of his spirit. Lily swallowed hard.

"Do you want to end us, Lily?"

Yes. No. Her stomach filled with angst.

"Just say the word and I'll walk away." His voice was curt with no hint of being affected by the possibility of their end.

Could it really be that easy? "Just like that?"

With his body still pressing against hers, he nodded. "If that's what you want."

Something buzzed insistently against her. Adam stepped an inch or two away, reached in the pocket of his jeans and pulled out his phone. His shoulders tensed up a bit as he frowned at the screen.

"No fucking interview," he growled, ended the call and dropped the phone on the counter.

"Another woman?" she asked, arms crossed over her chest.

"No other woman, Liliana. Just you, for as long as you want. I gave you my word." He walked over to the stove and poured the hot water into the cup with the tea bag. Then he opened her refrigerator to retrieve a piece of ginger and a lemon. Lily watched him move with ease and familiarity around her kitchen. He knew where everything was located.

She recalled the nervous feeling the first time he came to visit. Even after the half pitcher of sangria Minka had poured down her throat, her heart had been racing. And now here he was standing in her kitchen like he belonged. The fact that her condo was not even half the size of his house in Chilmark, or that their relationship was nonexistent didn't stop him from settling right in.

He brought out the cutting board to slice the ginger and split the Meyer lemon. Then he squeezed the juice into her tea, and stirred the pieces of the seed-bearing plant in the cup as well. He walked over to the other side of her kitchen to the liquor cabinet and poured a shot of whiskey into the cup and finished it with a tablespoon of raw honey.

"There," he said with a smile as he handed her the cup. "A hot toddy. This will knock you out for the night."

She took a sip of the warm liquid. Hot and sumptuous, with delectable undertones of sweet vanilla that awoke her slumbering palate and filled her with comfort. "Thank you."

He didn't move. Instead, his large body leaned against the counter as he continued to watch her. And the more he did so, the more she wanted to spread her legs and welcome him home. Especially since the last time they were together was a month ago.

Home. Ha! Not in a million years. Get over the romantics, Lily. She couldn't even fault Adam for that. He'd always been straightforward about their relationship—a physical commitment with no emotional attachment. *Sex with me only because I'm the alpha male. I rock your world, and I promise I will only have sex with you too* kind of commitment. Nothing serious. He never made promises or led her to believe they could be more.

Lily brushed away the thoughts. No thinking about possibilities. That was a definite no-no.

For four hundred and sixty-nine days. A year, three months and two weeks she'd been fine with their "committed but no chance for happily ever after" status. Lord knew it was exactly what she needed after her failed engagement. A relationship where the only thing she could count on was Adam's physical fidelity. Anything else would be too complicated and at this point in her life, complication was a major no-no. Except for that nagging void creeping up lately. Again, she dismissed it.

The question echoed in her head. What was she thinking?

Sex with no strings attached rarely resulted in uncomplicated. More like a complete disaster. Especially when feelings were starting to crawl their way in, never mind she was never really good at the just sex thing.

She blamed it all on her heart.

Treacherous heart.

"Should I call for a car to pick me up?" His voice interrupted her thoughts.

If she said yes he would not fight her, this much she knew. He'd walk out of her life the same way he entered. Totally unexpected, and it would leave her broken because as scared as she was of what ifs, she wasn't ready to say goodbye.

"You look tired." She gave him a coy smile. "You should at least stay the night."

He arched a brow. "Is that your excuse for me to spend the night?"

"I have a cold. I could use another hot toddy later." She took another sip of the drink Adam had introduced her to over the winter. A drink she'd come to associate with him. It even tasted like him, delicious and intoxicating.

Adam smiled. He walked over and erased the distance between them. "I see that." He brushed her bangs away from her face. "I'm still going to fuck you."

He better. "You might get sick."

His wide hands cupped her face. "Have I ever told you I like to live on the edge?"

Yes, as a matter of fact he'd established that right away. His thirst for natural rushes usually involved snowboarding, surfing, plane gliding and, let's not forget, the need for speed.

"Once or twice."

"Besides." Strong arms circled her waist and held her against him. "I don't get sick...ever."

Somehow she believed that.

"But if I were to get sick, I can't think of a more beautiful woman to get sick with," he continued with that sexy smile of his.

Adam had a way of making her feel as if she was the most beautiful woman in the world. One day she might start to believe him.

"You're worth me getting sick, Liliana. I need to lose myself inside you."

His hard-muscled body rubbed against hers. Desire flared and Lily convinced herself it was just physical. Never mind her head was spinning and she wanted him more than her next breath.

"Kiss me," she begged, her voice deep and husky.

Adam obeyed and their lips touched. A gentle touch filled with the promise of what she knew would follow.

"You're beautiful," he said low, lips inches away.

Her cheeks scorched, burning her skin. Her ex used to call her cute and pretty at times, but never beautiful. The past year, the word had become synonymous with her. Adam made her feel beautiful.

Too overwhelmed to use words, Lily circled her arms around his neck, drawing him back to the warmth of her lips.

In the year since they'd begun her desire for him had only intensified. Every time he touched her, she yearned for more. His tongue slipped inside her mouth to explore. The sound of his moan filled her head as he nipped her lower lip. She gladly went along for the ride.

"I want you naked," she said, fingers impatiently tugging on his T-shirt.

"Good, because I want to rip this dress off your body. We should burn it."

Her brows went up. She already knew the reason for his words. Adam took. Adam possessed. In some ways, she belonged to him. "You're not jealous because I wore it on a —"

His lips crushed hers. "Where's the fucking zipper?" he murmured.

She caught his hand and guided him to the side of the dress where the zipper was strategically hidden. With one quick motion, the dress fell off her body to the floor, leaving her standing in the middle of the kitchen in a pair of four-inch heels and a silk black bra with matching thong. Adam stepped back; his eyes swept over her body. The expression on his face shifted to one she recognized as hungry. Since shyness was not a trait she could ever claim, she allowed him to take in her nearly-naked body.

"Jesus, you wore that for your date," he said, his voice riled up, his displeasure obvious.

She took mental note of Adam's jealousy. She affected him. The realization caused one of those secret tingles only Adam had been able to garner. "No, I wore this," she emphasized, "because I love wearing sexy underwear and you know that."

His expression softened a bit at the reminder. "I think I need to buy you some grandma underwear," he joked, although Lily could tell by the way his eyes were shadowed, he was giving the thought of her in some unappealing underwear serious consideration.

Lily batted her eyelashes. "But you like my panties."

"Yes, but only for me."

Possessive. She liked it. Far too much, even if it wasn't due to emotions, but more like a kid not wanting to share his favorite toy kind of way. "I'm not getting naked for anyone else, Adam. I was just mad."

He nodded, then ran his wide hands over her bare shoulders before lowering his lips to kiss her skin. "Next time just talk to me," he suggested. His lips touched her skin again, this time a little further down past her collarbone. "A text, a call," he continued, "You have the international plan on your phone now."

The international plan she'd upgraded to just for him. Lily raised her head to give him easier access to her neck. Like a vampire his teeth found the little pulse throbbing under her skin, dug into it and sucked. The touch of his lips against her skin ran through her like wildfire. "Feels good," she said on a moan.

"Now we have to donate that nice dress," he continued. "Such a shame." His tongue trailed sweet, torturous circles along her neck to the back of her ear.

Had she been clearheaded, she would have argued about getting rid of the dress. Instead, a mess of aroused confusion ran through her mind but never found her lips. She was too high on Adam to care. She nodded in agreement. Her eyes dazed, no longer from the antibiotics or the cold, but as a result of Adam's mouth on her.

She wasn't sure when he unsnapped her bra. Lily only realized she was standing topless when he lowered his head, ran his tongue over her nipple like a hungry predator, then sucked it into his mouth.

"Perfect," he whispered. Her firm breast fit perfectly in his hands, his mouth among others things. "Absolutely beautiful baby, I love your breasts." Adam knew she thought they were too small, but to him they were perfect, capped with smooth honey areolas that surrounded the round shape.

A man of his word, he teased her right breast with his tongue then gently pulled the tip between his teeth while his free hand cupped and stroked the other. He couldn't get enough of her, jet-lagged and all. He wanted Lily. Never mind if she hadn't come home, he'd still be sleeping on the couch. Adam promised his body he'd give it a rest starting tomorrow during his flight back to Martha's Vineyard. Two days of doing barely nothing would be enough for his body to return to its normal biological rhythms after high-speed air travel through several time zones. Right now, he needed to take Lily and do sweet, wonderful things to that body of hers.

He scooped her willowy form up in his arms and placed her barely-covered bottom on the granite counter. Adam smiled as her lust-filled sugar brown eyes focused on him. She had that "come on Adam, right here" look on her face.

Oh, yes, sweetheart, right here in your kitchen because I don't have the patience to make it to your bedroom. They'd go at it again later. And if they were lucky, they'd be in bed.

Adam slipped between her legs. His fingers tingled as they skimmed over her soft, golden skin. She let out a throaty sound at his touch. Loving the familiar sensation that shot through him, he made himself at home. That was the problem lately. Every time they were together, he found himself thinking this was the only place he wanted to be. He attributed his thinking to the fact he'd never spent a year sleeping with the same woman. He was just getting comfortable. A year, three months and two weeks, he mused, but who was counting?

"Cold?" he asked, knowing the coolness of the marble counter would chill her cute, tight bottom.

She smiled at him. "Warm me up."

Her voice shot straight to his groin, causing his pulse to kick up. He took a deep breath trying to keep some of his blood in his head. Slow. Wanting to slow things down, he ran his hands over her thighs. She shivered, gooseflesh rippling her soft skin.

"Take me now, Adam."

"Patience," he drawled, not wanting to rush. While the desire to connect was fierce, he felt no need to speed up the process. He did a quick calculation of the last time they were together. Two weeks too long. He needed to prolong the pleasure and satisfy both of them in slow, torturous detail. Lowering his head, his lips brushed against her shoulder, and caught a whiff of light, fruity floral with notes of blackberry. "No more dating other men." Just the thought of her out eating, drinking with another man drove him mad. He kissed the nape of her neck, her jaw, the corner of her mouth.

Her lips parted for him, inviting him in. As much as he wanted to, Adam paused and waited, his mouth inches away from hers. Had it been any other woman throwing shit at him, he'd be pissed and end whatever agreement they had. But with Lily, it was important she trust him, come to him for answers, and not look for reasons to run.

Lust-filled eyes locked on his, the passion she never held back from him burning through them. Still, he waited. "Liliana, you need to trust me. I gave you my word."

"I trust you," she breathed.

His lips crushed down on hers, taking full possession. Her fingers were quick on his T-shirt. Adam drew back long enough for them to get the barrier over his head, dropped it mindlessly on the floor and went back to the frantic kissing. When her fingers fumbled over the buckle of his belt, Adam broke away for air once more.

"Your jeans are still on. They should be off," she huffed between hard, heavy breaths.

"In a little bit," he answered. He ran his thumb over the silk thong. "I don't like the fact you wore this tonight for another man." He didn't care he was showing jealousy or even downright claiming her as his.

In a way she was, wasn't she?

She opened her mouth to probably remind him once again she always wore pretty panties but he silenced her with a blistering kiss. "Tilt up a little," he instructed against her lips as his fingers caught the sides of the silky material. She did as he requested and slowly he dragged them down. "I love your body."

3

"Sex without love is a meaningless experience."
Woody Allen

*A*dam could look at Lily all day and never grow tired of it. Her eyebrows slanted sharply downward, creating a mischievous look that always lured him to her big, luminous brown eyes. There was something about her eyes—a flicker of fire, an almost honey color, shimmering beneath their rich mahogany tones. They shined and danced like moonlit waves when riled up, but focused when she needed to be. Right now they burned with sexual tension, screaming take me if you dare.

Typically he wasn't into women with short hair, but the no-fuss, hassle-free pixie cut suited the naked woman staring at him. He reached out and tucked a strand of dark brown hair behind her ear. Her full lips parted slightly at this touch.

Everything about her from day one had been uninhibited, candid with a no-holds-barred attitude. From the moment he'd asked why she still carried the engagement ring from her cheating fiancé, she went toe to toe with him and never backed down, her passion unbridled since the first time they slept together. At that time she'd been emotionally bruised and he tried his best to put aside how much he wanted her, to do the right thing. Then she reached out and kissed him. He hadn't stood a chance.

That night on the beach, with the moonlight flickering against the ocean, their bodies sought each other and she'd given him her all. A year later, he still couldn't get enough. The realization left him befuddled and often scratching his head, searching for an explanation. Earlier he told her he'd walk away if she wanted.

He'd lied.

His chest had tightened over the possibility and that left him conflicted. They were purely physical, which suited him fine. Easy and carefree with lots of uninhibited sex, that's how he liked a relationship. Their connection had been fierce, primal from the beginning, and their desire to ravage each other had only heightened over the course of the year.

That explained his nervous reaction earlier. Had to. Only an idiot would walk away from mind-blowing sex with a beautiful woman. Especially one he didn't have to use a condom with. First time ever in his life he'd done that. Since they had the "talk," which both stressed wasn't a commitment but out of respect. After that less than a minute conversation, she'd gotten on the pill. He loved the skin-on-skin connection.

Nope, one could search high and low and would never find his picture next to the word *idiot*. Brushing his thoughts aside, Adam smoothed the bangs away from her eyes, leaving her features unprotected and bare. Lips parted, skin flushed, she continued to look straight at him, daring him to take possession of her.

Bordeaux fingernails ran over the Maori tattoo on his shoulder to his upper bicep, down to the crook of his arm. A lingering touch that left him breathless. His muscles tensed, and a soft laugh generated from her throat. Physically, she owned him.

"Be more specific," she urged.

"About?"

"My body. What do you love exactly?" she asked huskily.

He loved her confidence. It matched his arrogance and leveled them. His gaze dropped to her lips. He loved her mouth. The fullness of them, especially when they were wrapped around his…

"How about I show you?" He claimed her lips, his tongue made wet trails over her soft mouth until she allowed him entry. Adam groaned, letting himself get lost in her with wild, fast abandon. She clutched his neck and met him with equal fervor. Reckless and soft at the same time, sending fireworks through his mind and shivers down his spine.

"You drive me crazy, Liliana," he whispered against her lips. He stroked her cheek. "You're so fucking beautiful." He kissed her once more even hungrier this time, out of desperation to quench the longing blazing inside of him for all the things he lusted after.

"Now, take me now." She pressed her chest against his.

A rush of heat shot through him. Adam groaned, he wanted more of her. His mouth moved to her throat, down to her collar. "Not yet." He slid a hand between her legs and groaned at the slick, wet heat between her thighs. Adam lowered his head to her sun-kissed legs and grazed his lips against one of her thighs, her waist, and her stomach. His fingers followed where his mouth had roamed many instances before and slipped between her thighs. "So wet and ready for me."

Done with the teasing, Lily squirmed a little closer. Slowly she ran her hands over his crotch. A rough sound escaped Adam's throat and every nerve ending in her body tingled with excitement. She wanted Adam. She needed him naked, couldn't wait to wrap her legs around his waist and let him fill her with his steely length. Greedy fingers trailed from his crotch and dipped inside the waist of his jeans. He chuckled and removed her hands, an indication he intended to take his time, to punish her for going on a date with what's-his-name.

"Adam," she cried out, wanting to feel him deep inside her.

He cupped her butt and pulled her to the edge of the counter, then dropped to his knees. His mouth kissed one inner thigh and the other before finding her core. Her immediate reaction was to reach for his head and hold him hostage as her greedy body demanded. But a deeper part of her, the woman within, wanted every single inch of him deep inside.

"Adam, later," she murmured, knowing they would seek each other again during the night.

Her words once again fell on deaf ears. His tongue stroked and teased her. As the pleasure assaulted her, Lily moaned from the delicious torture. Desperate to feel his heat, she lowered her gaze to the man who was making her feel so good and begged, "Now…please, inside me."

"Say my name again." His breath burned hot against her flesh as he inserted one finger slowly inside her, then another.

"Adam," she cried out, out of her mind and unable to take the teasing any longer. "I–I," she stammered. His mouth was hot and slick against her. Pushed to the edge, past all her limits she voiced words she never said to anyone, words she hadn't even acknowledged. "Need you now."

His tongue laved over her, pushing her over the tip. Weak from the explosion, her legs trembled. He placed steady hands on her thighs, as if he was trying to calm her. It didn't work. She wanted more. After a few passing seconds, she caught her breath, through hooded lids she looked on as he came to his feet, stripped out of his jeans and boxer briefs and stood before her, absolutely gorgeous and rock-hard.

Large hands slid under her butt to elevate her body and give him easier access. "Hold on to the edge of the counter. Wrap your legs around me," he commanded, voice rough with need.

Desperate to get him inside her, she'd do whatever he wanted to get there she followed his instruction to the T and drew him closer. He adjusted his frame between her legs, his free hand slid on her thigh, angling her hips properly to him.

"You're all mine, Lily," he growled in her ear. "Every inch of you belongs to me."

Then he was inside her, thrusting deep and hard, almost punishing. Her body pulsated with desire. She placed her hands against his flexed chest, bracing herself for the onslaught. She wanted more of his retribution. More of Adam. Her legs wrapped tighter around his waist and she rocked into him, matching his rhythm.

Skin against skin, lips seeking each other, they moved together. Oh, the ecstasy. As always, nothing could compare to their union. Chills shot up her spine, and she cried out his name. Her sounds of pleasure reverberated in the kitchen as she rode out the waves of pleasure.

"*Merda*," he swore in Italian before his head crashed on her shoulder.

She clung to him while their bodies spasmed in a savage fit until the final shudders faded. For a beat neither moved, their breathing equally ragged. He raised his head and brushed loose hair away from her face then placed one more kiss on her lips.

"Tired?" she asked with concern, not forgetting he was operating on little rest.

He smiled. "Jetlagged."

A few strings pulled in her heart. He flew from Morocco straight to her house because she hadn't answered his calls. He didn't utter the L word. It wasn't necessary. He cared and that was enough. She just had to remind herself to keep her feelings in check.

She slipped off the counter, lowering to her feet. "Let's go to bed."

With their fingers linked together, they walked down the hall to her bedroom leaving the clothes scattered on the floor of her kitchen along with all her reasons for breaking things off with Adam.

4

"Love is all fun and games until someone loses an eye or gets pregnant."
Jim Cole

Five weeks later, fatigued, anxious and terrified, Lily opened the brand new box—the tenth one—and hoped this would be the one to snap her out of this weird dream sequence. She sucked in a deep breath, exhaled and headed to the connected bathroom.

Even though she'd been thorough with the others, for precision, she cautiously read the instructions, never mind the step-by-step guide didn't vary much from the previous nine. At this point, she could recite each word with her eyes closed.

The first three steps were qualifiers, meant to educate the user on the variances between manufacturers. The length of time one needed to pee on the stick, the symbols used to indicate a positive or negative result, all the scientific information she needed to decide whether to invest in Gap maternity dresses or purchasing that fitted halter top she'd been eying from Anthropologie.

Step four tensed her stomach, even on the tenth one. Bold, chilling letters stared at her— *Prepare Yourself. Taking a home pregnancy test could be a nerve-wracking experience.*

No shit, Sherlock.

Ready to go, she chugged another glass of water, squared her shoulders and moved to the next act, the urine sample. After nine tests, she already knew what came next. She had to wait for the stated amount of time for the result. In this case, a whole three minutes, this meant eternity in pregnant or not-pregnant land. Anxiety curled in her stomach. Nerves tingling, Lily lowered her weight down to her knees and leaned against the wall for comfort.

She placed her phone on the floor, set the timer, and waited. The silver antique clock usually found on her nightstand now stood on the cream-colored tile floor, staring at her. Her gaze bounced between the two devices.

Tick. Tock.

The seconds faded away, determining her fate. Arms clutched to her chest, she had no choice but to abide by the rules of Father Time.

As she waited, Lily said a silent prayer to St. Jude, her mother's favorite saint, the patron saint of the hopeless and the desperate, the saint for those who felt trapped in lost causes.

She met all the required criteria.

While at it, she promised never to make another wiseass comment about how ridiculous periods were. Never again would she joke about being punished once a month for not being pregnant. Besides, a woman's monthly cycle was designed to rid the body of toxins. Technically, it was good. Now the stick just had to declare her not preggo and all would be well again.

Her phone vibrated and Minka's name appeared.

Hey, you're MIA. Call me.

Lily smiled sadly at the text. MIA was a strong word but fitting. The last two days, she'd avoided her family, Minka included. She was family; not all family was connected by blood. Hiding wasn't a trait she was fond of, but at times necessary, especially when life threw her a curveball so traumatic she couldn't even call her best friend of ten years.

They'd met in college and worked together until last year at an upscale private school in Princeton. Although Minka had moved to Martha's Vineyard they still talked on a daily basis. Minka was her confidant, her other half, the sister she'd always wanted.

When "What's his name" had ditched her, Minka had been the first to know. Even with about five hundred miles between them, they still managed to talk as frequently as possible, whether by a quick text or a long conversation. No, the distance had not weakened their friendship. As close of a relationship she had with her brothers and parents, Minka was her confidant, the sister she always wanted.

So why wasn't she confiding now?

Because if she told Minka, that meant what she'd been feared—the positive she'd been denying on every tossed aside e.p.t. would suddenly become very, scarily real. She couldn't be that girl. The one with the accidental pregnancy whose life went to the shitter. She was strong. Capable. Together. Shit like this only happened to other people.

She glanced at the screen. Still deciding.

And let's say hypothetically she did turn out pregnant. Never mind what the other tests have already proven she was as pregnant as pregnant came, but those had been indicators, two little plus signs. Hell, a little tilt of the stick to the left or the right might have caused a tainted result, which was why she bought and tried one last thing. This time the word pregnant would appear on the screen. No signs. Those were not reliable, at least not to her. In either case, she'd unload her troubles on her friend. But it'd have to be face to face. Some things were better delivered that way. Also, Minka wouldn't judge. That she was sure of.

Now her parents and brothers—yeah, nausea filled her just at the thought. She could see the disappointment in their eyes. Her family was tight, stable, but with all the love and warmth came expectations. She'd done a good job meeting all of them until now.

Graduate high school. Checked.

Go to college. Checked.

Do something you love. Checked.

Fall in love. Checked. Unchecked. Now in denial mode. But there wasn't a box for denial. Get married then have babies. Yeah, that's where she failed.

In two days she would be on the quaint island of Martha's Vineyard for her best friend's wedding, scheduled to take place in two weeks. A smile settled on Lily's lips, the gang was going to reunite once again. To think only a year ago she'd been introduced to Claire, Forrest, Jason, and Adam. She made a mental note to call Minka or the very least send her a text.

Later.

She still had the dreaded stick to deal with at the moment. Make that ten dreaded sticks.

She glanced at the stick. A blank window stared back at her. Lily did a quick time check. Not even a minute had passed. Time had a funny way of slowing down and moving at its own pace during urgency. Becoming more anxious with each passing second and in desperate need of a diversion, Lily picked up her phone and sent her friend a text in an effort to distract herself.

How excited are you about marrying that sexyfiancé of yours?

As she typed the words, Lily realized her hands were trembling and wrapped them around her sunken stomach. Minka was quick to respond.

I'm in heaven. I'm so in love.

Smiling, Lil typed back.

You and Jason are good together.

Her friend's response glowed on the screen.

So are you and Adam.

Minka the hopeful romantic. To think a year ago her friend thought she was in love with her twin sister's fiancé, now husband. Life was filled with wonderful surprises, well, at least surprises. The possibility of being pregnant with Adam's baby was not something she could categorize as one of those wonderful surprises, more like a complete, earth-shattering shock.

The decision to have a child, even when consensual, was momentous. To find yourself in the situation totally unexpected, your heart ripped open to unconditional love, the responsibility of a life in your hands, now that was a cruel joke.

She texted back.

It's just sex Minka. Purely physical.

Once again, she was reminded her relationship with Adam was nothing but sex. And the possibility of creating a life under such reckless abandonment made her throat tighten.

Her phone's screen came to life with another text.

**You both are so stubborn.
Anyway, I can't wait to see you.**

She quickly responded.

*Same here.
Give Jason my love.
Talk later.*

Her phone vibrated again. This time it was from her brother Zander.

***Hey, sis,
where have you been the last two days?
Call me.***

She ignored her brother's text. The last forty-eight hours, each one of them had called and texted. Each message had gone unanswered. They were a guarded bunch and would come knocking soon, but right now she needed to shut the world out until she could wake up from this nightmare.

Two days ago she woke up nauseous and headed straight to the bathroom. Initially she self-diagnosed a stomach bug and even mentioned it to Adam that night as they spoke. Only it didn't seem to want to go away. It wasn't until one of her colleagues casually mentioned that she might be pregnant did the possibility enter her mind. After work that day she went straight to the local supermarket and picked up a variety of pregnancy tests—ePT, First Response, and any other brand on display.

She glanced back to the thin plastic stick and realized while the instruction said to wait a certain amount of minutes, it'd changed before time.

Pregnant.

The word greeted her in bold for the first time.

Blood rushed in her ears and her pulse skyrocketed. Panic and reality bubbled in her stomach, making her dizzy. This time there was no denial; not a positive sign but the actual word confirming what the other previous tests had tried to tell her. Her eyes slowly slid away from the evidence before her. Her new reality.

She'd created a baby with Adam.

How?

The question she'd been asking over and over shuffled in her brain. She was on the pill; that was as baby-proof as one could get. Yes, there was that one to two-percent chance but Lily always saw that disclaimer as a CYA—Cover Your Ass type of thing, a just-in-case legal move to avoid lawsuits.

In nine months, give or take, she was going to have a baby. She'd be a mother. A life was forming inside her this very second. Her well-managed life was about to become chaotic, topsy-turvy.

The reality struck hard and her hand instinctively came to rest on her flat belly.

She wanted to move, yell, cry, anything.

Questions swam through her head.

How would she work or raise a child as a single mother?

She blew out a breath.

Her parents, and her brothers; she'd have to tell them. She'd failed them. The only daughter, the baby sister, pregnant and unwed. Don't forget single. Her Facebook status was *Single*. Maybe now she'd change it to *It's complicated.*

A soft chuckle escaped her throat while visions of her parents' concerned eyes flashed before her. Her overly protective brothers would want to beat up the bastard, of course. And then maybe marry her off. Her parents had two golden rules—Don't end up in jail and no babies out of wedlock. Her brothers had toyed but never broke the jail rule. She was the ballsy one. She broke one of the rules.

Lily continued to stare at the word for the rest of the allotted time until the buzzing of her phone pulled her attention away. Her eyes dragged to the printed screen.

Adam.

Back on the island.
See you in a few days.
We'll stay in bed all weekend.
I've missed that body of yours. Ciao.

In spite of the nervous butterflies in her stomach, she smiled. Adam had been in Italy for two weeks for a race and visiting his parents. He didn't have to return until next week but cut his visit short after the two agreed to extend her visit to two weeks.

Fuck! She was pregnant with Adam's child. A man who had nothing permanent in his life. A man whose ability to commit peaked at fuck buddy. A man with no home, no country.

Still, she'd have to tell him.

Tears welled up in her eyes. With her back pressed against the cool wall, she gasped, buried her face in her hands and wept. "I can't do this," she choked, rocking her body back and forth. The hot, salty drops dripped down her chin to her arms.

Lily wasn't sure how long she cried. She only knew by the time she entered her bedroom, night had fallen. She spotted the previous tests on the bed, each one with the plus sign. It crossed her mind to gather them and throw them away but drenched with fatigue, she shoved them aside and laid her tired body on the bed.

Just as she placed her phone on the nightstand, the tune *I'm Sexy and I Know It* by LMFAO echoed in the room. There was no need to look at the caller ID; she assigned that ringtone to only one man.

Nonetheless, her eyes came to rest on the small screen and watched Adam's name as the phone continued to ring until *MISSED CALL* appeared. He wouldn't leave a voice mail; she already knew a text would follow. Adam was not known for his patience; leaving a message to call back was usually out of the question unless she was teaching.

Liliana, I've missed you. Call me.

Even with words, the man had the power to generate a physical reaction from her. Her already tender breasts swelled at the thought of his lips against her... "Seriously, Lily, that's how you got here in the first place. Calm the fuck down."

While she didn't want to talk at the moment, she knew better than to avoid his text. She didn't want a repeat of five weeks ago when he appeared at her doorstep. No, she couldn't handle that tonight. Picking up the phone, she scrolled to his name, the first name on her contact list–something she blamed on the genius who decided to automatically alphabetize how names were entered and saved.

Hi, I'm okay.
A bit under the weather so going to bed early.
See you soon.

His next consisted of only two words but to the point.

What's wrong?

Leave it to Adam to try to get to the bottom of the problem right away. This one was a nine months problem.

Just a little tired and nauseous.

Oops, she slipped on the nauseous but her fingers had already hit the *SEND* button.
Her phone vibrated with his response.

Nauseous?

For a beat she contemplated not responding. Bad idea. Chewing on her lower lip, she texted.

Might have eaten something bad.

Okay, that was a lie, but not really because until today, she'd attributed the nausea to an upset stomach.

You need to rest. See you soon.

If she hadn't discovered she was pregnant, she would be talking to him right now, laughing and flirting over the phone. Her fingers tapped on the screen of her iPhone.

I can't wait to see you. Good night, Adam.

His response was quick. No words of love. That was never them.

Sweet dreams, Liliana.

Lily studied Adam's text for a few seconds, and smiled slightly with mixed emotions. Like it or not, she'd soon be someone's mother.

Maybe trade in her skinny jeans for high-waisted pants, drive a minivan to soccer games in last season's clothes smeared with dirt.

She released a deep breath. There was no time to retreat and go somewhere quiet to think. She'd have to face this head on. In two days, she'd be on that ferry crossing the Atlantic Ocean from Woods Hole and come face to face with her baby daddy. Overwhelmed with emotions, she rolled over and buried her face in her pillow. And then closed her eyes with hope to shut the world out, at least until tomorrow.

5

"Sex is like math—you add the bed, subtract the clothes, divide the legs, and pray you don't multiply."
Anonymous

*L*ily fought back the nausea bubbling in her stomach and entered the quaint little house that doubled as a doctor's office. As luck would have it, the waiting area was filled with pregnant women all sitting with hands on their round bellies. The men responsible for putting them there sat idle beside their significant other flipping blindly through magazines or playing whatever game on their smart phone.

She glanced around the room. Some of the women's faces were brimming with happiness, but most looked uncomfortable, their eyes tired, breasts swollen, and stomach protruding in various sizes of growing bumps. She took in their restless movement of tapping feet, tipping of water bottles, adjusting clothes. It seemed the bigger the bump, the more fidgety they appeared.

Women were supposed to glow; at least that was the myth. A lie. Instead, across from Lily sat a woman with her shirt falling in folds around the watermelon-sized bump where her stomach should be, her palms cradling the baby within. She looked as if she was ready to pop at any second. With the exception of one or two with clear, even-toned skin, the waiting room was filled with distressed-looking women sporting a nice case of acne or spotty skin.

Whatever happened to the contours of the body becoming more rounded and feminine with pregnancy? Another myth, she supposed. The pregnancy god had tricked all of these women to believe their bodies would gently swell and produce cute little babies. Instead, their skin stretched with a promissory note to never regain its elasticity.

Great, just great. This was what she had to look forward to. Swollen hands and feet and a watermelon for a stomach. One day, she'd have a conversation with the pregnancy god and confront him on the deception, that pregnancy was a beautiful phase in a woman's life. Because so far, based on the nausea alone, it was all false advertisement.

The revolving door swung open and Paige, the pretty nurse with Lily's chart in hand, greeted Lily with her usual welcoming smile. "Hi, Lily, good to see you again. Come in."

Lily returned the smile and quietly followed Paige down the hall where she was led to a patient room.

"Is everything okay? You said it was an emergency, so Dr. Mason will see you right away."

You better believe it. I got knocked up. Under normal circumstances, Lily would consider Paige a friend. Not on the same level as her friendship with Minka but close enough. Only one barrier stood between their friendships—Paige's close relationship with her brothers. As the head nurse of the OB-GYN who prescribed her birth control and the unofficial fourth member of the three musketeers, Lily always maintained a level of distance so that her brothers wouldn't interrogate the other woman. Too bad, because she always liked Paige.

"I appreciate it." The first thing she'd done this morning was call the office for an appointment. After a long hold, Paige had asked her to be there within one hour.

"Minka's wedding is coming up," Paige continued, her voice warm and pleasant as she took Lily's blood pressure, a common practice during each visit. "Rafa said you're leaving for the wedding tomorrow."

Lily nodded. Rafa was the oldest of the three Musketeers, also known as Rafael, Lily's older brother by five years.

"Blood pressure is a bit high." Paige's amber eyes studied her. Lily kept her expression as blank as she could. Eventually, the secret would be out and Paige would know her reason for the sudden visit. "I'll go get Dr. Mason. By the way, I checked your file. Your birth control is low. I'll call the pharmacy for a refill. Another year supply?"

"Um, I'm fine for now."

As expected, the other woman paused; realization for her emergency visit seemed to have sunk in. "Lily," the nurse said thickly. "Can you give us some urine?"

She nodded, although she could have saved them some time had she brought those darn positive pregnancy sticks still on her nightstand.

"I drank two glasses of water," she said, attempting humor for humor's sake.

Paige chuckled and led her down the hall to the restroom. "Leave the cup in the holder then come back to the room when you're done. Dr. Mason and I will be there shortly."

Less than five minutes later, Lily stood alone in the patient's room. She picked up a magazine. It read—*Pregnancy* in big, bold, red letters. She put the magazine down and stood alone with her thoughts, the renewed energy she experienced when she first woke up now merely a fraction of what it was.

On the radio, Gary Clark, Jr.'s piercing chords crooned the lyrics to "*Numb,*" a feeling Lily had experienced before when she discovered her cheating ex-fiancé's explicit text messages to his side piece. And now, sitting on the cold, hard exam table, she couldn't tell if the things happening around her were really occurring. All of a sudden life had thrown too much against her at once.

A hushed tone of knuckles on the door forced Lily to straighten herself as Dr. Mason entered with Paige close behind. Their eyes met and Paige gave her an understanding nod, easing away the fear that the whole patient confidentiality thing might be in jeopardy. An appreciative smile passed on Lily's lips as some of the tension left her body. She turned to the doctor for the inevitable.

"How are you feeling?" Dr. Mason, her OB-GYN for the last ten years, had a voice that always carried the same level of calm with no sign of surprise or disappointment. Today was no different.

Never had a simple question been so loaded. How did she answer that? Confused. Shocked. *Scared out of my panties.* No panties reference. *Nunca.* Never ever. "A little shaken," she answered as honestly as she could.

He smiled warmly. "You were on antibiotics a couple of weeks ago. That weakens the birth control," the wise doctor informed her.

Well, damn! Shouldn't that be in big bold letters on the prescription or the pill itself?

"Paige is going to take you to the exam room for an ultrasound. After that we can proceed with your options."

What options?

Ultrasound?

The words cluttered her brain.

Her eyes narrowed in confusion. "Options? An ultrasound?"

Dr. Mason pulled his chair and lowered his thin frame. "Part of my job is to make sure there's a heartbeat and ask if you're going to keep the baby. Not all unplanned pregnancies are kept."

Her heart tripped and her hand automatically landed on her flat belly. As petrified as she was, the possibility of not carrying the baby full term had not once crossed her mind. And of course there'd be a heartbeat. She had ten tests at home proven she was very pregnant. "I'm keeping the baby," she said in a low voice. There had to be a way to deal with her family. Maybe move somewhere very far. Now that was a tempting option. She looked at Dr. Mason. "Why the ultrasound? I took ten tests."

The doctor leaned forward. "There are occasions when there's no fetal heartbeat in a pregnancy. That usually ends in a natural miscarriage or a dilation and curettage."

She knew what a D&C procedure was, but shit, she hadn't thought of that possibility. All the emotions bottled inside paused for a moment as she processed this information. "I see." But really, she didn't.

Paige squeezed her shoulder. "That will take a few minutes. After that, we can do all the required blood work and go from there. Come to the front desk when you're ready. In the meantime I'll have the technician set everything up for you." With a comforting smile Dr. Mason and Paige slipped out of the room.

Once alone, Lily slipped off the table and reached for her purse. She choked on the lack of oxygen she had and released a deep breath in an attempt to stay calm, but the motion made her dizzy. Fear of what she may have to face alone consumed her.

The key to the Benz convertible fumbled between her fingers. Heartbeat—the word repeated over and over in her head. The possibility that the life forming inside of her had a chance to never experience living scampered through her thoughts. She let out a shaky breath and was about to exit the room when she almost crashed into Paige.

"Lily, I'm going to be in the room with you. I don't have to, but I want to. And no is not an option."

In spite of the situation, she appreciated Paige's offer. "You don't have to do that. I can go alone."

Paige shook her head. Her face set with determination. "Nonsense." She closed the door behind her for privacy. "I know I'm closer to your brothers than you, but I consider you to be a friend." She clasped Lily's hands in hers, no longer playing the role of a nurse but a friend. "I would never break patient-doctor confidentiality and tell your brothers any of this. This is for you to tell your family when you're ready. I promise I won't ask how, who, what," she finished with a reassuring smile. "You shouldn't have to do this alone."

Alone. The word bit through her. She'd never considered herself alone before. She was surrounded by friends, family, and maybe even Adam to some level. Only he wasn't the lean-on-me type. From that aspect, she was indeed alone. All they had was a physical connection. Nothing more.

Her shoulders dropped in defeat. Feeling powerless over the present or the future, she answered with a small nod, surrendering to the support offered. "I appreciate it, Paige. Thank you," she whispered just before the tears she had bravely tried to hold back began to cascade down her cheeks.

Less than one hour later and exactly six weeks pregnant, Lily sat in her car and scanned through the pamphlets one last time. A prescription of prenatal vitamins had been called in to her pharmacy which she had to pick up. Two weeks after the wedding she had a follow-up visit. She sent Paige a thank you text before dialing Minka's number. To her relief her friend picked up on the first ring.

"There you are," Minka greeted her on the other line. "I'm so looking forward to seeing you. How long has it been since we last saw each other?"

"A little over two months," she replied. And six weeks since she last saw Adam.

"Lily," Minka's voice automatically switched to concern on the other end of the phone. "What's going on? Are you still coming tomorrow?"

That was the kind of friendship they had. Even miles apart, words were not usually needed to detect when the other was in distress.

"Yes, of course. I am the MOH." Lily tried her best to sound cheerful, but knew she failed miserably. Not that she wasn't happy to be the Maid of Honor for her best friend. In fact, she questioned who was more excited over the fact that Minka had found true love with Jason Montgomery, one of Adam's close friends. "And I'm going to make sure you have the best wedding ever."

"Are you going to tell me what's wrong?"

She sighed. "Long story. I promise I'll tell you all about it tomorrow."

There was a slight pause on the other end. Lily knew what her friend was thinking. Tomorrow she was supposed to be with

Adam. "Do you think there's room available in Martha's Way for me to stay?"

A nervous chuckle came from Minka. "Why would you do that? I thought you were staying with Adam."

"I don't think that's a good idea."

"We saw him last night. He confirmed he was picking you up. Have you told him?"

Well, no. Not exactly. "Um, I will."

A silence fell between the friends. "I'm confused," Minka said at last.

So was Lily, but for a different reason.

"I don't think Adam has done anything wrong. Of course women constantly throw themselves at him, but—"

"Minka," she interrupted calmly, "I'll explain tomorrow. I just need to stay at Martha's Way for the next two weeks."

"Well, the inn is full this week. The island is pretty busy with the food and wine festival going on."

Oh, yes. She'd forgotten about the last hoorah on the Vineyard before it emptied out. "Oh, okay, well, I'll call The Fallon." Which would probably have no vacancy either, but hey, what the hell? It was worth a try.

"Don't be silly, you can stay with me and Jason. And whatever you're going through, please know I'll support you."

"Thanks. I appreciate it."

"But you need to tell Adam you're not staying with him," Minka continued, "You know he can be pretty stubborn."

Yes, she knew that too well. Stubborn and determined—two words she'd always associate with Adam.

"I'll tell him," she promised her friend.

"All right, send all the details to me and I'll pick you up. I love you."

After their goodbye, Lily texted the ferry information to Minka. From her contact list, she scrolled to Adam's name and studied it.

The second she heard the baby's heartbeat, she'd broken down in tears. Relief. Love. She fell in love instantly with the lentil-sized baby breathing life in her womb. And that's when she'd made up her mind to break things off with the man she casually slept with, the father of the unborn child. She'd tell him about the baby and expect nothing from him.

Her stomach tightened with nerves. Adam wasn't the type to go down without a fight. He'd never accept the "I'm pregnant with your child and we're over." But she'd never settle for anything less than the kind of love she witnessed from her parents.

Her mind was made up. She'd tell him about her pregnancy and walk away. Beside the physical connection, they had nothing. She'd give him the opportunity to be an active father, but should he choose not to, she'd raise her child as a single mother. An unwed single mother and shaming the Serrano name.

Pressing on the message option, she typed.

No need to pick me up tomorrow.
I'm staying with Minka and Jason.

As expected, her phone quickly vibrated.

Explain.

She wondered what he was doing. Knowing Adam, he was probably at his restaurant or at Vapor preparing for the food and wine festival. Ordinarily, she wouldn't refer to herself as a coward. But for once she was glad this conversation was taking place via text.

I'm throwing in the towel. We are over.

Her phone glowed with his response.

Like fucking hell we are.
Tell me that tomorrow when you see me.
Face to face. I'll pick you up.

Her inside quivered at the words. She wanted him, probably always would.

Adam, please, I don't want to make this trip about us.

Liliana, every time you come to the island it's about us.
I'm going to call in a few.
Busy with Guillermo for a bit.

Lily blew out a series of short breaths to gain control of the situation, of herself.

No need. Going to have dinner with my parents.
We'll talk soon.

As soon as she pressed the *SEND* button, the tune to *I'm Sexy and I Know It* started playing. It crossed her mind to press the ignore button and escape into her parents' house but she knew better. Besides stubborn and determined, Adam was also impulsive.

"What's going on?" he asked on the other end, his voice dangerously low and not nearly as calm as usual. Yet, it caressed her in places only Adam could. She leaned her head back against the cushion of the car seat and closed her eyes.

"We will talk, but not tomorrow. I need—"

"I need you," he spoke the words like a series of musical notes, making her knees wobble. Thank God she was sitting down.

"You don't need me, Adam," she argued, need implied an emotional connection.

"Oh, but I do, Liliana. My dick needs you and it's a part of me."

That was Adam. Raw and to the point. The admission should have stung, as it reminded her of what she already knew. But her body betrayed her and grew damp. She wanted him deep inside her, pumping, grinding, and shouting her name.

"I'll see you tomorrow," he said in a gentler tone. "First we have sex, then we talk about what's bothering you. And we will deal with it together. Together, Lily." His voice held a note of authority. "Not you alone."

"I have to go."

She quickly pressed the *END* button, threw her phone in her bag and practically ran inside the comfort of her parents' house. All the while praying for the strength she needed to walk away from the man with the strong hold on her.

6

"I keep myself busy with things to do, but every time I pause, I think of you."
Anonymous

Cilantro, garlic, onions, capers, Cubanese peppers—the indigenous seasonings of her mother's cooking greeted her the minute she entered their Victorian home in Somerville. Lily inhaled the intoxicating aroma of fresh, homemade *sofrito*. Her stomach, tempted by the delicious smell, growled in response.

Cocina Criolla, Creole cooking, that's how her parents had explained *Latinos'* cuisine, which could be traced back to the Arawaks and Tainos, the original inhabitants of Puerto Rico, her parents' birthplace. This made Lily and her brothers' first generation Americans of the Serrano family, but their Hispanic culture had been ingrained in them and for that she was grateful. They might not have grown up rich like some of the teachers she worked with at the private school in Princeton, but what they lacked in financial wealth, the tight-knit family made up with love.

She walked down the hall into the living room and found her oldest brother Rafa slumped on the cream-colored sofa by the fireplace, his face covered by his favorite New York Yankees baseball hat. His beloved black Lab, appropriately named Faithful, lay at his feet.

A smile curved her lips and she focused on Rafa's long legs. The urge to kick them overcame her as it had so many times as a child. His sandalwood eyes would shoot open, a moment of shock followed quickly by anger. He'd curse at her and threaten her with some bodily harm.

She laughed under her breath and stepped carefully around his sleeping form. The big goof. He could curse as loud as he liked and she'd still see right through him. All bark no bite. He loved her. All three of them loved her and she loved them right back.

The warm comfort of home seeped into her as she reminisced over memories growing up in the house with the Three Musketeers. Unlike today, their house had always been noisy, filled with laughter, fights between siblings, and music. They listened and danced to salsa or watched their parents dance the boleros of Rafael Hernandez.

If she closed her eyes, she could see a younger version of her parents smiling, dancing to the smooth beat of *No Me Quieras Tanto* in the kitchen, the table pushed aside and the dishes left for later. They never wanted more than what they had. They provided, shaped, and loved their children in spite of economic difficulties. And for that each one of them, in their own way, tried to make their parents proud. She'd done a pretty good job at that, at least she thought so. Well, maybe not once they found out she was knocked up.

"Why do you look like you're about to throw up all over the furniture?" Rafa's voice pierced her thoughts. He straightened his body and was now staring intently at her, his probing eyes missing nothing as he adjusted his baseball cap back on his head.

Lily ran her hands over her jeans and focused her eyes on a picture of the six of them framed on the mantle. Rafa always had the ability to read her, so she slapped on a smile. "I was just about to kick you."

He brought his body to a full sitting position. She surveyed him. Couldn't believe her brothers were all grown up. *So are you, and you've topped them. You're pregnant.*

"You look sick. Did another asshole hurt you?" His eyes narrowed, fully in big brother mode.

"Geez, Rafa, you don't have to be my protector. Nate was over a year ago."

"I still want to kick his ass."

Yes, she knew that. As a matter of fact, all three of them had threatened to remove one or two of her ex-fiancé's limbs. She cringed at the thought of what they might try to do to Adam. Her lover might be all muscled up and a total badass, but she doubted he could take all three of them, at least not at once.

"Well, I'm over Nate's cheating. Let it go." Although she couldn't control what they'd do to him if their paths happened to cross, she wouldn't mind if one of them punched the pretty smirk off his face.

"So what's bothering you then? Another guy broke your heart? I didn't know you were dating again," he said casually, as if she always made it a point to tell her brothers who she was dating. For the record, she typically avoided the topic and didn't bring Nate over until they had the "talk" and established them as boyfriend and girlfriend.

A nervous chuckle escaped her throat. "You guys need to stop treating me like I'm five."

"You weren't dating at five." Rafa grunted then seemed to think about it for a second and looked at her for confirmation, causing Lily to laugh.

Her brother came to his feet, stretching to his full six foot-plus height. Faithful automatically sprang to her paws. What a bitch. Shaking her head, she walked past her brother and his beloved dog.

"You don't see me all over your love life." In fact, she wouldn't set one of her friends up with any of them. They were handsome, charming, and what she referred to as male whores.

"Really, how old were you when—" Rafa asked in a low tone behind her.

"If I tell you, I'd have to kill you," she shot over her shoulder without stopping her stride. They didn't have to know that other than Adam, there had only been Nate and her college boyfriend. Her brother swore under his breath. Together they entered the charming European style eat-in-kitchen that had all the elements to be the heart of the home. Warm, peachy tones and creamy whites play nicely together. Her mother stood by the counter, kneading dough with bare hands, preparing to make biscuits. Her father came to join her mother, placed a glass of wine by her side. The two shared a glance then kissed.

Lily caught her breath over the intimate moment. It happened so quickly she almost missed it, but for one second, her father's hand touched her mother's back and pulled her into him. Their lips touched in a sweet, light kiss that spoke louder than words. The gesture exuded warmth, comfort, and their deep love.

The loneliness she'd been fighting all day resurfaced. Now she understood the reason behind it. Her parents had something that was out of her reach. They had love. As much fun as she had with Adam, their relationship was built on nothing of substance. And that was why she had to end it no matter how much he tried to sway her otherwise. And he would. She was sure of that. Women didn't walk out on Adam Aquilani. Subconsciously, one of her hands came to rest on her stomach, no matter what happened, they were forever linked.

"Stomach is upset?" Rafa whispered in her ear, causing Lily to visibly jump. "Who is the asshole?" The underlying threat in her brother's voice told her he suspected her little secret.

Lily shut her eyes. *Shit.* After counting to three, in Spanish and English, she turned to face him. His eyes reflected what she knew. Yup, he'd figured it out. "I'm just under the weather."

"Mom said you haven't been feeling well for about a month now."

Lily froze, counted to ten. "I ate—"

"Bullshit!" he muttered under his breath. "Some fucking guy knocked you up."

Her mother's chuckle forced Lily to turn and focus her attention on her parents. "*Hola* Mama, Papa," she greeted her parents with a smile.

"We're not done." Rafa whispered then walked away from her, Faithful followed her master. In a lot of ways, her brother reminded her of Adam. Strong, authoritative, and total alpha.

Ignoring the bowling ball sitting in her stomach and her brother's eyes searing into the back of her head, she walked over and kissed her parents. Lily had toyed with the idea of canceling her dinner date with her parents tonight, but since she was leaving for the Vineyard first thing in the morning and would not see them again till the wedding, she caved in. Now as her brother continued to watch her like a hawk, she wished she'd gone with her first instinct, maintained her stomach virus excuse and stayed away. Technically that wasn't a lie. Nausea had become her best friend the last few days.

"You look pale, love," her mother said, concern filling her voice.

Her father crossed the kitchen, squeezed her shoulder as he walked past her, and picked up a bottle of New Zealand Shiraz.

"Just tired," she answered in her most upbeat voice.

Her father seemed focused on filling the four wine glasses on the counter, but worry etched his face.

"Uh, none for me, Dad," she said in a nonchalant tone, ignoring her older brother who leaned against the wall, quietly witnessing the exchange.

"Still fighting the stomach bug?" Her father put one glass back in the cabinet.

Rafa snickered. Lily shot him a murderous glare. "I'm feeling better," she answered with a smile.

In true father fashion, Raul Serrano stopped and scanned her appearance. Lily's first reaction was to cover her stomach but told herself that would probably be a dead giveaway and kept her hands to her sides.

"*Tu madre* is right," he said in his always calm tone. "You still don't look like yourself. You work too hard."

Lily smiled. Her parents always thought she worked too hard. "Soccer season is over," she answered, referring to the kindergarten league she coached, in addition to the basketball league and the elementary literary group.

"You do too much," her father continued.

"I like keeping myself busy." *Because when I don't, I find myself fantasizing about a certain dark-haired Italian.*

"Still leaving tomorrow?"

She nodded. "Yes. And I'll see you guys next week."

"*Sí, sí,*" her father continued, the tone of his voice lifting just a tad with excitement. "Minka's fiancé called us yesterday and finalized all the arrangements for us at his inn. He's a good man. I want a good man for you."

Lily opened her mouth, nervous about what would come out and decided it was best to not address her father's statement. In two weeks, her stomach would still be flat. No sign of being preggers. The thought of having her parents on the island she'd fallen in love with sent her into rambling about all the places she wanted them to see.

"I'm glad you're coming." She meant it. Pregnant or not, she was determined to have a good time at the wedding.

"Are you staying at the inn?" The question came from no other than her pain-in-the-ass brother. Rafa picked at a fingernail, seeming uninterested. His casual manner didn't fool her. As an engineer who traveled over the world, he was well-rounded, worldly, and too damn clever. The smarty pants was trying to get a bead on her baby daddy.

"I'm staying with Minka and Jason." *Ha! I'm quick on my toes, big brother.*

He smiled. A sly smile, telling her he was on to her. Her phone vibrated from her purse. Lily's heart skipped. It could only be one person.

"Your phone," Rafa pointed out from the other side of the room.

Lily's gaze ping-ponged around the room, avoiding direct eye contact with her parents. She reached inside her purse and pressed the *HOME* button and ignored the message.

"Must not be important," Rafa cocked an eyebrow.

She kept her attention on her parents. If she ignored her brother, maybe he'd stop poking.

He stepped away from the wall and came to stand by her side, slung one long arm around her shoulders and squeezed the daylights out of her.

"By the way, I don't know if I told you but Minka invited us to the wedding too. And guess what, since we love you and Minka so much, we all accepted. I can't wait to get acquainted with." He paused. "How do they refer to themselves?"

She knew Minka had invited her brothers and was still waiting for their responses. Two of her brothers were out of town, Rafa had only returned home a day or two ago from India. Zander was a Navy SEAL. She didn't know his exact whereabouts, only he was somewhere in the Middle East and Max was doing some photography work for National Geographic in Russia.

Minka would have told her if they were coming. The light bulb switched on. Rafa—her nosy brother—had narrowed down Martha's Vineyard as the possible home of the bastard who had impregnated his baby sister. So he was going to do what any big alpha brother would do, recruit the other bad-asses and invade the island until they hunted down the bastard responsible for her fall from grace.

Her inside quivered. Lily twisted her neck as if sore and met her brother's eyes. "Locals."

He nodded, a satisfied smug on his handsome face. "Indeed. Locals. By the way, you've been going there a lot lately. You probably feel like a local yourself." He paused, seeming to think about his next words, then gave her one of his smiles that had brought many women to their knees. "I love you, sis." He placed a light kiss on her forehead then turned to their parents. "Mom, I've missed your cooking. Let's eat."

Since she couldn't escape to her old room to avoid more of her brother's probing comments, Lily smiled and nodded in agreement. But her mind was playing the worst case scenario. Her brothers coming face to face with Adam, because someone or two might not come out alive.

On a typical visit to the Vineyard, Lily always enjoyed the ferry ride sitting on the deck, sipping a glass of wine. Today, feeling dizzy from her third trip to the bathroom to vomit whatever she had left in her stomach, she slid her body on an empty chair close to the window and read Adam's text once more.

When I promised, I meant it. Remember, no regrets. See you tomorrow.

The words brought a stream of heat against her skin and took her back to that fateful night in Chappaquiddick.

Nate's cheating had still been fresh when Minka suggested she joined her for a weekend. Needing the escape, Lily had jumped on the idea. She thought she was going to spend a few days with her friend and get to know Jason Montgomery, the man Minka hooked up with, much to Lily's pleasure.

Instead, she got blindsided by Adam. From the moment he touched the engagement ring hanging around her neck, he'd penetrated her walls, forced out the reason for her sadness, then proceeded to tease her to laughter. However, it wasn't until he found her crying in the middle of the night on Jason's private beach in Chappaquiddick did she truly meet Adam Aquilani.

"Liliana," *his voice echoed against the crashing waves of the ocean.*

She turned and came face to face with Adam. A cool breeze rolled off the water and blew thick, black hair away from his face. The full moon illuminated his features. Dark eyes searched hers with no trace of the teasing laughter she'd endured from him all day.

"It's his loss, you know," he offered. "He doesn't deserve your tears."

Pain and humiliation swept over her and she let out a bitter chuckle. "Save the flirting for tomorrow. I can't do the bantering right now."

With a smile, he took a few steps closer. One long finger touched the ring then moved up to her cheek and brushed away a tear. He cupped her face, his thumbs caressing her skin. Perhaps it was that he found her at a low point in her life, but his touch affected her. It made her want to be kissed and touched, even if common sense told her everything about him was wrong for her. He was a bachelor, a playboy who spent half of his time in Italy or across the continents racing cars. And way outside her usual dating circle.

"Let's go inside," *he said in a low voice.*

Need You Now

Lily noticed the tightness in his voice. Not that it surprised her. Since the moment they'd met, Adam made it clear he wanted to sleep with her. And what if she gave in to the idea? As much as she'd sworn off men, his blunt offer to rock her world stayed with her all day. She, too felt the attraction.

Only she was too logical, too rational to give in to a momentary attraction. She knew the hottest flames burned the fastest and she would be yesterday's trick as soon as the sun came up. Because of that she fought the temptation to give in to the flirtation, the teasing. But in private, she wondered how his lips would feel against her own. His hands against her skin, exploring.

"Kiss me," she breathed.

She heard his quick inhale and for a split second the surprise registered on his handsome face.

"You're vulnerable right now."

He stood before her like a book of poetry. She was the starving artist, dying to read all the beautiful words written into his infinite space. "But you want to." And so did she.

He shook his head and took her hand in his. But she could tell he was fighting the temptation. "Not like this. When we kiss, I want you to only want to kiss me. Not when you are crying over some loser who couldn't keep his dick in his pants."

"And you could?"

With their eyes locked onto one another, he answered without hesitation. "When I make a promise, I mean it."

Somehow, she believed him. Lily let out a sigh. If there was a man who could make her forget and take away her pain, at least temporarily, it would be this gorgeous man standing here with her. Commitment wasn't in his vocabulary. Good thing she wasn't looking for one. The last two days he'd openly flirted with her, and now that she was throwing herself at him, he was suddenly making sense.

She stepped out of his touch and walked back toward the ocean, where she'd spent the last hour contemplating how to move on from the pain, the familiarity. For three years Nate had been a part of her life, he'd even moved in to her condo. They'd talked about babies, building a future together as husband and wife.

Some distance away, Lily sat on the cool wet sand. She brought her legs to her chest, leaned her chin against her knees and stared at the way the moon, almost too bright to look at, hung over the ocean; its light creating twinkling stars on the water.

"You should throw it in the ocean."

She glanced over to where Adam was now seating next to her. "What?"

"Your engagement ring. Throw it in the ocean and let go of the pain."

Funny. Only a few minutes ago, the same thought had crossed her mind but she'd dismissed it. No woman in her right mind would throw a ring worth thousands of dollars into the ocean.

Adam hoisted back to his feet and extended a hand to her. "Let's do it. I'll hold your hand the whole time. And maybe after I'll kiss you," he finished with a smile.

He was teasing, of course. He'd been doing that since they first met. Slowly, Lily placed her hands in his and came to her feet. In silence they inched closer to the waves. He leaned into her and removed the necklace holding the ring and slipped it into her palm.

"I'll be throwing away thousands of dollars." Really, she was trying to talk some sense into herself.

"It will make you feel better."

She inhaled the fresh salt air, and without giving it much thought threw the ring as far as she could. A fleck of water jumped in the dark and swallowed the weight that had been holding her prisoner. Lily stood, spellbound by the cleansing feeling that swept through her. The sea shimmered with indomitable power, granting her joy, freedom.

She turned to Adam. "Let's go skinny dipping."

Adam's laughter rang into the night like the strong currents of the uncontrollable waves of the ocean. "That good, huh?"

"I'm serious." Lily persisted and watched as the humor faded from his face.

"We would be naked," he said, his tone filled with sexual tension.

She nodded, well aware what skinny dipping implied. "Scared?"

"Liliana," he rasped, "I can't promise not to touch you."

Lily smiled. "Then don't promise."

With her gaze locked on Adam, she stripped out of her shorts, threw off her tank top and stood before him in her thong and bra. His eyes darkened, burning her skin. He muttered something in Italian. Whatever he said, she could tell he was losing the battle with control. He removed the crisp white tee, stepped out of his jeans and stood before her in white boxer briefs. Her breath quickened, fingers aching with the need to touch every one of his hard muscles.

"You might as well take those off too." Her eyes lowered to the fitted briefs that looked oh so delicious on him. "Once wet, I'll be able to see everything."

He arched a brow. "You're playing with fire."

"I'm aware." And to prove just how aware she was, she unsnapped her bra, wiggled out of her matching panties, and stood completely naked before him.

He sucked in a deep breath as his eyes took in every inch of her.

"Liliana, I need to know you're sure of this," he said, his voice very quiet.

She stared back at him. "I'm sure."

Absolute silence settled between them. She watched Adam's face, and her heart clenched at the raw desire in his eyes. Without a word, he slipped out of the boxers and stood gloriously naked in front of her with the most impressive erection. Now that they had officially crossed the line they had been teetering around the last few days, Lily found herself uncertain of what to do next. So she gawked at the perfection before her.

"First one in the water gets two orgasms," he shouted over his shoulders as he ran toward the ocean, giving her full view of his perfect ass.

She laughed softly. She heard the rush of the waves and caught Adam's silhouette floating. What the hell! She owed him two orgasms. She sprinted toward the ocean, the grainy sand tickling her toes. The second the water touched her feet, she felt a healing coming little by *little over her body and soul. She dove in and let the cool waves embrace her.*

"You owe me two orgasms," Adam shouted from the water.

Lily swam over to him. "You cheated."

"All is fair in sex and orgasms."

Facing him, she looked into his eyes. "So we're doing it." *While she was thrilled by the idea of rolling in the sand with Adam, there was the mental apprehension over the ramifications of her actions. Empty sex with strangers had never been her thing.*

He nodded. "If that's what you want."

Oh, she wanted. Especially after seeing all he had to offer. She really wanted. "I want."

"Me."

"You."

When his hand cupped the back of her neck and pulled her forward, she followed, completely forgetting the place and the denial of his attraction she was supposed to be harboring. His mouth brushed hers, his voice a whisper of feathers touching her lips. "No regrets."

Adam's lips felt hot on her neck, making her shiver. "No regrets," she repeated the words just before his teeth sank into her shoulder.

7

"Your heart and my heart are very old friends." Rumi Quote Art

"Welcome to the Vineyard! Leave your troubles behind and enjoy your stay on our beautiful island," the conductor announced as the ferry docked. This meant they were in Vineyard Haven, one of the main points of entry to the Vineyard. Lily breathed a silent thank you, her stomach had felt every ripple of the ocean.

Typically, this announcement shot excitement through her veins since it meant Adam was waiting for her. Today, she found herself chewing her nails several times. On each occasion, she'd forced herself to keep her hand from her mouth. It didn't quite work, as she found himself chewing again barely a minute later.

Nerves. She drew a deep breath for strength. There was no delaying their reunion.

She remained seated by the window as visitors, lost in their excitement, walked by lazily down the stairs to the lower level to retrieve their cars or bikes. Reaching for her overnight bag, she rose to her feet and lined up behind a mother trying to control three high-energy boys while supporting a baby girl on her hip. The woman dropped her shoulders in defeat and walked ahead of the boys, as if she were leaving them behind, which they seemed to find amusing. The boys giggled and ran after their mother. The scene made Lily wonder if that was how it had been for her parents.

How the hell did she miss the interaction between parents and children before?

That was birth control in itself. Pure, total abstinence. The best form of birth control because its effectiveness didn't vary based on whether or not one was on antibiotics. Well, it was better late than never because she had officially sworn off sex. *No más*—no more.

Nauseous and lightheaded from it all, she made her way into the waiting area and scanned the room, ready to come face to face with her baby's daddy. Only there was no sign of Adam. Lily reached through her purse and swiped the phone. No text. A pang of disappointment shot through her. She quickly reminded herself she was the one who ended things between them. Still, she hadn't expected him to throw in the towel so easily.

"I convinced him to let me come instead."

Lily recognized the soft, feminine voice right away. Smiling, she turned and fell into the arms of her best friend. After a long moment of silence, she finally pulled away from Minka and focused on her friend. "Wow, you look amazing, and so freaking happy."

Minka wore a red motif shirtdress with high brown boots and a denim jacket. Her curls, pulled away from her glowing face, giving the world full access to the happiness sparkling in her hazel eyes. One would have never guessed, the woman standing before her spent most of her life struggling with self-esteem and body image issues.

"And you look like you just saw a ghost," Minka observed, concern now on full display on her pretty face. "Or is it disappointment since it's me here and not Adam?"

Yes. No. Lily shook her head. "Maybe a little," she admitted. "But I'm so glad to see you."

Minka took the overnight bag from her. Which wasn't necessary, but Lily didn't argue. "Adam is at Vapor with Forrest. Jason is in Boston and due back late tonight," she said as they walked toward the door. "I was thinking we'd go back to the house, grab a bite, and you can tell me what's wrong."

Lily nodded. "When are Blake and Keely coming back?" Keely was Minka's fraternal twin who married Jason's friend Blake last summer. The circle was tight. By default, she automatically felt welcomed by them.

"They'll be back later in the week and Claire will arrive as well, but you know she has a busy schedule. Her visit will be short." Claire was Keely's BFF, and was raised by Jason's parents. Jason and Claire grew up like siblings in the same house.

She met Claire last year at Jason's photography show. They had immediately sparked a friendship. But other than that initial meeting, their paths had not crossed. The African-American/Asian singer and designer was always on the road. Their communication had been primarily through emails and text messages. "Yes, she mentioned she's on location shooting her movie."

"South America," Minka chided. "She's filming a romantic comedy and having a real romance with her co-star, according to the tabloids."

She tried to listen as Minka chatted about Claire's possible hot romance, but her mind drifted. South America sounded nice right about now. Sunny. Far away. She could run there and raise her baby, but the thought of Adam chasing her down made her shiver.

"How did she find time to design your dress?" Claire had also designed Keely's dress. Which made sense, since the ladies were BFFs. And from meeting her last year, it was obvious the woman had a heart of gold.

Minka pointed to her parked black Audi, side by side they walked over to the car. "She finds a way."

"Please tell me she finished your dress."

Minka smiled. "All done. She's bringing it this week for a final fitting."

Lily grinned with happiness. "Wonderful! I can't wait."

As they slid into the sleek car, Minka's face reflected all the happiness Lily knew her friend had found by falling in love with Jason and coming to terms with who she was.

"I'm excited," Minka announced with a huge grin.

Lily smiled, feeling her friend's excitement. In two days, this was the first time she was able to stop dwelling on her impending motherhood and not worry for one full minute. "You're going to be the most beautiful bride ever."

Minka slipped her arm in the crook of Lily's. "I asked Adam to give us a few hours. I literally had to beg."

The thought of Minka begging Adam for a bit of time to get to the bottom of things warmed her.

"But he's coming tonight to pick you up."

"I'm pregnant." The words left her mouth and made the whole situation real. Well, more real than ever. She watched the shock registered on her friend's face and let out a nervous laugh. "Yup. Knocked up. A bun in the oven. I'm having a baby." She choked on the words.

Minka slammed on her brakes and slid the car into a parking spot. Thank God the summer rush on the island had long dwindled. Otherwise, they would've taken at least three lives. After a long pause, her friend turned and faced her. Lily smiled weakly.

"You and Adam are having a baby, not just you."

Lily tucked a strand of hair behind her ear.

"Does he know?"

She shook her head.

"You'll have to tell him, Lily. He'll do the right thing."

It was the *right* thing that caused the muscles in her stomach to close in like tightening coils. "I don't intend on keeping him away. I just don't want to sleep with him anymore."

"If you weren't pregnant, would you still be sleeping with him?"

She didn't need to think about it. The answer was *hell-to-the-fucking-yes*. "You know I would. He's…" She paused, searching her brain for the right word.

"Non-committal," Minka finished for her.

"Yes."

"Fun and dangerously sexy."

Lily couldn't help but chuckle. Only a year ago, she'd spoken similar words to her friend. Now the role was reversed. "There's an irony here," she said with a smile.

Minka released her hand and chuckled, understanding the reference to her own situation with Jason only a year ago. She sat back and started the engine and started driving. "Do you want a commitment from Adam?"

"No," she answered just a bit too quickly. "I don't." She tried to sound a little more convincing this time.

"Why?"

"That's not what our relationship is based on."

"Jason and I started as fuck buddies."

Good point. But Lily was more pleased that Minka was now comfortable saying *fuck*. "You said fuck."

The blush on her friend's cheek told her Minka was still adjusting. "Jason likes when I say it," she admitted in a low tone.

And that made Lily laugh a little louder than she intended. She didn't care. She was relaxed with Minka and felt like herself again. Like coming home. She leaned back and adjusted her seat belt. Minka pulled out her phone and with quick fingers sent a text to someone. Adam.

"What did you tell him?"

"That I am stealing you for the night. And I'll bring you to him tomorrow."

Lily's heart squeezed. "Thank you."

Minka dismissed the words with a wave of her hand. "Tonight, we drink seltzer water and talk about babies."

"I'd rather talk about your wedding day."

"We can talk about my wedding day and your little bun in the oven," she said wrinkling her nose. "By the way, weren't you on the pill?"

"Did you know antibiotics weaken the effect of the pill?"

Minka nodded. Well, damn; apparently everyone had gotten the memo but her.

"What if Adam wants more than just a role in the child's life?"

Lily's heart kicked. Only one thing would make her consider permanence and that was the big L-O-V-E word, which was not part of the game she'd been playing with Adam. They had an agreement, and that word wasn't part of the equation. Nothing serious were the words they both used to describe their relationship.

"What do you mean?" she asked her friend.

"What if he wants a relationship with you?"

"Adam doesn't do relationships, remember?"

"He's been with you for a year."

"Just for sex, Minka."

Minka glanced briefly at her. "What about you, is it just the sex for you too?"

The whole thing stopped being sex for her a long time ago. She just never chose to dwell on it. Instead, she carried on and pretended she was not emotionally available, didn't trust men. Lily brushed away non-existent lint from her jeans and turned her attention to the road.

"Do I need to answer that?"

Really she didn't have to. Her friend knew her well enough. But to admit, say the words would make everything she felt more tangible.

"No."

With only remnants of the heavy summer traffic, the car slid onto Main Street with ease. Having visited the island on various occasions during the year, she knew after the wine festival, the island would become a ghost town with only the locals staying behind. Even some of the inns would close for the winter or open for a wedding here and there.

She rather enjoyed visiting during the season when there were fewer people around. Adam usually went to Europe for a week or two then stayed on the island. She visited often last winter, a lot of long weekends that should have tired her but instead made her feel alive.

They drove in silence, and for that she was grateful. Lily focused her attention on the road and admired the impressive private homes with sweeping ocean views. Adam's house in Chillmark was similar in setting. They turned on Beach Road and drove through Oak Bluffs, the town Blake grew up in and probably the trendiest of them all, with a very So-Ho like feel.

A smile settled on her lips as her gaze fixated on Jaws Bridge. The landmark was famous for visitors to jump into the ocean, something she'd done several times with Adam. Adrenaline pumped through her veins as she recalled the icy rush of the water, the feel of Adam's cold flesh slick against her own. She swallowed hard and pushed the memories away. There wasn't a part of this island that didn't remind her of him. She needed to get away. Far. Far. Away.

"By the way, Rafa called today."

Lily simply nodded. She already figured out what her brothers were up to. She only wished they didn't try to ruin her best friend's wedding. Her stomach turned at the thought.

"Let me guess, suddenly my three brothers are available to attend your wedding."

"He figured it out, huh?"

"And he thinks whoever is responsible for my fall from grace lives here."

Minka let out a soft chuckle. "Very perceptive."

"I won't let them ruin your wedding day."

Again, Minka waved her hand and dismissed Lily's concern. "Your brothers would never do that. They're gentlemen."

The words barely escaped Minka's lips before the car was filled with laughter. Her brothers were smart, fun, and successful. Some of her friends had even labeled them as sexy. But gentlemen? Nope. Not the Serrano brothers. And if they weren't the type to kill and ask questions later, Adam would probably fit right in with them.

---

*A*dam's eyes rested on the silhouette outlined by the down comforter. Fast asleep in true Lily sleeping state, the comforter pulled just below her chin. He ignored the immediate tightness in his chest and clenched his teeth. He'd been growing increasingly impatient since he'd received that crazy text. His mind had been spinning since he'd received her last text, he'd been frantic to see her. To feel their connection and make it real again. To find out what was wrong and fix it.

Yet here she was, completely relaxed, sleeping like a baby. As if he didn't exist at all, as if they'd never existed. Closing the door behind him, he invaded her space and walked into the bedroom. Now close enough to examine every detail of her face, he noticed a few lines under her eyes. Her usual honey complexion with the permanent glow she seemed to possess was replaced with an unhealthy hue. Adam's immediate reaction was to run the pad of his thumb against her cheek. He watched her stir.

"Adam." His name slipped out of her lips. He waited for her to open her eyes, to face him, and explain what the fuck was going on. But the slow, even breathing from her chest told him she was still in a daze and not even aware of his presence. He raked a hand through his hair and walked over to the window. The fight that raged inside him the last three days left him drained. He lowered his weight on the Lorraine armchair and checked his watch. It was well past ten. It wasn't like Lily to sleep this late.

Abruptly he came to his feet and charged down the stairs, down the hall and found Jason, now freshly showered from their morning run and dressed in jeans, chopping vegetables.

"What's wrong with her?"

Without looking up from his task, Jason shrugged his shoulders. "I already told you, I don't know."

Adam shook his head. His friend may be in the dark but he was willing to bet Jason's cute little fiancée was well-versed on whatever the mystery was. "Minka knows. If she knows, you know."

"Normally that would be a true statement." Jason placed the knife on the counter and opened the refrigerator to retrieve a box of organic eggs from Herring Creek, the farm owned and operated by Forrest's parents. "However, my fiancée has not said a word to me, nor have I asked."

Adam started to walk past his friend. Might as well find the second best source.

"Leave my girl alone," Jason warned in his usual badass attitude. If anyone could keep up with Adam, it would be Jason. "I told you we would drop Lily over today, but your impatient ass couldn't wait."

Adam leaned against the wall and crossed his arms over his chest. "She's avoiding me for a reason."

Jason snickered as he chewed on a piece of pepper. "You fucked up. Now you have to beg for forgiveness and brace yourself for the worst."

Uh. What? But more importantly who was this person talking to him? Surely, an alien had kidnapped his friend and taught him the word beg, because the Jason he knew didn't have such a verb in his vocabulary. Jason dumped the sliced vegetables in the pan over the eggs.

"You beg to Minka?"

His friend placed the pan in the oven, kicked it close with one leg then focused his attention on Adam. "I don't have to. I'm a perfect fiancé. But I would if I royally fucked up."

Adam dragged his fingers through his hair. "Jesus, I didn't fuck up."

Jason snickered. His friend didn't look the least convinced. "You didn't kiss anyone?"

"For the record, that woman kissed me. And I stopped her." And that was fucking six weeks ago. Since then, they'd spent days having sex in her apartment.

"Slept with anyone?"

Adam paced around the kitchen to the sliding door overlooking the large porch that Jason built himself. As a matter of fact, he refurbished this whole damn house by himself when he was in a pissed off mood. "The only woman I want to sleep with is upstairs and she doesn't want to see me."

"You're sexually frustrated."

He flipped his friend the bird. "I'm going back upstairs."

Another chuckle from Jason. "Seriously, if you beg, I guarantee you she'll say whatever you want when you make up."

"Lily already has a dirty mouth in bed."

Jason turned away and burst into laughter. Swearing under his breath, Adam walked out of the kitchen. Whatever happened to his cynical, moody friend?

Fucking love happened. Shit. That only made Jason more annoying than ever.

As soon as Adam opened the bedroom door, his gaze went to the empty spot on the bed. She was no longer there. Fuck. Surely she couldn't have left. He would have noticed, unless she snuck out with Minka. Double fuck.

He was about to walk out of the room when the bathroom door opened. Their gazes locked. Lily stopped mid-stride then took a step or two backward, a dazed look on her face.

Why the fuck was she surprised?

Did she really expect him to accept a breakup over the phone? The thought almost made him laugh.

"Adam."

Yup. That's me. In the fucking flesh.

"I was going to text you," she continued.

But he wasn't listening.

He was done listening. Done giving her space. It was time to speak the language they both understood. With urgent strides, he stepped into her personal space. "Fuck texting, phone calls, tweets, Facebook messages and all of that other bullshit. I want you with me. In my bed. On me. Under me." He caught a hold of her arm. "Wherever the fuck you want to be, Lily, it's going to be with me. Now let's go home."

8

"Just because I let you go, doesn't mean I wanted to." Anonymous

*E*verything about Adam told Lily to surrender. He stood before her with an unshaven jaw, in dark grey loose-fitted sweats and a blue retro crew neck with *Italia* printed across his chest. His broad shoulders stretched the material of the T-shirt. He was too close, his body almost touching hers from chest to waist. She needed to put space between them, yet her body could not, would not, move away from those hard lean muscles. She craved his touch. Adam was her drug. An expensive, illegal, soul-crushing, life-ruining, highly-addictive drug and she needed to leave him alone.

"I can't go with you."

One long finger came to rest under her chin and held her gaze. "You can't or you won't?"

Fearing that she might capitulate to the carnal desire burning in his eyes, Lily lowered her lids to shut him out. She hadn't been dreaming after all. Moments ago, stuck between sleep and consciousness she'd felt his thumb caress her face and called out his name. The touch had sent an electrical jolt through her, forcing her eyes open. She scanned the room for Adam and was greeted by silence.

Yet, everything in her had sensed his presence. For a while she'd remained on the bed contemplating how to handle the situation when they came face to face until the usual morning sickness flared again, forcing her to dash to the bathroom. Well, thank goodness she'd taken the time to freshen up afterwards. The warm water she splashed on her face even brought some color back to her skin.

"Liliana, can't or won't?" he asked again.

She shook her head. "What's the difference?"

"You're a teacher. You know the damn difference."

Crossing her arms over her chest, she walked past him to her suitcase and started pulling out her clothes. Hoping the small distance gave her strength. "I mean, does it matter?" she asked over her shoulder.

"Is there someone else?" he asked, his voice curt and matter-of-fact.

"No." She could have lied. That would at least cover the *can't*—an outside force making her unable to continue sleeping with him.

"Then this is your choice." That would be the *won't*—her own choice not to continue sleeping with him.

With her back to him, she nodded. Stillness filled the room as they processed the information. Lily herself was having a hard time accepting the reality of the curtain closing on their relationship, however casual it was.

"Tell me why," Adam asked into the silence.

Still clutching at herself, Lily fought the pain in the back of her throat and choked out the words. "We can't do this anymore."

She heard him move across the room as he came to stand behind her. The bedroom windows were cracked open, allowing a cool brisk air into the room. Still her temperature spiked from the heat of his body.

"Liliana," he said, his breath warm against her earlobe, causing her to visibly jump. He caught her wrist, spun her around and pulled her to him.

"Tell me how I fucked up," he demanded in a low rough voice, "and I'll fix it."

From any other man, the words might have come across as

begging. But not from Adam. Her gaze swept over him. His dark, brooding features set in a hard, determined expression, streaming with an abundance of testosterone and pheromones. Not an ounce of weakness. The man before her was an image of a fiery untamed steed, temperamental, and filled with determination. Not to mention sexy as hell.

She brushed her hand over the scruff along his jaw. His muscles ticked under her touch. "It's not you, Adam," she started gently, her heart twisting in pain to a degree she never thought possible.

He caught her wrist and pulled her hand away from his face. A short, bitter laugh came from the back of his throat. "Don't give me the 'it's not you, it's me' line, Lily. I coined that line."

His voice was loud, so thunderous, that she couldn't concentrate on what he said. The shortening of her name told her he was done playing nice. The few times Adam had used her shortened name were when he was near the edge over a disagreement between them.

"Tell me the truth." His voice cut her. "I, we," he motioned one hand between them. "Deserve at least that. Then I'll leave you alone."

I'm pregnant with your child. She wanted to say, but a small lump sat in her throat, taking away her ability of speech. He'd caught her off-guard. She exhaled, trying to release some of the tension built up in her shoulders. "We don't work."

His eyes narrowed. "From what I remember, we work pretty well together."

"There's more to life than great sex."

He looked at her as if she'd suddenly grown a second head. "Sex is a natural part of life."

Her lips curved into a smile. And like the predator that he was, he pounced on her momentary lapse. Adam slid a hand around her waist and drew her in, his mouth brushed against hers.

"Do you feel that?" he whispered against her lips.

His hand roamed over her back, manipulating her senses, making it impossible to think. She blinked and her lips parted. His mouth brushed over hers, a soft touch at first then sure and demanding, and the hunger she thought she had under control consumed her, scorching and chilling her insides all at once.

As if he was equally affected, Adam let out one low, inconsolable laugh and muttered against her mouth, "Chemistry. We have it. It's so strong we can incinerate this place."

Lily's heart pounded against the cage of her ribs. She couldn't deny the animal attraction between them, pure physical chemistry. Everything about Adam made her crave, the way he looked, smelled, tasted, the feel of his body and the sound of his voice. He was overwhelming and uncontrollable.

Still, he wasn't in her future, not the way she needed him to be, and she wouldn't let a baby sway her toward thinking they could be more. Their relationship was based on sex, really great sex. And God help her, she wanted more of him.

Leaning into him, she struggled to keep her eyes open. His mouth floated over hers as his gaze searched hers. "Don't look at me with those fuck-me eyes if you don't want to be fucked, Liliana."

He gave her an opportunity to deny him and waited. She stood frozen, waiting for his mouth to capture hers. When she didn't respond, he hauled her in against him. One hand palmed the back of her neck, the other pulled her hips against his. A low moan escaped her, and his mouth edged up in that sinful smile that always made her shake with desire. Today was no different.

He kissed her then, and the room fell away. At the taste of him, Lily realized she'd been starving for his touch. Lost in absolute, lustful ecstasy, her eyes slid shut and the space between them exploded. Her heart missed a beat and she wrapped her arms around his neck, and pulled him closer, molding her body to his.

They had kissed many times before but she'd never felt so lost in a kiss. It burned her alive. He kissed her as though he were famished. The kiss swallowed her, owned her. No one had ever made her feel so consumed. She heard a whimper. Hers. Any rational thoughts she had escaped her as she melted against the ridges of his body.

"You here, and me at home alone doesn't add up." His voice was low and husky as kisses trailed against the nape of her neck, leaving her head spinning. "Let's go home and I swear I won't stop making love to you until your legs are shaking." His lips brushed her earlobe, and her knees wobbled. "Let's go get lost in each other, Liliana."

Her body yearned, ached for him. She moaned.

He chuckled, a soft, sexy sound in her ear. "Hell, we can start here." He lowered his weight to his knees in front of her, lifted the silk top to expose her flat stomach. His lips moved down and settled against the flesh just below her navel, and planted a kiss there. Where their child lay. She gasped instantly, her whole body tensing.

Lily froze and gripped Adam's shoulders. "Please stop," she begged and quickly moved out of his reach, accidentally knocking a jar vase off the nearby table. The glass shattered and everything fell silent.

She saw the confusion cross his face, and then it was gone. With his eyes still on her, he came to his full height and dragged a hand through his hair, the muscles in his arms taut as he stood watching her. Silently screaming for an explanation.

"I…" she started, but a hard knock on the door drew her eyes away from Adam's. "Come in," she said in a shaky voice.

"Go away," Adam barked. His face set into a scowl, clearly irritated.

The door opened nonetheless and Jason stepped inside the room. His blue, assessing eyes shifted between them.

"Is everything okay?" His gaze was on Lily, studying her.

Unable to speak, she nodded.

"Jason, give us a minute," Adam said to his friend without taking his eyes off Lily.

She held her breath and prayed Jason didn't give in to his friend's request. The two men were close, business partners, childhood friends. She stood no chance. Dizzy and feeling weakness in her legs, she lowered herself to the bed.

"I think whatever it is the two of you need to discuss should wait another day," Jason said in an easy tone. "Lily looks like she's about to pass out. So why don't you both go into your respective corners and suit up for the next round, which I'm sure will come. She's here for two weeks, after all."

*J*ason's words forced Adam to look at Lily once again and take in her delicate appearance. She looked sucker-punched, her skin translucent. Her wide eyes, usually filled with life and laughter, appeared damp and overly bright.

"You want to end what we have together." The words were a statement more so for him than her.

Still, she nodded.

His stomach hit his throat and he shoved it the fuck back down. "Well, too fucking bad. We're not done. Not by a fucking long shot."

She looked at him with a dazed expression. Adam shoved his hands in his pockets then glanced at Jason, who remained silent. "I'll see you at Vapor tonight."

Adam stormed past his friend. He was breathless, sweating, and shaking like he'd taken a curve at 200 mph with no idea what was on the other side. Nothing made sense. He breathed heavily as he hurried down the stairs. All the trees on the island couldn't supply enough oxygen. He needed to get away.

"Adam," Minka called after him.

He stopped midstride and turned to face the woman who had become a friend. Her face was nearly buried underneath a mass of spiral curls. He impatiently brushed back a mane of hair to expose her pretty features. She flashed him an apologetic smile. In spite of all the tension inside him, he smiled back at her.

"Give her time," she said gently.

"She wants out."

Minka flinched. "Oh."

"What do you know, Minka? Tell me. She doesn't look well."

The two women shared a connection. They were best friends. He could tell by the way Minka was chewing on her lower lip, she knew what the hell was going on. He also knew no way in hell she was going to betray her friend.

"I can't," she said as he expected. "I'm sorry, Adam, but it's her story to tell. Not mine."

He understood the loyalty between the two friends. Hell, he had his own with Jason, Forrest, Blake, and Claire. "I'll see you tomorrow." He walked past Minka out of the house and hopped into the black Maserati GranTurismo convertible, put it in reverse and sped out of the driveway.

The convertible was Adam's latest addition to his collection of sleek, fast cars. Speed was his rush. He shifted gear, pressed on the pedal and the engine yielded to his command and accelerated. Good girl. His new baby. Dynamic and elegant, the perfect blend of freedom and passion, with enough practicality that his mother only frowned once when she saw the car. His argument—it comfortably sat four. Although, so far only Forrest had enough balls to join him for a test drive. Jason didn't part from his Jeep and Blake practically had two wives, his Mercedes SUV and Keely, Minka's fraternal twin.

But it was Lily he fantasized about, stripped naked and riding him with the top down under the moonlight somewhere. Only she no longer wanted to play. And she wouldn't tell him why.

Adam swore under his breath. Something was up and since it wasn't another man, he vowed to get to the bottom of it. Hell, as Jason said he would go back to his corner and get ready for round two, because they weren't done. Not by a long shot. But right now he needed an adrenaline rush to release the tension burning of him. Reaching for his phone he pressed Forrest's number and connected the phone to the car.

"What are you wearing today? Scrubs or farmer's shoes?" Adam asked when Forrest answered his phone.

"Which one do you like best?" His friend asked on speaker. "I hear wind. That means you're still not getting any so you took your baby for a ride?"

"You must be in scrubs. You're in doctor mode."

Forrest was the island's most eligible doctor. When he wasn't running his clinic, he was usually on his parents' farm working or catching waves with the boys, the reason for Adam's call. He checked the neon numbers indicating the late morning. The strong waves were long gone.

"Paddle boarding?"

"Can't. Two jerks came up with this idea of a wine tasting, food festival and every year, it gets bigger and crazier." Forrest complained with feigned frustration. "I'm closing shop in two hours and heading to the farm since we have to supply food to a certain restaurant in Menemsha and a bar downtown."

The restaurant belonged to Adam. Vapor was a partnership venture between Adam and Jason.

"How about tomorrow?" Forrest proposed. "First thing in the morning before the madness starts. We're supposed to get some strong waves."

Just what Adam needed, a fight with the ocean. The waves would be stubborn and try to take him down. He was ready for the battle. "It's a date."

Forrest chuckled. "I don't put out though."

"You're not my type. Apparently, I prefer willowy women with short hair."

Forrest laughed a little harder. "First Blake, then Jason, and now you. All the greats have fallen."

Adam snorted. "Don't confuse lust for the other L word."

"First sign is denial. You can't even say the word."

"Love," he muttered to spite his friend. "Happy, asshole?"

"And stubborn as hell." Forrest laughed again. "Yeah, you're a dead man. Gotta go. See you first thing tomorrow."

Adam disconnected the call and steered the car along the rolling hills of the island, passing sheep farms, winding country roads lined with vegetable stands and colorful harbors bustling with boats. He belonged in two worlds. All his life he balanced it well. In Italy, he kept a condo in the city and loved the fast life but Chilmark was home. His serenity.

He steered the car along the wooded area to his house and maneuvered the vehicle with ease along the roughness of the unpaved road. Once inside, he kicked off his shoes and welcomed the coolness of the wooden floor against his feet, and made his way to the laundry room to locate a pair of swim trunks before going to the shed house for his board. He hoisted it under his arm and walked down the hilly path onto the beach. Ahead of him, the calm, peaceful sea stretched out as far as he could see.

One of the perks of living on ten acres of land, and in a town with a population of less than a thousand people, was privacy. On most days he had the water to himself, like today. In Italy and the world of racing, he was considered famous, but on the island, except for an occasional tourist approaching him, he was left alone. He was a local.

He placed the board on the water and jumped in. Since he'd left his wetsuit behind, the icy water stung his skin, a welcome reprieve from the racing in his mind. Adam jumped on the board, adjusted his weight for balance, pushed off and began paddling, floating smoothly on the light waves.

And then there was nothing but the sound of his board skimming through the water, the occasional sight of birds landing smoothly on the sea, but soon returned to the sky, the splash of enthusiastic fish, and the freedom cry of seagulls filling the scene.

Peace.

He found that in three places, racing, the water, and buried deep between Lily's legs. He groaned. The taste of her sweet lips still lingered on his mouth like the smell of summer rain. He ached to kiss her deeper, to lose himself in her and feel her heartbeat against his.

Shit. Never in his life had a woman possessed so much power over his body. He inhaled and slowly released as the wind whipped his face. Keeping his breath steady, Adam paddled faster, and pushed harder until his shoulders burned. He felt his whole body working, his leg muscles warmed, cold air bit his lungs, and blood flowed into his limbs.

His muscles burned, then ached, then went numb. But he continued on, unhesitating. Catching wave after wave, relentlessly seeking the oblivion of physical exhaustion. Finally, he lay spent on the sand. Board by his side, he stared up at the crystalline sky and tried to appease his need for oxygen.

9

"My only nightmare is waking up in a world where you're not mine."
Unknown

*A*dam's eyes moved rapidly back and forth behind his eyelids. There was something, someone there, but he couldn't see it or move fast enough. His body felt heavy, as if he were dragging a ship's anchor behind him. He recognized his whereabouts. Small puddles of water welled in corners and seeped from walls, creating a strong presence of mold. The building was most dilapidated, beyond repair.

His eyes caught sight of the weathered door. Scratches etched their way along the bottom half of it and the edges were uneven and cracked. The door knob hung loose, waiting eagerly for him to step inside. It smelled horrid, and if you squinted hard enough, you could see tiny black bugs crawling in between the jagged scratches.

The door may be battered, but it was his freedom. He hurried his steps, but his only way out seemed further away with each step he took. As he reached for the knob, a skittering sound echoed behind him. Adam's scalp shivered. He quickened his steps and tried to hurry, but the hot breath of his tormentor burned the back of his neck.

There was pain, and a splattering of red. A chill washed over his body when a cold, metallic object pressed against his head. He was going to die. The room darkened slowly, and the sunset cast an orange glow through the window embellishing the grim scene. Accepting his fate, he squeezed his eyelids together.

The trigger released with a snap, and he jerked, sitting up suddenly in the dark quiet room, his heart hammering, cold sweat beading on his skin.

Another nightmare.

"Fuck!" he breathed shakily, sick to his stomach.

He remained still, looking around the room, reorienting himself from the dream. Then he dropped his weight back on the bed, allowing a second or two to settle his racing heart. After a few seconds, he rubbed his eyes, turned on the bedside lamp, and reached for the Panerai watch on the nightstand.

Five a.m. Perfect time to awaken from a nightmare. Forrest would be arriving soon for their early morning surf. Rubbing the back of his neck, he walked into the bathroom and splashed cold water on his face, and brushed his teeth before sliding into his a fitted black wet-suit.

He stepped outside. Patches of mist swirled above the colorful trees. He pulled the black skully down to his ears and inhaled the cool, crisp air. He just needed to breathe to rid himself from the dark thoughts in his head. He was in the process of fitting his board in the back of his car when Forrest's orange Jeep pulled next to him. Unlike Adam, who felt like shit, his friend looked completely at ease blasting *What I Got* by Sublime from the stereo.

"Hop in," Forrest hollered.

Adam shook his head. "Let's take my car."

"It's enough I'm going to freeze my balls early in the morning to help you relieve some stress. I want to at least be comfortable driving there, so get in."

Adam recognized a good argument when he heard one and dumped his board in the back of the Jeep.

"Gay Head or South Beach?" Forrest asked as Adam slid into the passenger seat.

Gay Head was located in Aquinnah and at this time of the morning the waves would be strong there. "Let's go to Aquinnah. Closer and better waves."

Forrest nodded and shifted gear to start the Jeep. "And further away from Lily."

"You're a fucking genius," he grunted. Jason's house was less than one mile away from the popular South Beach. The temptation to go there instead and demand an explanation from Lily would be too tempting. His friends knew him well. Resting his head against the cushion of the seat, he closed his eyes and enjoyed the fresh morning air.

"Has it occurred to you she just doesn't want to do this anymore?"

"She still wants me," he answered without opening his eyes.

Forrest snorted. "I mean, has it occurred to you she might want more? You know, a meaningful relationship with love, stability, and a real car?"

"Then she should say so."

"Except you don't want those things."

Adam slid his friend a sideways look. "What's your point?"

"What if she wants to take your relationship to the next level? Would you give it to her?"

He pondered Forrest's question. The possibility that she might want something more between them had not crossed his mind. When they started whatever it was they were doing, both had made it clear nothing serious was their only option.

"I don't do marriage," he muttered, "and neither does she."

"Who said anything about marriage?"

"We both decided what this was. If she wants to change the rules she should tell me."

"But you probably wouldn't want to continue playing."

"Is this the part where I point out that she's the one who doesn't want to play anymore?"

"No, this is the part you acknowledge that I'm brilliant."

"Or maybe a pain in my ass. By the way, Claire is coming to town. Are you guys going to give in to the tension and start fucking?" He purposefully turned the spotlight on Forrest, giving his friend a taste of his own medicine.

Forrest grunted and killed the ignition. "You look like shit."

"Thanks. Tell me something I don't know."

"The bags under your eyes are quite a delectable shade of purple. What brand is that?"

"Insomnia."

"Nice. Gotta try that some time. Tough night?"

Adam shrugged. "I'll eventually sleep again."

"I can . . ."

"No drugs."

"Actually, I was going to say have you thought about facing your demons?" When Adam didn't answer, Forrest slapped his shoulder. "Come on, big boy, let's go release some frustration."

Adam's legs were shredded from two hours battling strong ocean waves. For two days, he'd pushed himself and his body paid the price. But instead of feeling tired, the achiness energized him, a good thing too because he had a busy week ahead with the Food and Wine Festival.

He took slow easy strides down the path leading to the back of the restaurant he opened five years ago. The Wharf's Side was ideally situated half a mile from the port of Menemsha, and a short walk to the public beach. He took pride in hiring the best chef for this venture and partnering with Forrest's parents for a farm to table approach, allowing the restaurant to always serve the freshest produce in season. The move turned out to be a success. The Wharf's Side was now well established as one of the *must* places to eat when on the island.

He walked over to the edge of the dock, rubbed his hands together for warmth. The distinct crispness of the air sparked interest in lighting a fire and watching the sun set over the yellow, orange and red trees with Lily. They had done exactly that a year ago. The night had ended perfectly with her riding him until he exploded. The memory made him shiver with need.

An empty feeling settled in his stomach. He wasn't shocked by how much he wanted her; he'd accepted that fact a long time ago. Still, he shook his head at the memory and brushed any thought of her aside.

His phone vibrated in his pocket. His first thought directed to Lily. He extracted the phone quickly and glanced at the international number flashing on the screen. He dismissed the pang of disappointment and smiled.

"How's my favorite son?" His mother asked on the other end of the phone. Her voice filled with warmth.

"I'm your only son," he responded just as good-naturedly. That was the ongoing greeting between them and Adam would never grow tired of it.

"You made the news again here."

"Who am I marrying this week?" Both his parents took great pleasure over the Italian's media obsession with his love life. For the last year, every woman he was spotted with was the flavor of the week.

His mother cackled in laughter. "Ella."

Adam shook his head and laughed at the news. "She's family."

And on top of that Ella was happily married to Guillermo, his chef at The Wharf's Side. His interest in opening a restaurant on the island spurred upon meeting Guillermo and discovering his brilliant culinary skills. The couple split their time between Brazil and the Vineyard. As it happened she was in Italy the last time he was there and they met for lunch.

"I just wanted to let you know you're engaged to be married."

"Well, I love you even more for that. How's Dad?" he asked, picturing his dad chuckling in the background over the conversation.

"He's here laughing and pretending he's reading a book."

"Well, give him my love and thanks for making me aware of my engagement."

"The least I can do. How's that girlfriend of yours?

For no apparent reason, one morning during breakfast, he found himself casually telling his parents about Lily. They had asked the questions most curious parents interested in their only child's happiness would ask.

Who was she? How did they meet?

A teacher. Minka's best friend.

Was he in love?

It wasn't that kind of relationship.

After that they had not pushed. But from time to time he talked to them about her.

"I don't have a girlfriend," he replied, but Adam couldn't help but think of Forrest's words from earlier. What if she wanted more? "Liliana and I have an understanding," he said for his own self-assurance.

"Darling, I don't care how hurt she's been. A woman can't spend a year sleeping with a man and not become emotionally invested."

There were times he hated the frankness of his relationship with his parents. Right now was a perfect example. "So I've been told." He grunted.

"Will we get to meet her when we come for the wedding?"

Deep down, Adam was dreading that day. Not because he didn't want to introduce Lily to his parents, but he could already see their brains working, plotting to tie him down. "She's Minka's best friend. She's here. I will introduce you at the wedding."

"Not before?"

"It's not necessary." His parents knew him well enough to understand the discussion was final.

"Well, we love you very much. Call and let us know how the festival is going."

"*Ti amo*, and will do."

Adam hung up and stood staring at the blank screen of his phone. A cool autumn breeze pulled him out of his daze, tickling the barren trees where they cut across the sky. He looked down, noticing for the first time the piles of freshly fallen leaves raked into piles in front of him.

It was still early in the day but already the place bustled with activity and excitement. He spotted the Herring Creek Farm truck making the day's delivery for their farm to table menu at the restaurant. Forrest's parents waved at him. He waved back and started to make his way over when two black labs came chasing around barking in delight, scattering golden leaves everywhere before jumping on him for their usual greeting.

Chuckling, he reached in his pocket, lowered his weight to his knees, gave the dogs their daily treat, scratched behind their ears and patted their backs. They nuzzled closer.

"We have to head to Martha's Way," Luc called out to him from the truck.

"You're not wearing your seatbelt," Adam pointed out, knowing that was a constant debate between Forrest and his father.

"You sound like my son. We'll see you later." Luc whistled and the dogs jumped inside the truck.

From the backyard, the ocean air was brisk and he pulled the hood of his sweatshirt over his head. His thumb scrolled to Lily's number and pressed *TALK*. To his surprise, she answered right away.

"Adam," she greeted in a neutral tone.

The reception sent ice through his gut. "How are you feeling?"

"Better. I was going to text you but—"

"No more texting," he interjected in a rougher tone than he intended. "You're here on the Vineyard with me. From now on we talk, face to face. Got it?"

"Yes."

Her voice ripped through him. Adam squeezed his eyes shut as an awkward silence fell between them. He opened his eyes and focused his attention on the moving ocean. "I miss you and I want you. What is the American expression? Blue balls? Well, I think you can officially find my face right next to the term."

She laughed softly in his ear and he smiled. "I want to believe you're in as much agony."

"I am," she confessed. "But—"

"No buts, Liliana."

She let out a deep sigh. An awkward silence fell between them.

"Have the rules changed?" he asked, breaking the stillness.

His question was met by a gaping silence.

"What is it that you want, Liliana?"

"We have to talk," she acknowledged.

"Come to Vapor tonight. I'll be there." He needed immediate action and get to the bottom of whatever was going on. He'd suggest now, but he had commitments for the food festival.

"Don't you have an event there tonight?"

"We can still talk."

He knew her well enough to know she was shaking her head stubbornly at him. So he pushed. "I'm going to be busy all week with the festival, but I asked you to come here a week early to be with me, not to be at my fucking best friend's house. So we'll talk and you'll tell me what you want."

"What if I don't want anything? What if I want to stop sleeping with you?"

There was an uncertainty in her voice. Every muscle in Adam's body tightened. "Then grow some balls, face me, and tell me exactly that and why. You need to tell me why."

After a short silence, she let out a deep sigh. "Okay," she said softly. "I'll see you tonight." Her voice shook on the words.

"See you tonight, Liliana."

After he disconnected the call, he was about to head inside the restaurant when Guillermo appeared with two rakes in hand. Adam grabbed the offered rake and patted the older man on his back. Guillermo was a handsome man in his early fifties with tanned olive skin similar to Adam's and jet black hair sprinkled with a hint of grey. He was a brilliant chef and someone Adam considered a friend.

"Do they always have to cause chaos whenever they come here?" he asked, referring to Luc and Marjorie's two energetic Labradors.

Guillermo chuckled. "I think they love watching you squirm."

"They're not the only one."

"Problem in paradise?"

Adam shrugged. His relationship with Lily wasn't a secret. Everyone in his circle knew they were sleeping together. "Does Ella always tell you what she wants?"

The chef chuckled, clearly amused by the question. "After twenty years of marriage, I can tell you I still don't know what she's thinking.

The only thing I do know is when she says everything is fine, I'm in really big shit."

Adam swallowed his laughter, let the tension flush out of his body and started raking the leaves into a pile. Guillermo joined him.

"I think I'm in deep shit."

"Over you being engaged to my wife, who happens to be your cousin." Guillermo waved a dismissive hand in the air. "Tell Lily the truth. Ella is my wife."

"You're my cousin."

Guillermo shrugged. "Same thing. Family is family."

Adam nodded. Good point. "I don't think this is about another woman."

Guillermo stopped and rested his chin on the rake. "Then you need to beg and accept that you royally screwed things up."

"Jesus, what is it about begging and accepting fault?"

"Do you want to have sex again? With Lily, that is."

Adam let out a deep sigh. "At this point, I just want to have sex."

"Then go have sex. You have women tapping their fingers waiting for you to take them home."

"I don't want them."

"You only want Lily."

Adam curled his lips in disgust and grunted. "It will bring you great satisfaction to hear me admit to that."

Guillermo nodded with a smile.

"Fine. I want to have sex with Liliana, only her."

"So beg and accept that you royally screwed up. Now, let's talk about today's menu."

Adam nodded and switched to Portuguese as the two men discussed their dinner options for the night; all the while, his mind stayed on Lily. The need to touch her and the fact he still had about nine hours to go before they came face to face for round two made him feel edgy. This time, he had no intention of walking away empty-handed.

10

"Once you have tasted flight, you will forever walk the earth with your eyes turned skyward, for there you have been, and there you will always long to return."
Leonardo Da Vinci

In Lily's world there was one universal truth when it came to her relationship with Adam, it was easy for them to take off their clothes and have sex. Hell, people did it all the time. Only a year ago, she had shamelessly encouraged Minka to jump in the hay with Jason. But opening up your soul to someone, letting them into your spirit, thoughts, fears, future, hopes, dreams, now that was being naked. Adam and Lily had never been that exposed.

At no time had they shared childhood stories. Whatever intimate details she gathered of him had been a fluke. During a night out with their circle of friends, she'd learned his father was Christiano Aquilani, a famous retired Italian soccer player, who could easily rival Paolo Rossi or Baggio. Once off-roading with the group, it was casually mentioned his mother was Sophia Kensington, a former Miss America.

Adam didn't share anything personal. Not that she blamed him, she was as guarded and shared very little. Allowing herself zero chance to develop any sort of attachment. She even stayed away whenever his parents were on the island. Something, they did at least four times a year. Adam always casually announced when they were visiting, and Lily was smart enough to get the hint and stayed away. For all she knew, they didn't know of her existence, and that suited her just fine. Well, kind of.

There was that little pang each time she discovered a bit of personal information about Adam from his friends. Things that were common knowledge to the world, he never felt the need to share with the woman sharing his bed. A reminder, she was just a fuck-buddy.

She'd hooked up with him on a whim. They sought each other out when it suited them, no questions asked, no explanations needed. But then they'd started to talk and when they were apart, he'd text. That was where the trouble began.

At first she'd tried to ignore the messages. To acknowledge them would cause an expectation. Expectation led to disappointment. But eventually she'd caved, and their conversations went from a simple *Good morning* text, to a phone call in the morning, a text or two during the course of the day and a phone call at night.

No matter where Adam was, he called or texted. And although she never admitted it, she came to anticipate their daily interaction.

And then he had to go all chivalrous on her. Taking care of her when she was sick six weeks ago. Delaying his trip back to the island for three days. Making her laugh. Making her tea. Her belly did a flip. Damn his tea.

Why did he have to do that?

Belly flips were definitely not in their rule book.

She had willingly entered a dead-end relationship with him. And for a while it was exactly what she needed. Only now, she needed... wanted that crazy-out-of-this-world kind of love that she knew existed.

But not from Adam.

She turned left into the parking lot by The Shanti, the exact spot she caught sight of Adam strolling down the road over a year ago. She exhaled. She needed to tell him about her pregnancy. Lily exhaled a deep breath, dreading his reaction. She already knew what it would be.

He'd want marriage. Not because of love but because Adam took, Adam possessed. The same way he had taken her.

That feeling was wonderful in bed. Thrilling, stirring, electrifying.

But in real life? That would be settling. She never believed on settling, especially when it came to her heart.

No way. Not gonna happen.

Not in her life or her child's life. Unable to delay their impending conversation any longer, she stepped out of Minka's Audi and crossed the street from the large parking area by the pier, down the narrow path to Vapor. The evening was chilly but gorgeous, clear skies, and cool brisk air. The typical summer crowd had since dissipated, but the streets were filled with life. People young and old filled the avenue, crowding the local businesses participating in the Food and Wine festival.

The closer she got to Vapor, the quicker her heart raced. Nerves. She slowed her steps, drew in a deep breath, pushed open the door with a trembling hand, and proceeded to the bar.

She was met by the booming sound of excitement, deafening chatter, as one person spoke over the other. It appeared she'd found the party. Not that it surprised her.

Vapor was an honored sanctuary for Vineyard regulars and a familiar getaway for the many notables who frequented the island. The cool feel and warm finish of the brass bar and the Tapas-inspired grazing menu were enough to keep a loyal crowd. But the real reason people gathered at Vapor was to kick back, relax, and enjoy. Even in the winter, when the population was barely at fifteen-thousand, the bar was the place to be.

She wedged through the crowd, stomach flip-flopping, and made her way to the bar, where she knew she'd find him. A few feet away, she came to a halt at the sight of Adam. He stood next to Jason, who looked just as daunting and sexy in blue jeans and a Henley. But it was Adam who caught her attention. It was always him, had been since the moment they met.

He stood there completely unaware of her watching him. Tall, well over six feet with hard muscles, casually dressed in a white button-down oxford shirt with sleeves rolled to his elbows. Tonight he was sporting one of those I-decided-to-tuck-in-the-front-of-my-shirt-at-the-last-minute partial tucked into moss colored straight-fit cargo pants, with one of those skater, surfer belts. He looked as if he'd just stepped out of *GQ* magazine and could take on anything that came his way, including her.

He smiled over something a blonde woman said to him at the bar and tugged Jason playfully by his side. The two men laughed, nothing flirtatious. Being friendly to their clients was part of their job. Still, a pang of an avoidable loss lingered inside her. She missed his smile, his laughter, the way his eyes crinkled. She missed his kiss. She missed Adam. She wanted him more than her next breath.

At that instant, she knew as much as she'd like to deny it, pretend it wasn't so, she was head over heels in love. His world moved too fast and burned too bright. Still, she fell. The realization wasn't earth shattering, almost expected really. What was not to love? But she didn't know how to feel about her feelings.

He poured a shot, pushed a drink across the counter. Something in his casual movements and easy smile made her feel like she couldn't live without him. Only she knew better.

Adam was not about commitment. She knew he was trouble the minute she'd spotted him walking down the pier over a year ago with a woman on each arm. So shame on her. Once again, she'd fallen for the wrong guy and found love in a hopeless place.

Had they not been interrupted by Jason yesterday, she would have freely given herself to him with no regrets. It was simple, he consumed her. She couldn't help it. He was just too damn . . . hot. A beautiful raging storm filled with total hotness. And the minute she let the cat out of the bag, he'd come in like a tornado and Lily, like a tree with many branches, but weak roots, would be thrown to the ground.

In love or not, she needed to be strong. If not for her, for their growing baby. She couldn't help falling in love, but she still had a choice on how to go forward. Adam was impulsive, he didn't do commitment. He belonged in two worlds but not really rooted in either one of them. She needed–wanted–a foundation and stability. The baby wasn't responsible for this epiphany, it was who she was. Her relationship with Adam, the casual, non-committed, no promises teeter-totter they rode wasn't her. She'd pretended long enough.

Adam suddenly looked up and their gazes clashed. Her feet moved at their will and headed to the bar.

"What's your poison?" Jason asked in his usual calm, cool, and collected manner.

"Tonic water," she answered.

Jason's eyes narrowed. He paused.

Yikes! Did she just let the cat out of the bag?

Her heart was pounding, her legs suddenly restless, and her palms slippery with nerves. But she gave him a cool smile. To her relief, he poured her the tonic water with a twist of lime and went about his business.

"Jay, can you handle this for a bit?" Adam called over his shoulder.

To alleviate the sudden dryness in her mouth, she took a sip of her drink.

"Yeah, I got it." Jason answered, shot glass in hand.

Heart in her throat, she watched Adam put away the bottle of liquor and walk to the edge of the bar where she stood. He took her hands in his and smiled. Lily could have died that instant and she wouldn't have cared. Instead, her lips parted with an overwhelming need to be kissed by him.

He didn't kiss her.

"I didn't think you were going to come," he said in a low voice.

"I said I would." Okay, her voice shook just a bit, but overall she had to give herself brownie points for sounding relatively calm.

"Let's go talk." He placed a hand on her back and guided her past the shuffle board to the stairs that led to the lounge.

As usual the lounge was quieter, less crowded, with a smaller bar. With a nod, Adam acknowledged the pretty bartender she knew as Maxie. He led her to the opposite end of the room, away from everyone to an empty table.

"What's on your mind?" he asked once they were sitting and facing each other.

She blinked. Loneliness, fear, the fact that she was about to walk away from the man she loved, all plagued her mind. He reached and grasped her hand, automatically their fingers entwined.

"You said things have changed." His voice was low and raw.

She nodded.

A painful silence settled between them.

"What do you want from me? From us?"

She met his gaze briefly and then looked away. "You race cars." The words were spoken so softly, so out of the blue. She turned her attention to Adam. He sat, watching her, waiting. "It scares me." She gave him a small smile, as surprised by this revelation as his expression said he was. "It's dangerous."

In the dimly lit room, she saw something flicker in his eyes. Annoyance. Anger. She wasn't sure.

"Life is dangerous," he responded. "You either live it or let the unknown cripple you. I chose to live."

"But you could die. Look what happened to Sean Edwards, Allan Simonsen." She named a few race car drivers who'd died recently.

He leaned forward, his elbows on the table. "Everyone dies, Lily." There was emptiness in his voice she'd never noticed before. As if he were numb. "I live for now."

She shook her head. "I need more, Adam. I need stability and tame."

He sat back. "Tame," he repeated.

"You're not tame," she said sadly. "You can never be tamed."

He brushed a hand over his jaw and let out a breath. "You want boring."

Silence.

He pushed his chair back, came to his full height and extended his hand to her. Puzzled, she looked at him. "I'll walk you out."

With a slight lip press, she absorbed the unexpected shock of disappointment and lowered her head to keep it from reflecting on her face. What did she expect? For him to fight for them, or even worse, try to convince her to stay.

"I want you, Liliana," Adam admitted, his voice very quiet. "When I touch you, I melt. When I think of you touching me, I lose myself."

Life needed to go easy on her. It just wasn't right for him to tell her things like that. To utter words as if she were the love of his life while he was breaking her heart.

"But I don't fit the mold of your ideal guy. I can never be that person."

There was a hint of regret in his voice that pulled at her heart. Lily glanced at him, his expression clouded. When she didn't place her hand in his, he dropped his extended hand to his side and waited for her to join him.

This is it, she thought and stood. The end. No more Adam. No more secret smiles or early morning phone calls. She walked ahead of him, heading for the exit. Her heart beat a slow ache in her chest. She stumbled, almost tripping down the stairs. She quickly reached for the wall to catch her balance but he was already by her side, strong arms around her waist. Their faces inches away.

"Don't fall," he whispered. His gaze on her mouth.

The warning came too late. She already had.

Then he was kissing her, deep and hard. Lily's arms instantly moved to his neck. Warm, soft lips matched hers. Her body ached all over, her head spun, and she forgot all about why Adam wasn't the one. When he pulled back, he lingered, clearly not wanting to stop. The band had arrived and was singing a great cover of *"Ain't No Sunshine"* by Bill Withers. Dazed, she remained still.

He released her. With clenched jaw, he ran a hand through his hair. "I'll see you around." He walked past her and opened the door for her to leave.

11
―――――

"If you've deeply resonated with another person, the connection remains despite distance, time, situation, lack of presence or circumstance."
Victoria Erickson

Two days later, Lily sat in the passenger seat next to Minka, fiddling with her phone. There had been no word from Adam. Not one single attempt. Her fingers scrolled to his name, too chicken to press *SEND*, she chose the text option and stared at the empty space.

What exactly was she going to say?

I miss you.

I love you.

I'm carrying your baby.

She typed the words and stared at them on the screen.

And now what?

Press *SEND*?

She pondered over the message. It was a lot to communicate via text. Besides, hadn't she been the one who chose to walk away? In the end, she didn't even have the strength to let her fingers do the talking and discarded the phone in her purse.

"You miss him," Minka said gently. "I don't understand why you broke up with him."

"There was nothing to break up from."

That was a lie. She knew it and so did her friend.

Minka pulled the car into the entrance of Martha's Way and parked in the reserved spot. The stylish yet chic inn owned by Jason was hidden in the pastoral town of West Tisbury on seven acres of spacious immaculate lawns, surrounded by a whirlwind of colors. Dark reds, bright oranges, and traces of crisp yellow leaves drifting down from the thick branches of the surrounding trees lent a perfect combination of autumn to the scene. Around each bend on its grounds were benches where one could relax amongst the flowers and fountains and take in the afternoon sun or the night sky.

"Looks like Keely and Claire are already here," Minka informed her, pointing to the parked orange Jeep. "Adam will be here later. Will you be okay?"

The answer was a resounding no, but she couldn't ask them to exclude him. They were a tight knit circle that she'd somehow managed to weave herself into. Besides, she knew going in this day would eventually come. "I'll be fine," she replied.

"He needs to know."

They stepped out of the car. A light breeze passed, making the falling leaves twirl in the air and evoking fond memories of jumping into piles of leaves with Adam last autumn. A soft smile touched the corners of her lips. "I'll tell him. I just need the right moment."

Minka took her hand and squeezed it. "I'm worried about you."

"Don't be. I'll be fine." She smiled. "And I will tell him."

Minka nodded, tucked her curls back behind her ears. "Jason hasn't asked me what's going on, so don't worry about that. You can stay with us as long as you want."

Lily nodded. Jason hadn't asked her any questions either, but during dinner, he no longer offered her wine. He had to know. He was a perceptive man. Jason and Minka, as expected were perfect hosts, but she couldn't help but feel she'd be in the way for two weeks. The wine and food festival was over, the remaining crowd was dwindling, and soon the island would consist only of locals. She made a mental note to speak to Nora, Martha's Way manager, to book a room for this week and next.

Lily stopped her strides, bent down and picked up a leaf from the ground. "Autumn is such a perfect time for a wedding." She brushed the dry, brittle foliage against her fingers. "It's going to be absolutely beautiful. You're going to look amazing."

"You think so?" Minka asked without a hint of the insecurity she'd worked so hard to overcome.

"Hell, yeah. I can't wait to see the dress. Come on, let's go try on some wedding dresses, my friend." She hooked Minka's arm in hers and the two women chuckled together.

They found Keely and Claire in the front living room sitting by the crackling fire, leisurely drinking a glass of wine. As Minka's longtime friend, Lily had met Keely before. But it wasn't until last year, during Lily's visit to the island, that she'd really gotten the chance to know Minka's sister and develop a friendship with her. "Here comes the soon to be bride." Keely hugged her sister, then Lily. "And Adam's kryptonite."

The women chuckled. Lily had become accustomed to them teasing her about Adam. "I'm not his kryptonite," she said for probably the hundredth time.

Claire chuckled. "He talks about you all the time, you know."

No, she didn't know that. "Adam and I are not together." She might as well put it out there. Their relationship had never been a secret.

"Right. Just sleeping together."

"No, I mean." Lily paused. "We broke up."

Claire's pretty face turned into a serious expression. "Oh. I'm sorry to hear that. I was looking forward to the two of you making beautiful babies."

All the air left Lily's lungs. She tucked one side of her hair behind her ear.

Keely brows knotted. "You were good for him. He's a fool. We'll be sure to give him the stare down later."

Lily felt Minka watching her. She walked over to the vintage leather chair by the fire and sat down. "Adam didn't do anything." Technically he hadn't.

Claire and Keely's eyes bulged in shock.

"You dumped Adam." Keely's voice went up on the last word.

"Wow, that's a first," Claire added. "Let's drink to that." She picked up the open wine bottle.

"Um, no wine," Lily stammered, causing the two women to give her a strange look. Lily twisted her neck as if sore and rubbed the back of it. She knew they picked up on her hesitation.

"Oh," Claire and Keely said in harmony.

She offered a tight smile. "I'm pregnant."

"And she hasn't told him," Minka added.

Lily shot her BFF a look. Minka smiled.

"He should know," Keely said gently.

Claire nodded in agreement. "We are here for you, Lily, whatever you need. But he needs to know."

Friends were like that. They were loyal, priceless. They shared your happiness and sorrows with you and call you on your shit when you were being a coward.

"I am going to tell him."

They exchanged another round of hugs. When the tears fell down her cheek, she chuckled and tried to bring the attention back to the reason why they were there on the first place. She glanced at Minka. "Let's go try on that dress of yours."

As Claire placed her wine glass down on the antique coffee table, the bohemian bracelets on her left arm drew Lily's eyes to the black ink inside her wrist.

"You have a tattoo," Lily remarked. "Can I see it? I've always wanted one."

Claire hesitated then pulled the bracelets back, revealing the delicate black loops of the infinity sign.

"It's beautiful. Why do you hide it?"

Something crossed Claire's face but it disappeared quickly. "I've had it for a while. Most of the time I forget it's there." She exhaled, smiled brightly. "Let's go try on your wedding gown, Minka."

Lily picked up on the tightness in Claire's voice. Whatever story was behind the tattoo, the other woman wasn't ready to get into it. She understood that and didn't press on. They all had their secrets. They walked up the stairs to the main suite where the gown Claire and Keely designed was carefully displayed on the bed. A gasp escaped Lily and Minka's lips as they rushed forward.

A hopelessly romantic creation, the ethereal gown was covered from head-to-toe in intricate Chantilly lace carefully placed to create an ultra-flattering silhouette.

"Wow," Minka's voice trembled. The emotions clear in her voice.

Keely batted her eyelashes, fighting back tears. "Come on, try it on," she urged her sister.

Seconds later, Minka stood circled between her twin sister, her friends and her new BFF—the wedding gown.

"Wow, check out the back," Lily exclaimed.

Minka spun around revealing a deep V leading to a modest train.

Keely walked over to her sister. "You look so beautiful, Minka," she said softly, her voice choked with emotion.

Minka brushed her eyelashes as if something was caught in them. The two women chuckled, looked at each other and hugged. Tears rolled down their faces. Lily stepped back and took in the moment. The tension that once existed between the two sisters now seemed like a figment of her imagination.

"It's perfect," Minka said with a beaming smile once Keely stepped back. "Thank you." She tipped her head to Keely, Lily, and Claire. "To all of you. I love it. I love you."

Another round of hugs and sniffles were exchanged. No problem for Lily, tears came easy nowadays. Her phone chirped, she walked over to the bed and picked it up.

Adam.

Her heart somersaulted.

"Lily, are you okay? You look pale." Keely remarked.

"It's Adam," she whispered.

"You should answer," Minka said.

And so she did, with all three women watching her.

"I can't stay. Come downstairs." His voice was low, gruff, and sexy.

She felt the blush race up her face. Lily smiled grimly at her friends. "Adam is downstairs. I'll just be a minute. Be right back," she said over her shoulder, already stepping out of the room.

Heart in her throat, she entered the large living room and stopped. He stood gazing into the fire, his posture stiff, tension vibrating from his body. A pair of low slung, dark denim jeans clung to his hips. A three-buttoned hoodie with a white crewneck beneath fit perfectly to his broad back. The tips of his too-long hair peeked out of a heather grey beanie. Only Adam could make a sweatshirt and a beanie look like an Abercrombie centerfold. He turned and met her gaze. His gave nothing away.

"I thought you were coming to dinner later," she said, trying to break the thickness in the air.

"I want you, Liliana."

His voice, the words, ignited desire inside her.

"Adam..."

He held up a crooked finger. "Come closer."

Of course she shouldn't. Dark eyes stayed on her, daring her. Lily took one step forward, then another, until she stood merely inches away from him. His hand cupped the back of her neck and pulled her in to him. Then he was kissing her like her lips were air and he was drowning.

She took in the sweet taste of him, the feel of him pressing against her, the robust sound of his groan when she brushed her tongue to his. Drenched with the feeling of being desired, even just physically, she brushed her tongue against his. The act garnered a groan deep from his throat.

His hands moved over her, melting her away. She touched him too. Everywhere and with hunger. She lost track of time, how long they kissed. When he pulled away, her head followed so their foreheads leaned against each other. She didn't open her eyes until she felt him place what felt like a key in her hands.

"I'm leaving you my car," he announced, his voice husky. "I want three things; to see you, kiss you, and fuck you. I want it all tonight. Come to me if you want me as much. If not, don't come and I promise I'll leave you alone."

12

"Love is the answer, but while we wait for the answer, sex raises some pretty good questions."
Anonymous

It was late, well past midnight, when Lily pulled into Adam's driveway. During the course of the night, she'd managed to convince herself over and over she wouldn't come to him. And here she was, questioning her sanity. There should be a relationship status for *I don't even know what's going on.*

This was a booty call, of course. Her head knew walking away was the right thing to do. Leave that door closed. Her thoughts on the other hand went southward, heat blitzed between her legs. Adam wasn't the only one who craved that physical connection.

As she stepped out of the Maserati and made her way to the house, lust hummed through her. Part of her wanted to run, yet she knew she hadn't come this far to flee just yet. Last time, she told herself during the drive. Farewell sex.

She glanced at the house, pitch black with the exception of one flickering light in the family room. He was watching TV, waiting for her. He knew she'd come. What could she say, Adam was her weakness.

The front door opened just as Lily fumbled through her purse, searching for nothing specific. Slowly, she lifted her head and took him in—beautifully sculpted hair-roughened chest, lean muscles bulging everywhere to narrow hips in loose black sweats sitting low on his hips. So low she could tell there was no barrier beneath. He left her breathless.

Words were not spoken, they weren't needed. The reason she was at his doorstep was clear. Adam leaned over, wrapped his arm around her waist, pulled her inside, on the brink of man-handling, and pinned her against the wall. He kissed her as if there was nothing else he'd rather be doing. As if she was his whole universe…and the moment was eternal. It was overwhelming.

"I'm not tamed," he said when he finally broke the kiss. His sweet, warm breath lingered just above her swollen lips. Their faces so close they were sharing air.

"Or boring," she acknowledged, loving the feel of his hard chest against her breasts.

Unruffled, he smiled and nipped at her lower lip. When he finally released her, Adam stepped aside and kicked the door closed. She walked past him into the house, to the large family room. The television was frozen to a shot of Adam's last race. His face hidden behind the headgear he wore for protection, but she'd recognize the sleek silver race car anywhere.

She was that predictable. Why else would he be awake in the middle of the night? "You knew I'd come."

He picked up the remote and slowly moved the race car to another curve. "No. I was hoping you'd come. I chose to work while I waited."

With her eyes still glue to the television screen, she asked, "Does it bother you that you didn't win?"

Adam had come in third. Not that it mattered, he'd racked up enough points for the year to keep him sitting pretty at the number one spot.

"I don't need to win every race. I just like to understand what I can do better the next time around. Like everything I do."

Lily nodded. He was talking to her as well. Their relationship. She ran her fingers over the back of the leather sofa. "What if I didn't come here tonight?"

"Then I would have jacked off and called it a night," he answered without giving it a thought. "A man can only hold on for so long, Liliana." He gave her a meaningful look. "It's been six weeks."

Lily knew the time frame all too well. She had a little lentil growing inside of her because of it. Adam turned off the television, threw the remote on the sofa, and came to stand in front of her. "You're nervous."

She shook her head.

"Do you have doubts?" he continued, his eyes on her. "I won't have sex with you if you're not sure you want me."

Oh, she wanted every inch of him inside of her. But she still had to tell him about the little pregnant situation. And that worried her.

"You don't think I want to have sex with you?" She removed the scarf around her neck and slowly unbuttoned the denim jacket she'd worn to shield her body from the cool autumn breeze. Dark eyes stayed at her until she placed the jacket on the sofa. "I want to taste you." She edged in closer, kissed his neck, and he let out a tortured groan. "Feel your skin against mine. I want you to take me."

He didn't touch her. Instead, he leaned his big frame on the arm of the leather sofa and crossed his arms over his chest. "No more games, Liliana." His voice carried a level of warning. "We do this because you're sure. You want us as we've been."

Temporary. Fleeting. He didn't say the words, but the message was clear. She looked into his eyes. Dark, deep, and intense. He wasn't going to touch her until she agreed to his terms. She was treading on dangerous ground. Everything told her to come forward and tell him about the baby, but that'd have to wait. Which was irresponsible on her part, she knew that. She'd tell him in the morning–after their last night together.

Right now, Adam was on her to-do list. And because she desperately ached, needed that physical connection with him at least once more, she uncrossed his arms, walked into him, pressed her lower body into his and faced him straight on.

"Make love to me," she breathed.

With a swift movement, he picked up the remote on the sofa next to him, pressed the power button and the room went black. But she saw every twitch of his muscles. The moonlight trickled through the window, leaching color from all it touched, casting a silver organza veil over the room, shimmering, dancing.

Adam took over then. His mouth closed over hers, fierce, demanding, and hungry. Lily let out a whimper and wrapped her arms around his neck. One hand smoothly moved up to sink into her hair, the other drew her even closer. He sucked on her lower lip and she parted for him, wanting to lose herself with the father of her baby, the love of her life, ready to give him whatever he wanted one last time.

"And the fuck-me boots are hot. They stay on during the first round."

Her head dropped back as she chuckled. "First round?"

His lips left hers to nuzzle her neck. "Don't intend to sleep tonight. We are not stopping until you're sore. I promise."

The words drove her mad. His breath was hot on her neck, making her shiver with need. His hands roamed over her body, touching every inch of her through the material, stopping at her hips for a slight squeeze before cupping a cheek in each hand.

"You drive me fucking insane," he growled and rocked her into his erection. "My addiction, Liliana. That's you."

His voice surged through every vein in her body, making her lightheaded. Addiction. The word wasn't even strong enough. How would she live without their passion? Without Adam? The thought caused an ache behind her heart and lent desperation to her actions. She needed this. Him. One last time.

She arched her back as his fingers grazed her thighs to the hem of her dress. His hands moved upward to her thong, teasing through the material, then brushed the tiny swatch to one side and slid two fingers inside of her. On the edge and dying to have him inside her, Lily let out a breathless whisper as he lowered his head to kiss her hard, driving her over the edge.

"The dress. I'll buy you another one." She heard him say roughly. Lily was still shuddering and slow to react. The front buttons popped and she heard them bounce off the hardwood floor. Her eyes flew open in shock, fascination, pleasure.

He shoved off the sweats and just as she imagined, he wore nothing else underneath. The sight of that part of him, beautifully erect, so incredibly male, made her moan.

They tangled in a kissing, touching war. Her feet moved blindly as Adam pushed her against the wall. "Hold on tight, darling."

He brushed what was left of her dress up to her waist. Large hands gripped her ass, squeezing hard, and scooped her off her feet. Lily instantly wrapped her legs around him and shivered.

"Cold?"

Oh, God, no. She shook her head. And even if she was, she wouldn't have admitted to it. Not when she was about to have up-against-the-wall-sex with Adam.

He lowered his head, ran his tongue around her nipple and tugged it between his teeth. The sensation sent prickles of awareness over her skin. She grabbed a fistful of his hair as her head fell back against the wall.

"Fuck me, Adam," she begged, panting for the torture to end, and wanting more of it as well.

Adam sank his teeth into her shoulder then claimed her lips in a deep, sensual kiss. His hands tightened around her ass as he tilted her waist a bit to allow him access, and then he was pushing inside of her.

"Oh, God." She screamed as her body stretched to accommodate him.

"No, sugar," he muttered against her lips. "It's just me." And plunged deeper, filling her up.

She tightened her thighs around him and took all he had to offer. Her breasts pressed against his chest and Lily forgot the entire world. Just her and Adam, and the butterflies in her stomach. Filled with hunger, she tried to rock into him but he held her still.

"Don't move," he ordered roughly.

She felt him throbbing inside her, struggling to maintain control. "Don't stop."

"Liliana." His voice was hoarse, tortured.

Not caring if she was acting like a caged wildcat, she tilted her hips and drew him closer. Wanting to give as much as she was getting, and needing to feel every inch of him, she dug her nails into his shoulders and he winced.

"Please," she pleaded.

She heard him swear savagely. His hands moved to the back of her thighs, and slowly withdrew. In one sure stroke, he filled her up again. He repeated the motion, again and again. Each time with more urgency. His hard length pounded into her, each thrust deeper than the last.

"I'm going to come, Adam."

"Good, that makes two of us."

His gaze stayed on her, intense, claiming, watching her reacting to him as he pushed her over the edge once more. His mouth crushed against hers and she exploded.

"Adam," she cried out his name as shock and pleasure rippled through her body.

She was deep in euphoria when she heard Adam say *fuck* and joined her. Shuddering in her arms, he let out a low, hoarse sound and squeezed her ass as he lost himself in her.

For a moment, neither of them moved. Adam buried his head into the crook of her neck, his broad shoulders rising and falling against her body as he caught his breath.

With shaking legs, Lily attempted to adjust the heel of her boots from his back, but he held her still.

"Not yet," he said against her neck. He was buried inside her, his hands still cupping her ass.

"You'll cramp up."

He chuckled, his breath hot against her skin. Then he lifted his head to see her face. "You underestimate me. I'm tougher than I look."

It was her turn to laugh. Since she'd met Adam, she'd never questioned his toughness. Everything about him screamed brute strength. Still, he slowly withdrew from her and brought her to her feet.

"Let's go to bed."

Lily smiled. "You're done with me?"

Raw desire flashed in his eyes. "Liliana, I intend to violate that beautiful body of yours in the most sensual way. I meant what I said, no stopping until you're sore."

He kept his promise and took her over and over. Starved with an insatiable appetite only Adam could satisfy, she let him. Passion, rich and lush, flooded every sense as she met him move for move, giving as well as receiving. Their harsh breathing and muffled groans filled the room; the salty smell of sex flooded her nostrils and filled her lungs. She wanted to go on forever. To never end. To be lost in this sensual dream with him for eternity. Much later when they finally collapsed on the bed, out of breath, Adam rolled unto his back and brought her with him and pulled the covers over them.

Every muscle in Lily's body ached. Pain had never felt so good.

"I need to text Minka."

"Why?" he asked, eyes closed.

"To let her know I'm spending the night."

"I bet you one million dollars they're not expecting you back."

She scraped her finger nails across his chest. "You're so cocky."

He chuckled. "I like when you say cock."

"I didn't say cock."

"You just did," he said. His eyes still closed.

Lily smiled. He was teasing her. The old Adam was back. Her heart did a little dance.

"We'll drive over and get your stuff tomorrow. Now sleep." He nudged her with her elbow and tightened his grip on her. "I sleep better when you're around."

"I bet." She chuckled against his chest.

"It's true, Liliana. You bring me peace." He placed a kiss on her head. "Now sleep."

With her thigh between his, Lily tried not to make too much of the way her heart swelled. Of course he liked her. Even if their relationship was only on a physical level, she'd always known he cared.

In the night, she listened to Adam's even breathing, fast asleep next to her. She touched his chest and his arm automatically tightened around her. Lily smiled in amazement at how a person who was once a stranger could suddenly, without warning, become her entire world.

When she stirred and opened her eyes, it was morning and she was in Adam's arm. She peeked at him, still asleep. She slipped out of his grip and as quietly as possible, pulled one of his T-shirts out of the dresser and over her body. She glanced back at him; still sleeping. She walked over to his side of the bed and appraised his appearance. His hair wildly tousled and stubble darkened his jaw. He looked disheveled, feral, sensuous, a perfect reflection of their night together. She lifted a hand to touch him but stopped. Her chest tightened with guilt and her stomach flooded with nausea.

Shit. Morning sickness. Lily turned toward the adjacent bathroom but quickly realized that was too close for comfort and rushed down the stairs. She walked-ran hastily down the hallway, hands over her mouth to the closest bathroom and heaved.

Clinging the porcelain toilet, she hurled again and again. Infinitely grateful that Adam was fast asleep, she took her time coming to her feet. Splashed some cold water over her face and rinsed her mouth. She needed to sit down and reflect, better yet, find her purse, take her prenatal and think of a way to tell Adam the truth.

She pulled in and then slowly released a deep breath, opened the door and gasped as she almost bumped into Adam. He stood there in low slung jeans, his face a dark mask, holding her hostage at the threshold.

"Adam."

He tilted his head. "None other."

The coldness in his eyes chilled her to the bone. He leaned back and she walked past him, refusing to look at him. She made her way to the family room and located her purse. She knew he followed. His presence was not something she could ignore. Still, she tried.

"I'm going to give you two minutes to tell me what I've finally figured out."

Heart in her throat, she found the pre-natal bottle and palmed it in her hand.

"I need water," she said and escaped into the kitchen. To her relief, he didn't follow. After swallowing the pill, she pulled out her phone and scrolled to Minka's name.

Hey Minka, I'll be over soon.

Her friend texted back.

Tell him.

She placed the phone on the counter, took a deep breath and squared her shoulders as she walked into the family room. She found Adam standing by the large window overlooking the private beach, his back ramrod-straight.

"It crossed my mind last night," he said, his back to her. "Your breasts are different. Fuller."

Damn. She hadn't given much thought to the slight changes of her body. Truth be told, she didn't think he'd noticed.

"I know every inch of your body, Liliana, probably better than I know my own."

The hitch in his voice tore through her. Pain...she paused, analyzing the sound. Disappointment, that's what it was. She'd disappointed him. Unsure of what she should do, Lily wrapped her arms over her chest.

"I'm pregnant," she said softly, her heart hurting with each word for not telling him right away. "Starting my seventh week."

He turned to face her, his gaze cold and unyielding. "When were you planning on telling me? Or was that not part of your equation?"

No. He had it all wrong. Of course she wanted to tell him. She started to take a step forward but stopped. Tension crackled in the air. Everything about him told her not to dare come too close. "I tried…"

He sneered. "When did you try? Was it the time you broke things off via a fucking text?"

He looked at her, rage in his eyes, skin bloodless beneath his tan. She looked away.

"Or maybe the other night at Vapor? God damn it, Lily! You've had how many opportunities to tell me?"

The sound of her shortened name cut her. She could count on one hand the times he'd addressed her by it. They had disagreements before, but over mundane things. Her heart pulsated against her chest. The last thing she wanted to do was to cause him grief.

"I'm sorry, Adam. I had every intention of telling you. I just needed…some time to sort things out."

"And did you sort them out? Was us fucking all night part of the sorting out?"

There was a strange note in his voice. In spite of her pain, she smiled. "No. We fucked because you're my weakness," she admitted. "A weakness that I was trying to overcome." She waited for him to interject. When he didn't she continued. "You touch me and set my body on fire. I want you in the worst way, your taste and the feel of your skin next to mine. You're not the only one who is addicted, Adam, but physical attraction is not enough to raise a child." Lily exhaled. "That's why I didn't tell you."

He just looked at her for what seemed like eternity, his eyes blazing. "There's something else. Tell me what it is. Tell me the whole truth before I lose my fucking mind."

"I knew if I told you, you'd want to marry me. I don't want to marry you."

13

"It is much easier to become a father than to be one."
Kent Nerburn

The silence in the room was deafening. Lily braced herself for the explosion, the questions, maybe even accusations. What she found was even worse—a stoic expression, revealing nothing. Adam stood there, his posture stiff. The only hint of some sort of reaction was the way his rigid bicep muscles flexed involuntarily.

He didn't say anything, but she felt the tension vibrating from his body. She'd hurt him. The realization made her queasy because honestly, she hadn't realized she could cause him any type of anguish.

"I'm pregnant." Her voice cracked on the word this time.

After what seemed like eternity, he let out a short breath and ran a hand over his face. His palm moved to his corded neck and stayed there for a beat. The act was unintentionally sexy and just so totally Adam. Her heart twisted.

"I had every intention of telling you," she said quietly.

His eyes flicked through the room then moved back to her face. The hardness in them sent chills down her spine. He took a step forward, she shuffled back.

"I found out two days before I arrived here."

He said nothing.

For good measure, she added. "And he's yours." Somehow, it seemed fitting to refer to their baby as *he*. A version of the man standing before her.

"I don't believe I questioned you about that." His voice was deceptively calm.

She didn't trust it. The way his jaw flexed, eyes sharp and cold just like the rest of his facial features, told her he was fired up and ready for war.

An awkward silence settled in the room while they stared at each other. Lily eventually looked away, grabbed her purse and turned to walk out of the room. As she brushed past him, one hand caught her waist and held her still. The movement caused his T-shirt she wore to ride up a bit, exposing her bare thighs.

"Where are you going?"

She cleared her throat. "To get dressed. I booked a room at Martha's Way."

"Cancel it."

"Adam—"

"We're not done," he said in a menacing whisper. "I let you speak. Now you're going to listen."

Lily swallowed, her gut clenched with anticipation. His hand fell away from her waist, but he was still standing way too close.

"We are getting married," he said, his voice low and definitive. "It is not about what you want. You're pregnant with my child. We get married. End of story."

What? No. And just like that her temper flared. "I told you I don't want—"

He cut her off. "I told you, this is not a choice to be made. Not for you or for me."

Because she needed all the strength she possessed, Lily stepped back, tilted her head up and looked at him. He was totally serious, not a hint of amusement on his handsome face. This couldn't be happening. "You're willing to be miserable for the rest of your life for the sake of a child." It wasn't a question. This had been her fear all along.

He looked unperturbed. If anything, she caught a hint of a smile. "We won't be miserable. The sex is good."

She let out a chuckle, not of amusement, more out of the ridiculousness of their conversation. "We're over, Adam, and now you know why."

A do-not-fuck-with-me look crossed his face. "We're not over. We are just beginning."

The finality of his words made her stomach hurt, but more than that, it made her mad. If Adam wanted a fight, then he'd get one. One of the many things she learned growing up with three pain-in-the-ass brothers was a woman needed to grow a pair once in a while. Chin up, she walked right to him and stabbed a finger into his hard chest. "You don't get to tell me what to do," she said between clenched teeth. "We're over." She turned on her heels and walked past him.

Lily reached the doorway when Adam caught her hands. The whole thing happened too fast. His fingers laced in hers, chests pressing against one another. With his weight he directed her to the wall, raised her arms up over her head, and caged her in. Not one to cower, she looked straight into his eyes.

"You don't love me," she whispered.

His jaw tightened, but he made no attempt to dispute otherwise. Her heart scattered in tiny little pieces. She hadn't expected a declaration of undying love, but the reality still stung.

"I need love, Adam. That mad, passionate love. It should be experienced at least once in a lifetime." She examined his stoic expression, and her posture sagged. The fact she was forever bonded to a man who didn't love her smacked her in the face. It shouldn't. She already knew that. But…still, reality sucked. "That's not who we are."

She waited for him to speak.

He didn't. Instead he sent her a long, pained look then slowly released his grip and put some distance between them.

Lily swallowed hard, her heartbeat slowing to a grinding thud. This was her life, pregnant and in love with a man who wanted to marry her for the sake of their unborn child. Feeling small, weak, and defeated, she turned to leave.

"What about you, Liliana?"

The question ripped through her. She stopped, but didn't dare look at him. Still, she felt him move to erase the distance between them once again. His hands gently grabbed her arms and turned her to him.

"Look at me."

Slowly, she tilted her head and met his gaze.

"You've told me how I feel." His gaze swept over her face. "But you haven't told me how you feel."

The heart had a way of wanting what it wanted. Of aching to override reason and common sense. Even now, wounded, dulled with sadness, hers still ached for Adam. Hearts were wild creatures that way.

I'm in love with you.

The pain in her chest hurt like a deep gash. She took a deep, laboring breath and tried to get a grip of her emotions, but the liquid sadness flowed down her cheeks, leaving a wet trail in the path.

Oh, damn. Adam could taste the tears as if they were his own. And true enough they were rolling down her cheeks. He could handle a lot from a woman but tears. Yeah, he was fucked. He reached for her, but Lily turned on her heels and ran down the hall. Seconds later, the door slammed, hitting him like a sucker punch.

All of a sudden the room felt too large. He stood there feeling smaller and smaller as he searched for the right words, the right action, and the right way to feel.

A cannon ball had blown through him and left a gaping hole in his stomach. He was going to be a father. Dad. *Padre. Pere. Vater.* It didn't matter what language he translated it into, it was scary as hell.

They had to marry. No ifs, ands, or buts about it, but bringing Lily around to the idea was clearly going to take some work. His gaze landed on his cellular phone on the coffee table. He picked it up and pressed on the names of the three men he viewed as brothers.

> ***Meet at Vapor in twenty.***

Within seconds the phone buzzed back. He scanned their responses.

> ***Can't. Patients. Full day today.***

Forrest's office was always busy with so-called "sick" patients. Blake's text followed.

> ***In a meeting with Jason and his father.***
> ***Sorry, bro.***

Adam responded.

> ***Twenty.***

Blake and Forrest responded almost simultaneously.

> ***Noon.***

Jason added.

> ***This better be good, asshole.***

Adam checked the time on his cell. He had less than two hours to kill. His thoughts on auto drive, he started toward the bedroom and stopped. A vision of Lily's quivering lips still fresh in his mind. He'd give her time. Hell, he needed time.

Changing direction, he made his way down the stairs to the laundry room. From the clean bin, he pulled out a wrinkled, long-sleeved T-shirt and changed into sweats. Tension caused his leg muscles to tighten. A good run and a cold shower should bring him some relief.

At exactly noon, the four men sat at the round table on the far left of the bar. Other than a few stragglers left for the last wave of the foliage, the place was empty. Maxie placed chilled beers on the table.

"Thanks, Maxie," Adam muttered.

"Want some food?"

All four shook their heads. She smiled at them then walked away leaving the three other men waiting for Adam to explain. He took a swallow of cold beer then let out a breath.

"You look like you just saw death," Jason was the first to speak. "Want to spill it?"

"Lily's pregnant."

His three friends nodded. None of them appeared overly surprised by the news. They usually took great pleasure teasing him about hooking up with Minka's best friend. He caught them exchanging quick, solemn looks. Apparently everyone knew about Lily but him. What the fuck!

"Why does it feel like I'm the last one to know?"

After an endless moment, Jason spoke. "I didn't know for sure. Minka never said anything."

"She looked a little pale last night during dinner," Forrest added.

"She stopped drinking," Jason said, then took another sip of his beer.

Adam remembered Lily choosing sparkling water the other night at Vapor. Shit.

Why did he not pay closer attention?

He already knew the answer. The last few days, he'd been thinking with his other head.

"I thought you two were casual," Blake said carefully.

"You've never heard of those little things called condoms?" Jason added.

"Has she seen a doctor?" Forrest, the forever practical one, asked.

Adam's head pounded from the questions thrown at him. He

shrugged and answered in one breath. "I don't know. We are casual and she's on the pill, so I don't know what happened."

"I'm guessing the usual age-old thing." Jason grinned. "You know, boy and girl got naked, rolled around, and stopped thinking."

He shot his friend a long, hard look. Unfazed, Jason leaned back and continued to drink his beer as if he were at a parade.

"You're the one who was having sex with Minka without any protection. Do I need to bring up Chappaquiddick?"

"Hey." Jason waved his hands defensively but still looking relaxed in his chair, "That was only a few times. She went on the pill for a while."

"A while?" Adam asked.

"We want to start a family but seems like you're a few steps ahead of us." Jason tilted his beer to Adam and took a swig.

"And us," Blake chided.

"And you should know antibiotics lessen the effectiveness of birth control," Forrest said, shaking his head.

Adam frowned. "Speak English."

"Last time you went to visit her, you told us she was sick as a dog and on antibiotics. I'm sure that didn't stop you from—"

"I got it," Adam growled, cutting his friend off. But shit, how did he not know about how antibiotics and birth control worked before? Because he'd always used condoms in the past, that's how. But with Lily, they had thrown that extra caution to the shit. They relied on her being on the pill. He was screwed.

"So what are you guys going to do?" Blake asked

"I told her we're getting married."

His friends sat a little straighter. All three placed their bottles on the table. A dull pain hit Adam in the back of his head. He rubbed the still stinging spot and turned to Blake. "What was that for?"

"For being an idiot," Blake snorted. "First of all, you told her to marry you."

The others nodded in agreement. Fuckers.

"Second, you don't ask a woman to marry you because she's pregnant."

What. Why not? "She's pregnant with my child."

Jason leaned his elbows on the table. His sharp blue eyes never wavered from Adam's face. "You do realize we are living in the twenty-first century, right? The *me man, you woman* approach no longer works."

Adam took a swig of his beer, ignoring Jason.

"You're missing Blake's point, dude," Jason continued. "What was her reaction when you *told* her to marry you? Did she jump into your arms with joy?"

Adam groaned and shook his head. "No. She cried and locked herself in the bedroom." He stared blankly at his barely touched beer.

"You're still not getting it." Jason shook his head in dismay, which drew an amused smile from Forrest and Blake.

"Love," Forrest said after a heavy sigh. "You know, Blake and Keely, Jason and Minka kind of love."

"You and Claire too." Adam added just to be an asshole. On days like today when he was obviously the butt of the joke, he didn't mind going for a below-the-belt shot.

Forrest sat back on his chair. His grey eyes dark. "Claire and I are not together."

There was always a high level of tension between the two, which Adam found exhausting. He would have pointed out to his friend mental love still counted, but chose to let it go for now. "Are you even getting laid?" he asked instead.

Forrest laughed. "Are you offering?"

Adam flipped him the bird.

"Have you seen all those women who are always sick?" Blake put his hands up for the in air quotation, "sick."

A pretty brunette approached the table and made small talk with Forrest. She reminded him of her appointment then sashayed her tight butt away to the bar, confirming Blake's observation.

"Back to you," Jason said, once the brunette was out of view. "You're an idiot for telling Lily to marry you."

"Fuck you," Adam responded automatically. He rubbed his brows, the tension slowly leaving his body.

"No thanks, man. I'm getting ready to marry Minka. Oh, yeah..." He smirked. "We're getting married because we love each other, not because of a child."

"While I'm happy you found happiness, I don't believe in that love shit."

"What did you do for her birthday?" Forrest asked.

Adam searched his brain. Oh, yeah. "Flew to New Jersey. Bought her flowers." Spent the weekend naked in her apartment.

Blake nodded but didn't look that impressed. "Did you take her out to dinner or spend the whole weekend screwing her brains out?"

"Jesus, Blake!" Truth be told, he'd done exactly that. Surely, he'd taken her out to dinner at least once, although at the moment he couldn't remember one occasion where just the two of them had been to a restaurant. Whenever they went out they were always surrounded by the three Stooges along with Keely and Minka.

How the hell had he never taken Lily out to a restaurant before? He'd done so with women he liked much less. Adam took another swig of his beer.

Blake shrugged. "What do you know about her?"

Let's see, he knew she had long, toned, beautiful legs that he loved best wrapped around his waist, whether standing up or lying down. He loved her legs. And her lips around him, he loved that too.

"Besides all the wonderful things she can do to your body," Blake added.

He searched the faces of his friends. They were looking for answers with substance. Adam drew a blank. He couldn't think of anything. He groaned.

"She needs a cup of coffee every morning," he said, picturing Lily without her cup of caffeine in the morning.

"She has three brothers," Blake added.

Adam's eyes widened. Three. He knew she had brothers but he never took the time to ask how many.

"You didn't know that, did you?" Forrest drawled, sounding almost disgusted.

Adam was starting to regret reaching out to them. He could do without the interrogation today. "I knew she had brothers. I imagined two."

Blake grinned. "Three big bad-asses. I think one is a photographer, one is a Navy SEAL and the other is a big-shot engineer."

"How the fuck do you know so much about her?" Adam growled. He didn't like the tone of Blake's voice.

"She's Minka's best friend," Blake answered, like *duh*. "You don't even know what college she went to, do you?" He paused, waiting for Adam to answer.

Shit. Adam regretted calling them.

"She went to Yale with Minka. That's where we met." Blake shook his head in obvious disgust.

"And her brothers are coming to the wedding," Jason announced. His voice filled with pleasure.

Adam swore under his breath. "A photographer isn't a badass in my eyes, and that engineer one, I bet you I can take both of them." The third one, whoever he was, had Adam's utmost respect. The military required a certain breed, a certain level of toughness.

"You've been together for a year now, how did you celebrate your anniversary?" Blake continued to probe.

Anniversary. That word was for couples.

Jason smirked. "Fuck buddies celebrate anniversaries too, at least they want to. They just don't say it."

"Like you did with Rita," Adam mumbled, reminding his friend of the incident between him and Rita before Minka came into his life.

"Touché. See, that's how I learned my lesson. Even fuck buddies have expectations."

"We don't celebrate anniversaries," Adam grunted. "We don't celebrate anything. We fuck."

"And now you're having a child with her." Forrest added, his voice low and controlled. "I suggest you get her to like you, maybe even love you a little, if you really want her to consider marriage."

What was happening? The man who couldn't get the woman he had a thing for to look his way was giving advice on relationships.

"From what I know of Lily, she's her own person and stubborn," Forrest continued.

"Like most women," Jason added for good measure, and Blake nodded in agreement. Adam shared their pain.

"But," Forrest paused, choosing his words carefully, "she has to feel something for you to continue this no strings attached but exclusive bullshit. No woman can go that long without getting somewhat emotionally invested."

Adam heard those words before from his mother. If he didn't know how alpha Forrest was, he would have insisted he turned in his Man Card. The other two dumbasses nodded their heads as if Forrest's words were gospel. Okay, so maybe his friend had a point.

"You just have to make her want to admit it. And perhaps you should try to look beyond her ability to fuck your brains out on a daily basis. You know, try liking her back." This came from Jason, the man who spent most of his life thinking with his dick first.

"I do like her."

The admission didn't surprise Adam. It was true, he did like Lily. Otherwise, sex or not he would not have hung around this long. But he'd never admitted it before. He never even considered whether he liked her as a person.

"Then show her." The three men said collectively, as if they'd spent their whole lives waiting for this moment.

"I fucking got it," he growled, though now he was a whole lot less pissed off.

Jason was the first to push his chair back and rise to his feet. "Good, because Blake and I have work to do and Forrest has sick fake patients to see. Good luck, bro. That's some deep shit you're in but fun for me to watch." He patted Adam's shoulder then started toward the door.

Blake and Forrest did the same, leaving Adam sitting by himself at Vapor. He reached for his phone and scrolled to Lily's number. She was quick to answer.

"How are you feeling?"

"Better," she answered in a low voice.

For the first time he detected a naked vulnerability in her tone. It made his heart squeeze. "I'm stopping by Jason and Minka's to get your luggage then coming home. Let's talk."

She sighed. "Adam, I'm not marrying you."

"No marriage." *For now.* "Let's just talk. Can we do that?"

"Yes," she answered after a beat.

"Good. See you soon, Liliana."

After he disconnected the call, Adam ran his palm over his face. He felt as if he'd been shoved off a cliff and ended up under a boulder. A heavy weight bore down on him, making him more unsettled and off balanced than he cared to admit. Maybe, just a little spooked.

In a few months he'd have a child. And if he succeeded at getting Lily to marry him, he'd be a husband. Adam let out a quick breath and scraped a hand through his hair. He rose from his chair, took one last swallow of his beer and headed for the door, ready to embrace the last thing he ever wanted to be in life…someone's father.

14

"No matter how attractive a person's potential may be, you have to date their reality."
Mandy Hale

Tired and weary after her fourth trip to the bathroom to heave, Lily had hoped the shower would help. It didn't. She slipped into another of Adam's T-shirts, stepped inside the sunlit bedroom and came to an abrupt halt. There sat Adam on the bed, with his back against the ecru upholstered headboard, one leg hanging off the edge with the other planted on the floor. He vibrated tension and looked morose, a complete contrast to the room's relaxed, sophisticated atmosphere.

His gaze swept her from head to toe, rested on her bare thighs, then went back to her face. For a brief moment, she caught a glimpse of the passion that existed between them, but it was quickly masked as he brought her attention to the dress in his hands, the one she wore last night. At some point, he'd torn it from her body, she just couldn't remember exactly when that occurred.

"I'm sorry about your dress," he apologized, his voice quiet. "It looked good on you."

Tension filled the room, not the good sexual kind. More like, *shit you're pregnant with my child* kind of tension. It made her uncomfortable. Not quite sure how to react, Lily walked over and took the dress from his hands. "It's not a big deal."

"Liliana."

The way his voice rippled her name in that seductive accent caused her insides to quiver with apprehension and she clutched the dress for comfort.

"I assume you've been to the doctor."

She nodded, her posture rigid.

"I am going to ask Forrest to stop by later to check up on you."

"Adam, I'm fine."

But his fingers were already typing away on his phone.

He looked her over once more. "You look pale." He noted. "Let him check your blood pressure or something." He put up a hand to stop any incoming argument. "For my own sanity."

This made her smile. "Okay, if it will keep you sane." She walked over to the battered Ludlow trunk at the end of the bed and placed the dress on top of a mocha-colored cable-knit throw. "But you do realize Forrest is a family doctor." She glanced over at him, a small smile touched his lips and her heart squeezed a little.

"Did you cancel the room you booked at Martha's Way?"

Lily shook her head and his jaws clenched.

"What do you want from me, Adam?" she asked after a moment of silence. It was time to address the big elephant in the room. He did say he wanted to talk, so might as well get to it. "I mean, I won't keep you away from our child. That was never my intention."

"Then what is your intention?"

She shrugged because really she had no clue. "I don't want to be the one to turn you into someone you're not."

"And what is that someone?"

"A father, a husband," she answered without a beat.

He rose from the bed, walked to where she stood, cupped her face in his hands and kissed her fully on the lips, rocking her universe and claiming her and their child in the process. Automatically, her hands thrust into the silky strands of his hair and Lily opened her mouth to urge him in. When he finally broke for air, she leaned into him, craving his touch.

"As of today, we are officially dating," he said, with his arms around her.

Caught off guard, her body stiffened and she squeezed her eyes shut. Once again, Adam was taking over and mentally she was too weak to fight. Space. She needed to put space between them so she could think clearly. With a little shove, she broke away from his hold and walked to the opposite side of the room and sat on the bed.

"You said no marriage," he continued, "so I won't push. But we deserve a chance to see if we like each other. I'm asking that we try."

"Would you have suggested that if I wasn't pregnant?"

Adam glanced at her and she met his gaze straight on.

"Probably not," he answered. "But," he quickly added, "It's not because I don't like you, Liliana." He paused. "It's because I'm not the type of man a woman dates, falls in love with, or marries, for that matter."

"From what I can see, you're pretty dateable."

"You don't know me," he answered, his expression etched in stone.

The words floated in her head and pulled at her heart. There was something in his voice, if she didn't know better, she could label as pain but dismissed it. From the outside looking in, Adam had the perfect life, rich, carefree with doting parents, and a wonderful group of friends. For the first time, she wondered if there were more layers to the man she'd been sleeping with.

"Are you still hung up on that cheating asshole?" he asked when she didn't speak.

The question surprised her so much that she almost laughed. "It's been over a year. I think it's fair to say I'm over the whole disaster."

"I'm your rebound," he reminded her.

From the bed, she glanced at him and was surprise to read the seriousness on his face. Maybe that night on the beach he'd been, but somewhere along the way he'd stopped playing that role. "You're not my rebound," she said gently.

He shoved his fingers through his hair then came to sit next to her, his thighs brushed against hers. His hand reached for hers and netted their fingers. "I'll stay committed to you."

She chuckled because he didn't have a clue how fast he made her heart race. "You make it all sound like a business deal."

He shook his head, a small smile tugging at the corners of his lips. "No, this is the start of our story."

Had it been up to her, Lily would have never opened herself to another man again. Been there, done that with Nate, the two-timing bastard. There was no need to end up with another engagement ring in the ocean. And this time, there would be no Adam to turn to, make love to; he'd be the reason for her heartbreak. Not that she was afraid to take a stab at love again, maybe just afraid of getting hurt all over. The pain would be more intense this time around, and it scared the crap out of her because there wasn't one person in the world she wanted more than the man holding her hands.

Loving him terrified her.

Still, she was more afraid of the idea of walking away without giving them a chance.

With their fingers laced together, she glanced at her left ring finger and exhaled. Maybe there were no right moments, right guys, right answers…maybe sometimes one just had to say what the heart was feeling.

"All right," she said quietly. "I will date you, Adam."

She just had to stick to her initial decision and not let him convince her into a loveless marriage. But hell, at least there'd be guaranteed great sex.

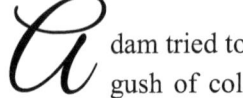

---

*A*dam tried to focus on anything but the relief that hit him like a gush of cold air. Only his mind went flying to how hot she looked and how easy he could have her naked. With one swift movement he could tear off the small barrier of clothing between them and jump her. Shit. Semi-hard, he jerked upright and released her hand. He needed to have another talk with his conscience.

"You said you've been to the doctor," he repeated the words from earlier. Baby talk should do the trick.

Her eyes narrowed. "Yes."

"Ultrasound to make sure…" His voice trailed off the last words. Just the possibility of not discovering a heartbeat gave him agita.

"All done."

"By yourself?"

Staring at him, she shook her head. "No. One of the nurses stayed with me. She's a friend."

But her voice trembled and Adam cursed himself for letting her go through such an ordeal technically alone. "From now on I go to all doctor appointments with you. Is that understood?"

She gave him a faint smile. "I live in New Jersey, Adam. How do you intend to do that from here or wherever you may be?"

"I'll be there. Just tell me and I'll be there."

She held his gaze. "You'll drop everything to be by my side for our child?"

"Yes."

She stood up and came to stand in front of him. His friends' words echoed in his mind. During the drive back to the house, the sudden thought had hit him like a snowball made of granite—no more sex between them. He needed to quench his desire to own every inch of her and connect on a deeper level besides the physical intimacy. Whatever the fuck that meant in guy-land.

Just to be on the safe side, he took a step back but Lily was already pressing her sweet sexy body against him. She kissed his ear. He could hear her breath as she did so, making things more intense.

"Let's use the next few days to discover each other."

Her voice carried implications as she wrapped her arms around him. For a brief second, he thought about going at it once more. What was once more? He sucked in air and released her arms from his neck. A frown crossed her face.

"We have one rule though."

Her head fell back. Eyebrows squished together, lips pursed, she gave him a look. "So no more any-strings-attached-but-exclusive rule. That's out the window, right?"

"Right."

"But there's a new rule to us dating?"

"Yes."

She rolled her pretty brown eyes, tucked a handful of hair behind her ear and laughed. She never looked more beautiful to him. And everything about her was screaming take me. He ached for her. This was going to be harder than he thought.

"Liliana." He tried to sound curt but failed.

She cleared her throat. "Oh boy, I'm scared. You look serious." One delicate hand touched her flushed face. A sigh slipped through her lips. "Okay, give it to me."

"No more sex."

Her eyes widened in shock. "What?"

"Liliana." He reached for her hands but she swiped him away.

"Don't call me that."

"That's your name."

"Yeah, but…" she let out an exasperated sigh. "When you say it in that sexy Italian drawl, I immediately get wet. And now you're saying no sex." She paused, crossed her arms over her chest. "What do you mean no sex?"

"Sex will cloud our judgment." Yeah, even in his own ears his excuse sounded weak.

Her teeth caught her bottom lip, mulling over his words.

So he decided it was the best time to lay the ground rules. "We've been having sex for over a year now and barely know each other. All I'm asking is for a chance for us to do that."

Who the fuck was this person talking? Adam wanted to know. And while at it, he'd like to get his balls back.

"And after that?" she asked in a low voice, filled with suspicion.

"We continue as we were." *And I intend to kidnap you to an island and keep you there until you become Mrs. Aquilani.* But she didn't have to know that.

"Continue having sex, you mean."

He huffed. Shit, he was beginning to feel like the one being used. "Yes, continue to have sex if that's what you want, but you'll be pregnant and all."

"So."

He stared at her.

She tossed up her hands. "Pregnant women still have a sex drive, Adam. As a matter of fact, it increases."

That's right; he read about that once somewhere. "Like now?"

She nodded. "Yes." She released a deep breath. "Thank God I brought Bob."

Now he was lost. "Who the fuck is Bob?"

With a jutting chin she deliberately raised her eyebrows. "Battery Operated Boyfriend, also known as BOB," she spat out the words.

He frowned, his muscles and veins straining against his skin. Lily had a dildo. How the hell did he not know about that? His thoughts tumbled in his head, making and breaking alliances like underpants in a tumble dryer. "You have a dildo."

It was a statement, but she smiled and gave him a dismissive nod. "You're not always around. A girl has needs."

"Okay, then play with your dildo. But—" He stopped and stared at her. "I get to watch."

She shrugged. Whatever. Crossed her arms over her chest, gave him another uneasy look before dropping her sweet ass on the bed and turned her back to him. From any other woman, he would have found the act irritating and annoyed the shit out of him. But not with Lily. For a minute, he studied her, sighed and put both hands on his forehead. He was torn between the devil and the angel sitting on his shoulders. One wanted to remind her a fucking dildo couldn't do the job, not like he could, and the other wanted to take care of her. Finally, he walked out of the room and didn't look back until he was by the door.

"You and I are going on a date tomorrow," he announced.

She didn't answer. Adam swore under his breath before closing the door behind him. Thoughts of Lily pleasuring herself in the room burned his brain. His friends were idiots, which made him an even bigger idiot for believing he could be around her and not want sex.

15

"Life begins at the end of your comfort zone. Take risks."
Anonymous

The salted sea air was solid in the village of Menemsha, a small fisherman's town in Chilmark, where Adam's restaurant, The Wharf's Side, was located on the historic harbor. As they drove through the light breeze of the early evening, Lily admired the fishing cottages. Being on the quiet coast, the town felt like a remote oasis, secluded from the bustle of tourists and shoppers typical of Edgartown and Oak Bluffs.

She'd been surprised upon learning their date was to be at his famous restaurant, the "must" place to dine when on the island. Not only had she never been there, it was one of those things she learned about Adam in passing. Today, she was entering his world for a glimpse of all the little things personal to him. In fact, this was her first time in the town located just fifteen minutes away from his house.

Her heart began to race the moment the car pulled into the reserved parking spot. With anxiety curled in her stomach, she ran nervous hands over the skirt of her dress. This was it. Their first date.

He turned to face her, and those gorgeous, breathtaking eyes caught a wink of sunlight. A perfect blend of molten chocolate marbled with rich flecks of gold, they seemed full of life as his mouth opened in a broad smile.

"Ready?" he asked.

She breathed in the ocean air, plastered a smile on her lips, and nodded. In return he frowned and caressed her face with his thumb. The slight touch gave her an electric jolt.

"You don't look well," he observed, his voice calm, showing no sign of nerves. "Are you feeling sick?"

Her heart was a jackhammer rattling within her ribcage, but other than that, all was well. "I'm fine."

His gaze swept over her once more, then he got out of the car. In a pair of urban slim fitted black chinos with layered blue and heather grey buttoned down Henley, hugging all of his muscles, he looked handsome, daunting, and sexy as hell. He moved swiftly and opened her door. He extended his hand and she placed trembling fingers in his. Hand in hand they walked in silence into the restaurant.

"Stop being nervous." He squeezed her hand. "A date is supposed to be fun, at least that's what I've heard."

She steadied her breath and tried to calm the panic. "You've never taken a woman out on a date?" she asked, distracting herself with the conversation. Not that the thought of Adam sharing an intimate meal with a woman was comforting.

He chuckled. "Of course. But often I get bored within thirty minutes."

"Why am I not surprised?"

He glanced over and smiled at her. "It's always an interview. I don't care for a Q&A session," he said as he opened the door for her.

She could only imagine the poor women with their questions. *Do you want to get married? How many children do you want? How rich are you? Are you as good in bed as I imagine?*

At least she knew the answer to the last question.

Lily stepped through the door and was greeted by an interesting blend of modern design stainless steel, combined with traditional brick walls and repurposed barn wood on the floor. The restaurant was surprisingly filled. The atmosphere was cool with a welcome feel perpetuated by the friendly staff. Most waved or nodded an acknowledgment to their boss and smiled warmly at her. Even some of the patrons waved at Adam. A quick introduction was made between her and the maître d' before Adam led them up the stairs to the second floor.

Unlike the first floor, which had a more formal and serene atmosphere, the upper level deck was filled with life—a bar, a small area for a band, two elegant sofas in the corner, and dancing fire flames from lanterns projecting enough heat for those who dared to venture and dine outside.

"I reserved the most romantic table for us," Adam said with easy charm, and led her to a table at the far end of the deck overlooking the harbor.

As he pulled her chair, Lily caught a few women glancing appreciatively in his direction. Some lingered a little longer, forgetting their spouse or date sitting across from them. She understood the pull he had on her gender. Everything about him exuded sexuality, confidence, and promises if one dared to look deeper. He seemed oblivious to it all, almost as if he only had eyes for her.

"We should have time to catch the sunset after dinner," he said as he sat across from her, "You haven't caught a sunset until you see the one here."

Who was this man?

She knew he was meticulous, thoughtful, and detailed. Even during sex he'd pay attention to every inch of her, pleasing her until she couldn't think. But there was something about the way he was making her feel today. It felt intimate. "You've thought of everything."

"This is our first date. I'm trying to impress you," he said, his voice calm and sexy as hell.

Their eyes met with a flare of heat, causing her to blush. He leaned in for a kiss, and possessed her inner soul. It was a gentle kiss, like cotton. The soft caress melted her heart. When he sat back, she turned her gaze to the stunning view of the harbor.

People sat on carts along the pier eating lobsters, drinking beer, and laughing. A sun-beaten man covered in bright orange overalls with knee-length black fisherman boots stood at the end of the pier, slicing his catch of the day. Lily observed a mother leading her son over to the fisherman. She was too far away to hear their words but by the gentle gesture of the mother, she guessed the woman was explaining the art of fishing to her young son.

A smile formed on her lips as her gaze traveled to the filled parking lots, the beach-goers as they walked in easy lazy steps from the sandy shoreline to the nearby shops and the multi-generational family take-outs. Her attention wandered back to the water. Boats lined along the dock rocking gently to the rhythm of the ocean. Everything and everyone around them seemed happy, carefree, lost in the moment, but sadness swept over her in waves.

"It's so beautiful here," she said in a flat, monotone voice.

"Then why do you look sad?"

The question forced her to look at him. "If it wasn't for the baby, you would have never brought me here."

"If it wasn't for the baby, you would have never been open to coming here with me," he said with an expression that gave nothing away. "You were just as emotionally unavailable as I was."

She couldn't deny that. Still, he'd gotten under her armor and captured her heart. "And now you are," she paused, not sure if she could say the word. "Eh…emotionally available."

"I'm working on it. Can you do the same?"

The problem was, she was already emotionally involved. Unable to speak, she wet her lips, nodded and picked up the menu. A young, handsome waiter with olive complexion and black hair similar to Adam's came to the table. Adam rose to his feet and shook the young man's hand.

"Lily, this is Claudio. He works here until we close next week for the winter break. He'll be our waiter." Claudio beamed at Lily. She smiled at him. "Do you mind if I order something for us?"

Just the fact that he asked her first was enough. "Please do."

"Let's go with a plate of the fresh mozzarella, a bowl of steamed little neck clams and a bottle of the non-alcoholic Fre Brut," he said to Claudio without glancing at the menu.

The gesture touched her. She batted her eyelashes to hold back the tears that threatened to flow. Damn it. Her hormones were all out of whack this evening. To her relief, Claudio quickly approached their table. He poured their wine, waited for Adam's taste test before filling her glass. Once they were alone, Adam raised his glass to her.

"What should we toast to?" he asked, his voice light and teasing.

There were so many things she could toast to. Her family. Minka and Jason's upcoming wedding. Nate cheating on her; without that, she would have never met Adam. Their unborn child. But as she stared at the sexiest man she'd ever known, she could think of nothing more than to celebrate the start of their next chapter.

She raised her glass. "To our first date."

"And to the next." He winked at her as they each took a swallow of their wine.

Oh, he really needed to stop being so charming. In an effort to keep herself from drowning under his spell, she tried to dispel what they were experiencing. "I'm sure you've been here before with another woman, not that it bothers me," she added quickly.

"Actually, when I do eat here, it has been alone."

Putting the wine glass on the table, Lily peered at the few women sitting at the bar. She caught a few staring in Adam's direction. "Do you usually go home alone from here?"

He sat back and appeared to ruminate over her question. "Before you, no, not always."

A little bit of pain pulled the strings of her heart and squeezed around it. Things like that shouldn't bother her. He was a handsome, rich bachelor, and she was sure women flocked to him. She should be appreciative of his honesty. But, most of the time the truth was often the hardest to digest.

"Liliana." He caught her hands. "I don't mean to hurt you with my answers, but I won't ever lie to you."

Again she wanted to cry. "I appreciate that."

He took another sip of his wine. The waiter appeared with the appetizer they ordered. Adam asked for a little more time to order. "So tonight I want to know about Liliana Serrano. What grade do you teach?"

Scanning the selection of elaborate main courses on the menu, she peered over it and asked, "Is this going to be a Q&A session?"

He chuckled. Understanding she was using his words on him. "But I'm asking the questions."

"What's the difference, it's still Q&A."

"Fair enough."

"Third grade," she answered anyway.

He smiled. "Do you enjoy it?"

She nodded and smiled at the thought of her class. Her last group of students had been an interesting bunch, a bit much at times but each lovable in their own way. "Yes, very much."

"I'd love to see you in the classroom."

She put the menu back on the table and looked at him. Adam grinned, mischief twinkling in his eyes. Lily thought of a typical day teaching, what she often referred to as her happy chaos. "It's rather boring."

He chuckled. "Every man wants to do a hot teacher. Here, taste this." He forked a piece of fresh mozzarella and placed it in her mouth.

Perfectly seasoned fresh cheese with basil and a touch of salt and vinegar met her palette. Lily closed her eyes savoring the flavor. "That's delicious, and I'm not hot. At least not when I'm teaching."

Releasing her hand, he leaned back in his chair and watched her, his handsome face fully exposed under the beautiful evening sky. Claudio approached their table with a plate.

"Compliments of Guillermo," the handsome young man said with a smile as he placed a plate of grilled chorizo in caramelized onions on the table, then left.

"Guillermo will cater Jason and Minka's wedding," he explained. "This is the best chorizo I've ever had. You must try it."

The aroma of the grilled Spanish sausage pierced through Lily's nostrils. As he'd done with the mozzarella, he sliced the chorizo and fed her a piece. The minute it entered her mouth, her palate came to life with the robust blend of paprika, chili powder, and whatever other secret spices Guillermo used. Picking up her fork, she reached over for another piece. Lily closed her eyes, savoring the flavor of the spicy sausage. When she finally opened her eyes, Adam was watching her. His eyes rested solely on her lips.

"I did say no sex, right?"

The question made her laugh. His idea, not hers. She was still processing it.

"You know that's every boy's fantasy," he continued.

"Well, good thing you're not a boy."

He shook his head and laughed. A rich laugh that made her skin tingle. "We are the immature sex. Therefore, I'm still hung up on that."

"You've already done me."

He grinned. "But not a teacher fantasy. How about a college student and a professor?"

Still laughing, she shook her head. "How did we get to this conversation?"

"You're a hot teacher."

"Okay, I'm a hot teacher." She surrendered and accepted his compliment. They sat back and discussed the menu. Adam told her some of his favorites. By the time the waiter came, Lily decided to go with the grilled snapper and leeks. Adam chose sea bass with chanterelle mushrooms. Then he recommended she try the little necks. At first she was reluctant to use her hands to clean the clams, soak them in hot water, then the butter sauce, but within seconds, she found herself enjoying the moment.

As they ate, the conversation became light and easy between them until her family came up.

"Jason mentioned your brothers and parents are coming to the wedding."

"That's what I've heard," she answered with a slight smile.

"Do they know?"

"The oldest one, Rafa, thinks he has it all figured out."

He smiled. "So he's coming here to seek me out."

"I'll control the situation."

He shrugged, unperturbed by the idea of three men coming to an island specifically to hunt him down. "I've dealt with worse. I can take it."

Again, she noted the slight strain in his voice. She searched his face. His eyes were dark with secrets that she'd never felt close enough to uncover.

"You have secrets, Adam."

"We all have secrets, Liliana," he said, his voice void of emotion.

An awkward silence fell between them, like a vacuum, creating an overwhelming sense of emptiness. Lily finished the last piece of clam and tried to focus her attention on the water, but she couldn't, not with the questions that suddenly twisted her heart in knots. No matter what Adam said, the truth was he wasn't ready to put his heart on the table. With the slightest probe, he'd shut down.

She was grateful when a tall, lean-built, handsome man with jet-black hair similar to Adam's but sprinkled with grey approached their table with Claudio. Adam smiled; the tension her words brought seemed to have left his body.

"Liliana, meet Guillermo, the best chef on the island."

Guillermo took her hand in his and lowered his lips to hers. Lily couldn't help but giggle. She heard of the Brazilian chef before from Minka. He had catered Keely and Blake's wedding and would be doing the same for Jason and Minka's.

"It's a pleasure to finally meet you, Lily. You drive him crazy, and I love it."

"Guillermo also has a big mouth," Adam mumbled. "He enjoys watching me suffer. One day I'll have to fire him."

The chef seemed unfazed by the threat. He laughed and waved his hand. "His bark is bigger than his bite. Deep down he's a teddy bear. I do have to borrow him for a moment if that's okay. I don't mean to interrupt."

Adam glanced at her and she waved away his hesitation. "Please, that's fine. I'll be right here."

With a nod, he pushed his chair back and walked away with Claudio and Guillermo. As they did so, she thought she heard

Guillermo speaking Portuguese to Adam. Which made no sense, but then again, most Europeans spoke many languages. She watched them. There was an ease between the three men, but what struck her the most was the similarity between them. It wasn't one of those hey you are brothers kind of resemblance, but their mannerism, the broad shoulders, the dark hair.

What's your secret, Adam?

She picked up her fork and toyed with it between her fingers. Lost in her thoughts, she nearly jumped when someone touched her shoulder. She looked up at Adam, his eyes held hers. Another intense connection settled between them. Adam ran his fingertips up on her forearm, leaving a trail of goose bumps blooming in their wake.

"You're okay?" he asked with a slight frown.

He leaned a little closer and brought one hand to her face. His thumb ran along the curve of her cheekbone. She couldn't fight it. She nestled her face into his hand, feeling his warmth seep into her.

"Yes, sorry. I drifted," she answered.

His lips brushed her head, then he released her and walked over to his chair. "My apologies, kitchen issues."

"Is everything okay?"

"An irate customer." He shrugged. "We ran out of the catch of the day. I went and talked to him." He checked his watch. "Let's eat and go catch the sunset."

Adam kept the conversation light while they ate. She learned about the Aquilani charities helping battered women and troubled teens. He told her about the investment he, Jason, Forrest, and now Blake put into the Vineyard to provide activities for the children on the island, especially during the quiet season when the population was about fifteen thousand or less. She learned a little about his life in Italy, his condo in Rome and house in Verona. He even shared childhood stories of him and his parents. He kept her laughing.

As they left the restaurant for the beach, he took her to the kitchen to say goodbye to Guillermo, who hugged her tightly and made her promise she would come back again. Feeling giddy from the food and the company, Lily promised to return.

"Let's go catch the sunset," Adam whispered. She tucked her hand in the crook of his arm and allowed her body to fall to the rhythm of his steps to the beach. Their contact was broken momentarily for her to remove her strappy heels.

The cool sand floated between her bare feet. She followed Adam and sat on the cooling dunes. A comfortable silence settled between them as they watched the seagulls walking along the shoreline. The sandcastles slowly dissolved, the waves washing away all signs of the children's efforts that day, as shadows crept over the land. A few beachgoers smiled at them. Some locals waved at Adam but left him alone.

"I've been to many places, but the sunset here is one of the best I've ever seen." His arm came to rest on her shoulder and pulled her closer to him.

Lily focused her eyes on the magenta sky. The sun was setting on the horizon, painting the water with the reflection of brilliant pink and orange that spread across the sky. The silence continued, but that was okay. Mesmerized by the beauty of the scene, she nestled a little closer to Adam and gazed at the place where the sun went down.

"Breathtaking, isn't it?"

The words, heavy with sexual desire, ate through her like a wildfire in a desert. The yearning inside her burst forth.

"Yes, very much."

But it was autumn, the ocean breeze was cool, making her shiver.

"Let's go home," he whispered huskily in her ear. As he came to his feet, with arms extended he gently pulled her up with him.

His arms wrapped around her comfortably, sending sparks flying, heart fluttering, emotions building. Lily heard the soft whisper of his breath as he exhaled. Before she could say anything, Adam tilted his head down and kissed her, sending a shiver down her spine.

"I never agreed to the new rule," she said once their lips were finally disconnected.

He shook his head, reaffirming he was going to stick to this no-sex nonsense. His arm slid along her back to guide her closer and held her to his heart. His chin pressed gently on top of her head. "I discovered something tonight," he said in a low rough voice.

"What's that?"

"I'm liking you a lot more than I originally planned."

His steady, strong, powerful heartbeat drummed in her ear. Lily closed her eyes and lost herself in the moment. Her fears over his lifestyle and career choice still lurked in her conscience, but she knew she needed to stop being afraid of what could go wrong and focus on what could go right.

16

"Boys, if you like her, if she makes you happy, and if you feel like you know her, don't let her go."
Nicholas Sparks

*A*dam's stomach felt like a whirlpool ready to engulf him with no remorse. He couldn't breathe, the oxygen suffocating his lungs.

"Não!" he screamed the word 'no' in Portuguese, the weight of his heart bringing him to his knees. Black tears fell easily from his eyes and rolled down his cheeks as he watched the light fade from her eyes. Her soul slipped through his fingers as her body lay there stiff.

He examined the woman's lifeless features, her lifestyle etched harsh on her face. She was a prostitute, a drug addict. No one would miss her, not her pimp or her clients. Except for him, she gave him life. He loved her. Even with all of her flaws.

With trembling hands, he brushed the matted black mane away from her face and swiped his hand over her eyes. His gaze lingered on the empty syringe on the floor, a drop of blood still trickling from her vein. Inches from her body lay what finally ended her life. He reached over and gripped the cold metal. Young adolescent fingers wrapped around the gun as he rose to his feet, and headed for his fate.

The door creaked open. He spotted his target right away. There on the bed, waiting to be hunted. Blinded by fury, he took aim. With the strength of a man, his eight-year-old body held the semi-automatic pistol as steady as possible. His finger pulled the trigger and bullets spat relentlessly, one after another.

As his body fell further into the abyss, a soft feminine voice, like the harmony of angels, called out to him. He recognized the sweet sound right away. It breathed life into him. *Lily.* But it wasn't enough to pull him free. He closed his eyes and gave himself away to the darkness. Her voice grew stronger, nearer. Soft hands touched his naked arms—not the thin skinny limbs of him as a child, but of him as a man.

He tried to emerge from the dream, but his head was filled with images. Lily's smile, her face in the throes of passion, his parents and a baby wrapped in a wool towel with a mass of dark hair similar to his. He couldn't tell if it was a boy or girl. Not that it mattered, it was his child. He walked over to pick it up. The more steps he took, the further it moved out of his reach. Adam blinked and rushed his strides as images of the black curls faded away.

He came to a halt, paralyzed to the spot, a menacing aura holding him in a tightening grip. He spotted the infant. Brown trusting eyes glanced at him. Then they turned to look into the face of a dark-haired man. A knot formed in Adam's throat. He tried to move forward, to run and snatch the child to safety, but his feet would not allow him to do so. He opened his mouth to speak, to beg, and spare a life, but terror sucked the breath from his mouth and silenced his scream. Adam stood, ice-cold, as the man stroked the baby's arm, the end of a syringe shining in his hand.

A sudden, sickening sensation ran through his body.

Fuck!

Not another addicted baby. He needed to stop it. He fought against his weight, but heaviness kept him deathly still.

"Adam. Adam." Lily's voice was subtly sensual and smooth, a velvety whisper.

He struggled to open his eyes.

"Adam." Her voice had a little more urgency this time.

He woke up with a gasp, covered in sweat, and breathing heavily. His mind reeling.

Shit!

He closed his eyes momentarily and grabbed hold of his consciousness. When he opened them again, Lily was sitting by his side, her short hair tousled from the night. The thin straps of the little thing she slept in slipped off her slim shoulders. Her face masked with concern. The sight caused his heart to stop.

"Liliana," he said when he was sure his voice would not shake. "Did I hurt you? The baby?"

She shook her head, but grief reflected in her big brown eyes. He knew she wanted to break his exterior defenses. He felt it last night for the first time. He wasn't ready for that, and God damn it, she needed to understand that.

He swung his feet to the floor and sat on the edge of the bed. Sunlight seeping through the curtains touched his face, as Lily's hands traced down his back and found the curve of his waist. She pressed her face against him. Her lips followed—sweet and tender, kissing away every second of the memories that flooded his mind like waves of destruction.

"Liliana." It wasn't fair to take from her. Not when he couldn't show her everything that he was. Still, he sat there and got lost in the feel of her lips for what seemed like the millionth time.

"Are you going to tell me what that was about?"

"No."

A long sigh came from her lips. Her breath caressed his skin. "You're not ready." Her hands moved to his shoulders and slowly started to work out the kinks. "But when you are, you'll find out I'm a big girl." She let out a nervous chuckle. "I can handle things."

His hand moved to hers and held it still. "Like unexpectedly getting knocked up."

She laughed.

A little laughter, like the sun breaking through stormy clouds. It illuminated the darkness inside him. He edged over a little more so he could face her. "You're sure I didn't hurt you?"

---

*L*ily scanned Adam's face, his eyebrows drawn together. Beautiful and haunting, yet full of sadness and pain. She was seeing the man behind the cool, laid-back exterior for the very first time.

He was a puzzle and just maybe with some broken pieces. Still, she was permanently in love with him, always and forever, with all of the secrets and smiles. Everything. She'd fallen hard and just wanted him. Her fingers stroked the scar above his left eyebrow, the first time she allowed herself to touch one of his perfect imperfections.

"Not physically, you didn't." Emotionally, her heart had been ripped out of her chest as she sat there watching Adam struggle to emerge from whatever dark hole he'd fallen into. This side of him was new to her, it shook her a bit. Not out of fear, this much she knew. But a confirmation in so many ways that they were strangers. "How did you get this scar?"

"Playing *fútbol*." He rose from the bed and moved across the room. The hardwood echoed his pressured steps. His long arms leaned against the window sill on the opposite side of the room. The muscles on his back turned rigid, shutting her out once again. "I'm going gliding," he announced over his shoulder.

He meant plane-gliding, another one of his extreme sports, cheating death each time. He was Superman and life was his stage.

"I can think of better ways to release tension."

He turned and stared at her, long and hard, as if contemplating her invitation, before his lips cracked into a genuine smile. "Don't you have to meet with Minka and the others?"

"I can push it back." She shrugged. "Say three hours."

He laughed and Lily saw some of the tension leaving his body. She sank on the plush mattress, inviting him to come join her. After a slight hesitation, several long strides brought him to her side of the bed.

"I'd need more than three hours."

"You have that much tension?" she questioned with a brow raised.

He nodded. "A full load." His eyes were serious, as was his tone.

"Good thing I'm around to help you release."

His hands found her hips and pulled her to the edge of the bed. Her skin bristled at his touch. Needing to be closer, Lily hoisted herself to a full sitting position and clamped her thighs around his. Her fingers found the waist of his boxer briefs and slowly ran her hand over his crotch. He groaned.

"You want me," she whispered, and lowered her lips to tickle the fine hairs that cover his lower abdomen.

His muscles tightened under her touch. "Yes," he said low and husky. "But—"

"No buts."

He released a heavy breath then gently pushed her back on the bed. He stood still as his eyes took in every inch of her. Lily's hands found the hem of her delicate cotton nightie and inched it up high, exposing crystal pink hip-hugger lace panties.

His eyes darkened and dropped to her thighs. Under heavy lids, she watched him struggle to maintain control. Then his hand brushed her inner thigh, spreading her legs just a little wider. He stroked a thumb over the thin material, teasing her swollen flesh. Hypersensitive to his touch, every nerve in her body tingled with pleasure as her hips rocked in gentle motion.

"More," she begged.

But he pulled back and stepped out of her reach. Lily searched his face, his eyes burned with emptiness. A boiling fury swelled inside of her. She rose to her feet and walked up to him. Chest to chest, she glared at him.

"What's that about?"

"We agreed—" he began in that typical cool as a cucumber voice.

"No," she stopped him, her voice louder. This time she was the one who moved back and stepped out of his reach. Needing a moment to breathe, she gave him her back. After a second, she whipped around and peered at him. "You made that stupid rule, Adam. I didn't agree to it."

"What do you want, Liliana? You want me to fuck you to release my demons? You want to be a substitute?" The questions hung in the air. A look of great bitterness swept across his face. "Well, too fucking bad. You've never been that."

"Then talk to me."

Time stood still like never before.

"I can't." He walked past her and slammed the bathroom door behind him, leaving her standing there fuming.

Three hours later, Lily's whole being still seethed with anger. She slumped on to her chair, alongside Keely, Claire and Minka at West Chop, a steakhouse restaurant on the pier overlooking the Atlantic Ocean. After picking out the floral arrangement for the wedding, lunch had been suggested. Lily wasn't sure if she agreed or not, she just found herself sitting there and for once she wished she was anywhere else. All day, her mind had been preoccupied with thoughts of Adam.

"Earth to Lily," Claire said with a wave, flashing her colorful bohemian bracelets. "Whoo-hoo! Over here, honey."

"You're not sitting straight," Keely said gently.

Without looking at her friends, Lily ran her fingers over the rim of the teacup. She inhaled the ginger and citrus aroma of the tea. Although this one was not laced, it still made her think of Adam and his hot toddies. "So?"

"That means you're sad." That great observation came from none other than her BFF Minka.

"What's eating you, girlfriend?" Claire asked. "I thought all was well in Adam and Liliana land now."

She took an appraising look around the table, and then focused her gaze on Claire. "You grew up with Adam, right?"

"Technically, I grew up with Jason."

"I don't mean in the same house. I mean around them. You're that pain in the ass little sister, right? No offense," Lily added.

"None taken." Claire shrugged. "That's how they all describe me."

She took a sip of wine. "I am close to Adam but…" Her voice lingers. "He spends half his time in Europe."

Lily sat a little straighter. "What happened to him?"

Claire blinked. "What do you mean?"

"He…" She caught herself and looked at Claire, Keely and Minka. Concern filled their faces. They were her friends, but she didn't want to betray Adam. "Never mind." She brought her attention back to her tea.

"Have you ever Googled Adam?" Minka asked after a brief silence.

"No, why would I?" Lily asked without lifting her gaze from her tea.

"You Googled Jason," Minka continued.

Lily looked up then and smiled at the memories. "Yeah, but that's because I was being a concerned friend. And I was dying to see what he looked like. Total hotness by the way, but I've told you that like a million times."

Claire feigned choking on her food. Keely and Minka chuckled.

"And you know," Lily continued, "Adam and I were pure sex."

"So let's look him up now," Keely suggested and started to reach for her phone.

But Lily's hand quickly covered Keely's. "No. I'd much rather he tells me."

"Good thing," Claire said, "because what's on the internet is not the full story. Only Adam can tell you everything."

Lily sat back. "So you know something."

Claire shrugged. "We all know the minute details. I thought you did as well."

Lily took a calming breath and tried to control the searing pain in her heart. "I don't know anything." Her voice trembled. "I'm in complete darkness."

Claire squeezed Lily's hand and smiled at her. "Don't give up on him. He's not perfect, but he's a good guy."

"He refuses to have sex with me too," she said softly. "Something about getting to know each other, blah, blah, blah." She rolled her eyes.

Her friends laughed. Lily broke out in giggles.

"No sex," Keely said between chuckles. "That's a problem."

"Tell me about it. When I'm not nauseous, I want to have sex. Hell, even when I'm nauseous, I want sex. I'm naturally horny and this pregnancy thing just quadruples my horniness level."

"Horniness?" Minka asked, hazel eyes twinkling with humor.

"I made that up." Lily grinned. "Brilliant, right?"

Another round of laughter touched the table. "So how long has it been? I thought you guys made up that night you left after dinner?" Minka asked, her lips curved into a smile.

Lily sighed. It felt like forever. How the hell did they use to go weeks without sex? Oh, yeah. They used to have major phone sex. "Uh…I guess today would make it two days."

"And you're complaining." Claire's eyes shot up with disbelief. "Try months, my friend. Well, at least with an actual person. Toys don't count."

Lily laughed. "You're lying."

Claire shook her head. "I wish."

"But all of your boyfriends," Minka said. The tabloids always had Claire dating someone.

"All lies. Pure fabrication. If I smile at someone, I'm dating him."

"According to the latest tabloid, you're hooking up with your co-star. What's his name?" Minka asked with a frown.

Claire waved a dismissive hand and Lily caught a glint of her tattoo again.

"What's the story behind the tat? Why do you hide it?" Lily asked and silence fell over the table. "Okay, what do I need to know?"

Minka shrugged. She looked just as clueless, but Keely and Claire exchanged a quick look.

"I fell in love once," Claire said, sadness filled her voice. "I was young and foolish." Her pretty face grew solemn. "It's the past, a place of reference."

Claire's tone told her this piece of her history had long been buried and forgotten, no longer a place of residence. Lily understood that. Over a year ago, Adam had helped her let go of Nate and start the next chapter in her life.

The front door of the restaurant opened and Forrest strolled in looking like no doctor Lily had ever known, in sea-green, broken-in chinos, a white shirt, fitted dark grey wool blazer, and black frame hipster glasses. His chestnut hair a bit tossed by the wind. In typical women's fashion, they gawked silently. He didn't notice them. Good thing because they got to watch him flirt with the pretty bartender.

Lily leaned closer to Claire. "Is Forrest in the brother zone too?"

"Totally," Claire answered without a beat, but her gaze lingered on him a little too long. He turned abruptly in their direction and their eyes locked. After a second, she looked away.

Brother zone. That was total bullshit. Seeing through her newfound friend, Lily waved at Forrest and signaled for him to join them. As he approached their table, he removed his glasses and slipped them into the pocket of his blazer. Too bad, she liked the look.

"Why don't you join us?" Lily suggested. "We're having lunch."

He glanced at their faces, but his grey eyes lingered on Claire. "I don't want to interrupt."

Lily chuckled and waved away his concern. "Nonsense." She scooted her chair to make room between her and Claire. "Grab a chair. Besides, we can't let you flirt with the pretty bartender when there are four of us here."

He smiled. "You're all taken."

Right. She forgot about that. "Not all of us."

Minka kicked her from under the table. Keely glared at her. And Claire looked like she wanted to die. Forrest wasn't fooled either. He smiled, totally on to her scheme. But he pulled a chair and settled between her and Claire.

"I'll join you for a little, but I'm meeting someone here."

Shit. He had a date. The realization dawned on Lily too late. A tall, pretty redhead dressed in skinny jeans and what Adam would call "fuck-me" boots walked into the restaurant. She glanced at the bar, checked her watch and bit her lower lip seductively. Yikes. Forrest was going to be someone's lunch.

"Thanks for the invite, ladies, but I have to go. My date is here."

He pushed his chair back, then stopped and looked down at Claire. "When do you leave, Claire?"

"After tomorrow," Claire answered without a glance at him.

"Let's all meet tomorrow at the farm for dinner then. I'll even cook something." He smiled. "Any special requests?" He asked the table, but clearly the question was directed at Claire.

"Umm, whatever," Keely answered. Minka and Lily nodded in agreement.

Claire shrugged, but she lifted her head and met his gaze. "You know what I like. Surprise me."

Their eyes stayed on each other for a beat. "As you wish."

Oh, damn. He was quoting Westley from *The Princess Bride*. Totally swoon-worthy.

"Sorry." Lily fanned her face. "Pregnant hormones are making me a little warm."

Forrest's hand rested on Claire's back for a moment then he smiled and walked into the hungry redhead's arms.

By the time Lily pulled Adam's sleek Porsche GTS Cabriolet into his driveway, darkness had fallen. After lunch, Minka convinced her to head back to Martha's Way and help her with seating arrangements while Keely and Claire worked on the finishing touches of the bridesmaids' dresses. Between work and lots of laughter, they had lost track of time.

She spotted the black Maserati and glanced at the house. Once again, the light from the family room was on. Ready to make amends, she walked inside the house and headed down the hall.

Adam sat on the sofa, casually dressed in a T-shirt and worn jeans, nothing fancy. Yet his mere presence affected her, and her heart did that little dance only reserved for him. He was jotting down notes as he glanced back and forth to the large television screen of his last race. Even from the door, she could detect he was focused.

"I went back to Martha's Way with Minka and we lost track of time," she said, announcing her presence.

"No problem," he muttered, picked up the remote and froze the screen to the part where he was knocked out of the lead. "My parents are on the island," he said over his shoulder.

She froze in place. "What?"

With his back still facing her, he nodded. "You'll meet them tomorrow at the farm."

The morning's tension still hung thick in the air. Feeling a sense of heady anticipation, Lily let out a nervous chuckle. "You knew they were coming?"

She waited. He didn't answer.

"Adam."

He placed the remote on the sofa, stood up and closed the space between them. Flat black eyes with a lifeless look to them greeted her. Her immediate reaction was to hold his hands, kiss away whatever he was struggling with. But she held back.

"I'm sorry I didn't tell you. It didn't seem important then."

Translation—they weren't important, at least not until the baby. Lily swallowed back the pain. Too late for her ego to be bruised, she already agreed to date him and explore the possibilities of them becoming more. "Let's go to bed," she suggested in a choked voice.

His lips brushed hers. "Go ahead. I'll come in a few."

She hesitated, but Adam was already on the sofa, his attention back to the television screen. The walls were back up, shutting her out once again.

Well into the night, Lily stared blankly into the darkness of the bedroom. A terrible weight fell onto her shoulders as she lay still on the bed. She waited, hoped, Adam would join her. But eventually, her eyes felt heavy. Eventually, she fell asleep. Alone.

17

"Is this love or a deception of feelings?"
Warlock

*S*imple things tended to become complicated when one expected too much. Twiddling her thumbs, Lily glanced over at Adam, his mop of unruly dark curls blowing against the autumn breeze. With his vision hidden behind a pair of black onyx sunglasses, she couldn't quite make out his expression. But everything about his composure screamed he was in complete control and was once again back to his sexy cool, laid-back self. Unlike her.

In silence, he maneuvered his little baby of a car on their way to Herring Creek, his thumbs thumping to the tune of *Transliterator* by Devotchka. They had not spoken much today. By the time she woke up, Adam had already left for his restaurant and spent the whole day there preparing to shut down for the winter season.

There had been no mention of why he hadn't come to bed. But Lily already knew the answer. Fear of showing any vulnerability. The possibility of having another dream and exposing whatever monster oppressed him during sleep would indicate a sign of letting his guard down a bit, and expose his internal wounds. She caught a glimpse of them during his nightmare. He was now guarded.

In either case, that conversation had to wait. Right now, more pressing things occupied her mind. Like the fact she was about to come face to face with the two people who molded him into what he was today. Her stomach had been tied up in bunches since Adam dropped the news his parents were on the island.

Yep. She blamed her tossing and turning all night on them and that gorgeous man sitting inches away from her.

"You're nervous again," he noted without a glance in her direction.

She squirmed in her seat. "I'm not," she said, then bit the corner of her mouth.

He smiled. "You're fidgeting."

Okay. Maybe she was. But it was his fault. She clasped her hands together. A little warning would have been nice. And she didn't mean the "Oh, by the way, my parents are here," type of announcement. Nope. Lily needed…she searched her mind for a decent prep time. Two weeks would have been fair. Just like he had for her family.

The car turned smoothly onto a dirt road leading through acres of land. Brightly painted farm buildings stood near rows of glowing green, ripe red and pure purple crops. Bold red letters marked a sign nailed to an oak tree, Herring Creek Organic Farm. The early evening sun, full and bright, combined with the earthy scent of compost made the farm smell like a secluded forest. She took in the beauty of the land. It was an agricultural paradise.

"How long are your parents here for?" she asked, ignoring his comment.

"They're here for the wedding."

Yeah, he'd told her that. Actually he texted her that bit of information earlier today. The Maserati drove past a rusty metal plough standing opposite a bundle of hay.

"The wedding is over a week away."

He shrugged. "My mother is from Boston. She spent a lot of time on the island before moving to Italy. And they still come back. You know that."

Yes. She did. But she'd never been around. And they usually stayed with him. More importantly, she usually stayed away.

"They volunteered to stay here," he informed her.

"Why?"

"They know you're staying with me. I don't know." He shrugged again. "Dad said something about not wanting to intrude."

"Do they know?" Her hands automatically folded over her flat stomach.

Adam glanced at her, caught hold of one of her hand and brought it to his lips. "Yes."

She sighed heavily.

The Maserati made a sharp left behind a red barn and came to a halt among many parked trailers and trucks.

"Look at me, Liliana."

Reluctantly, she turned to face him as he pulled his sunglasses off. Once again, she found herself drowning in the intensity of his eyes.

"My parents came yesterday. I would have told you but we didn't talk much during the day." A smile touched his lips. "They've known about you for a while now. Naturally, they are excited to meet you. And that was even before I told them about the baby."

Wait. What? Had the pregnancy affected her hearing as well? What did he mean they'd known about her? That implied she'd always existed in his world. Too bad she couldn't say the same.

"They've known about me?"

He nodded. "We discussed you a few times. Does it bother you?"

Oh, to have had been a fly on the wall during those discussions. "Um...no. I just didn't think they knew I existed."

Adam brushed a strand of hair from her forehead. "Like your parents don't know I exist."

Guilty. Her chin dropped and her gaze darted downward, with one finger he lifted her face back to his.

"I don't know why I told them about you," he said in a gentle tone. His gaze bore into hers. "But I understand why you never told your parents about me. It doesn't bother me. So stop thinking and let's go have fun. Everyone is here tonight."

"Everyone?"

He smiled. "Jason's father and Claire's mother are here as well. What started as us getting together turned into a party."

"I see," she answered, fighting back the sour taste in her mouth.

"The island is small,'" he continued. "We all grew up together and our parents are good friends. Everyone knew they were coming for the wedding."

She nodded tightly. Once again, she was the last to know. "One big, happy family."

His eyes searched hers. "You're part of our family now. Might as well get to know everyone."

Lily drew in a deep breath. It didn't matter that he owned her heart, or that in a sea of people her eyes would always search for him. She wasn't part of the family. They were still in the discovering phase. Baby or in love, she had to keep afloat. Of all people, she knew love was fleeting, merely a madness. It erupted like a volcano and then subsided.

But the little voice that knew she was on the brink of losing all sense of rationality reminded her she lost that power a long time ago.

"Stop thinking." Adam leaned into her. His focus was intense and unnerving.

His mouth swooped down to capture hers. And like every other time everything in her surrendered to him. Passion and desire exploded throughout her body, between them, like the twists of a rope, mutually mixing one with the other, and twined inextricably around her heart.

"Come on, my parents are watching us," he whispered against her lips.

What! Her head whipped around to follow his gaze and landed on a couple hugging and smiling in their direction. Lily groaned miserably and Adam chuckled as he stepped out of the car. He came by her side, slipped his hand in hers and led her to his parents.

Lily surveyed them with each closing step. They were a beautiful couple and something about them generated warmth and tranquility. She guessed they were in their mid-fifties. His mother, a former Miss

America, looked beautiful in a silk poppy dress and knee-length cowboy boots. She was tall, with a fair complexion, lustrous blonde hair, and smiling blue eyes. Physically, the two men didn't look that different from each other, and could easily pass for father and son. They were similar in height, same bronze complexion and dark hair. Only difference, his father's hair was sprinkled with a hint of grey. But as she got closer, she realized, although the man was handsome, the two bore no resemblance.

His mother pulled Adam in her arms and planted a kiss on each of his cheeks. The two men shared a warm hug. She smiled at the obvious love Adam shared with his parents. After he pulled back from their embrace, he reached for her hands and introduced her. "This is Liliana." He nodded at the couple.

Curiosity sparked in their eyes as they appraised her appearance. Smiling, she extended a hand to them, but she was pulled into four arms. Hugs and kisses soon followed. The warm embrace left her rather speechless and a little nervous. But she liked their warmth; it reminded her of her parents.

"What a pleasure to finally meet you, Liliana," his mother said, still assessing her and smiling. "Congratulations on the upcoming wedding."

A little disoriented by what she heard, Lily chuckled. Surely, there was some confusion. "Oh, we're not getting married. Jason and Minka are."

His parents frowned, their eyes darted between her and Adam.

So that's what a deer felt like when caught in headlights.

After an awkward silence, his father spoke in a slight Italian accent. "Yes, of course. Their wedding is next weekend, but yours is soon after, no?"

Lily's blood boiled in rage. Anger couldn't cover all that she felt. Hurt. Betrayed. Lost. She waited for Adam to set the record straight. When he didn't, she glanced at him, and his jaws clenched. "We are not getting married. Not anytime soon." she said in a flat tone, and then smiled weakly at his parents. "Please excuse me."

Grievously troubled in mind and vexed in soul, she unlaced her fingers from Adam's and slipped away from his touch. He made no attempt to hold her back, and her heart dissolved to her toes.

He just let her go.

With autumn leaves crunching under her feet, she nearly ran toward the converted barn house where Forrest's parents held most of their social functions. Numerous windows and a trim of translucent siding kept the indoor illuminated with natural light. Wood-clad walls displayed bright, bold, local art pieces, giving the place a warm environment. She scanned the room and the familiar faces. Cheerful chatter surrounded her as Maxwell's *Urban Hang Suite* played from the built in surround sound system. The singer's sensual, Neo-Soul voice filled the room as he cataloged the stages of adult romance through his songs.

Jason had one arm draped over Minka's shoulder as they engaged in a conversation with his father. Whatever was said between the three of them caused Minka to touch her cheek and beam. The couple looked relaxed, in love, and their apparent happiness pulled at Lily's heartstrings. Claire's mother was laughing with Forrest's mom, Keely and Blake. Distance away, she spotted Forrest talking to his father. Claire was nowhere in sight. With the exception of Adam's parents, she met them all around the same time last year at Jason's art show, honoring his mother's photography.

Yes. One big, happy family. Adam's family. Not that anyone had ever made her feel less than welcome. If anything, she was greeted with a warm reception from day one. But it wasn't about everyone in the room. Her problem was with the man she loved.

Baby or not, no love, no marriage, she reminded herself. And the first step to achieving love was to establish trust. Call her selfish, but she wanted it all from Adam. His intensity and vulnerability. While she was drawn to his unguarded way of living, the reality was Adam had surrounded himself by walls.

"Every time I see you, you look miserable."

Claire's voice startled her. Lily turned and smiled weakly at the other woman.

"What did Adam do now?" Claire chuckled. "Still no sex?"

In spite of the bitter taste of sadness inside of her, Claire's question brought a smile to Lily's lips. "You look beautiful, Claire," she remarked as Claire spun in full circle to give her a complete view of the modern, yet ethereal indigo backless dress. "Wow! I love it!"

On any other, it might have come across as trying too hard, but the pretty singer looked effortlessly beautiful and elegant.

"Thank you." Claire smiled. "So what's wrong?"

"Nothing," Lily answered with a slight shake of her head. "Everything, I guess. Adam's parents think we are getting married."

"It could be a misunderstanding," Claire answered, her eyebrows furrowed. "But what would be so bad about that?"

"Would you marry someone just because you find yourself pregnant?"

A smile touched Claire's lips. "You're in love with him."

Lily remained quiet.

"And you want him to love you, except Adam, like most men, is slow in the love department."

The slow part wasn't the problem. Their relationship was in a transitional phase, and she'd been willing to go for the ride. That is, until the nightmare occurred. Lily peeked at Forrest. He was still engaged in a conversation with his father. His mother and Jason's father walked over and joined them.

Claire chuckled. "There's nothing going on between me and Forrest. We are friends."

"Right." It was clear Claire had no intention to divulge whatever was going on. At that exact moment, the hair on the back of her neck prickled. Lily turned toward the door and her gaze collided with Adam's. He gave her a long calculating look, but didn't come to her. Instead he headed to where Jason and Blake were now engaged in a conversation. "He has these dreams that he won't talk to me about," Lily said in a whisper. "I'm mad at him."

"You need to give him time, my friend," Claire whispered. "Has he opened up to you yet?"

Lily's gaze dropped to the floor as she shook her head. "Quite the opposite. He has completely shut me out."

Claire squeezed her shoulder. "You know I love all of them, right? But," Claire continued, "Adam is being really stubborn right now." She paused for a breath. "However, let me say, the baby is a complete curve ball. For both of you. The only difference is you've already fallen for him."

"It's not enough. His walls are so high, I can't reach around them."

"I'm going to tell you a little story, and then we have to go mingle," Claire said, her gaze on the couple now talking to Keely and Minka. "I once did an interview for this premier magazine in Europe, the reporter thought he was clever and shifted the topic to Adam. It was then I learned there is no record of his life from the age of eight to ten."

Lily's mouth opened but words couldn't find their way out.

"Naturally," Claire continued, "I immediately became guarded and asked that we kept the conversation on my upcoming record." She shrugged. "I love each one of them as they are. They've done the same with Jason after his mother's death. Anyhow, the point to me telling you this is I warned Adam and the next day the reporter was assigned to cover fashion or something. Last I checked, he was still calling Adam for an interview."

Lily peered at Adam. He smiled at something Blake said and patted Jason's back. On the outside one could never tell he carried wounds. She was still clueless of their depth.

"His parents are very influential in Europe," Claire informed. "They love him very much and would protect him at all cost," she said with admiration.

"That was pretty low of that reporter to try to get information through you." But even she had to admit Claire's words had piqued her curiosity.

Claire shrugged and seemed undaunted. "People are always snooping. I'm going to mingle. Are you going to stay here sulking over Adam's dumb-ass move or enjoy the night and get to know his parents? They are a nice couple. I love them."

Lily chuckled. "You love everyone. Even Charles," she said, referring to Jason's father.

Claire smiled. "Hey, he raised me. And he's a good guy. Just made a stupid mistake. We all do. And look." She tilted her chin in Jason's direction, who was once again talking to his father. "It seems all is well between the evil father and the angry son."

The two women chuckled. For someone she only met recently, Lily liked Claire's easy confidence and attitude. "You're back in L.A. tomorrow?"

Claire nodded. "I'll be back for the wedding. After that I have a year of touring ahead of me to support my movie and new record drop." She rolled her eyes to the ceiling. "By the time I see you again, your little bundle of joy will actually be a couple of months old."

Lily admired Claire's talent and was a fan of her music, but the idea of spending a whole year on the road made her cringe. "Do you love the whole thing that comes with the fame?"

Something crossed over Claire's delicate features, but once again it was quickly buried. "It comes with sacrifices, but I love what I do." She pulled a hand on Lily's back. "Come on. Let's go join the fun. One more thing, have you told Adam you're in love with him?"

Just the thought made Lily cringed. "Oh, God no."

"Well, don't look, but the big bad wolf is coming this way."

She looked of course and caught sight of Adam's imposing figure approaching them, holding her gaze prisoner the whole time.

"I'll leave you two alone," Claire said as Adam closed the distance between them.

"Come with me," he summoned in a controlled tone and took her hand in his. The gesture was filled with such an innate claim that she could only follow as he led her outside. He turned to face her. "All right, say what's on your mind."

The authority in his tone removed Lily from the spellbound trance she was under. She gazed up into the sky. The light of day had oozed away. "Your parents." She paused and cleared her throat. "You told them we are getting married."

He released her hand and took a few steps away from her. "You already know that's what I want."

Lily exhaled and glanced at him. Adam was leaning against the wall, one foot planted on it. Eyes closed, he tilted his head back to rest against the wall that braced his back. Static electricity vibrated off his body.

Her brain pulsed agonizingly. Her heart followed. "Yes, but..."

"We're dating, Liliana. We're getting to know each other."

Only they weren't. He was shielded in his armor.

"You've shut me out since that dream. You didn't sleep next to me last night." Lily paused and swallowed the loneliness inside. "You don't trust me enough to share your pain with me." She walked over to him and slid her hand over his face.

He opened his eyes only to narrow them at her.

"Why can't you just tell me what you feel?" Her fingers traced his lips. "I need to know what's inside you, Adam."

He caught her hand and held her still. "Liliana," he said in a gruff tone.

She shook her head and watched him. "How you act is confusing me. I need you to trust me." Under the evening sky, she searched his face, the pained expression that met her. "You don't trust me enough to let your guard down and be vulnerable."

Adam straightened himself to his full height and turned his head away from her piercing stare. "Let's go eat."

And just like that he closed the door on her once more. One strong hand came to rest on her lower back as he guided her back to the room.

The aroma of the dinner prepared by Forrest filled the house. Lily followed Adam to where his parents sat. They smiled at her and she caught a hint of concern in both of their eyes. As Lily sat, she caught a glimpse of Claire walking over to where Forrest was working a bottle of wine. She uncorked another bottle and the two fell into a natural routine.

Adam leaned into her, his lips brushed against her ear, and Lily trembled with awareness. "For the record, I do trust you," he whispered in her ear. "But all of this is new to me."

18

"Let's misbehave."
Anonymous

*L*ily adjusted her eyes to the glaring morning sun seeping into the bedroom. Realizing she was still in the dress she wore for last night's dinner, she glanced at the empty space on the bed.

Another night of sleeping alone. Sighing, she pulled her weight to a sitting position. Images of the drive back to the house were a blur. They had stayed out late and fatigue had taken its toll on her body, but she remembered Adam's voice gently telling her to close her eyes as he carried her to the bedroom. She asked him to stay but he slipped out of her grip and left the room.

She took a deep breath and exhaled.

On the nightstand, *I'm Sexy and I Know It* ringtone echoed in the room, immediately causing her heart to skip a beat. "You didn't come to bed again."

"I left you coffee," he said, ignoring her words. "Decaf."

Lily would never understand decaffeinated coffee; it was like sex without the orgasm. Oh yeah, she wasn't getting that either. "Thanks."

"One cup," he warned. "Forrest said—"

"Adam," Lily interrupted. "I never have more than one cup, and my doctor said I can drink regular coffee, you know. It's not like it's a drug."

"I would rather you didn't," he said after a beat.

The strain in his voice tore at Lily's insides. "I won't," she whispered. "I promise. Where are you?"

"At Vapor right now."

The bar normally didn't open until lunch time. Lily scrubbed her hand over her face. "You're avoiding me?"

"I have a meeting with the guys to go over Vineyard Sound for a couple of hours." Vineyard Sound was the center the five of them opened in Vineyard Haven to support abused children. "Then the four of us are going to test the cold water in a paddle boarding race. Nothing serious."

He meant nothing too dangerous. His way of reassuring her that he would not flirt with death today.

"You're feeling okay? You were pretty tired last night."

"Yeah," she answered with a chuckle. "I'm always tired, but I'm okay." She paused, wanting to say the words bottled up inside her, tell him she loved him, or worse ask him to spend the day with her. "I guess I'll see you later."

"Yes. Take it easy today."

She had to meet Minka, but other than that her calendar was empty. Because all of her time was supposed to be with Adam. That was the reason she came a week early.

About twenty minutes later, freshly showered, she wiggled into a pair of broken-in jeans. Lily paused to catch her reflection in the mirror and examined the little roundness of her belly.

No baby bump yet, but her waist had changed, making the jeans a little difficult to snap closed.

She flicked the thin silver bar going through her navel, wondering how long she'd be able to keep the belly ring. Smiling, she slipped into a black silk camisole, grabbed a pair of beige pumps along with an oversized cardigan from the closet, and made her way down to the main floor.

Like everything about Adam, the kitchen was an exciting mix of classic and up-to-date amenities, keeping the room timeless in style but modern in functionality. Vintage wide-plank French oak floors, Old Masters oil painting as featured art wall in the kitchen, and a marble-topped island added a farmhouse style.

She stopped and glanced at the picture of Adam and his parents on the counter before walking over to make her coffee. The sound of a car engine caught her attention. She peeked out the open window and caught a glimpse of an old pickup pulling into the driveway. Seconds later, Adam's parents stepped out.

She gripped the coffee mug and tried to breathe slowly, telling herself to calm down. She'd tell them Adam was out and make a dash for it. And of course use Minka as an excuse. It wouldn't be a lie; she was scheduled to meet her friend. They didn't have to know she still had three hours to kill. Putting on her brave face, Lily walked out of the kitchen to greet Adam's parents.

When she opened the door, a delighted look stretched across their faces. Lily nodded in their direction, but they reached over for a warm hug.

"Liliana," his mother said as she took in Lily's appearance. "You look much better. We were worried about you last night."

Lily found herself smiling. "I'm fine. I was a little tired. Please come in." Wait. She didn't mean to say that. The plan was to make a run for it and avoid any marriage conversation. "Adam's not here," she added for a little sanity check.

"We know," his father responded. "We wanted to make sure you were all right."

Geez, could two people be any nicer?

They were running a close second to her parents. "Thank you. I was about to have a cup of coffee. Decaf," she added with a smile and they chuckled. She sensed they knew Adam had something to do with it. "Adam has strong views about me having caffeine," she said as they entered the kitchen.

"We're not surprised," his mother replied. "Although a small cup is fine."

"But that's our Adam," his father quipped.

No shit, thought Lily as she found two extra coffee cups. "I don't know how you like your coffee."

"Don't worry about us, we can make our own," his mother said as she sat on the stool. "We wanted to talk to you."

Lily quickly glanced at them.

"Come sit with us, dear," his mother continued, her voice warm and encouraging.

She edged a cautious inch closer. "I'm sorry if I came across a bit rude yesterday, but . . ."

"You were caught off guard," his father chimed in.

"I didn't realize Adam told you we were getting married soon."

"You don't want to marry Adam?" his mother asked with a thoughtful expression.

Lily cleared her throat with guilt. Put aside the initial shock from last night, she liked Adam's parents. They were warm and obviously loved their son. "It's not that. It's . . ." she let out a deep breath. "It's complicated."

His mother smiled. "You love him," she said then turned to her husband and beamed. "See, I told you she was in love with him."

His father nodded, leaned over and kissed Adam's mother. "That's the best news we've heard," he said, his gaze now on Lily. "When Adam told us the two of you were getting married, we were concerned." His father ran a hand through his hair.

The motion made Lily smile. It reminded her of Adam. "I can't marry someone who doesn't love me. I'm sorry."

His mother stood up, walked over and hugged her. "Adam is difficult. We love him. But he's built walls."

"A fortress he lets no one penetrate," his father added.

The words described someone who had been deeply hurt and was refusing to allow himself to feel love again. A forced solitude. Lily nodded and batted her eyelashes in an attempt to hold back the tears that threatened to spill down her cheeks.

"Why?" she asked, wanting to know what brought him so much hurt.

His father smiled warmly at her. "It's for him to tell you. It's not our story."

"You're a strong person, Liliana," his mother said gently. "Give him some time."

Lily winced. "He won't even open up to me. I don't know."

His mother rubbed her shoulder. "We didn't mean to make you sad. We wanted to make sure you were all right. No matter what happens between you and our son, we look forward to getting to know you. And —" She smiled brightly. "—we can't wait to meet the little boy or girl. How many weeks are you?"

"Seven."

"You guys have time. Don't be sad." She glanced over at her husband. "How about we take Liliana out for breakfast?" Her attention returned to Lily. "Are you up to it?"

"Oh, as much as I'd love to, I have to meet Minka. Maybe another time?" To her surprise, she found herself a little disappointed. She liked Adam's parents even if the state of her relationship with their son was out of their control. "Maybe we can do dinner soon."

"That would be great. Why don't you confirm with Adam and let us know a day?"

Lily nodded.

His mother clapped her hands. "Well, we must be going. I'm glad we were able to talk Liliana." She leaned in and hugged Lily. "Don't give up on him. He's a good person," she whispered.

By the time Lily returned from meeting with Minka, it was dark. She stepped onto the paved driveway and the night swallowed her into darkness. Stars blossomed in the blackness. Not a light was lit in the house, but she spotted Adam's Maserati.

Opening the door, she walked inside and made her way to the bedroom. The room was empty. Her heart fell. She went to the kitchen and switched on the light.

Nope. Not there either.

She crossed the hall, turned left and entered the den. She caught his silhouette sitting in the dark with a drink in his hand. She flipped the switch and he looked up sharply, his face a black mask. The mere presence of him caused her stomach to contract, and a rush of heat flooded her entire body.

"Come to bed with me." She waited. Her heart pounding against her ribs as if trying to fulfill a thousand beats.

"I was adopted. My mother, Sophia couldn't conceive."

His eyes locked with hers. There were no words to sum up the intense wave of emotion that shot through her. He was opening up to her. Ready to spill his secrets. She rushed over to him and dropped to her knees between his legs.

"Adam," she said through quivering breaths. "It's all right. We can talk in the morning," she pleaded, unable to bear the anguish in his voice.

He chuckled, a dry, lifeless laugh. It shattered her heart and she wrapped her arms around him.

"My mother was a prostitute."

His voice was void of emotion, but Lily felt every bit of his pain. A dark, sickening grief filled her heart. She bit her lip to keep from crying.

"A drug addict," he continued and paused again. "I was born an addict."

A gasp escaped her throat, as the shock washed over her like a tidal wave. Images of Adam as a baby, born addicted, a result of the drugs used by his mother. She didn't know much about it, but she remembered Paige talking about it once. The drugs traveled the placenta, causing the baby to become dependent on the substance, developing an addiction just like the abuser.

Her stomach quivered and she fought back the nausea that threatened to take over her body. Lifting her head, she caressed his face. "Adam, oh, Adam." Her voice shook with pain.

"There's more," he added harshly.

Lily clung to him like a lifeline and shook her head. "No more. Not tonight."

"Liliana," he said her name in a tortured voice.

She shifted her body and leaned into him. Their faces inches apart. "Please," she mumbled breathlessly against his lips. "Let me comfort you."

He tilted his head down and kissed her hard with an urgency that was almost rough, burning her lips with his mouth. He tasted of bourbon and warmth. And something else. Love. Yes. Most definitely love. She loved him.

It was her turn to rip apart clothes. With hungry hands, she tore open his button-down shirt, unbuckled his belt with one hand using the other to run her fingers over his stomach.

His hands caught her arms and held her still. "Liliana, no sex."

She met his gaze. "This isn't sex."

He raised an eyebrow and exhaled a long breath. "No?"

"Foreplay." She smiled at him, eyes still wet with tears. "You said no sex, but foreplay is totally okay." She paused. "No penetration, no house rules broken." She licked her lips and unzipped him.

The sight of Lily on her knees between his legs stunned Adam. Oral sex, blow job, whatever the fuck one wanted to call it was nothing new to them. Lily had always given as much as she got and always left him winded and wanting more. But something shifted tonight. He opened up to her. At least he started to, but she stopped him from putting everything on the table.

Adam tilted her chin, and caught a glimpse of the pain that coursed through his veins in her eyes. Only hers were a little feral and mingled with lust, even through the tears still glistening on her cheeks. Brushing his thumbs against her face, he swiped them away, leaned into her and kissed her. She met him with fierce passion. Briefly their teeth clashed, then she sucked on his lower lip, teasing him with her tongue, telling him who was in charge.

"I won't be able to stop," he whispered in a raspy voice against her lips.

"It's not up to you." Her voice was a little labored, but filled with determination as she pressed her hand against the firm bulge in his pants.

A low groan escaped his throat. He was a goner, completely fucking gone and at her mercy. Even with the faintest touch, he'd be sure to explode.

"Don't try to stop me," she warned.

He needed to stop her; otherwise, he'd be fucking her until daylight. But the tension was still burning through his veins and he craved the physical contact. Eventually, he'd have to gather his balls together again and give her free access to everything that he was, but not tonight.

Emotionally exhausted, he wanted to take everything she was willing to give. "I'm not."

She licked her lips once more, her intentions clear. Adam felt his muscles tighten with anticipation and moved his hips upwards from the sofa to assist her in achieving her goal. With quick, yet smooth motions, she undid his pants, and pulled down his boxer briefs. His cock sprang up, completely enlarged and rigid.

Her hand coiled around his erection, and Adam sat frozen. Waiting for the brush of her lips. Needing to feel the softness of her mouth wrapped around him. She leaned forward, brushed one side of his shirt aside and slowly started to kiss his stomach. With each brush of her lips, he took one step closer toward madness.

He needed to touch. Shift control over to him. Impatiently, his fingers brushed across her shoulders, letting the straps of her top fall, giving him easy access to her breasts. With ease, both hands slipped underneath her blouse and cupped each breast. He molded them in his hands, tugged on her nipples, and she moaned with pleasure. All the while dragging her lips from his navel down the trail that led back to where her hand was kneading him.

The rosy tip of her tongue swept over the throbbing head of his swollen manhood and licked away his creamy nectar. He grew stiffer, larger. Adam inhaled sharply.

"Don't stop, Liliana," he mumbled, and dropped his head back against the cushion of the leather sofa in resignation.

She tasted him once more, her tongue slid along his length, causing his breath to grow louder. She repeated the motion, exploring every throbbing pulse before taking as much of him as she could in her mouth.

God damn it!

Adam grunted.

She continued the slow and steady motion, sliding up and down his engorged flesh. Every nerve in his body responded to her touch. With fingers knotted in her hair, his body melted with pleasure. His legs muscles grew warm, fresh air entered his lungs and blood flowed into all his limbs. He would've fallen, had he not been sitting down.

"Liliana." His breath came in short gasps.

Adam pulled himself up, his eyes fixated on her lips. With each blow, she preyed on him a little more, took him a little deeper, mauled him with her tongue, while her fingers touched and fondled his thighs and everything in between.

Knowing he was about to go over the edge, he gripped her arms to pull her to him. He'd bend her over and take her from behind and plunge deep inside of her. Instead he met resistance as Lily continued to increase the speed of each of her strokes.

"Fuck!" he swore. "Liliana. I can't stop."

Her eyes fluttered open and met his momentarily, and he knew what she wanted. Not that he could control himself any longer. *Jesus!* His fingers tightened through the strands of her hair as he crested. His body collapsed, releasing all the tension loaded inside of him, leaving behind nothing but a shiver.

"Come here," he said a few seconds later, pulling her to him. "Your turn."

She shook her head. "Tonight was all about you."

Her unselfishness caused his gut to tighten. But he'd never been a selfish lover and now that he was a bit more relaxed, he wanted to pleasure her just as much.

"Come on, let's go to bed," Lily said, repressing a yawn.

He studied her face. Her cheeks flushed to the color of scarlet, and she smiled at him.

"You're okay?" he asked, suddenly concerned. He'd forgotten she was constantly struggling with nausea.

"Of course," she answered, dismissing his concern with a wave. "We've done this before."

"But you've never . . ." He paused, not quite sure of the appropriate word.

Lily chuckled. "Swallowed."

He laughed. "Yes, swallowed."

"I wanted to," she said, holding his gaze. "Besides, in the past, you've never let me finish."

Adam pulled his boxers back on, picked up his pants and rose from the couch. With one arm over her shoulder, he drew her closer to him. Her arm leisurely circled his waist as she nestled closer to him. The connection felt good.

"Think you'll sleep tonight?" she asked as they walked down the dark hallway.

Her voice was filled with concern, causing a strange flutter of expansion in his heart. Leaning over, he placed a light kiss on the top of her head. "I think I will."

19

"You can't start the next chapter of your life if you keep re-reading the last one."
Anonymous

*A*dam entered the bedroom, feeling refreshed from his first night of sleep in two days. His gaze automatically went to Lily, and his heart constricted at the sight before him. She sat on the bed in a grey camisole, striped cotton sleep-shorts riding high up her thighs, legs crossed, and typing away on his laptop. Her face wore a determined look. She paused, scratched her temple and went back to typing.

He examined her body. It was different, more curvaceous, and softer. Even more so than when he realized she was pregnant. The changes were subtle, but he noticed. The vision of Lily in his bed with his child growing inside her rattled him a bit.

The jolt he felt inside went beyond the pregnancy. He trusted her. Not the no-sex-with-anyone-else trust, it ran far above their physical agreement. It was the kind of trust that resonates, forcing him to bare his soul and let her see the wretchedness behind his smile. Her delay in telling him about the pregnancy bothered him, but he understood her reasoning. She was scared, so was he. It didn't shake his trust.

His heart swelled in his chest. Everything about Lily and their situation shook him up—the good kind of tremors. The kind that made him want to snatch the computer away and pin her on the bed, under him. In an attempt to stop his thoughts from taking over, Adam walked across the room and picked up a faded black Henley.

"What are you doing?" he asked.

"Making sure my students are doing their work while I'm gone," she answered, still typing away.

He smiled. "Are they?"

She looked up from the screen, an expectant look on her face. "For the most part." She chuckled and closed the MacBook Pro. "I also had to confirm my doctor appointment."

"In New Jersey?" he asked, a reminder they were still a long way off from marriage. Not that he expected last night's event to sway her decision. Well, maybe he did. But more so, he'd wanted to confide in her.

She nodded, confirming his thoughts.

He pushed away the disappointment that stirred his insides, walked over to his side of the bed and picked up his cell phone. "When is it?"

"The Wednesday after I return home," she answered. Her voice revealed nothing.

Adam glanced at his calendar. Shit. He was scheduled to fly to Russia the day after the wedding for the Russian Grand Prix, one of the last three races of the season, and was planning on going back to Italy for a few days. In his mind, Lily would be by his side during this trip. He sat on the bed and ran a hand through his hair. "Come to Russia with me."

She let out a shaky laugh. "What?"

"After the wedding, I have a race in Russia." Adam caught the sudden stiffness of her body. His racing was not particularly ranked high on her list. He realized that at Vapor when she tried to break things off. What was it she said? He searched his memory for her exact words. Yes, she wanted tame. Racing wasn't tame, but he loved it. Speed helped control the rage inside him. For the first time since he went on his quest to get her to marry him, he found himself wondering how much he'd have to give. Not wanting to dwell on the reality of their situation, he took her hand in his. "Come with me and we can fly back together for your appointment."

"Adam, that's crazy," she said, glancing over at him in shock.

"Why?"

She laughed again. "Well, for one I have to go back to work."

He opened his mouth to tell her she no longer had to work but thought better of it. "Extend your vacation," he said instead.

"It's tempting, but I can't."

"It's only three days."

She shook her head. "I have to work, Adam. I don't have millions in the bank."

He stayed silent. No need to point out he'd earned enough in his thirty-one years that neither ever had to work again.

"Besides," she smiled. "I may need to use my days later as the pregnancy progresses."

"Liliana, I want to be a part of this. Don't deny me that."

She slipped her hand out of his, cupped his face, leaned forward and kissed him. Adam exhaled, releasing some of the tension building in his shoulders.

"Never." She held his gaze. "But I understand you have a race, so come after if you're not too tired."

"I can't change your mind?"

She shook her head. "Not on this one. But—" Her hands brushed over his head and settled on the back of his neck. "—I'm willing to try to change yours."

Knowing she was referring to his no-sex stance, Adam chuckled. "You're not going to give up on that, are you?"

"Nope. A girl has needs."

"What happened to Bob?" The battery powered boyfriend he'd gladly help operate.

She laughed. "He's not nearly as sexy as you are. And frankly, if I were to rank the satisfaction level, I'd say you're much better at hitting the spot."

Adam laughed, amused by her persistence. Not that he wasn't regretting his decision. Hell, last night he would have taken her, and just a few minutes ago he had to fight back another strong temptation. She lowered her head to his neck and nuzzled his skin, trailing open-mouthed kisses along the underside of his neck, sending hot shivering tremors down his groin. He sucked in a deep breath and gently pulled her away. Disappointment crossed her face. For safety reasons, his own, Adam stood up. She glanced at the aching bulge in his pants, and met his gaze. Amusement flickered in her eyes.

"All right. Get up, we're going out," he said hoarsely.

She laughed, a nice, warm laugh. "How long do you intend on keeping this up?"

"Until you say yes."

Her eyes narrowed. "To marrying you?"

He held her gaze.

"What if I never say yes?"

He shrugged and pretended her question didn't affect him. But it did. "Then we no longer have sex. Come on, get dressed."

"Where are we going?"

"To my restaurant."

"Why? I thought you closed."

He shook his head. "Officially this weekend. Come on, we're spending the day together."

Lily noticed the small group gathering in front of The Wharf's Side the minute Adam pulled the Maserati into the restaurant's entrance. She glanced at Adam and his jaws clenched but he continued to park the car. She looked back at the faces. They looked like tourists, stragglers, mostly women in tight pants and fitted shirts, exposing ample cleavage. Groupies. And they were waiting for Adam. Her man.

"Looks like some of your fans are waiting," she said, looking back at Adam. For the year they'd been together this was her first encounter of this side of his life. At times, she'd even forgotten he was famous.

Adam didn't answer. He turned off the ignition and walked over to open her door. Within seconds, they were mobbed by screaming female admirers.

"Adam, can you take a picture with me?" A woman with a British accent asked.

"Can you autograph my breasts? Mine are bigger than hers," another said.

Ouch. That hit below the belt. No need to pick on her B-cup breasts.

"Who is this with you, Adam?" Another asked.

"Is this your girlfriend?" The questions continued.

"Relax," Adam whispered in her ear. "It's all part of the career I've chosen, roll with it." He squeezed her hand. "I got this. I got you." With that he turned to the small mob around them. "This is my girlfriend, Liliana," he said to the crowd. His voice was calm and unhurried.

A low rumble swept through the group, upward roll of eyes. A few wrinkled their noses or pursed their lips in disappointment. All of this because Adam, the superstar Formula One racer, had publicly bestowed the title *girlfriend* on her.

The announcement was news to her as well. The words stunned Lily, causing her heart to thump like a pistol. Girlfriend. They had officially entered relationship territory. When did that happen?

She already knew the answer. The day he found out she was pregnant.

"I'll sign a few autographs and take a few pictures," Adam said to the group of women, "but after that I'd like some privacy."

Heads nodded with understanding. They smiled at him, completely under his spell. Lily grunted.

"Give me ten minutes," he said while pressing against her.

Adam released her hand and walked into the crowd. Lily stood back and took in the scene. A beautiful blonde threw her arms around him as her friend snapped a picture. Then two pretty women with a pair of magnificent racks crushed their forbidden fruits against him. Through it all, Lily had to admit Adam looked completely unaffected, and in his element. He draped his arms over their shoulders and smiled for the camera.

The madness continued for about five more minutes. But for Lily, it felt like eternity. Adam continued to laugh, smile, and pose for pictures. Arms crossed over her chest, she kicked a few leaves with the tip of her boots and tried to ignore the burning desire to walk over and kiss her boyfriend until he was breathless.

Boyfriend. Ha. She stifled a chuckle.

There was still so much to learn about him.

Who was his biological father? Was he still alive?

Did he even know the man who impregnated his mother? Was it one of her clients?

And more importantly, did he carry any side effects from the condition of his birth that might have been passed on to their child?

On the external he appeared to be in good health but Lily knew not all wounds were obvious. Not that it mattered, her love for him ran deep and unconditional. Her phone vibrated. Knowing she hadn't connected with Minka yet, Lily smiled and fumbled through her purse until her hand found the phone. Her eyes stared at the number, she glanced over the text and her stomach turned icy.

Lily, I miss you. I love you.

Nate. She had deleted all of his information from her contacts, but after three years together, she'd recognized that number anywhere. Even after a year and well over him, the sudden text caught her by surprise. Still holding the phone, she stood for a couple seconds, contemplating how to tell her ex-fiancé to go screw himself.

Common sense told her to ignore the text and hope he got the message but this was the same Nate who decided his goods were too good to only share with her and decided to spread the wealth. The same Nate she kicked out of her apartment. The same Nate her brothers were still threatening to kill.

She glanced at Adam and their eyes met. He smiled at her. Not the dreamer speed chaser smile, but the one that gave her a piece of him. Unanswered questions or not, she was his girlfriend. They had crossed the *just fucking* phase. She was pregnant with his child, desperately in love with him, and her past had just come knocking.

Only Lily knew it was best to leave some doors closed. She was about to text Nate back, probably with a polite *go bark up another tree you fucking cheater* when Adam signed one last autograph, said something to the herd of women, to which they all sighed. And then he headed over to her. Lily would bet all of her savings that all of them had wet their panties. No need to check hers, she wasn't drooling, at least not openly.

She placed the phone back in her purse with a mental note to respond with a simple *Please don't contact me again.*

"Liliana!"

Adam's scream caught her attention but Lily became aware of everything too late. A cacophony of sounds hit her ears like a tidal wave as a black car swirled to her left, inches away from where she stood by Adam's Maserati. With barely any time to react, she shuffled back, one foot caught on a small dip in the pavement. She staggered in her heels and fell forward.

From a distance, she heard wild notes of hysteria from the group of women standing not too far away. Normal reflex dragged her hands up in front of her face. Her arms grazed along the ground and skin tore from them, pain screamed through her palms in a horrible sting, her head bumped her arm shortly afterwards, then her body connected to the concrete, hard.

For a split second, Lily went numb, then winced at the stabbing flash of pain that needled from her knees, throughout her body. Everything hurt. She lay on the ground, and tried to catch the breath that was knocked out of her when she fell.

"Fuck!" She was on her hands and knees when she heard Adam swear from somewhere nearby. Then his strong arms circled her waist protectively and scooped her against him. Adam. He was here. He'd make everything okay. She clung to his broad shoulders, and lifted her eyes. His features were fuzzy but she felt safe.

"Liliana," he said her name delicately.

Even in pain, his voice rippled in that seductive accent in her ear. He pulled her against his chest and Lily felt his heart accelerating.

"Please tell me you're okay," he whispered in her ear, stroking her hair.

Her head hurt like hell and maybe spinning. Yes, definitely spinning, but other than that, she felt fine. She nodded. "Help me up."

"No." His voice was stern. "I'll call Forrest."

A shadow fell over them. Lily squinted until Guillermo's face came into focus.

"Lily," Guillermo called out, slumping over by her side.

She smiled and hoped it was a reassuring one. "I'm okay, just a little sore. Help me up please."

Guillermo looked at Adam for confirmation. After a slight nod from Adam, the two men slowly helped her to her feet. Feeling dizzy and sick, she leaned a little on Adam to gain her equilibrium. Once she felt somewhat stable, Lily straightened herself, wiped her hands down the thighs of her jeans, and tried to make herself unseen as she noticed the shocked and concerned faces of the women who had just violated Adam.

"Go inside with Guillermo," Adam said, gave a chin jerk toward the restaurant, and then stared straight ahead.

Lily followed his gaze and surveyed who she assumed was the person responsible for her fall. The man was of olive complexion with dark curly hair under a fedora. Not particularly tall, but he walked with purpose as he approached them. Something about him made her stomach churn.

He looked at her, Guillermo then at Adam. A mad glint lingered in his eyes.

"Adam." She gripped his arm, crippling with fear.

He continued to stare at her. His eyes were deep and dark. Adam said something to Guillermo in the language she recognized as Portuguese and nudged her into Guillermo's arms. He took one step forward and looked down at the man. Everything about his vibe told Lily he was ready for a fight. In whatever form it came.

"No fucking interview," he said, his voice dangerously low, reserved to chill the bone marrow.

Lily shivered.

"Get off my property or I'll call the police."

"You can't continue hiding," the man said in a shifty voice.

There was a hint of an accent Lily couldn't place.

"If she's hurt," he glanced over his shoulder at her, then back to the man. "You're a dead man."

The stranger sneered. "This isn't Italy. Your parents have no power here."

"Get off my fucking property." Adam waved a dismissive hand.

"I know your secret," the stranger said in a menacing tone. "You can't bury the past."

"Go fuck yourself."

Lily's head flinched back with confusion. What the hell was going on? Feeling overheated and dizzy, she held on to Guillermo.

"Adam," Guillermo shouted, his voice alert with concern.

Guillermo continued to speak in Portuguese. Whatever he said caught Adam's attention and he rushed to her side, face pale. He scanned the rest of her body then met her gaze. Feeling a little warm, which Lily attributed to the effect he had on her, she smiled.

"I was right, you do speak Portuguese," she said, turning to Adam and flinched at the sharp pain in her stomach. Something was wrong. "Adam."

Everything stopped and nothing made sense. She followed his gaze to the brown stain on her inner thigh. Blood. But she couldn't tell where it was coming from. Something sharp jabbed into her side and Lily tried to adjust herself but the pain . . . oh, the pain.

"Oh," Lily said. Paralyzed with shock, the world circled around as her body fell so fast that all she could see was a blur.

20

"Sometimes the smallest things take up the most room in your heart."
　　　　　　　　Winnie the Pooh

Lily's consciousness came back with a start. Loud sounds rushed into her ears. She scanned her surroundings through blurry eyes and immediately spotted the ambulance, and the black Dodge Charger police car responsible for the deafening sound. Uniformed men and one woman stood talking, exchanging notes. She steadied her breath and tried to calm the panic stirring inside.

Not too far away, Adam's brooding figure caught her attention.

Tension oozed off his broad shoulders. He stood there…frozen. And then the man responsible for her fall spoke. The distance between her and them was too great for Lily to hear their words.

Things got a little out of control from there. Adam hurled himself toward the man and gave him a sharp round punch to the chin, knocking the other man to the ground with a loud cracking noise. Adam took another step forward, crowding over the sagged figure, ready to inflict more punishment suited for the situation.

"Shit!" Lily heard someone shout as the policemen, the male EMT and Guillermo rushed toward the two men. The female EMT was quick by her side.

Lily gasped. "Adam," she called. Still weak and disoriented, she tried to come to her feet only to realize she was belted to the stretcher. One of her arms heavily bandaged to protect the cut she acquired from the fall. She exhaled and rested her elbows on the gurney to support her weight.

Guillermo placed a hand on Adam's shoulder and tried to pull him away. With a hard shrug, he pushed his friend's hand off. Lily watched the rapid rise and fall of Adam's chest, his body vibrating with anger and ready to kill.

"You can't beat him up," Guillermo said. "Then he'll win and the police will be on your ass."

"Get off my ass!" he said without looking at his friend. He grabbed the man's collar and dragged him to his feet, their faces inches apart. "You hurt her, you fucking asshole. I should beat the shit out of you." His voice came out cracked and loud.

The man snorted, unfazed by the threat. "Go ahead," he challenged, and spat a mouthful of blood on the pavement.

"Adam," she called out again, pleading for him to come to her, her voice trembling.

His body tensed. She held her breath. After a second or two, his head turned in her direction. Lily's eyes fixated on his face, and her heart broke into a thousand pieces at the distress of emotion that greeted her.

After what seemed to be an eternity, he sucked in a breath, exhaled, shoved the man off, and let his hands fall to his side as the energy escaped him. He took two small steps back and hurried to her side.

"Hey." A faint smile touched his lips. He entwined his fingers with hers, and gave her hand a little squeeze for reassurance.

"The baby," she said, giving life to the tangible fear creeping inside of her.

Someone cleared their throat. Lily looked up at the two EMTs approaching them. A pretty brunette and a muscular man with short cropped black hair came to stand by her side. Both looked to be in their early thirties. They nodded at Adam with an air of familiarity.

"We have a call into the hospital," the man spoke in a calm voice. "I'm Gus and this is Mary." He introduced himself and his partner. "We are going to take some notes and check your vital signs. Feeling okay?" he asked in a gentle tone.

"The baby," she repeated. "Is the baby okay?"

The man known as Gus smiled warmly at her. "We are going to take you to the hospital. They will do a fetal ultrasound." He glanced at Adam. "We need to take a look at your hand."

Adam absently rubbed a hand over his knuckles. "I'm fine."

Gus nodded. "We still need to document everything." He glanced at the two police officers now talking to the intruder. "The police are here for a report and in case you want to press charges."

"We have to take your blood pressure." The pretty brunette smiled down at her then focused on Adam. "You have to let go of her hand for a sec, Adam."

He obliged and stepped back. Mary placed the cuff of the monitor around Lily's arm as two uniformed men approached them and shook Adam's hand.

"Is Liliana going to be okay?" Adam asked. His voice was rough and strained.

Gus nodded.

Adam glanced back at her. "And the baby?"

"I don't have that answer," Gus answered in a controlled voice.

"You can press charges if you want." One of the police officers advised.

Adam nodded and dragged his hand over his face. He glanced at the man standing next to the police car. "No charges. Let's just file the incident."

"You're sure?" One of the cops asked.

Adam nodded again.

"150 over 90," Mary said over her shoulder as Gus jotted down the number.

Gus lowered himself to Lily's side. "That's above normal." His eyes limped with sympathy. He smiled at her and squeezed her shoulder. "All right, we're going to take you to the hospital now. Adam, meet us there."

"I'm not leaving her side. I'm riding with you," Adam responded.

Neither Gus nor Mary argued.

Lily could only describe the ride to the hospital as ordered chaos. Even with the seatbelt around her, she felt every sharp turn. At one point, Gus took a corner too fast, sending equipment flying while Mary sat by her side, looking unaffected and writing down notes. Adam continued to hold her hand. With the other hand, he stroked her bangs away from her face.

"It's going to be all right Liliana, no matter what."

She nodded. The words were comforting but couldn't stop the tears from coming. His thumb stroked her cheek and brushed the tears away.

By the time they pulled up, the hospital seemed to know what to expect. Staff were mobilized and standing by. Adam stayed behind to talk to Gus and Mary. A nurse around Lily's age approached her with a friendly smile. "Hi, I'm Gwen," she said, introducing herself. "We are going to take you into a room and I'll be back to get some information." She glanced at the papers in her hand. "Do we need to contact the father of your baby?"

"I'm the father," Adam's approaching voice announced.

Lily noticed a brief look of surprise on the woman's face, but it was quickly masked. She had the feeling the two knew each other on a more intimate level at some point.

Great. Just what she needed. A close encounter with one of Adam's pretty ex-lovers, while she looked like she'd been dragged by a caveman.

"You're going in for an ultrasound in a little bit. Hang in there," Gwen said with a warm smile before Lily was rolled away to a private area in the emergency room, and transferred to a hospital bed.

"How many weeks are you?" Gwen asked. She drew the curtain hanging from a track on the ceiling closed for privacy.

"Seven," she answered.

Adam slumped into a chair.

"Your blood pressure is high. We are going to weigh you in, check it again and test your urine for protein."

Lily let out a nervous chuckle. "I'm fine. I fell. I'm fine."

But Gwen was already shaking her head. "These are important for detecting preeclampsia, which could be very dangerous to you and the baby." She glanced at Adam then back at Lily. "I'll get some reading material for you and give you a few minutes to change into the hospital gown. We need the open side facing front." She handed Adam the gown and slipped out of the room.

Adam was quick by her side. He tore open the plastic and pulled out the gown. His hands covered hers as she fumbled to undo her jeans.

"Let me do this," he advised. His voice was quiet and controlled.

With one swooping motion, he removed her shirt, leaving her in her bra. He paused. Through hooded lids, he took a cursory glance at her rising chest.

"God, Liliana," he groaned.

He swore softly. Then his fingers unsnapped her jeans and helped her slip out of them. His gaze rested on the brown spot on the jeans for a brief second then folded them neatly and put them out of view.

"I'm still bleeding," she acknowledged. "I need something to put on."

He nodded, understanding her request. "I'll tell Gwen."

"We're coming in for some tests," the nurse announced and entered in the tight space.

A horde of people followed and rushed into the room. An IV was inserted in her arm. Nurses and assistants buzzed around her, asking questions, poking her arm for blood, checking temperature, and blood pressure.

Once they were alone, Adam leaned forward and buried his face in his hands. Lily took a deep breath. Realizing Adam was probably experiencing the same level of fear as she was, she exhaled, inhaled again. Her head swam with thoughts.

What if the baby failed to survive the fall?

What would become of her and Adam?

She'd done the unimaginable and went down that slippery road from lust to love.

Even as Lily tried not to let the reason for their growing closeness occupy her mind, the reality of the situation was, without a baby, Adam would have never opened himself to her or to the possibility of them.

Their dating was a result of her pregnancy.

Big mistake.

"You look like shit," she said, trying to defuse the tension in the room.

He looked at her and chuckled. "So do you."

She laughed and turned her head to the television hung in the corner of the room. "Thanks."

"But still beautiful, Liliana. You'll always be that to me." His voice warred with emotion.

Her heart stumbled before finding its rhythm once again. Tears threatened to spill, but she swallowed them back. This man, so dark and mysterious, had managed to capture her soul, and made her forget her heart was ever broken or that he could easily crush it again.

After announcing their presence, two men drew the curtain. "Time for the ultrasound," one said. He glanced at Adam. "You can come or wait…"

Adam rose to his feet. "I'm coming."

The distance to the exam room seemed endless. Adam walked by her side. Not a word was spoken. Fear weighed heavily in the air between them. Besides the squeaking sound of the wheeling bed and footsteps echoing on the checkered linoleum floor, it was so quiet Lily could hear her heart banging against her chest.

A door propped open and her bed was pushed inside next to the electronic machine with odd wires leading from it. She looked around. Cold. Sterile. Basic.

The technician greeted them and explained the process of the ultrasound. Lily nodded with understanding. She'd already gone through that about a week ago. Adam came to stand by her shoulder, reached for her hand and brought it to his lips. Then the cold object was inserted between her thighs.

She winced, shut her eyes and let the tears flow.

The room screamed in silence, creating an overwhelming sense of emptiness.

Then Lily heard the steady sound waves beeping from the monitor.

Her eyes snapped opened and peeked at the sound waves on the screen used to create an image of their unborn baby. She looked at Adam. A frown creased his brow. Lily smiled. She saw the confusion in his eyes as he glanced over her to look at the technician.

"What's that sound?" he asked.

"That's the heartbeat. Strong little guy," the technician said and smiled at them.

Tears welled behind Lily's eyes once more. A feeling of relief soothed her body. She looked at Adam again. He drew a deep breath through his nose, releasing all the tension inside of him. He leaned in and kissed her forehead, then took hungry possession of her mouth, his tongue dipping in, kissing her with a passion, which took her breath away.

She was drowning in the passion until Adam pulled away. Dazed, she looked at him. He now had a smirk on his face.

The technician cleared her throat. "Sorry, I have to take a few more pictures." She looked at Lily. "I need you to be calm."

Oh, right. And that meant no kissing Adam.

About one hour later, the curtain drew open again, the doctor along with Gwen entered. Adam stood up and the two men shook hands.

"Good to see you again," the doctor said to Adam. "Forrest called. I told him everything is okay." He turned to Lily. "Liliana, my name is Peter."

She shook the man's hand and narrowed her eyes. A feeling of dread crept up from the pit of her stomach. "What's wrong?"

He smiled. "Nothing," he answered. "But we are going to keep you overnight for observation."

"Why?" The question came from Adam.

"You suffered severe trauma," Peter said, speaking directly to Lily. "Typically after the adrenaline and shock wear off, the victim experiences some pain."

"I'm fine."

"We need to monitor your neck and head, and give you something if necessary. Also, we need to stabilize your blood pressure."

"No drugs."

The finality in Adam's voice cut through Lily. She knew his fear was related to his birth condition.

Peter looked at Adam then at Lily. "It won't be anything strong."

Adam's face was set in a hard, determined expression. "No," he said, his voice rougher.

After a brief moment, the doctor nodded. "There are different types of shock. Some are dangerous and may cause damage to Liliana or the baby." He stopped and gave them a moment to process the information. "I'll leave the two of you to discuss our options if required."

"What about the bleeding?" Lily asked with concern.

"The blood is brown, left over from your last cycle. That is common. It should stop in a day." His gaze went to Adam then back at Lily. "However, you have to refrain from intercourse for a few days."

That was the easy part. She already wasn't getting any. She glanced over at Adam and searched for any kind of humor in the situation. His face was stoic.

"We are going to admit you," Gwen said. "In the meantime, elevate your extremities to increase blood flow to the heart."

Once they were alone, Adam pulled the chair closer to the bed and sat down. The color once again drained from his face. He slouched forward and took one of her hands in his.

"No drugs, Liliana."

With her free hand, she caressed his face. "Adam, what happened to you was different." Grief swept through her system, enveloping her body. A dark, sickening pain filled her heart over Adam's agony. "I'm sure the hospital will follow every protocol."

He heaved a sigh. "I'm at seventy-percent chance of becoming an addict. I've passed that to our child. I don't want to increase a statistic like that."

"Have you ever done drugs?"

"I was born an addict, Liliana." He dragged a hand through his hair. "I won't even take a Tylenol unless I'm dying."

"You turned out okay."

He shrugged. "So far. But I live in fear over that knowledge every day."

"Our baby will be okay. We will deal with whatever comes our way."

"Together. No matter what, Liliana."

She understood the implication in his words. The M word–marriage. What he'd wanted the moment he learned of her pregnancy. He spoke no word of love. They liked each other and, as he pointed out, the sex was great between them. Still, settling for anything less would leave a void inside her for the rest of her life.

"No matter how we end up, Adam, we will always deal with our baby together." She propped herself on the bed to a sitting position, and patted down the empty space by her side. Despite the ache inside her heart, every piece of her wanted him closer. "Come here."

He gave her a weak smile. "There's no room. You need to be comfortable."

"I need to feel you next to me. I need for our bodies to touch."

He reluctantly lifted from the chair and lowered his weight on the bed. Lily shifted to allow more room for him.

"Liliana."

"Sshh," she silenced him. "Just hold me."

"I want to do more." His hands skimmed over her breasts.

Heat ripped through her. "Me too. But apparently we can't have sex."

"We weren't having sex anyway."

"But I was hoping things would change for the better."

He laughed, slid his hand through the front of the gown and cupped one of her breasts.

"That feels good." Lily moaned, her whole body trembling with longing. "I want more."

Adam lowered his head and bit her nipple. Lily gasped over the tingling sensation. He released her and closed the gown.

"You don't play fair," she complained, her body still quivering with desire.

"Neither do you."

"I did nothing."

"No?" He took her hand and placed it over his erection. Lily wrapped her hand over the bulge in his pants and stroked him. Adam cursed softly. "You do a lot to me, Liliana. Even when you do nothing."

21

I'll tell you my sins and you can sharpen your knife."
Hozier – Take Me to Church

The metallic shower head hung above Adam. He pulled the lever to the right and a stream of cold water rained onto his skin like an electric shock. The hair on the back of his neck prickled. Goosebumps slithered up his arms and legs. He clenched his jaws and reached for the shampoo, washed his hair, and rinsed off the suds.

He grabbed the soap, scrubbed his neck, and closed his eyes. Typically, he preferred a steamy hot shower but damn it, he'd been fighting a raging hard-on since Lily was released from the hospital. Actually, since he'd fondled her in the emergency room.

Sick. Fucking sick.

Who fondles a woman while she lays on a gurney waiting to be admitted?

Me.

He dragged the soap over his body. The action soothed his skin but failed to alleviate his desire or aching bulge. Instead it caressed him like Lily's kisses, running along his torso.

Something else had emerged inside him. An ache that clawed at his limbs, not the sexual one, something deeper. Although he'd been scared out of his mind over the possibility of her miscarrying, Lily's well-being through the whole ordeal had been his main priority.

She affected him.

His mind wandered to the woman in his bed, and his breath caught. He was feeling shit he never wanted to experience. Feelings. Emotions. Those things had made his birth mother weak, caused her to do some dumb crazy shit. Because of feelings, she became dependent on a pimp and sold her body for money. Those who didn't pay in cash had provided her drugs to satisfy her favorite pastime.

Disgust and anger washed over him.

He should probably run in the opposite direction as fast as he could and drop his marriage quest. Time and time again, Lily had made it clear she would not settle for anything less than the whole enchilada. She wanted love.

Yeah, he should definitely run. He didn't do love, at least not the kind she asked for. He loved his parents, his extended family and friends, but the love Lily wanted meant getting the heart involve and becoming exposed, vulnerable.

Run wasn't the word. He should be sprinting out of her life.

But something told him it was too late. She had already penetrated his layers.

His gut tightened. Needing to numb everything inside, Adam turned the knob to the max, and hissed. The bitter cold water spread over his back and his muscles flexed in response. One hand planted firmly on the wet tile facing him, while the other tightened around his throbbing erection, and glided over firm flesh. His head fell forward as he continued the slow and steady motion, sliding up and down. Images of Lily stimulated the searing heat inside. His speed increased.

Shit. His hand loosened around his shaft.

"What the fuck!" He shook his head with disgust, not because he was ashamed of jerking off. Hell that had been his go-to move since he was fourteen. The first night he woke up with a hard-on over some girl in school. But he enjoyed it most when Lily watched him while she touched herself.

Yeah...that's what he needed. A little jerking off while she gently stroked the delicate softness between her thighs. But she couldn't do shit. Completely out of commission for at least two more days. The bleeding had stopped a day after they returned home, but Peter had advised they continued to sustain from intercourse.

Intercourse. The word sounded so technical.

He and Lily fucked. Hard. Anywhere they could. And since her fall he wanted to throw that bullshit *no sex* rule out the window, slide inside that moist, needy place he called home and pummel himself into her fiery furnace.

He was an asshole.

On top of the accident, the nausea had returned full force. Even now while she lay in bed, pale as a ghost, all he could think about was having her legs up in the air, preferably resting over his shoulders, or maybe have her on her knees. Take her from behind this time with her sweet round ass in the air.

Yup, that made him an asshole. A thirty-one year old horny, fucking asshole.

He needed to control his desire to fuck her brains out every second of the day and think. Slowly, his world was shifting off its axis and she was the culprit. The horror of her fall, fear for her safety, and the thought of what they might have lost. All of that had consumed him, making him less guarded. Another wall was lowered. But not all. There were still things he needed to tell her, expose what existed inside and show her all that he was. He needed to walk down that street completely naked and vulnerable. He let out a ragged breath. At least his hard-on was under control. Well, sort of.

Turning off the water, he quickly dried off and wrapped a towel around his waist before stepping into the bedroom. His gaze automatically went to the bed where she was half propped under the covers with her cell phone in her hand and a slight frown on her forehead.

He fought the longing to go over and kiss her, pull her in his arms as they usually greeted each other. Instead he walked over to the nearby chair and picked up his favorite pair of grey sweats. His lounging sweats; no underwear needed for those.

He felt her honey-colored eyes watching him. "How are you feeling?" he asked while tying the knot of his sweats. She continued to watch him.

"We need to talk."

The seriousness in her voice caught his attention. He met her gaze and a heavy numbness invaded his chest. "Whatever you read on the internet is not true."

"I didn't Google you. I'd much rather you tell me." Silence fell between them as her gaze fixed on his face. "Everything, Adam. I want to know who this man was and what he wants."

He picked up the towel from the armchair. "He's a reporter."

Recognition flickered in her eyes. "The one who badgered Claire with questions about you?"

He nodded.

"Your parents had him demoted."

"I can't control how my parents react to things."

She smiled. "They love you very much."

"Yes they do." He'd never deny that he got lucky in the adoptive parents pool.

She continued to watch him. Adam waited for the questions to come. It was inevitable and he was ready. Well, as ready as he could ever be. But she picked up the cell phone again.

"I did some research on your birth condition."

"Addicted babies," he said in a low, rough voice. "Say it, Liliana, then everything about who I am becomes real."

She flinched at his words, but said nothing. His lungs burned.

"You can still abort if you want." Adam watched Lily. She struggled to shift her gaze but his eyes were locked on hers, willing the connection to hold. Even in his ears the words sounded callous. But shit, that was an option they should have talked about from the moment he found out she was pregnant with his child. "I never wanted to be a father, so I'd understand."

Her face glazed for a split-second and then she frowned, her lips pursed together and her eyes were unblinking. At that moment, if her eyes were a weapon, the piercing look in them could have caused serious destruction. She became a lioness. He had come into her territory and she was about to attack.

Although Adam's voice grazed with pain, the words still delivered a massive blow to Lily's chest. She surveyed his stance. The hard ridges of his chest flexed with controlled anguish. The sweatpants hung low to his hips. The material clung to him like a lover, outlining that part of him that made him male. "You think that's what I want?"

He shrugged with indifference. "It's something we should have talked about."

His eyes stared at her with such intensity that it made her uncomfortable, and she squirmed and writhed under his gaze.

"It's an option."

Funny, the possibility of terminating the pregnancy; however, unanticipated, never crossed her mind. Sure her life had taken a surprising twist, but she'd adjust. Yet, here Adam stood, admitting he never wanted to be a father and giving her a choice to cut their ties. "I don't want a fucking abortion." Her chin spasmed and Lily bit the inside of her mouth to control the anger knifing her insides. "I want this child. With or without you. And all of whatever flaws you think he may have."

"Liliana." He took a step forward in her direction.

"Don't." Her voice trembled and she buried her face in her hand. "Don't say my name in that voice. Don't touch me." She paused, exhaled, and lifted her face to meet his eyes. "Don't do anything."

Lily shifted her gaze to the window so Adam couldn't see the amount of pain his words inflicted. "I need a few minutes alone."

He hesitated then walked out of the room. It wasn't until the door closed that Lily let the hot torrents of grief course down her face. Frustrated, she punched the pillow with her fist and buried her face in it as the deep emotions stirred with no other outlet but through her long-lasting sobs.

Paige had sent her several links on drug addiction in infants. The statistics were grim. More than fifteen-hundred babies were born addicted to heroin, crack cocaine, and other drugs every year, approximately four babies a day born dependent on something through no fault of their own. The findings shocked and horrified her.

Adam fell in that statistic.

The images she saw on the internet and the reality of what Adam had to endure as a baby in the womb, innocently absorbing the nutrients laced with coke or whatever else his mother injected into her system had not been easy to absorb. Lily's stomach bubbled like the sea boiling in a storm, wanting to heave the visions of the man she loved as a baby screaming, shaking with withdrawal pain.

Several times she'd rushed out of the room to the nearest bathroom and relieved the disgust in her chest. Although physically sickened, she kept on and read all the information. She needed to familiarize herself with the side effects Adam experienced as a child. Easily irritated was one of them, and appeared to still be a work in progress. She loved him, a man she was still learning about. She loved him, with all his flaws and traits. She loved Adam Aquilani.

Through no choice of his own, he had suffered an addiction that came straight from what was meant to be the most perfect environment —his mother's womb. Instead, Adam, and these other faultless babies born into the trauma of addiction were given a tragic start in life. And because addiction had an inherited component, passing down from parent to child by way of genes, their baby without a choice, through no fault of theirs, had become a fallen heir.

She understood Adam. He was haunted by fear, by his past.

Still, to hear him admit he didn't want to be a father was a terrible blow. She felt empty and joyless, like a sheet of white paper.

"You're crying."

With her face buried on the pillow, she sniffled. "Go away."

His weight dropped onto the bed next to her. "I don't like to be the reason for your tears."

"I'm crying because I'm an emotional wreck. My hormones are out of whack. Not because your words hurt me." She sniffled again. "Or because you admitted to what I always knew in my heart."

"What's that?" His hand stroked her back. The touch made her inhale sharply.

She turned her face and peered at him through heavy lids, tears still tickling down her cheeks. "I trapped you. We are here because of a baby you don't even want."

His eyes grew darker. His expression had all sorts of emotions. "I want the baby, Liliana."

"Don't say things you don't mean," she pleaded, her voice trembling.

"Had it been up to me, no, I would not have chosen to father a child. But I did." He removed his hand from her. "You and I have made a permanent mark and when I thought you could have miscarried, I was scared shitless."

He expelled his breath in a slow, steady hiss. "Guillermo and I are related."

She watched him. He was opening to her again. The look on his face told her it wasn't an easy thing for him to do, but the fact that he was doing it anyway pulled at her heartstrings.

"He's my mother's cousin. Claudio is his son. I found them when I lived in Brazil."

Lily brought herself to a sitting position and brushed the tear stains from her face. "You're Brazilian?"

He smiled and shook his head. "I guess in a way, yes. My mother was Brazilian and my father was American. But I was born in Queens, New York with two junkies for parents." Disgust twisted his mouth into a sneer. "I learned Portuguese when I lived in Brazil. My parents, adoptive parents," he clarified, "insisted I learned about my Brazilian roots."

"You said was." She swallowed. "Both of your parents are…dead?"

He nodded. "I lived in hell for eight years of my life. Due to the drugs in me, I was a fussy child, slow at developing and had difficulty processing things." Pain grated his voice. He raked a hand through his hair. "I got hit a lot."

Lily leaned into him, and gently caressed the scar on his left eyebrow. All the things she had in her life, peace, stability, loving parents and siblings. For eight years of his life, those things didn't exist for Adam.

"That's really from playing *fútbol* or soccer as it's called here. But my nose was broken from a blow once."

Lily's spirit quivered. "God, Adam…my heart hurts for you."

"After my parents' death, I became a part of the system. I moved from foster home to foster home. Some were nice, some not so much. And some," he shrugged. "Just weren't equipped to deal with someone like me."

A solemn tear fell down her cheek. "I'm sorry you had to go through all of that."

"I was a handful. Very hyperactive." He chuckled. "I still struggle with that now." He admitted. "Hence all the crazy things I do."

She smiled. "I thought it was because you wanted to die."

He shook his head, scrubbed his face again then met her gaze. "Maybe I do deserve to die. But that's not why. The racing and everything else help control everything else inside me. Actually, so do you, Liliana." His eyes darkened and grew more intense. "You bring me peace."

Butterflies went crazy low in her belly, and her heartbeat raged out of control. She remembered the first time he uttered those words to her. Lily had dismissed them as a result of mind-blowing sex talk. Now she understood how heavy that admission was for him.

So many unspoken questions, but *no más*. No more. They had time. Possibly a lifetime. She pressed her body against his bare chest, wrapped a hand around the nape of his neck and drew him into a hot, tongue-thrusting kiss.

"We can't have sex, Liliana," he said, disconnecting their lips.

Lily heard the torment in his voice. Just for confirmation, her fingertips traced the bulging muscles in his back. "What if we could?"

He groaned. "Then I'd be buried inside you already." His mouth took a hungry possession of hers. "And you're not doing me any favors today."

She smiled and tightened her arms around his neck. "I'm very selfish, Adam. I love having you in my mouth."

"You can't say things like that." He cupped her swollen breasts through her tank and molded them in his palm.

Lily moaned. "More," she begged, her lips trailing open-mouth kisses along his neck. "I want more."

Adam wrapped his fingers around her wrist, stopping her movement and gently pulled her away. He stood up, looked at her once more then walked over to stand by the window. "There's more, Liliana. I want to tell you everything."

A fluttery, empty feeling sat in her stomach. Lily pressed her lips together and waited.

"My mother died of an overdose," he said over his shoulder. "She was shooting up with my father. He was her pimp."

A dark, sickening grief filled her heart. "Adam." She wanted to touch and comfort him but he was sending her that stay away vibe.

He turned to face her, across the room, their eyes locked. "That night I shot him. I killed him." He let out a tortured breath. "At the age of eight I shot and killed my father."

An involuntary gasp escaped her lips. Lily felt her heart trampled beneath her feet. Not out of shame or disgust, but love and pain.

"There." He exhaled, dark eyes continued to strip her soul. "I've laid down my armor, Liliana. If you want, come slay me."

22

"When love is not madness, it is not love."
Pedro Calderón de la Barca

For several seconds Lily sat silently, hunched over with a sense of loss so powerful that her muscles wouldn't respond to commands. First her limbs went numb with absolute shock over Adam's revelation, and then replaced by waves of pain. Her stomach churned over as grief swept through her system, enveloping her whole body, leaving her with nothing but physical pain.

The only time she'd ever shot at someone was during a game of paintball. Zander, her Navy SEAL brother, insisted that she learn how to fire a weapon for protection, took her to a shooting range. She'd felt the recoil of overwhelming force in her hands, the destruction that came from the other end of the gun. The evidence of its power, the sound, and the holes, fluff blasted and torn from dummy targets had left her shaken. She never applied for a permit, didn't want one in her home.

Yet, here Adam stood before her, confessing to have pulled a trigger and to have taken a life, all at the tender age of eight. His innocence lost so early in his lifetime. She drew a deep, shaky breath. As more tears came, more thoughts of Adam going through the motion of life, like nightmares whirled through her head.

Her phone vibrated next to her on the bed. She swiped her face with the back of her hand, broke her connection with Adam and eyed the screen.

Lily, it's me, Nate. Where R U?

This was Nate's second text in two days. She failed to respond to the first one, not for any specific reason, only she'd forgotten about it, about Nate. And right now was not the time. Not when the man she loved had opened up to her and laid himself bare.

Lily turned her attention back to Adam. He leaned on the wall, motionless by the window. His gaze was still on her, holding her prisoner. She looked him dead in the eyes. He was no longer unflappable. Fear, worry—emotions he kept bottled inside for so long—greeted her. He'd chosen to break free from them because of her, their unborn child, and all the possibilities. His willingness to be vulnerable, to trust her with everything that made him the person he'd become, won her heart over a million times.

She was head over heels in love with Adam and all of his little things.

Permanently so.

Nothing could change that.

Her phone vibrated again. She made a mental promise to strangle Nate for choosing the most inappropriate time to be persistent. Picking up the phone, to type Go to hell in all caps, she noticed Rafa's name on the screen. Lily almost laughed at the absurdity of the situation. She needed to give Adam all of her attention, all of her, but her world had come crashing. She read the text from her brother Rafa.

¿Cómo estás? See you in two days.

How could she forget?

Her fingers expeditiously moved across the small keyboard and typed.

Can't wait. Luv U.

Her response was pure sarcasm, except for the love part. As much of a pain in the ass and all in her business her brothers were, she loved them. But Rafa was on to her. Lily pressed *SEND* and dropped the phone back on the bed.

She willed herself off the bed and closed the space between Adam and herself. His eyes dropped to her. "I almost forgot my family will be here in two days."

"What do you want to do?" he asked in a dangerously low voice.

Puzzled, she frowned. "What do you mean?"

"About us." He signaled between their bodies. "What do you want to tell your family? The ball is in your court."

Lily glanced up and touched Adam's face, and a muscle in his jaw ticked. "Do you expect me to walk away from you now?"

Silence dominated the room.

She captured his hand in hers and guided it to her chest. Lily closed her eyes so that she could feel him with her heart. "I carry you here." She opened her eyes. "I could never slay you."

His head tipped forward and pressed his forehead to hers. "Liliana." His voice was rough, ragged, leaving Lily intoxicated. His arms curved around her waist and pulled her into him. "You're busy tonight," he said, his lips oh so close to hers.

She blinked. "I can be if we think outside the box."

Adam let out a chuckle, released her and dragged a hand through his hair. "Your phone."

"What about it?"

"Someone is trying to get your attention."

Oh. She'd been so lost in his arms once again that nothing else mattered. Now that he mentioned it, Lily became aware of the buzzing sound on her bed and let out a sigh of frustration. Why was everyone choosing tonight to call her? The vibration of the phone settled in the room. Probably Rafa again or another one of her brothers in their own protective way reminding her they were coming to the island for Adam's neck. Well, good luck with that.

"Ignore it," she urged.

The sound ceased but picked up again seconds later. Lily let out a long breath.

"Whoever is calling is pretty persistent. They must need you. Go." He gave her butt a gentle nudge in the direction of the bed.

She leaned on the bed and swiped her finger on the phone. The screen lit up. To her surprise, Minka had called several times. Thinking back to last year when she reached out to her friend after finding out about Nate and his cheating ways, she picked up the phone and read the text.

I need my friend.

The desperation of the words made Lily's heart thump. Oh God no. What could possibly be wrong? She glanced back at Adam. He was still standing at the same spot, looking a little less tense, but not relaxed either.

"What's wrong?"

"It's Minka." Her mind already racing to all the things that could be wrong. Of course, she was imagining things. They were only days away from the wedding. Jason loved Minka and vice versa. Still, in the year the two have been together, this was the first time Minka had reached out to her with such urgency. "If your friend fucked up, I'm going to kick him in the nuts."

He smiled. "I think Keely already got that covered."

"I don't mind contributing."

Adam walked over and pulled up to her. He brought his hand up to cup her face. Lily closed her eyes and nestled into his hand, feeling his warmth seeping into her.

"Go to her. Sounds like she needs you," he breathed against her lips.

Torn between walking out on this moment they were sharing and going to her friend, she continued to look at him. Some things only happened once, and she sensed she may never get this again. "You and I." They had so much to talk about. "You need me too." She exhaled and pressed her face on his chest. "I don't want to walk away from this. It may never happen again."

He gently pulled her away. "I'm not going anywhere. We can finish this conversation another time."

"You asked what we should do about my family."

He nodded.

"My parents will love you. My brothers, on the other hand, will probably try to hurt you."

He smiled. "I can handle them."

She nodded. "What about us? Will you let me love you?"

He stared at her with a blank expression. His eyes gave away nothing, making it impossible for Lily to understand the depth of his emotions. "We can't have sex. Go to Minka."

She meant the perfect, amazing, beautiful, strong emotional connection, and just plain awesome kind of love. Not just the physical act. But she understood. One step at a time. One conversation at a time. Adam may have lain down his armor, but that didn't mean he was ready to hand his heart over on a silver plate. It was all due to fear, she understood that now. He was crippled by his past.

Twenty minutes later, Lily entered the house Minka shared with Jason. The second her friend opened the door, she was able to tell Minka had been crying and filled with angst. "Where's Jason?" She had not spotted his Jeep on the driveway when she pulled in.

"At Vapor."

Adam had closed his restaurant for the winter over the weekend. And from what she knew of the island, most of the tourists should be gone by now. For Jason to be at Vapor around ten at night meant something was wrong. "What did he do, Minka? Keely and I can hurt him really bad. I'm sure Claire would help if she was around."

"Have you looked at Jason lately?" her friend asked in a throaty voice.

She knew what her friend meant, not to only see the outer appearance but to see all the little things beneath. What she failed to do with Adam. To look so deep to see the person's soul, his fears, dreams. What made him tick. Nope. She'd been so consumed by her own physical needs and resisting the pull of getting emotionally attached to pay attention. Love had smacked her right in the face anyway and left her pregnant on top of it.

But she looked at Jason, all the time. At first it had been out of concern, to make sure he wasn't an asshole toying with her friend's feelings. Because no one knew how deep Minka's insecurities ran more than her.

After a while, her scrutinizing became admiration. She marveled at the way Jason used every opportunity to touch her friend, his fiancé. There was no shame in his love for Minka.

At times, it made Lily think about her fuck-buddy relationship with Adam. Even Nate. She gave all of herself to him, unconditionally so. He cheated on her with some floozy. Sure, her ego had been bruised, but her confidence had not been broken. Neither did the experience change her outlook on love. Not when she witnessed the beauty of such deep connection every day in her parents, in Minka and Jason, in Keely and Blake.

Jason was handsome, rich, and constantly surrounded by beautiful women, whether at Vapor or traveling for Montgomery Corporation. That was all a part of who he was, just as everything that came with loving Adam. But there was no doubt in Lily's mind about Jason's feelings for Minka.

"Jason is crazy about you."

Minka let out a soft chuckle. "I know that." She paused. "I should know that." They entered the living room. Minka immediately dropped her body on the sofa and released an exasperated sigh. Lily sat beside her. "I'm not skinny. I will never be skinny."

"You're healthy. It doesn't matter what the scale says."

"I know that." Minka let out another soft chuckle. "Once in a while my insecurities rear their ugly heads."

"Like tonight."

"Like tonight," Minka confirmed.

"The two of you have been together for a year now. I think he sees you and loves you as you are. Jason is in love with everything about you. Not just your ass." She teased her friend. Normally tight-lipped, Minka once slipped and told her about Jason's obsession with her backside. "You do have a nice rump."

"You're killing me," Minka groaned. "Jason and I got into a fight. I said some nasty things."

"Like how nasty, on a scale from one to fifty."

"One hundred," Minka admitted in a brittle voice.

Lily cringed. "Should I dare ask what you said and why?"

"I questioned his love for me. And I didn't use the kindest words."

The sadness in Minka's voice ripped along Lily's heart. She clasped her hand over Minka's. "Oh, hon."

"What if he wakes up one day and realizes he can do better than this?" She waved a hand over her body.

"Minka, I thought you were over all of that."

"I thought so too. But…"

"With days to go, the fact that you're about to marry this hunk of a man is too real." She understood Minka's anxiety. She was about to sign a contract of vows that should never be broken, it was normal for insecurities to creep up. "You deserve all the happiness that you and Jason have found. Don't let anything screw that up. But if you're having doubts, we can make a getaway tonight."

"I love him."

"I know you do. And he loves you. Why don't you call him and tell him to bring his ass back home where he belongs?"

"I'm scared." Minka's voice shook on the words. "Just a little, but scared nonetheless."

Minka turned to face her. Her eyes leaked with insecurities, uncertainty. Lily felt the tears well up again. She really needed to stop crying, but shit, this was her best friend. "You're going to make me cry. I can't cry anymore tonight." She let out a chuckle and touched the corner of her eyes. "Damn it, I'm crying."

They fell into each other's arms, and cried a river, with ragged currents flowing down their cheeks onto the wilted collars of their shirts.

Minutes later, emotionally drained, they fell back on the sofa, wiped their eyes and let out a shaky laugh.

"I love you, Lily."

"Ditto, my friend. Do you feel better?"

"A little."

"Good."

"I know Jason loves me," Minka said with a little more certainty.

"It's okay to doubt." She understood doubts. Only a week ago, she questioned her relationship with Adam. It felt like eternity. "Call your fiancé and remind him how much you love him."

Minka nodded. "I will. Sorry for calling you so late. I could have called Keely but—" Minka shook her head. "Still work in progress there."

The sisters had made a ton of progress on building a stronger relationship. However, after years of resentment, specifically from Minka, it would take time to mend something so fragile.

"We are closer and no more jealousy from me anymore, but…" She paused. "I hurt her for so long, you know."

Lily touched her friend's shoulder. "Keely doesn't hold grudges. She loves you."

"I know. And I love her. I'll get there one day." She exhaled and smiled at her friend. "What's going on with you and Adam?"

"He told me everything tonight." It wasn't her story to share, regardless how close she was with Minka.

"Is he okay?"

She nodded. "I think so. I still have questions."

"Are you okay? I mean so much has happened to you in over a week." She let out a deep breath. "That was pretty selfish of me to text you so late."

Lily waved a dismissive hand. "Technically, I'm at your service this week. This is your wedding week. And I'm okay. The baby is well protected and fine." She patted the small roundness of her stomach. "Just a lot to process." Lily chewed her bottom lip. "I'm so in love with him."

"So you'll marry him then?"

"Is it that simple to marry someone? I mean, you and Jason are in love. You're not settling. I can't say I wouldn't if I were to marry Adam."

"He loves you, you know."

"He cares for me. I know that. But love, I don't think he's there."

Minka smiled. "He's there. You're just not looking close enough."

Maybe. But she was looking now at his vulnerability, his trust in her. The front door opened, indicating Jason had returned home. Lily glanced at her friend. Swollen eyes smiled at her and Lily relaxed. Everything was going to be okay.

Jason entered the living room, looking as handsome as ever in a casual dark blue wool jacket, blue plaid shirt and faded blue jeans. His daunting blue eyes settled on Lily and he nodded. "How are you feeling?"

"Much better."

"Adam sent me a text to tell me you were heading over."

Lily smiled. "Yeah, I was just leaving."

"I'm not kicking you out but…"

As always, he looked in total control. He glanced at Minka and their eyes locked.

Lily stood up. "I'll leave you two alone."

Minka rose to her feet. "Jason…Oomph!"

He pulled Minka against his chest and crashed his lips against hers. Minka's arms quickly wrapped around Jason's neck and welcomed him back home. Heat ignited between the two. Feeling her temperature rising, Lily fumbled through her purse to find her keys and tried her best not to stare, but she looked and she saw an ardent love, passion, trust, respect and lots of fucking heat. Jason's feelings raw on his face, hiding nothing from Minka. All the things she had with Adam.

It hit her then. Adam loved her. In his own cautious way, he loved her. And he showed that to her tonight by showing his vulnerability and opening himself to greater possibilities. He trusted her. It scared him, she could tell. Because trusting her meant he was giving her ways to hurt him, still he laid down his armor.

"I'm in love with you. Don't ever doubt that, Minka," Jason said once they finally broke for air, bringing Lily back to reality. And right now she felt like a peeping Tom.

"I'm sorry," Minka apologized.

"Show me," Jason said, his lips on Minka's neck.

Oh boy. Lily cleared her throat. The sound fell on deaf ears. "Um... I'll see my way out." Jason was now nibbling on Minka's ear. "Well, yeah...Um...okay. Have fun."

She slipped out of the room, walked down the hall and made her way into the Maserati. Once in the car, she pulled out her phone and texted Adam.

Why tonight?
Why did you tell me everything tonight?

His response was quick.

You want all of me.
I'm giving you what you want.

She blew out a breath and brushed her bangs to the side.

Because of the baby?

She pressed her eyes closed and waited for her phone to vibrate again. *Please say no.* This time his response took a second or two. When her phone finally buzzed, her heart kicked. Slowly, Lily read the words.

No. Come home.

Lily counted to ten as slowly as she could to calm herself down. Never mind she was alone in her car, in the dark, in Jason's parking lot. And Adam couldn't see how giddy those words just made her.

When her heart finally settled, somewhat, she answered.

Ask me to marry you again.

23

"Family is like underwear. Some crawl up your ass. Some get a little twisted. And some actually do cover your ass when you need them too."

Anonymous

Two days later, hand in hand, Lily and Adam walked outside Peter's office at the only hospital on the Vineyard. Once in the hallway, she tugged on his shirt and he pulled her into his arms for one of those heart-racing kisses. Adam's hands instantly circled her waist and held her.

"What was that about?" he asked once they finally stopped for air.

"I can officially have sex." She grinned. "That means we can have sex." She glanced at her watch because her family was due to arrive in a couple of hours. The way she was feeling fifteen minutes would do. Hell, the quicker, the better. "Like right now."

He laughed, a soothing, light and easy sound.

"If we go back to the house, you're not seeing your family today."

He hadn't proposed again, but he'd only just returned from Boston helping Jason with last-minute wedding stuff. Another chuckle came from him with a twinkle in his eyes. Since their conversation two nights ago, they seemed to be laughing constantly, touching more, smiles, jokes. The way they were when they first discovered each other, but hotter now, more in sync, more connected.

She pressed closer to him. The evidence of his words poked her. "Just to be clear, we're over the no-sex thing, right?"

"Totally." To prove how totally serious he was, he squeezed her ass.

"Oh, hi guys."

Lily froze, she recognized that voice. Gwen. Straightening herself, she tried to pull out of Adam's embrace. He kept her in his arms, though he reluctantly removed his hand from her ass.

"Good to see you again, Gwen," Adam said warmly.

Yeah. They totally used to be bed buddies. She could tell by the way Gwen tucked her hair behind her ear. Which only meant one thing…Adam had rocked her world.

Lily wriggled her body, Adam tightened his hold.

The pretty nurse smiled at them. "Feeling better?"

"Yes," Lily answered as warmly as she could; only she was plagued by jealousy. Not that she should. Hell, she'd slept with other men before Adam. Two others to be specific, but whatever, there were others. "My arm is bandage-free." She extended the arm she scraped during the fall. She hadn't needed stitches, just something to protect the cut from infection.

"That's wonderful." Gwen smiled brightly, a little too bright. Lily squirmed. Adam held her still. "Well, it was nice to see you both. I need to check on a patient."

They stood in silence until Gwen made a left turn and disappeared. "You totally slept with her."

"Is that a question?"

She shot him a look. He smirked. Not that she was jealous or anything. "Just for my sanity, in case I ever make this place my home. I mean just in case you ever ask me to marry you." Oops, she didn't mean to bring the M word back up. Especially since he hadn't acted upon her request for him to ask her again. "I mean…"

"My past doesn't matter," he said somewhere deep in his throat.

In other words—yes, we rolled around naked once or twice.

Yeah. She was officially jealous.

"I haven't wanted anyone else since the first time we kissed on the beach." He leaned a little closer and brushed his lips on her ear. "Just you and me. No one else matters."

Lily felt her knees giving in to the weight of his words. One hand went up and clung on to Adam's steely bicep.

"You're okay?"

She nodded.

"Good. Let's go find something to do before I meet your family. Do I look presentable?"

His tone told her he was teasing. Probably because he already knew he looked good enough to eat. Dressed in a plaid shirt tucked under a long-sleeve grey Henley and toasted brown slim fit khakis, with a two days scruff, he looked relaxed, casual and as if he just stepped out of a magazine. No, *presentable* wasn't the word to describe how Adam looked. She could think of other words. Strong, delectable, delicious, yummy. But presentable. Nope, he was too dangerously sexy to ever look presentable.

"You already know you look so good it's a sin. Why do you think I want to jump you all the time?"

"I thought it was my charm."

Well, that too. Once she saw past the *I'm an asshole* façade, he was quite charming.

Adam laughed and slung his arm over her shoulder. "Come on, let's get out of here."

At exactly two in the afternoon, Lily sat in the Maserati beside Adam in the Martha's Way parking area. Her eyes immediately spotted Rafa's black Land Rover. Her heart sped up. She scraped a hand through her hair.

"Breathe, Liliana." Adam took her hand and brought it to his lips. "If you want I can stay with you the whole time."

She shook her head and flashed him a smile. He had errands to run with the other guys for part of the afternoon. Which worked; it'd give her time to really talk to her parents. She closed her eyes and took a calming breath. This was it. Time to tell her parents they were going to be *Abuelos*.

"Ready?"

She nodded. "Yes." But her voice shook. Damn it, her nerves were getting the best of her.

Adam ran the pad of his thumb over her cheek, her lips. "You and me, we're in this together. I'll cancel with Jason."

She met his eyes and saw the determination, the stubbornness. He had her back. No matter what…just like she had his. "No need to cancel. I'm ready."

From the outside, Lily appeared in total control, but Adam sensed her nerves. She held his hand a little tighter and her smile was a little too quick. This side of Lily was new to him, and he wished he could take away the anxiety he knew was eating her inside. Instead, he squeezed her hand back and headed to the large sitting area where laughter and busy chatter could be heard down the hall. He recognized the voices of his friends Blake, Jason, and Forrest, all there welcoming Lily's family. Minka and Keely were in Oak Bluffs picking up their parents. Claire was due back on the island today as well and Jason had sent the inn's car service to pick her up.

Voices of other men reverberated in the room as well, strong, masculine voices, similar to his own and his friends, but belonging to Lily's brothers. He felt her tense next to him and his gut tightened. Not out of nerves, but for the first time in a long time, he felt helpless. This was one of those moments Adam wished superheroes truly existed, and that he had superpowers—at least telepathic, so that he could transmit thoughts to her family. They entered the room, all eyes turned on them. It became as quiet as a graveyard in the night.

Adam took a quick survey of the room. His friends stood by the bay window, circled in a group with three other men. Her parents stood by the fireplace a few feet away. His eyes fixed on an exact replica of Lily. Her mother looked like a version of Lily from a different time, before she cut her hair. The woman's peaceful beauty gave him a glimpse of what Lily might look like as she age.

The Musketeers, as Lily fondly labeled them, resembled their father more. Bronzed and standing around six foot plus, they had their dad's hair coloring in various lengths. One was sporting a military buzz, muscles straining his shirt. Zander. Adam noted. He was the SEAL, the second oldest. He glanced at the second one. He was leaner, in low-slung, fitted black jeans and a vintage black T-shirt. His hair tousled. Maximus, or Max as often referred by his sister. The youngest of the brothers, just a little over a year older than Lily. Then his eyes clashed on the oldest of the Serrano brothers. He had sun-kissed brown hair, his mouth compressed to a hard line. Rafael. None of them gave him a welcome vibe, but Rafael, or Rafa as Lily often referred to him, looked the most pissed-off with lots of attitude.

Their eyes went to Lily's hand, the one Adam was holding. Then at Adam's face, their sister, then back at him. Yeah, they wanted his head on a platter. Too bad, he wasn't ready to be anyone's dinner unless that person had long, tanned legs and was named Liliana.

Adam squared his already broad shoulders, silently sending them a message. You want a fight, come get it. With Lily at his side, he ignored the boys and walked straight ahead to her parents. Like hyenas, they continued to watch him. *Assholes.* He continued to ignore them... on purpose.

"I'm Adam Aquilani," he said to her parents, extending his free hand. "I'm going to marry your daughter."

"What?" That came from Zander.

Adam didn't even flinch. He caught the surprise on her parents' faces. Their gazes went to their daughter, then back at Adam.

"Oh fuck no!" That was Rafael.

"Rafael." Their mother scolded without even looking at her son. The strength in her accented voice surprised Adam. "Sorry about that." She smiled warmly at Adam. "My boys can be a bit..."

"Rude," Adam finished just for kicks.

All three muttered something under their breaths. Adam was able to make out the words break and neck. He held back a smile.

"This is my husband, Raúl."

"Mr. Serrano," Adam acknowledged the older man. The two shook hands.

"How long have you been dating my daughter?" her father asked, like his sons, there was concern in his eyes and not as much warmth as his wife. Adam didn't blame him. He'd react the same way, or worse.

"A little over a year."

Raúl looked at his daughter, then back at Adam. "A year. That's a long time. I can't say we ever heard of you, Mr...."

"Adam. Call me Adam."

"Oh, for God's sake." Rafa approached them. "They haven't been dating. They've been going at it like two fucking teenagers."

"Rafa, watch your mouth." Their father scolded the angriest of them all.

This time Adam even heard Zander and Max snicker.

"She's pregnant," Rafa continued, ignoring his parents' words. He glared. "He got her pregnant and now he's trying to do the honorable thing." He laughed. "At least you're not as much of an asshole as I imagined."

"Jesus, Rafael," his mother said sternly. "Sit down."

Rafael let out a long slow breath then slumped into a chair. Adam almost laughed. He caught a glimpse of his own Wolf Pack trying very hard not to laugh.

"We need a few minutes with our daughter, Mr. Aquilani."

"Adam."

Lily's mother smiled at him and nodded. "Okay, Adam. And you can call me Carla."

Adam turned to Lily, looking for the okay that he could leave. She smiled at him. A faint smile, but one that said she could handle things from here on. He lowered his head and kissed the corner of her lips.

"Jesus!" All of the Musketeers hollered in harmony.

"I'll be back around six to pick you up."

"You're not staying here?" For the first time Max spoke, his voice dangerously low. "You're sleeping at his house every night, with him?" He threw the words without looking at Adam.

Need You Now

Adam dragged a hand through his hair, silently telling himself to keep his temper in check. He failed. "For Christ's sake, Liliana is not a child. Stop acting like she's ten."

Blake was quick by Adam's side. "Let's go. We have things to do."

"Liliana?" Rafael scoffed. "You call her by her full name?"

Adam ignored the other man and focused his attention on Lily. "I'll pick you up at six." He nodded at her parents. "I'm going to marry your daughter, with or without your consent. I'd prefer to receive your approval. Come have dinner with us Thursday night. I'd like for you to meet my parents."

"We don't get an invite?" Zander muttered.

"Nope," Adam responded without looking at them.

"Well, too bad. We're a package deal. If you invite our parents, we come too." Rafa grumbled.

Adam could have sworn he'd never met anyone angrier than this guy. Even more so than when Jason went through his I-don't-give-a-fuck phase.

"We'll be there, Adam." Lily's father answered. "We'll talk more when you pick Lily up tonight."

He shook the older man's hand, leaned over and placed a kiss on Lily's mother's cheek. A bold move, he knew that, but hell, that was a part of his culture, Lily's as well. More importantly, he wanted to send the message he was here to stay. Like it or not. Adam took one last look at Lily. Her skin was flushed. She looked a little sick. He glanced over at Jason. They had a full list of things to do. But damn it, he didn't want to leave her.

"Go," she whispered. "I'll see you in a few."

Adam fought the need to pull her in his arms once more. "If your brothers give you a hard time, call me. I'll be right over," he whispered in her ear. "You and me, together. Got that?"

She nodded.

Once Adam stepped out of the room with his friends, the voices of Lily's brothers sounded all at once. He stopped and stood in the hallway, ready to go back inside and beat the shit out of her brothers. His friends, as expected, stayed by his side. Then he heard Lily's voice.

"Adam's right, you know. I'm not ten. Get out! I want to talk to Mom and Dad alone."

"Over our dead bodies," Zander said.

"We came here to kill him," Rafa grunted.

"And I promise we'll make it quick," Max said.

Adam snorted.

"They'd have to go through us first," Jason said in a low voice. "They're as big as us, but I can take at least two of them down."

"Leave us alone with Lily," their father ordered. "And stop acting like immature thugs."

"What!" All three echoed. "He's…"

"*¡Dios!*" Their mother said, the frustration in her voice loud and clear. "I don't want to hear the F bomb again. Go wrestle each other and let us talk to Lily."

After a lot of moaning and groaning, the room grew silent. The door opened and the three Serrano brothers came face to face with Adam, Forrest, Blake, and Jason. They sized each other up.

"We're going to kick your ass." Zander looked fixedly at Adam.

"Unfortunately, we're a team here, family," Jason said calmly. "You'd have to beat up all of us, and I promise you that ain't gonna happen."

"It's not you we want," Zander informed Jason. "We like you." He shrugged. "But if you don't mind getting your pretty face smashed."

Jason laughed. "Try me."

Rafa smirked. "Flag, then."

"What the fuck is flag?" Adam questioned between clenched teeth. All of them purposely keeping their voices low, so not to disturb the conversation going in the other room.

"Football, pretty boy," Max informed. "Flag football."

Adam chuckled. "You're calling me pretty? You're standing here in a pair of skinny jeans and a pretty designer T-shirt."

Max pulled lightly at his shirt. "My jeans are tapered, and this is a vintage tee."

Adam scoffed. "Still pretty."

"And you look like you just stepped out of *GQ* magazine."

Adam waved his hand. "All three of you can kiss my ass." He turned to leave just as the front door opened. Claire stepped inside. She looked at the three men, clearly appreciating the view. She was officially a traitor.

"Claire," Max said with a note of recognition.

Claire did a double take, then smiled and threw herself in the man's open arms. This time it was Forrest who snorted.

"Oh, my God, I never made the connection," Claire said in awe, "You're Lily's brother."

"What are you doing here?" Max asked. There was warmth in his voice. Adam grunted, so did Rafa.

Claire finally turned to look at Jason and the others. "Well, I grew up with these guys. They're family." She flashed Adam and the others a smile. "This is Max."

"We know," Adam muttered.

"Max and I met a long time ago, and he shot my fall cover for *Vogue*."

"You were naked," Forrest pointed out dryly.

The big lug had been quiet during the whole exchange. Another man recognized Claire and apparently took naked pictures of his woman and he was suddenly alive and ready for some ass kicking. Adam shook his head.

"I wasn't naked. I had a sheet over me."

"It was pretty obvious you were naked underneath." Forrest waved a hand toward Max. "And this is the guy who took that picture."

Claire crossed her arms over her chest. Her almond eyes shooting fire at Forrest. "Not that you have any say in the matter, but Max is good at what he does."

Rafa and Zander let out a chuckle. Claire turned and gave them the same look. The two men cleared their throats.

Rafa stepped forward, took Claire's hand and brought it to his lips. "You're famous, aren't you? A singer. A friend of mine likes your music."

Claire smiled at Rafa. "Thanks."

"Let me take you out to dinner tonight," Rafa continued.

Oh, hell no. Adam moved forward to wipe that arrogant smirk off Rafa's face, but Forrest beat him to it. He grabbed Claire's hand and pulled her against him. For a brief moment, Claire looked like she was going to check him, but thought better of it and stayed in his arms.

"Stay away from Claire," Forrest warned.

Rafa shrugged carelessly. "Is she yours?"

"Claire is busy."

Rafa raised an eyebrow. "Doing?"

"Him," Adam, Blake, and Jason said together, looking in Forrest's direction.

Claire threw her hands up in frustration and stepped out of Forrest's hold. "Hello, I'm right here." She let out a breath. "What did I walk into? The battle of the biggest balls?"

No one answered.

She picked up her black textured Mulberry overnight bag and threw it over her shoulder. "Well, go on. I'm out." She stopped and surveyed each one of them. "Where's Lily? I haven't talked to her since the accident."

"You hurt my sister?" Zander asked.

Unable to continue this conversation any longer, Adam raked a hand through his hair. "Listen girls, I got shit to do with my friends. You want to take your frustration out on me then flag football it is." He walked up to Rafa. "I'm going to allow you one good hit tomorrow. And that's only because I understand why your panties are in a bunch. After that, you hit me hard, I hit you hard back." He assessed the other two men. "You girls can decide who gets that one lucky hit tomorrow."

24

"Without exception, all epic loves start with a massive dose of lust."
Anonymous

*P*anic clawed inside Lily's gut to her throat. Wringing her hands, she glanced at the large industrial clock on the wall. Barely fifteen minutes had passed and her parents had not said a word. She glanced at the door. No Adam. Lily inhaled a deep breath and put on a brave face. "Say something," she said at last. "I've broken one of the Serrano rules. Tell me how much I've disappointed you."

"Is it true, bebé?" her mother asked. "Is Rafa telling the truth?"

She looked at her parents; no disappointment in their eyes, only concern. "I'm starting my eighth week." As if the baby had always been there, Lily ran a hand over her stomach and smiled. "I was scared when I found out, so I didn't tell you."

"You can tell us anything," her father said.

Lily smiled weakly. "I know, but I'm single and pregnant. Not exactly an ideal situation for me." She tried to sound brave, calm. Instead her voice cracked, on the verge of tears.

Her father touched her shoulder. "Parents want their children to make their own path and find happiness. But our expectations should not drive your happiness."

A small silence settled between her and her parents.

"Is that why you're going to marry that young man? So you won't be single and pregnant?" Her father continued.

"Adam. His name is Adam. And the answer is no." Even with all trepidation over failing her parents and their expectations, she'd never marry Adam for the sake of their child.

"You don't marry because of a child." Her father continued. He didn't appear to be convinced by her answer. "Marriage is about love, the heart." He touched the left side of his chest. "Feeling like you're home when that person holds you."

Moved by her father's words, Lily once again felt the tears coming. She brushed the corner of her eyes. "I feel that way with Adam. He owns my heart."

Her father's hands cupped her arms. He leaned in and kissed her forehead. "And you own his? He never said he's in love with you. Although he's determined to marry you." As he spoke, his voice was calm. It carried Lily away, like it always did.

"I wouldn't marry him if I didn't think he did."

"It's not about what you think, *querida*," her mother said, coming to stand next to her. "It's about what he lets you see and trust. You need to be his hope as he is yours."

She nodded, letting her parents words sink in.

"Why haven't we heard about him, *querida*?" her father asked.

Because until recently our relationship was based only on sex. But she couldn't tell her parents that. She was their darling. "Adam and I were complicated."

"We understand." Her father studied her face. The love they have for their children clear in his eyes. "We never want you to settle," he continued. "No matter what the situation is, never settle for anything less than the whole enchilada."

By the whole enchilada, he meant love. The love her parents shared. The fact that she'd broken a Serrano rule was now an afterthought. As always, her parents' main concern was for their children to be happy. Unwed, pregnant and all.

At that moment, she knew things were going to be okay. "You'll give him a chance?" she asked just to be sure.

"If he's important to you then he's important to us."

Tears immediately began streaming down her face. Relieved, she fell into her parents arms for a long embrace. "*Te amo.*" Her mother's gentle laughter reverberated in her ear like the sound of angel wings flapping.

"He seems like a nice young man," her mother whispered in her ear. "He's very protective of you."

Lily chuckled. "Just a little."

"Well, if this isn't a Kodak moment."

Lily froze at the sound of Rafa's voice. Well, one hurdle down. Now time to deal with her brothers.

"Rafa," her father warned.

"It's okay, Dad." Lily stepped out of her parents arms and eyeballed her brothers. Their faces were a crimson shade, and their eyes seemed to spark with fury. "Why are you so angry with Adam? It takes two, you know."

"Thanks," Zander muttered. Muscles and veins strained against his skin. "We needed that mental image."

"He doesn't love you," Rafa said.

Ouch. The words stung, so much so that she gasped. Her mother stepped forward and shot Rafa a stern look.

"You've gone too far, Rafael. I expect you to show Adam respect."

All three of her brothers uttered a grunting sound.

"Your mother is right," their father spoke. "You need to show some respect."

"I called in a favor to a friend to run a background check on him," Zander said, as if nothing else mattered.

Lily's eyebrows shot up in shock. "What?" She glared at them, unable to believe what she was hearing. "Why would you do that?"

Zander shrugged. "You got burned with Nate. It's not going to happen again."

But she wasn't thinking about Nate or his cheating ways. She could care less about that chapter of her life. It was her past. Adam was her future. The world circled around her as her thoughts scampered to what Zander had started. A reporter might have not been able to get all the information, but Zander could. Zander would if she didn't put a stop to it. She had no intention of keeping Adam's past buried, but one obstacle after another. One day she'd tell them everything, but not today.

"You need to call your friend and ask that they stop." The urgency or rather panic in her voice caused her brothers to look at her. Knowing they would be able to see straight through her, Lily looked away.

"Is he married?" Max asked.

"My God!" She whipped around and shot them an angry piercing stare. "You guys are idiots. Do you really think I would shack up with someone who is married?"

"So then what are you hiding?" This time it was Rafa who spoke, his dark eyes narrowed on her. "You're hiding something about him."

"Just stop whatever you started." Her voice cracked.

"Lily," Zander said, approaching her. "What's going on? Tell us what's going on and I'll stop it."

But she couldn't. Adam trusted her, she could never betray him. "Please." She pleaded, feeling herself drowning in fear. "Just stop whatever you started." She herself was still learning about Adam's childhood, the fact that he took his father's life. She still had no clue what happened after that, she only knew this reporter was going to great lengths to expose him. There had to be a reason, which she intended to find out but at her own pace, not by her brothers' overbearing ways.

"Zander," her mother said, "call your friend and close your background check." She looked at her daughter. "Lily is a grown woman. We trust her to make the right decision."

"He could be a fucking killer!" Rafa said through clenched teeth, sounding disapproving. He threw his arms in the air. "Just because he's some famous rich boy doesn't make him greater or bigger than us. You guys..." he looked at his parents, "may have decided to drink the

Adam Kool-Aid, but we haven't. Zander will not stop digging until we find out what Lily is refusing to tell us."

Feeling light-headed and a bit disoriented, Lily grabbed her purse to find her phone. She scrolled to Adam's name and pressed the *TALK* option just as Zander extended his hand to her.

"Liliana?" Adam's voice was filled with questions, concern. And the muscles of her heart tightened with an incredible force.

"Give me the phone," Zander said. "Let me speak to him."

She looked at her brother. The arrogance now replaced by uneasiness.

"I'll be there in ten," Adam said.

Zander took the phone from her. "She's fine. She'll see you later." He disconnected the call and handed Lily the phone. "I'll call the investigation off."

Rafa released a guttural roar. "Are you kidding me?"

Zander turned to his brother. "Relax, bro. Lily's our sister." His eyes searched hers. "But if he's in trouble, know that you can trust us."

Thanks, she mouthed.

Zander nodded and threw an arm over her shoulder. "Come on, let's catch up."

Lily hesitated, not trusting her brother. He pulled his phone from his pocket, went through his contact list and typed.

Drop it.

For confirmation he showed the text to her and pressed *SEND*.

"We would never hurt you Lily. We are just concerned."

"We're still kicking his ass in football tomorrow," Rafa muttered, his displeasure in full display.

Sometime during the course of the day, Lily began to relax around her family. Rafa's nostrils were still flaring, but for the most part his rage seemed to have gotten under control. Especially when Keely and Minka arrived with their parents and the wedding became the main topic of discussion.

They were all gathered in the garden, when Adam and the others pulled up and headed in their direction. Jason and Blake greeted their in-laws. Their women like magnets went into their arms. Claire was engaged in a conversation with Max. She looked up and her gaze collided with Forrest's. Tension thickened the air between them until Claire broke their connection and turned her attention back to Max.

Adam had either gone swimming with his friends or freshly showered. His hair was wet and looked like he ran his fingers through for some sort of manageability at the last minute. He'd changed into a fitted heather grey sweater, clinging to every muscle on his chest and emphasizing his broad shoulders; cuffed, dark denim jeans accenting brown, rugged boots; and a rustic cashmere scarf thrown around his neck, adding a great layer to his outfit. He embodied the fall weather.

His eyes stayed on her as he took slow, deliberate steps toward the group. He looked alert, tough, and in complete protective mode. Lily could only stare, heat churning in her belly.

After a short, polite conversation with everyone, he took her hand in his. "Hey." His mouth smiled, but his eyes searched hers, silently asking if all was well. She smiled at him and his shoulders relaxed a bit. "Let's go home." He glanced at her brothers and Lily held her breath. "Shave your legs for tomorrow. See you at three."

"What's that about?" she asked Adam once they were in his car.

He chuckled. "Your brothers challenged us in flag football."

"Oh, Rafa said something about beating your ass tomorrow."

His laughter deepened, as if no way in hell any of her brothers could touch one hair on his skin. She believed it. He backed out of the driveway onto the main road. "I promised them I'll give free aim to at least one good hit."

"Have you ever played?"

"I've played football. Same thing."

The concept was the same but there was one major difference, no physical contact. The main rule of flag football was instead of tackling players to the ground, the defensive team must remove a flag from the ball carrier to end a down. Something told her all of them had no intention to follow the rules. "You're just as bad, you know."

He glanced at her, an innocent *who me?* look on his face.

Lily rolled her eyes. "Jason is playing too?"

He nodded.

"He's getting married in a couple of days. He can't get bruised."

Adam shrugged, not seeing her point. "What does bruising have to do with getting married?"

She huffed. Men. Some things they just didn't get. "Because," she said slowly, very slowly. "Minka will not be happy to have her husband photographed with a black eye, or any other mark that she didn't personally put on his skin."

"I promise you Jason won't be sporting a black eye. It's me they want, you know." He reached for her hand. "How come they never went after your ex?"

"They tried." She groaned, thinking of the many times her brothers tried to *accidentally* meet up with Nate.

"You stopped them from rearranging his face?"

"What's the point? He means nothing to me."

"If you were my sister, I'd beat him up."

Lily threw her head back and laughed, all anxiety from earlier leaving her body.

He brought her hand to his lips and turned the car to the street leading to his house. "I have a surprise for you."

She glanced at his profile. The muscles of his face was relaxed, his cheekbones soft, a slight smile curving the corners of his lips. And her heart did that little dance again.

Adam parked the car and was quickly by her side. He took her hand in his. "Let's go to the beach."

Puzzled, she looked at the direction of the water. The mellow autumn sunset lingered over the ocean, sending a cool breeze in the evening sky. She was wearing a light jacket and automatically began to pull up the zipper. Adam quickly removed his scarf and placed it around her neck. "I'll keep you warm."

His voice was low and incredibly sexy. Lily moved closer to him. Not because she needed the heat, his mere presence would warm her even if they were stranded in Antarctica. But as always his emotional pull was strong.

In silence Adam led her to the private beach. Lily paused when she spotted the blanket and picnic basket on the sand. "What's this?"

He smiled. "I made you dinner."

"A picnic?"

"I'm trying to be romantic."

She laughed, tip-toed and pressed her lips to his. She released his hand and almost sprinted to the grey blanket with the Martha's Vineyard emblem in its center. She sat and crossed her legs. Chuckling, Adam followed and joined her. He leaned in, planted his hands by her legs, and kissed her neck, nibbling on her skin. Arousal surged through her body and she tugged at his sweater, pulling him closer.

"Can anyone see us?" The beach was private, but he had neighbors, not many or too close, but they had access to the beach as well.

"Still too early," he whispered between kisses that were now going up and down her neck, melting her bones away. "But I intend to make you come right here tonight."

"Promise."

He let out a short whisper of a breath as he exhaled. "It's a matter of life or death for me."

For her too. She needed to feel every inch of him inside her. Lily removed the scarf around her neck, slid her arms around his and lowered herself on the blanket, bringing his big body along. His lips grazed her collarbone, her jaw toward her mouth. He paused, brought his face to hers, his intense dark eyes holding hers prisoner. And the emotion she read in them rocked her axis. Adam ran the pad of his thumb over her parted lips.

"I've missed this." His voice was gruff, filled with need.

Then his lips crushed against hers with urgency, his tongue dipping in, kissing her deep and hard. She knotted her fingers in his hair, electricity pulsing through her veins. "Now, Adam," she panted and kept kissing him. "Let's go inside." She tilted her hips and rocked right into his erection.

She heard him groan and slowly peeled himself away from her. "Not yet." Arms by his side, his head tipped back, he drew out a deep breath into the cool air. "In my head this goes a certain way."

She sat up. "What happened to being spontaneous?"

Dark, heavy-lidded eyes turned to her. "I don't mean sex."

Okay, he was confusing the hell out of her. "Speak English."

"Stay with me, Liliana."

"I'm trying." She really was, but there was that space between her legs that wanted, needed him right there.

Adam hoisted himself up. "I made you dinner."

She peered at the picnic basket then smiled at him. "It's very sweet."

He ran a hand through his hair, obviously frustrated. "I never want to be sweet."

"Okay then, you're not sweet. Let's go inside and I can show you how unsweet you are."

He grunted.

Lily rose to her feet and walked into his arms. "I'm trying to stay with you, but you're confusing the hell out of me."

He tangled his fingers in her hair, slanted his head and kissed her once more. "I told your parents I was going to marry you," he said against her lips.

"Okay."

He smiled. "The other night, you told me to ask you again. I spent all of yesterday shopping for a ring."

Lily blinked. Things were slowly starting to make sense. The sudden trip to Boston with Jason. The picnic. The beach. They first made love on the sand to the sound of the ocean in Chappaquiddick on Jason's private beach. But a beach was a beach. Adam was being romantic. She smiled, tiptoed and wrapped her arms around his neck and shouted, "Yes!"

His arm circled her waist and brought her against his chest. "I haven't asked."

"Ask me, then."

His dark eyes grew serious. He brushed his lips against hers one more time then released her. Lily watched as Adam lowered himself to one knee and took her hand in his. Her eyes clouded. *Shit. No tears. Not now.*

"Liliana, in your arms I'm rooted. Will you marry me?"

She fell to her knees beside him. The tears were now flowing down her cheek but she didn't care. She cupped his face in her hands and let out a shaky laugh between her tears.

He kissed the palm of her hand. "Does that mean yes?"

Through stream of tears, she chuckled. "Yes." She could have sworn he looked a little relieved. Like she would ever say no.

Adam pulled her into him with such force that it knocked them both off their balance. His back hit the sand and she landed on his chest. "I'm going to make love to you all night and maybe all day tomorrow."

She laughed. "You have the football game."

"Football break to kick your brothers' asses, then more of you."

25

"Intimacy is the act of connecting with someone so deeply, you feel like you can see their soul."
Anonymous

After another deep, wet kiss, Lily gave Adam a gentle shove and pulled up to her feet. She slipped off her jacket, yanked her sweater over her head, tossed it somewhere on the ground, and stood in a body-hugging black tank. Still lying on the cool soil, he watched her, eyes twinkling with amusement.

"What are you doing?"

Instead of answering, Lily kicked off her boots, pulled off the tank. In bra and a fitted pair of jeans, she threaded her fingers to the waistband of her pants. Adam braced himself to his elbows. Dark brown eyes heated to a whiskey color, no longer amused. She threw the jeans to the side and stood bravely in matching black panties and bra, sending a clear message of her intent.

He rose to his feet, removed his shoes then stood still for a beat. His thick hair tousled from the light breeze with strands blowing in his perfectly carved face. He was intoxicating. Lily watched him take two easy strides to close the space between them. She stood there, with their bodies oh, so close, goose bumps on her skin, not from the coolness in the air, but with desire, and the heat he generated.

"Our neighbors are going to think you're crazy," he said in a low, gruff voice that only increased her arousal.

"Do you care?"

"No," he answered without giving the question much thought.

She didn't think so. "I'll race you to the house." She grinned and he smiled. A slow dangerous smile that told her she stood no chance of winning whatever game she wanted to play. "Winner gets to do whatever they want."

He raised his eyebrows, curiosity piqued. "Anything?"

She smiled wickedly. "Anything."

"I'm going to win," he assured her.

Adam was bigger, taller, and definitely faster. She knew all that, but at this moment her heart was beating more profoundly, dancing with joy. And she felt like living on the edge.

He playfully pulled a strand of her hair. "Can BOB come out and play? I'd like to watch, or maybe help him find your sweet spot."

The idea of pleasuring herself while Adam watched sent a sensation down the pit of her stomach to that hyper-sensitive area between her thighs. "You'd have to win the race," she said over her shoulder and bolted toward the house. Lily didn't think Adam made any effort to move until she was halfway there. Still he caught up with her.

"Oh, this is going to be fun," he said by her side, not even out of breath.

Adrenaline coursed through her veins, keeping her breathing steady, she pushed harder and sprinted a bit quicker as the cool air bit into her lungs. He stayed by her side with no effort, slapped her ass playfully then left her eating his dust. "You cheated." Her playful scream was met with ripples of laughter.

Lily entered the house a few seconds, okay, minutes after. While her breath came in short gasps, Adam looked as if he barely moved. "You cheated," she repeated.

He chuckled, came to stand in front of her. His fingers delved into her hair and held on. "You're a sore loser." He kissed one corner of her mouth, then the other. "Pay up." In one swift movement, he swept her off her feet into his arms and carried her up the stairs, drugging her with a molten-hot kiss.

Somewhere in the back of her mind, she heard Adam kick the bedroom door open then plopped her on the bed. He stood back, tilted his face down, and with smoldering eyes drank in her body.

"I'm beginning to show a little bit."

He nodded, eyes hooded. "I'm taking it all in." His hand slid under her, cupped her behind and pulled her to the edge of the bed. Deft fingers glided over the thin silver bar going through her navel, the round of her stomach before finding her silky thighs and slowly removing her panties.

"Do you like?"

Adam placed one knee on the bed, his arms resting on each side of her body, holding her prisoner. He gave her a very hot look. "I'm feeling a lot of things right now, like is the least of them." He claimed her lips into a hot, tongue-thrusting kiss.

At the words, the touch, her body liquefied. Her immediate reaction was to arch her back and pressed her chest against his, deepening their kiss which garnered a low, sexy growl deep from his throat.

And then her bra was gone, tossed carelessly aside somewhere in the room. Adam's teeth scraped over her nipple. He then took one brown bud into his mouth and sucked vigorously as he slid a hand into the liquid heat between her legs.

"You want me?" he asked.

"Always."

He smiled. "Show me."

She knew what he meant. Sex between them had always been uninhibited, free, and easy. They had no problem pleasing each other or themselves while the other watched. He took her hand, entwining their fingers, and led her to the liquid heat between her legs.

"No BOB, just you and me."

When she started, he pulled his hand back and watched her stroke the delicate spot. It went on for a beat, their gazes locked on each other the whole time. But then she increased the speed of her stroke and lost herself in the sensation. She couldn't help but close her eyes. Oh God, her body edged to the point of ecstasy. "Adam." She let out a fervent plea.

"Open your eyes, Liliana," he demanded and she obeyed. Adam removed her hand, captured her finger in his mouth and suckled on it, tasting her.

Lily arched her back, needing to fill the void. He responded by sliding his own blunt masculine fingers deep into her delicate softness, then another, making her buck forward.

"Adam."

"Tell me what you want, Liliana."

"You," she stammered, "in me."

He shook his head. "Not yet," he said, before sliding to his knees between her legs. He cupped her ass again and pulled her a little more to the edge of the bed, placed her legs over his shoulders. "So fucking beautiful," he rasped, then ran his tongue over her mound.

Lily let out an incoherent cry, her muscles tightening against him. Adam stroked, touched, and licked every single inch of her until she was breathing like a lunatic as her body floated into ecstasy. It took a few minutes before the shaking stopped and her breath settled. But she wanted more, so much more.

When she was finally able to open her eyes, he brought himself up to his six foot-plus height. He quickly stripped off his clothes and stood magnificently naked with a raging erection. So when he brought her legs to his chest, shoulders, dragged her further to the tip of the bed and made room for himself between her thighs, she hoisted her hips then closed her eyes to welcome him home.

"Open your eyes, Liliana." He smoothed her bangs away from her temple and tilted her chin so their gazes locked. "I need you to see me, us. Look with me."

His voice was thick with desire and need. She opened her eyes to see just the same intensity reflecting in his eyes. A need she knew that didn't come easy or readily displayed, but he was letting her see all that he felt. Wordlessly telling her he loved her.

Adam needed her as much as she needed him. This generated a

cocktail of emotions within her. Her gaze lowered to where he was positioned between her thighs and watched as he pushed himself inside her damp entrance with a slow thrust, stretching the walls of her body until he was lost so deep she felt him to the depth of her soul, causing her heart to slip at their stark connection.

"Fuck," he groaned. "You feel so good."

"Harder."

"Slow."

She lifted her hips and rocked against him. "No, fast and hard."

Adam swore, expelled a slow, steady breath, then began to thrust, long and deep, holding her gaze captive as he increased the speed of his stroke, pounding her with rigorous strength until the orgasm rippled through her in stunning waves, sending her flying. With one more masterful thrust, he came along with her.

"Wrap your legs around me."

She obeyed. His body collapsed over her, chest pressed against her breast. She could feel the thunderous beat of their hearts dancing to the same chaotic rhythmic tune. Lost in their euphoria, neither made an attempt to move. At least not until her stomach reminded her she hadn't eaten. Even then, she kept a firm grip around his neck.

"You need to eat," he said, against her throat.

"I'm fine." She didn't want him to move. Not ever.

Her stomach screamed out of hunger again. Adam laughed softly, lifted his head and brushed a kiss against her temple. "Come on. We have a picnic at the beach waiting."

Oh, yeah, she'd forgotten all about that. "It's still good?"

He loosened her arms from his neck, walked to his dresser to grab a fresh pair of boxer briefs and slipped into his favorite black pair of sweatpants. "Should be, but there's leftover in the fridge. Let's take it to the beach and eat. I have to clean up anyway or the seagulls will find a way to open the basket." He picked up his jeans from the floor, dug into the pocket and retrieved a small black velvet box. "Your ring."

Her heart leaped in her chest. They'd never gotten to the ring part of the engagement. "Oh."

He turned to her with a worried look on his face. "You don't want it?"

"God, yes." She let out a short laugh. "I was just so…um…horny I skipped the ring part."

Adam approached the bed, took her hand in his and took the ring out of the box and slipped it on her finger. "Does that mean you'll still be my wife?"

She laughed, a deep laugh filled with joy. "What do you think?"

One hour later, Lily was full and had eaten way too much, but she didn't care. Dinner had been delicious, simple but thoughtfully prepared by Adam himself. Fresh avocado dip with crispy crunchy pita chips, roasted eggplant, red onions and bell peppers in a wrap, fresh squeezed lemonade and a baked blueberry pie from Herring Creek farm for dessert. Between laughter, touching, lots of touching, a kiss here and there, some lingered, some quick, and the mellifluous sound of waves rushing to the shore, they ate everything, and had lost track of time. But that happened when one's heart was dancing with joy.

The sun had completed its tour for the day, and now replaced by a myriad of stars, which dotted the sky and danced against the ocean. The cool breeze caressed her skin and Lily hugged her knees, wriggled her toes in the soft velvety sand beneath her feet. She peeked once more at the cushion-cut white diamond ring encircled by a row of pink and white bead set of diamonds Adam had slipped on her finger. Classically elegant, it was perfection.

"Cold yet?" Adam asked not too far away as he tidied up the remnants of their picnic.

"Come warm me up."

He dropped to the sand beside her. "Want to go back inside?"

She fixed her eyes on the ocean. "No, this is perfect."

He took her hand in his. "I know you're worried about my career and the danger it presents. Do you want me to retire?"

She turned and got a look of his expression. Her heart stuttered at the seriousness on his face. He was ready to walk away from the career he loved for a chance to have a future with her. No, she wouldn't be that woman who made him choose. She'd just have to learn to accept

Need You Now

with love comes danger, fear and joy. It was a package deal. "I couldn't ask that of you."

"You didn't ask. I am offering."

And she loved him for that. "You love your career. I can't take that away from you."

A silence fell between them for a beat. Then he asked, "Tired?"

Her heart squeezed at his concern. She rested her head against his. "I don't want this to end, Adam. This moment right now is perfect."

Everything was perfect. Her ring. Adam. Dinner. His hand holding hers as they stared out at the sea...no one there, just them.

Perfection.

Sometime in the night, Lily reached for Adam, only to find his side of the bed empty. Her eyes flew open. She threw the comforter aside, a shiver of apprehension crisped her skin. Barefoot, she rushed down the stairs; the wood creaked under her feet. She didn't bother turning on any lights; she was familiar with the landscape and made her way to the family room. She found him lounging on the sofa, sipping on a beer, gaze glued to the TV screen. She walked over and sat next to him. "Another dream?"

"You should be sleeping, Liliana."

Yeah, definitely another nightmare and he was shutting her out again. "What was this one about?"

She waited. After a long beat, he placed the beer on the floor next to him, picked up the remote and turned off the television. "One day I came home to my father slapping my mother around." His voice was roughed with pain. "I rushed over and pulled him off, well, I tried to."

"Oh, Adam." Her throat tightened in pain for him.

"He pushed me off. I was small and weak. So I fell, but then he started kicking me, bruised a few ribs, then he put a gun on my head. Right here." He pointed to the center of his forehead. "That's one of the few times my mother ever protected me."

Lily let out a disgusted sigh, unable to imagine the horrible pain he'd suffered as a child. "I can't take away your childhood, but I wish I could."

"These are my dreams, Liliana. Except they are not dreams. They are my nightmares to live with."

Lily moved into Adam's arms. He shifted his weight to make room for her and she cradled against his muscular body. It felt so good to be in his arms that for a moment she just stayed with him, breathing him in. But Adam was in pain. Her Adam. Together they needed to make him okay. "What can I do? Please tell me. I can go to counseling with you. Whatever. I'll do it with you."

"No counseling."

"Your parents never took you to one? They can help."

"They all want to give me meds. You can't give narcotics to an addict."

Still in his arms she turned so that they could be face to face. "Your birthing conditions don't mean you'll become addicted."

His lips twitched in a weak smile. "You're willing to chance that?"

She didn't answer.

"I'm not," he answered his own question. "I never want to be what my parents were."

His face was set in a hard, determined expression. She caressed his brooding features. "We will make you better," she said and kissed him softly on the lips. "Just don't shut me out. I couldn't take it if you were to shut me out again." Her voice trembled on the words, remembering only a week ago, he had shut himself from her.

His large hands cupped her face and forced her to meet his gaze. "Liliana," he murmured her name. "My instinct will always be to protect you. Even from me."

"Can't you see, Adam, I don't need protection from you. I just need you." She smiled then.

His mouth crushed against hers, and he kissed her hard. But this wasn't about kissing—it had everything to do with need, hunger, and the darkness inside Adam.

"Hold on to me, Liliana," he murmured against her lips.

She did as he requested and locked her arms around his neck.

Adam hoisted her up along with him to a sitting position, with her on top of him. Their eyes met, his gaze dark and intense, almost wild. "Ride me."

With her sitting on his thighs, he lifted up his hips and slipped off his sweats, then proceeded to shove her shorts and panties down. Adam pushed up her silk camisole and she lifted her arms to ease the process for him. Within seconds, she straddled him with his hard length thick between them. Skin on skin, flesh on flesh.

He lifted her slightly and placed her warm entrance on the tip of his erection. "Now, Liliana," he said, and lowered her body over his length.

Lily cried out at the firm contact, and began moving on him. He thrust up into her, making her feel him even deeper. And as the pleasure inside her mounted, she couldn't help but think maybe, just maybe in a way, she was healing him, however, temporary it was. So when he leaned in and took one breast into his mouth, her love for him took over. Her fingers slid through his hair and gripped a handful. She heard him wince but she didn't care. Lily's breath grew shallow, the speed of her movement increased, until cries of ecstasy filled the room.

A little while later, Adam rolled to his side and pulled Lily's back against him. He turned the television back on and her heart sank because that meant he was once again avoiding sleep.

"Go to sleep," he whispered in her ear.

"I'm not leaving you."

He turned off the television. "Okay, you win. Go to sleep."

In the dark she smiled and pressed her back a little closer against his chest. "I love the feel of you."

"The feeling is mutual." He kissed her shoulder. "You do something to me I can't explain. Now sleep."

Love, she thought. It heated their soul, energized their spirit and supplied passion to their lives. It was their connection.

26

"Let your past be your springboard, not your quicksand."
Steve Maraboli

Half hour before game time on a sparkling but cold island afternoon, Lily walked onto the football field at Martha's Vineyard Regional High School in Oak Bluffs with Adam's arm slung possessively over her shoulder. Her brothers, dressed in white with navy trimmed Lacrosse shorts and grey fitted graphic tees were huddled with comparable size men in black athletic shorts and fitted T-shirts in the middle of the field with their cleats on, ready for battle, completely impervious to the chill in the air. Apparently a uniform coordination had taken place sometime before the match because Adam was dressed in black shorts like the rest of his pack with a blue cotton tee with the words *Put Up or Shut Up* on its front.

As they approached the group, she could hear the banter going back and forth between them, which included a push-up challenge between Rafa and Jason. Side by side, the two men dropped to the balls of their feet on the ground, palms down under their shoulders, and back straight. In perfect alignment, they elevated themselves then lowered their weight, still in perfect alignment, as low as they could go.

By the time Lily and Adam joined them, the two men were still going with easy, economical speed. They turned to eyeball each other and kept going until both dropped to the ground, rose to their feet and elbowed each other, and then shook hands.

A quick race across the field broke between Zander and Blake, or whatever else to show their physical prowess while Keely, Minka and Claire looked on, openly enjoying the view. Even Lily had to admit seeing that level of testosterone huddled together would have been a mesmerizing sight if three of the toned bodies didn't belong to her brothers.

"Men are so immature," Claire murmured, but she didn't look away from the muscles bulging everywhere.

"Finally," Zander said over his shoulder. "We didn't think you were going to show up."

"And miss kicking your asses? Never," Adam jested.

Rafa and Max sent hyena-like stares at Adam's arm over her shoulder. To show her brothers his ego was just as inflated or perhaps superior, Adam pulled her closer against him in the see, she's mine kind of hug.

The whole display was further proof of her theory. Men never really grew up. In order to get laid, they learned to act in public and fooled women into believing they were no longer snot noses. But really they were.

"What's with your boyfriend?" Max asked tossing the football up in the air and catching it. "He looks like shit." He stopped and studied his sister. "You too. Not as much as him, though."

The words were casually thrown at her, to appear indifferent, but she noted the hint of concern in her brother's voice. He was worried about her. And maybe even a little about Adam. Ordinarily, she'd run into his arms and give him a big little-sister hug, but as payback for their bad 'tude yesterday, she rolled her eyes and replied, "Geez, thanks." While she eventually did fall asleep, she knew the exact time Adam ultimately drifted to sleep. By then, the sun was starting to rise.

"Lily," Claire exclaimed. She was quick by Lily's side and took her friend's hand in hers. "What a beautiful ring."

All three of her brothers' gaze went to her left hand and huffed. Max slung the football in Adam's direction; Adam quickly removed his hand from her shoulder and caught the approaching ball to avoid getting hit in the chest. Max flashed a smug smile. Mission accomplished.

Keely and Minka circled them, pulled her into tight hugs and both tiptoed to kiss Adam on the cheek. The guys followed. Her brothers continued to breathe fire, although the heat level had subsided a bit.

"You're really going to marry this guy?" Zander asked.

Blake placed a hand on Zander's shoulder. "Accept it, man. Adam is one of the good guys."

"Welcome to the family, Lily. You need new brothers anyway," Forrest teased.

"Remember, I saw your girl naked," Max threw back.

"I'm not anyone's girl." Claire looked fixedly at Max. "And you didn't see me naked."

"If you're not doing him…" Rafa tipped his head in Forrest's direction.

Claire sighed, raised her hands and stared Rafa down. "You need to stop it too."

He focused on Claire and flashed a very bad-boy smile. The kind of smile that had melted women. "I still want to take you out to dinner."

Claire crossed her arms over her chest, not the least bit affected. "Not happening."

Rafa laughed, a good-natured sound that Lily was so familiar with and loved. She couldn't help but smile. They might be coming across as assholes, but they were the good, caring kind of assholes.

Adam extended his arms and stretched wide. "Are we playing football or what? You have the flags, Forrest?"

Forrest reached into his backpack and pulled out three pink towels. "For you guys."

Jason and Adam snickered. Her brothers took the towels, studied them and hung them off their hips.

"Since you guys are outnumbered," Blake pointed. "I'll be the ref."

"Wait," Minka called out, "Aren't there rules?"

Jason circled Minka's waist and pulled her against his chest. "Not really." For reassurance, he placed a lingering kiss on his fiancée's lips.

Blake cleared his throat. "Sorry, Minx." He furrowed his brows together. "Let me go over the rules for the concerned fiancée." The guys muttered under their breaths, voicing their displeasure. "QB gets the ball and either keeps and runs with it, hands off, or passes in order to get to score. Defense stops these plays from happening." He struck the palm of his hands against one another. "Enjoy!"

In other words, tackle the hell out of each other. The men seemed pleased with the rules. As they separated into their respective teams, Lily and the others made their way to the stands.

"You think they'll be all right?" Minka asked with obvious concern.

Before Lily could answer, Adam's body banged against Zander and Max, making the sound of a train crashing into two planes. She felt Minka wince next to her. And even though Lily grew up with siblings wrestling around her and was used to boys playing rough, her body still shook a little at the hit. Adam hoisted himself up from the ground, wiped his lips with the back of his hand and tossed the ball in an impervious manner to her brothers. First down.

"That's your one hit," he yelled over his shoulder to her brothers. "Now all's fair."

For the next hour, Lily watched her brothers try to go to war with her fiancé and his friends. The problem was, war always failed to determine who was right—only who was left barely standing. Instead of simply yanking the flags as they were supposed to, each team tackled the hell out of each other, then snatched the towels off their opponents, thrust them with great triumph in the air and fist bumped their teammates. A simple flag football game was now a pulse-pounding event.

"Nothing good can come out of this," Minka murmured, her tone full of worry.

At that instant Zander tackled Jason. Rafa jumped in just for reassurance. Minka flinched. Blake signaled them to play on. Apparently the late hit rule also didn't exist.

"They are beating the hell out of each other." Claire leaned forward, fully immersed in the battle of muscles.

"I'm glad Blake isn't playing." Keely shivered after Max tackled Forrest.

"Jason might lose a tooth," Minka said partly to herself just as Jason grabbed Zander and brought him face down to the ground.

On the last play, Lily didn't take her eyes off Adam. He lined up on the far right of Forrest, who was their quarterback. Knees bent slightly and leaning forward, he zoomed down the field, caught the ball thrown by Forrest and dashed to the end zone. The steady pounding of her brothers' footsteps echoed in her ears as they chased Adam down. She watched hard bodies collide and when Adam hit the ground, she put a hand over her mouth to stifle a scream.

She held her breath until Adam pushed himself up to his feet, spit out some dirt and grass and spiked the ball on the ground as a sign of victory. They won by one point. His teammates high-fived him and pulled their shirts over their heads. Her brothers did the same. All of them stood shirtless and covered in sweat oblivious to the cool autumn air. Keely and Claire let out a low mercy sound. But it was the scribbling in black ink on Forrest's forearm that caught Lily's attention. An infinity tattoo similar to Claire, but his appeared to have words scribbled, only he was too far away for her to decipher the damn thing.

After handshakes were exchanged, all seven men made their way to the stands. Adam kept his gaze on her the whole time, then flashed a victorious grin. Lily walked straight into his arms and kissed him. She didn't care her brothers were right there or that Adam was covered in dirt and sweat.

"Aren't you supposed to be some sort of European pretty boy?" Rafa asked. His voice was void of the anger from yesterday, even from one hour ago. He wasn't warm and fuzzy, but less angry was always a step in the right direction.

Adam laughed. "I have many talents."

Rafa shook his head. "Do you always have to point out you get to see our sister naked?"

"How did you get that from what I said?" Adam shook his head. "I say let's go to Vapor for beer and food. Our treat to the losing team."

"We lost by one point, that barely makes us losers," Zander muttered.

"We have the W and you have the L," Jason teased. "So yeah, that makes you the losing team."

"Claire," Rafa called. "You're coming too?"

Lily turned to Forrest. "Can I see that?" she asked with a smile. "Your tattoo." She added when his eyebrows creased in question.

He smiled. "Sure. At times I almost forget it's there."

He extended his large muscular arm and she peeked a little closer to the tattoo on his forearm. The words in black bold letters—We were and in that moment I swear infinite—curved seductively in the form of the infinity symbol over his skin, permanently glued to him. *Holy crap.* Claire had the same infinity tattoo, maybe not the words, but Lily hadn't been able to get that close. The tat was always strategically hidden underneath the layered bracelets she wore, but the infinity symbol was etched in the inside of her wrist. She looked back at Claire and was surprised to find the other woman watching her. She searched her friend's face for some clue, but Claire's eyes told no story.

"Claire?" Jason asked

"No," Claire answered. "I'll pass."

Forrest drew his breath and released it before speaking. "Why?" His voice was thick with frustration, emotions.

Claire's eyes wavered from Lily to Forrest. "I..."

"You have to leave," Forrest cut her off. "You always have to leave. Not tonight, Claire. Come with us."

An awkward silence settled within the group. No one moved until Zander's phone started to ring. He retrieved the phone from his pocket and frowned. "I have to take this," he said and walked away.

"I'll come for a little while, but I can't stay," Claire said to the group.

Zander returned quickly. Lily examined her brother. His big, muscular body was now rigid with tension. He picked up his shirt and put it back on, then smiled warmly at her.

"Is everything okay?" she asked her brother. He had a dangerous job, and she always worried about his safety.

He nodded. "Yeah, it was work."

"Beer or not?" Adam asked.

"Beer." The men answered.

"Shower first," Max said, which generated a cough from Adam.

"Fine, pretty boy," her fiancé teased, laughter in his voice. "See you all in about one hour."

Hand in hand, Lily walked back to the Maserati with Adam and everyone just as a black Ford pulled up. The same reporter jumped out of the car and hurried toward them. Adam stopped and held her close to him.

"I am seriously contemplating getting a restraining order," he said under his breath.

In the fear of the moment, time stood still and yet it raced. Her brothers watched with curiosity. Zander leaned against the Range Rover with his arms crossed over his chest, quietly taking in the event. Jason, Forrest and Blake looked ready to attack.

"Pereira Cooper," the man said smugly.

Lily glanced at Adam. His eyes twitched. A new, uncomfortable perplexity began to invade her.

"What do you want?" he asked, tone stern.

"You already know what I want. The truth."

"No interview."

The man looked at Adam then gave Lily a quick once-over. She stared back at him as he moved closer.

"You should know who you're going to marry," he warned.

"Leave her out of this," Adam growled low in his throat.

But Lily released his hand and stepped forward with one desire and that was to protect Adam from whatever this man had over him. "I'm with my family. I'd appreciate it if you'd leave."

"You don't know him."

She knew he was a big puzzle with damaged pieces, but nothing they couldn't put back together. Yeah, some pieces might bend, curl at the end or have to be squeezed back into their spots, not fit as they once were, but none of that mattered. No one was perfect, and she loved Adam with all of his perfect imperfections. Lily smiled. "I know enough."

But the man looked over her shoulder to Adam then whipped his head to the others watching like hawks. Even her brothers seemed guarded. Finally, Zander stepped forward, placed his hand over the stranger's shoulder.

"I don't really care about him." Zander motioned to Adam. "But my sister seems to care." He flashed the man a warning smile. "I suggest you leave now or if he chooses to rearrange your face, all of us might join him."

The man sneered. "Is that a threat?"

Zander shrugged casually. "Yeah. And don't worry, I always deliver on my threats."

Lily looked at Zander. He gave her a reassuring nod. Whatever reservation he had about her relationship with Adam had taken a back seat. He and the other imposing figures all ready to attack, except Rafa. He leaned back watching the whole scene unfolding.

"I can take care of my own business," Adam said to Zander.

"Yeah, I see that," her brother responded in a calm tone.

"Show is over," Adam announced. He pulled gently on her hand. "Come on, let's go home. See everyone in one hour."

They drove in silence to the house. From time to time she glanced over at Adam's profile. His face was set in a stony expression, completely shutting her off. Or at least trying to.

Once inside, Adam stripped out of his clothes and went straight to the shower. Lily dropped her purse on the floor, kicked off her sneakers and sat on the bed, listening to the sound of the water running. Her stomach spasmed for Adam. Another reminder behind his smile was a hurting heart, filled with torment.

Her phone buzzed. Lily fetched it from her purse and glanced at the text.

I'm still in love with you. Nate.

Frustrated, she blew out a breath and texted back.

Please Nate. Not now.

And let her body fall back on the bed with her eyes fixed on the ceiling. When the door opened and Adam stepped into the bedroom, she turned to look at him. He stood stark naked for a moment, then walked away to retrieve a pair of black boxer briefs and slipped them on.

Silence clung to the room.

"You're shutting me out again," she said into the silence.

"Not my intention." He came to stand at the side of the bed, eyes dark and personal. "Ask me the questions and I'll answer."

Lily brought herself to a sitting position. "Who was that man? What's his name?"

"Marcos Souza." Adam lowered himself to the bed and sat next to her.

"Why don't you give him the interview and move on?"

"It's my story, my past. I don't feel like sharing it with the world. My parents have two years of my life pretty much sealed. From age eight to ten. They wanted to give me a chance to create my own path without being judged."

She gripped his hand and held on. His gaze rested on their connection.

"I think," he started again, his voice thick, "the Internet states I was an orphan until the age of ten when I was adopted. I don't know for sure, I never really looked." His jaw clenched. "Souza is digging for that. He'll get what he's looking for soon enough."

"The accident with your birth father is not public?"

He turned and held her gaze. "It wasn't an accident, Liliana. I shot him. I took his life. I had no right to do that, no matter how much of an asshole he was."

She looked at his profile, so harsh and wounded. "You were eight and beaten down." From what she'd learned physically and mentally. "Eventually you have to take a deep breath and let it go. Sometime the way to do that is to face it head on." He taught her that lesson that night he found her crying.

No response.

"Anything else I need to know?" she asked into the echoing silence and tried not to think of worst-case scenarios. But then again, what could be worse than taking the life of your own father?

"Not really." He raked a hand through his wet hair. But there was an edge in his voice. "My father was taken to the hospital where he died of exsanguination. Severe blood loss," he explained. "My lawyer was able to convince the jury that I acted in self-defense." He shrugged. "So I walked. I was under psychiatric care for a while. Went to a few foster homes and eventually was adopted by my parents."

Lily let out a breath and tried to process everything she'd learned, but she was too physically and mentally exhausted. And sad. Too damn sad. "You've been through so much," she said with tears in her eyes. "Just too much."

"I survived."

He lay on the bed and pulled her into his arms. She cuddled against him and ran her fingers over his solid wall of male chest.

"And who is…" she paused, unable to remember the first part of the name the reporter mentioned. "Cooper."

"Pereira Cooper."

She nodded.

"My birth parents' surnames," he said thickly. "Maria de Lourdes Pereira and Timothy Cooper."

"Cooper is your last name."

He nodded. "Once upon a time I was Adam Pereira Cooper. My parents dropped them once I was adopted." He ran his hand over her arm. "How come you never asked about that?"

Her hands gracefully moved to his waist, slipped beneath his briefs gripped his virile masculinity. "Many reasons."

He waited.

Her entire body was now vibrating with need, but tried very hard to stay calm and give him the security and comfort he needed. Because those things were part of loving someone. "Because that's your past. Not who you are now."

"My past shaped me."

She tilted up and kissed his chiseled cheekbones. "Yes, a part of your story. A couple of chapters in your life." She lowered her lips to his chest where his heart beat. "Don't give it too much power."

"And this is all okay with you?" he asked. His hands slid to her hips and stayed there.

"What you went through as a child will never change how I feel about you. It's the man you've become who has a hold on me."

With a sweeping motion, Adam pinned her under him. He pulled her to him and kissed her with a hunger so strong it made her knees wobble. "I'm going to make love to you very slowly," he promised against her lips.

"Aren't we going to meet everyone?"

"They can wait."

And he kissed her with a hunger so strong, Lily was glad she was lying down; otherwise, her knees might have given out on her. A soft laughter rushed from the back of her throat, she wrapped her arms around his neck. "Is sex the gateway to get you to talk to me?"

He smiled, a very sexy smile filled with promises of things to come. "It works. No one loses."

27

"Every saint has a past, every sinner has a future."
Oscar Wilde

It turned out marathon sex with Lily was the cure for nightmares. After they returned from Vapor, they'd barely made it inside the house when she tore his shirt off. They didn't quite make it to the bedroom at the first go. He'd taken her on the floor and had the bruises on his knees to prove it.

That suited him fine. And Lily hadn't complained. One of the many things he loved about her. She was always ready to take a trip on the wild side as long as he was by her side. Once they caught their breaths, she dragged him to the bedroom, straddled him and made both of them climax so hard, Adam thought the earth shook. He loved that too.

Sometime in the night, they'd eventually collapsed in bed half-delirious with pleasure and completely satiated. He slept hard, and no dreams, at least not the kind that left him covered in sweat. In fact, he remembered nothing from the moment he kissed her goodnight.

Trusting, warm Lily had brought him peace. He loved that too.

Love. There was that word again. Lately, it had become synonymous with Lily. From the way she smiled, her touch, her resilience.

He'd known for a while his feelings ran deeper than their physical connection, but like any other man not looking to put his heart on the table, he fought. And it worked. At least until the moment he chose to walk down the Lily path naked and exposed too much of his heart, his mind, and what existed on the inside. He showed too much of himself; surprisingly, that was when he started to get it right. To think, only a week ago, she told him she wanted nothing but mad, passionate love. Slowly, but surely he'd given up control and surrendered to her wishes. And she'd become his deepest, most desperate desire.

She stirred and his arms automatically tightened, holding her close to his heart.

"Adam," she called his name, eyes still closed.

"Yeah."

"Did you sleep?"

"Yeah."

A smile touched her lips. "Good. I'm tired." The words were a slur of exhaustion.

"Then sleep."

"Hold me."

"I am."

He drew her naked body closer and she snuggled against him, still sleeping, breathing softly, cozily installed in his lair. Skin on skin. He glanced down at her body; his gaze rested on her stomach, and became overwhelmed with a sensation that went beyond anything he ever experienced. The fire in him that only she could ignite flared up. His first thought was to roll her on her back and spread her legs. He wanted to hear her cry out his name again and again, but damn it, there was no need to wake her up. Come to think of it, he'd been rather on the selfish side for beating her body so much. He'd make sure they took it easy today. No sex. Well, at least nothing rough, or hard as she often requested, and who was he not to oblige?

Adam grabbed the comforter and yanked it over them. He placed his free arm under his head and fixed his eyes on the ceiling while Lily's head rested on his chest, one of her legs slung over his Tonight was dinner with her family and his. That ought to be fun. Because he cared for the woman in his arms and knew deep down she'd want her pain in the ass brothers to get along with him. He made a silent vow to be at his best behavior.

During the football game and even at the bar, he'd caught Lily smiling a few times while he interacted with the big goofs. As long as Lily didn't expect him and the knuckleheads to break out into *Kumbaya,* the evening would be a success. To be fair, Zander and Max seemed to have warm up to him. Rafa, on the other hand, was still a fucker. His bad attitude made it easier for Adam to dislike him. But then again, he detected the feeling was mutual. A vision of his mother sitting across from him, giving him the now-Adam-behave stare down flashed before him. He smiled. How many times in his life had she whipped him into shape with only that look?

The morning slowly drifted. Adam lost track of how long he lay there with Lily in his arms. It wasn't until she stirred and mumbled, "I can stay in your arms forever" did he make any attempt to move, but even then, he stayed still until she broke their contact and sat by his side. She rubbed her eyes with the back of her hands.

"Do you feel sick?" He was constantly worried about her health, whether she was consuming enough food.

"Nope." She stretched.

Adam gaze rested on her perky breasts. "Stop doing that."

Her eyebrows squished together in confusion, then she realized his eyes were on her breasts. She laughed breathlessly. "Oh, I was stretching."

But the twinkle in her eyes told him she enjoyed torturing him. Well, two could play the game. He chafed his thumb over her dark pink areola. She immediately stopped laughing and moaned instead.

He lifted his weight enough for his lips to touch her stomach, circled his tongue over the tip of her navel ring then kissed the spot below. "Hey, little guy."

He felt her body freeze. "What are you doing?" she asked, her voice filled with emotion.

"I'm saying hello to our son."

Her fingers slid into his hair, giving him a shiver. "Or daughter," she added, her voice hoarse.

"It doesn't matter to me." He kissed her belly again, circled her waist and fell back on the bed, bringing her along with him. Her breasts crushed against his chest. "What time do you have to meet Minka today?" he asked, trying to figure out if they had time for a quickie.

"What time is it?"

He grabbed his phone on the nightstand. "Eleven."

She froze, jerked upright and leaped out of the bed, gloriously naked. "Shit. I'm going to be late. How did you let me sleep that late?"

There were a few reasons. He wanted her to rest, had no clue at what time she was supposed to meet with Minka, but most importantly, she had felt so damn good in his arms. "I like the feel of you against me."

She looked down into his face for a long moment.

Enjoying the view, he leaned back with his hands behind his head. "What?" He laughed, feeling light-headed and…Adam searched his brain for the appropriate word. Happy, he was happy.

She shook her head. "I'm going to shower." She stopped by the door and looked at him. She looked relaxed and happy. "Any nightmares?"

"No."

She smiled and disappeared into the shower. Adam lay there with his hands under his head, smiling for a few minutes. His phone beeped on the nightstand. Barely moving, he reached for it and answered his mother's call.

"Are you in front of a television?"

The panic in her voice cause his gut to tighten and his smile faded. "Do I need to be?"

"Does Liliana know everything?"

"Yes," he answered without a beat. There was nothing else to tell, so much so that at this point he didn't even care if Souza dug deep enough.

"What about her family?"

He froze. He never gave her family much thought about his violent past. *Shit.*

"Adam?"

He shook himself and rolled out of bed. "I'm here. What's on the news?"

"Souza found your trial. The shooting. It's in the news."

He closed his eyes momentarily. This meant Lily's parents and brothers were probably aware of everything. He swore. He didn't like being bamboozled or cornered. Not that his past was still that anchor holding him back, he was learning to let go with Lily, for Lily, for them. But fuck, even unexpected as the pregnancy was, everything that happened so far had been on his own terms. "I have to go."

"What do you need us to do?" his mother asked.

What his mother didn't say was *Do you want us to sue Souza's ass? We can find a way.*

"Nothing," he answered without a beat, no longer caring about Souza. His mind was on Lily and her family. They had to get to them and put everything on the table. "I have to go."

"Adam."

He paused.

"We love you."

"I know. I love you too. See you tonight."

For a moment he stood in the middle of the room, waiting for Lily to come out of the shower, contemplating his next move. His phone vibrated in his hand.

What do you want me to do?

He read Jason's text. Jason was the first to befriend him when he started coming to the Vineyard with his adoptive parents. He hadn't bought the chip Adam carried on his shoulder. Because of that the two had become friends since the age of ten. The following summer, he met Blake, Forrest, and Claire. Since then, they had become inseparable, family. They had each other's back.

I'm sure there's a law somewhere this asshole has violated. We will get him.

He glanced at Blake's text and would have chuckled if he wasn't too fucking riled up. The only law that was broken was exposure. Last time he checked, that wasn't a crime.

Surfing tomorrow? Whatever. I'm available.

Forrest was always up for an adrenaline rush.

Adam, Does Lily know all of this?

He could sense the shock in Claire's text. For some reason he and the boys had shielded her from his past. For no particular reason, except when he did open up and confessed, she hadn't been around. After that night, the topic was never discussed again.

Lily stepped into the bedroom wrapped in a towel, her hair slicked back. She took one look at him and stopped.

"We're going to Martha's Way to see your parents."

Her brows furrowed. "What's going on?"

Before Adam could answer, her phone chirped. She walked over to retrieve it, looked at the screen then back to Adam. "That's Rafa asking me to come to Martha's Way. Tell me what's going on."

"Apparently I made the news. I take it your brother caught my face plastered all over."

Lily exhaled a deep painful breath. He watched her type away on the phone then placed it back on the nightstand. She walked up to him and wrapped her arms around his neck. "We're in this together." She repeated the words he once said to her. "I'll get dressed while you shower."

Rafa's dark expression confirmed what Adam had told her. She studied Zander and Max. They surprisingly looked calm. Her parents were sitting holding each other's hands, their faces crammed with concern. She captured Adam's hand in hers.

"Mom, Dad."

Her parents glanced at her, then at Adam.

"How can you feel safe with him?" Rafa spat.

"Come on man, don't be a dick," Zander said, surprising Lily.

"Sorry," Max said to his parents, "but boys curse. So there's going to be a lot of cursing going on here."

"He's a murderer," Rafa continued.

"You're out of line, Rafa," their father said sternly.

"Adam was a child," her mother pointed out.

"Seriously, man." Zander shook his head.

"For Christ's sake, Rafa!" Lily's voice shook.

"Lily," Rafa warned, glaring at his sister.

"Liliana," Adam said, his tone telling her he had a handle on the situation.

Both men called to her with barely a glance. She squared her shoulders and stood firm. "I'm not a child," she said between clenched teeth and whipped her head back and forth between the two. "You," she glared at her brother. "Stop treating me like I'm a child." One finger hit Adam's wall of a chest. "And you stop treating me like I'm a fragile little thing. Haven't I proven to you that I'm not?"

Neither man spoke.

"I trust Adam with everything. My life, our baby's. Why are you so against our relationship?"

Rafa's eyes snapped around the room. "So you're all comfortable with her marrying this guy." He chuckled. "Well…"

Silence. The atmosphere saturated with disaster.

"It was self-defense," Adam's voice cut through the thick air in the room.

"Premeditated," Rafa scoffed.

Adam released her hand and buried them in the pockets of his sweats. "I didn't catch the news, but did it mention that my birth parents were both drug addicts?"

"It touched on that," Max responded.

In other words, Souza made Adam out to be the crazy kid. Adam fixed his eyes on Lily's parents. The expression on their faces silently telling him they were willing to listen. One of the many reasons she loved her parents. They taught her to always give everyone a chance and now they were demonstrating it as well.

Adam ran a hand through his hair and moved forward in the room. "My mother was a prostitute, my father was her pimp." He paused, giving them a chance to digest that little bit of information. "They were drug addicts, and abusive to one another and to me."

"That doesn't give you the right to take a life," Rafa said thickly.

"Rafa," Lily interrupted. "Adam is not responsible for Lea's death."

Another heavy silence filled the room. The air grew thicker with tension. Adam looked at Lily then Rafa. Her brother's face was a dark mask of anger.

"We can't bring her back," Lily said, sadness heavy in her voice. She knew the words hurt Rafa. Lea was a fragile topic that hadn't been touched or discussed since her unexpected death. She was all too familiar with her brother's pain of losing his wife. But as much as she wished she could take away the guilt, agony, it wouldn't bring Lea back.

"Your brother is right, Liliana." Adam's spectral voice interrupted her thoughts. "I was eight, and I made a mistake."

Rafa sneered. "It's bigger than a mistake."

"I can't edit or erase my past. I can only accept it. Liliana has helped me a great deal with that." He paused. Another wave of silence filled the room. All of the Serrano eyes stayed on him, waiting to hear his side of the story. "I was born an addict."

"*Dios mío*," her mother whispered.

"For eight years, violence and drugs were my normal," Adam continued. His gaze swept over each one of her brothers. "You're lucky to have never lived through that. You'll never know what's it's like to not want to come home because you may catch your mother with a needle up her arm, or a client walking out of the dingy house with his fly still open."

"Why did you shoot him?" Max asked.

"You need more reasons," Zander spat.

"I came home one day and found my mother on the floor dead with a needle in her arm, gun by her side. It's easy to give a reason or to hide behind the fact that I was eight, but..." he released Lily's hands and shoved his own into his pockets. "I became a product of my environment for a while. I was angry, tired of being abused. It wasn't until later did I find out that my father had held a gun to her head and tried to sell me off. As crazy and sick as she was, she refused to do it."

He walked over to where her parents sat. "I care a great deal for your daughter."

Lily watched her parents stand up. Her mother took his hand in hers. In her loving way, she touched his face. The gesture made Lily's heart squeeze. "We know you do. We wish you and Lily had told us everything."

"Me too," Adam answered thickly.

"Do you love her?" good ole Rafa asked, his gaze intensely fixed on Adam.

Because she'd learned so much about Adam in the last two weeks, Lily detected the muscles in his neck and shoulders tensed. Time seemed to have stopped, waiting for Adam to answer. Lily stood still, heart thundering.

Adam said nothing for a long moment. When he spoke, it was in a voice of breathtaking, ice-cold venom. "Love is a word used too much, too soon, and too carelessly."

Her heart jumped. But she dare not move. Rafa shook his head, gave Lily a long look, glanced at Adam, then back at his sister. "You asked why I'm so against your relationship and this is why. He doesn't love you. He doesn't know how to."

The words stabbed her in the gut. Pain as strong as one hundred daggers sank into her stomach. She met Adam's gaze and searched, pleaded for some indication that the last two weeks were not a figment of her imagination. Adam's jaw clenched. He stood rigid. Unwavering. And her heart dissolved to her toes.

"You're an asshole," she heard Max say to Rafa.

"Fuck off," Rafa replied.

She stood still in the room. Tears, large and profuse, flowed down her cheeks. All the faces around her blurred.

"Adam and Lily need time to talk. Let's give them that." Her father extended his hand to Adam and the two shook hands. "Our hearts tell us you're a good man. Thanks for coming to us today. It meant a lot." Reaching for her mother's hand, the two stopped to give her a hug then walked out of the room. Her brothers followed.

Once alone, they stood in silence for what felt like hours. Her eyes fixed on Adam's face.

"Let's go home."

Adam reached for her, but she took two small steps backward.

"Liliana."

In her heart of hearts, she knew he loved her. She'd seen it in his eyes on many occasions. Yet, he stood there in front of her parents and acted so cold. "I love you so much that it hurts my heart," she said, her voice breaking as she did so.

A frown fell upon his lips and she let out a soft bitter laugh. Her gut wrenched in pain for him, for her, and their baby. "I thought you loved me. I thought," she paused, fighting back the cascade of tears she met his gaze and let out a low bitter laugh. "I saw it in your eyes." Adam walked over to the large bay window. Gray clouds blanketed the earth. He turned his back to her, shoved his hands into his pockets and focused his gaze into nothingness.

"You're scared to love me, or at least to say it, because if you say it then it becomes real."

She waited for him to say something. Anything to prove her brother wrong and confirmed everything she thought she saw in him. He said nothing and the blow of defeat painfully clobbered her heart against the cage of her ribs.

"I can't settle, Adam." She took a deep breath to stop herself from breaking down again. "I love you too much to ever give you just a portion of me. It's all or nothing."

From the sheltered corner where he stood, Adam turned to meet her gaze. His expression told her once again he had shut down. With her emotions strangling her whole, she dragged herself away from the scene, with a broken heart and a battered soul.

28

"When you meet the one who changes the way your heart beats, dance with them to that rhythm for as long as the song last."
Kirk Diedrich

*L*ily adjusted the shoulder of the haven blue dress. She studied her reflection in the mirror; the fluid cut fit her perfectly. She blew out a breath and strands of her bangs danced away from her eyes.

"Ready?" Minka whispered in her ear.

She smiled. "Yes."

The door to Martha's Way that lead to the acres of land swung open and she stepped into the sunny afternoon. A hush settled over the crowd. With slow strides, she walked down the aisle. Her parents blew her a kiss, her brothers smiled. She caught sight of Adam's parents sitting a few rows over and they smiled warmly at her.

It was early October. The leaves, having lost their green hue, seemed to be a mirror for the sun that day as both burned a delicious shade of orange. A sunny day with a few puffy, white clouds. A perfect day for Minka and Jason's wedding.

Claire and Keely had already walked down the aisle and were now standing on the opposite side of Jason and his groomsmen. Blake blew a kiss across to Keely. Forrest and Claire made brief eye contact then eventually broke the connection. She peeked at Jason. He stood under the oak tree, strong and stunning in the navy shawl-collar Italian wool tuxedo with his three best friends at his side, patiently waiting for his bride. Then her eyes drifted to Adam. His face was carved in a granite expression. He returned her gaze, sending a startling jolt through her limbs. She hadn't seen him since the whole ordeal with her parents; that was two days ago. He even skipped the rehearsal dinner. Her immediate reaction had been to go to him and made sure he was okay, but she sucked it up and stayed away.

She took her spot by Keely. Minka's sister took her hand in hers and gave it a small squeeze. Lily smiled, appreciating the warm gesture. They all knew she and Adam were on the fence.

A pleasant breeze rustled in the surrounding shrubs. The smell of fresh cut flowers filled the air. Claire stepped forward to the microphone and her plangent voice drifted through the crowd as she sang the lyrics to *I Feel That Too* by Jesse Baylin. Guests and family members came to their feet, all heads turned to face the far end of the walk to greet the bride. Down the aisle, Minka stood in the beautiful embroidered gown. She held a bouquet mixed with rich reds, fiery oranges, and beautiful yellow fresh flowers. The combination captured the exquisite fall hues. Her father held her left arm and smiled at her as they reached the bottom step. The lighter-than-air floor length veil border of dainty crystals subtly flashed as the wind gently batted at the ends of her dress.

When Minka and her father reached the bottom step, her father leaned and placed a kiss on his daughter's cheek then brushed his eyes. He shook Jason's hand, let out a breath and placed Minka's hand in Jason's. Minka's father was visibly shaken. Lily understood and shared the sentiment. Minka was her best friend, the sister she never had.

Claire's voice faded, the clergyman stepped forward and so did Jason and Minka. Lily watched. Her eyes became moist; she didn't care to brush them away. She caught the faint sound of Keely and Claire's sniffles and knew they were all in the moment just as she was.

"Family and honored guests, thank you for coming to witness the beautiful union of Jason Montgomery and Minka Greene," the clergyman's voice carried over the crowd.

Lily steadied her breath and tried to compose herself, but Adam's intense gaze drew her back to him. His eyes lowered to her left hand and she realized his gaze was fixed on the engagement ring she was absently rolling with her thumb. When he looked at her again, a hint of a smile teased his lips.

Her body reacted to him as always, but it was more than that. Her mind was aching for him too. *I need you to love me.* Shaking her head, she looked away, but not fast enough to miss the way his brows creased.

Lily watched the couple exchange rings. "By the power vested unto me I now proclaim you husband and wife." Everyone came to their feet. A wave of applause echoed through the crowd. "You may now kiss—"

The word bride was never spoken. Jason wrapped one arm around Minka's waist and pulled her to him. Their lips sought one another and they kissed passionately to a thunderous standing ovation.

Arms linked, Jason and Minka, with identical smiles on their faces, walked down the aisle as husband and wife for the first time in their lives. Blake and Keely held hands. Claire slipped one arm in the crook of Forrest's. They stopped near the end of the walk, forming the start of the receiving line.

Lily stood still for a beat, her body tensed and very aware of Adam as he came to stand next to her. He reached out with arm extended. She bit her lower lip with hesitation.

"Liliana."

"I can't touch you..."

He stared at her, brow arched. "Why?" he asked in a husky voice.

"Because I'll give in," she confessed. "But I need to be..."

"Stubborn," he finished.

She shook her head. "It's more than that, Adam."

Adam leaned into her a little bit, his lips brushing her ear. "I miss you."

A whimper slipped through her lips. Her body would have collapsed had Adam not place his hand on her lower back for stability.

"Adam—" she started in a tortured tone.

"Sshh...later. Right now, it's about Jason and Minka." He gave her a gentle shove ahead of him. His hand stayed on her lower back until they reached their friends.

Shortly after family and guests filed down, pausing for hugs and kisses and congratulating the married couple.

---

*A*dam watched Lily take center stage with microphone in hand, ready to make the traditional Maid-of-Honor speech. Her bangs swept to the side, giving everyone full access to her face. Her eyes were bright. Her lips, the color of a red rose, smiled and lightened the room. She looked happy with no care in the world. This was the Lily he'd known for the last year, always ready to face the world head-on. She didn't dwell on obstacles, even if the obstacle was him. His heart clenched at the sight of her, just as it had done earlier when he watched her walked down the aisle. She made him feel way too fucking much. He lowered his gaze to the aged scotch in front of him, brought the glass to his mouth and let alcohol burn his insides.

"Life is about risk. Love is risky. Often time it leaves us heart-broken and empty." Her voice flowed like a river in the room, grabbing everyone's attention. "Common sense tells us not to expose so much of who we are to another person. Our insecurities, fear, wounds, and even what makes us happy. Because really then we become exposed, naked." She lets out a little chuckle. "But then love tends to happen. Usually we stumble upon it. And everyone knows falling in love is a crazy roller-coaster ride."

Heads nodded in agreement. Voices echoed her sentiment. Adam continued to look on.

"When we fall in love, our heads tell us we're going to die." She paused, glanced at Jason and Minka and smiled. "But our hearts tell us that it's okay to become less guarded and to trust because we can fly."

She absently touched her stomach and Adam's heart bumped against his ribs.

"I've watched this beautiful couple fall and learn to fly together. Neither was looking for love, but the best things in life tend to happen unexpectedly." She smiled. "I." She paused, waved a hand toward the crowded room. "We celebrate your love. Your trust in each other. Kiss often, and don't ever stop showing or telling each other the love you carry in your heart. I love you both."

Applause exploded in the room. Adam's blood rushed through his head. Once upon a time he used to not feel anything deep for the female gender. Lily had managed to change that. She got to him, big time.

As she walked back to her table, she looked in his direction and their gazes collided. She paused, studying him for an exceedingly long minute, then walked back to her table and joined her family. They sat distance away facing each other but her attention now belonged to everyone but him. Max placed an arm over her shoulder and pulled her to his side. The two exchange words, Lily smiled and reached for her purse. She pulled out her phone, frowned and excused herself from the table.

Adam counted to twenty, pushed his chair back and left the room.

"Stop texting or calling me."

Adam slowed his steps at the sound of Lily. The pitch of her voice rose slightly with anger and frustration. She stood in the garden of Martha's Way, under the smeared autumn red sky, with her back to the door. He had followed her with the intention to talk and make her understand they didn't need damn words to express anything between them. Now he stood stiff, listening to her talking to whoever was on the other end. "You had your chance, Nate," she continued after a slight pause.

Nate. Her fucking ex-cheating fiancé. Adam stepped closer and leaned against the doorway. She stood in the garden with her back to him, one hand holding the mobile phone to her ear, the other rubbing her bare arm. He fought the urge to go to her and warm her with his heat.

"No, I'm not angry at you. Not anymore. I haven't been for a long time." She paused again, giving the jerk a chance to say whatever he needed to say. From what Adam gathered, the asshole was trying to get her back. Well, too bad. She was unavailable.

"You're my past, Nate, not my future." Another pause, this one a little longer. She gave her body a little shake under the cool breeze. "I'm pregnant." She exhaled. "And no, it's not rebound sex. I'm in love." Her voice trembled on the words, tearing Adam's inside. Another pause. "Yes, that mad, crazy love I've always wanted." She paused again. Adam imagined the cheating bastard was probably measuring the love she once had for him. "I let you go, Nate, a long time ago. Now it's your turn. Goodbye." She disconnected the call and stood there for a beat.

Adam remained by the doorway, fighting the urge to throw her over his shoulder and take her back home where she belonged.

"You can come out now," she said over her shoulder.

He closed the space between them and pressed up against her back. "I wasn't eavesdropping." His hands ran up and down her arms and she shook a little from his touch.

"What do you want, Adam?"

"You," he answered without a beat. He'd missed her terribly the last two days. Everywhere he turned, Lily's face was there. Her smile, her laughter.

She whirled around to face him, their faces inches away. Her heart-baring eyes searched his. "For sex."

The sharp-edged words cut him. He deserved her venom in a way. His hands fell to his side and he took a step back. "You know it's more than that."

There was a beat of silence, as if she was processing the weight of his words. "Where were you last night? You didn't come to rehearsal dinner."

"I flew to Italy Thursday after we talked to your family."

Another silence.

He shoved his hands into his pockets. "I had to do some damage control after Souza's piece, so I gave an interview to a local station there. It will be aired in a couple of days."

"When did you come back?"

"Around two this morning."

"How do you feel? I mean, are you okay?"

The concern in her voice made his heart clench. He stroked a finger along her cheekbone, then tucked a loose strand of hair behind her ear for the sheer pleasure of touching her. "I'm fine." He leaned in. "I want you home with me."

She stepped out of his grasp and walked in silence. She stopped next to various shades of Chrysanthemum plants. From the distance she studied him. "I saw it in your eyes that night. I'll never forget that."

"Liliana."

She held up a hand. "You never want to say it, do you?"

Adam released a deep breath. And she let out a soft chuckle.

"I can't, Adam. As much as I want you and me, I can't."

Pain poured out in her voice like a river. And it hurt because he didn't want to be the reason for her heartache. He took a step closer. She took a step back. An overwhelming silence dominated the space between them. She was a woman who needed to hear those words. She believed in them. Everything in her life was about love. Her family, her friends, Even her damn brothers.

"I see it in your eyes," she repeated. "I feel it when you hold me."

"Isn't that enough?"

She smiled, a sad smile. "I wish it was, but you see I never want to have doubts. I have no problem telling the world how I feel about you." She held his gaze. "I need the same from you." She shook her head. "And you're not there, Adam. I want it all. I'm greedy like that."

Another long awkward silence fell between them. The autumn breeze filled the trees with a rustling murmur and swept the dried, crispy leaves across his path. Lily shivered, let out a deep breath, then walked past him into the warmth of the inn.

Hours later, well after the speech, toast, and all the things that newlyweds did to celebrate their love, Adam loosened his tie, sat back and watched Lily dance her ass off on the floor doing the conga line.

She moved as if she was connecting to the song, swaying her sexy curves left and right, as the rhythm carried her feet across the dance floor. One of Jason's friends Adam had met and actually liked until now, jumped behind her and held on to her waist like it was his lifeline. Lily turned, made eye contact with the bastard and laughed. Adam winced. This was going to be a long fucking night.

Since their conversation in the garden, she'd gone out of her way to avoid him, and it was driving him nuts. He downed the last drop of the scotch in front of him, and pushed his chair back. What was that, his third now? He couldn't remember. The alcohol wasn't doing its job, he wasn't numb.

He glanced at the dance floor again, the music switched to *Moves like Jagger* by Christina Aguilera and Adam Levine. Lily kept on dancing. That same asshole wrapped his hand around her waist and pulled her against him close enough to feel his junk. She turned to face the asshole, placed a gentle but firm hand on his shoulder and put some distance between them, setting some boundary.

Too fucking late. Adam removed his jacket and slung it over the back of the chair. He rolled up his sleeves. The fucker now had his hand on her lower back. That same spot he'd kissed many times in the last year. The bastard said something to her and she laughed again. Yeah, someone needed to wipe that smirk off this guy's pretty face. As for Lily, evidently she'd forgotten they were still engaged. She was still wearing the damn ring, for Christ's sake. Total disrespect.

Adam paddled through the crowd and headed straight toward Miss Happy Feet and Sir Touch-A-Lot. Halfway there, he passed his parents and Lily's parents dancing and laughing. Lily's father was doing some fancy dance move with his mother while his father and her mother applauded. *One big, fucking happy family.*

"Adam, darling," his mother called after him, breathless.

He stopped, gaze on Lily. The dude was still trying to cop a feel.

"Lily's parents are wonderful." His mother continued smiling. "We are going to have dinner with them next time we're in New York."

"Great," he said, not really caring his voice showed he had no desire to hold a conversation with his parents and in-laws at this time.

As the music switched to *Cupid Shuffle* by CUPID, the asshole spun Lily so she ended right in front of him. Adam swore under his breath. He spotted her brothers, dancing away like major goofballs. Neither one tried to step in and stopped this asshole from manhandling their sister.

"What's wrong, son?" His father followed his gaze and chuckled. He was already moving to the right, to the left. Adam stepped away to avoid being kicked.

"I have to go." He kept moving.

The "Cupid Shuffle" was in full swing. Adam dipped, leaned back once or twice to avoid crashing into a dancer or two as he crossed the dance floor. Jason, Blake, and their wives were leading the whole mess. He shook his head in dismay. Some songs paired with a specific wedding dance should be prohibited at weddings. The "Cupid Shuffle" topped the list.

He reached Lily just as she took two steps to the left and crashed right into the wall of his chest. Her eyes widened and her lips formed into an *O*. He caught her wrist and started to drag her off the dance floor. Adam secretly admitted that was very caveman-like, but he didn't care.

"What are you doing?" She planted her feet firm on the floor, her lips pressed into a thin, angry line.

"I'm taking you away from sticky fingers."

Sir Touch-A-Lot walked up a little too close to Lily. Adam's shoulder accidentally checked him. He would have liked to pop him too, but this was one of his closest friends' wedding after all. So he played nice. Sort of.

"Hey man, we're dancing," Sir Touch-A-Lot said.

Adam pinned him with a look. "That's my fiancée you've been groping the whole night. She's also very pregnant with our child." The asshole looked at Lily for confirmation. She grinned. Asshole backed off. Adam gestured her to the empty table. "Come on."

"Why are we going there?"

"To talk."

"I'm not walking off this dance floor." She stood firm, hands on hips, challenging him. "Unless you're ready to tell me you're in love with me." She held his gaze. "Are you?"

Adam raked a hand through his hair.

"I thought so." She smiled at him.

He couldn't read her. The vulnerability he caught earlier was now gone. A server approached them with one flute in the tray. Lily snagged it and gulped it down and thanked the server by using his first name. Bryan, the handsome waiter, beamed at her. Everything now made sense. She was drunk, and pregnant with his child. Adam silently counted to one hundred very quickly to stop his head from blowing off.

"Are you drunk?" He watched her frown and realized his voice sounded more accusatory than he intended.

"This was seltzer water. See?" She tip-toed close to his face and blew warm, minty breath on his face. No trace of alcohol and the move was erotic as hell. "Geez, Adam, I tend to be on the responsible side, in case you haven't noticed."

Oh man, she made him feel like an asshole for doubting her. He shoved his hands in his pockets. "I'm sorry, Liliana. You just look like you're having a good time."

"Actually, I am, and I don't need to be drunk to have fun. Don't you know me at all?"

Her honey eyes shot him a you're-an-idiot kind of look. Since he had nothing of substance to say, he stayed quiet. To his surprise, she slung her arms around his neck and pressed against him.

"This is the only way you get to talk or touch me. So dance."

He put his hands on her hips. "You're still my fiancée."

Something crossed her face but once again, it was quickly masked. The mood of the music changed to something slower. Adam wrapped his arms around her. Her chest rose against him. Sparks flying, emotions building.

"This is our first dance," she said. Her face buried in his neck so deep that her lips brushed against his skin.

He was sure they'd danced before but at the moment with her so close, her scent filling his lungs with every breath he took, his mind became fuzzy. More and more of her became a part of him. He couldn't think straight. "Is it?"

"It is," she breathed on his neck.

His gut tightened. How had he never danced with her before? Adam jerked her closer, and pressed his lips to her temple. "Then no more talk. We dance."

Lily could feel his hands touching her waist as the rhythm of the song played. Her mind in tune with his hot breath against her neck, he stepped forward and back, she followed. The tempo of their bodies was as trance inducing as the moist, intoxicating air their sensual bodies emitted toward one another.

"Do you feel that?" he asked, his voice deep and husky.

This was not merely a dance. His body firmly pressed against hers was communicating his deepest feelings, wordlessly telling her he loved her. She nodded, rested her head on his shoulder and closed her eyes, losing herself to the intense heat that radiated between them. At that moment, she became oblivious of the world around them and lost herself in Adam's arms. They continued to move like that until Lily lost track of where her body stopped and where Adam's began.

"Liliana."

"Hmm."

"The music stopped."

Still dazed, she slowly opened her eyes. They stood on the dance floor alone with Adam's arms still wrapped around her. She caught the amused stares of Keely and Claire. Lily squeezed her eyes shut. Once again, she'd lost herself under the Adam spell. The man was addictive.

She sighed and stepped away from him in an attempt to minimize their body heat, but he jerked her back up to his chest. Before she could say anything, he tilted his head down and kissed her, sending a shiver down her spine.

"I need you home with me," he said, gravelly against her lips. "You belong there. You're everywhere."

She looked up into his face, emotions on full display "I was only there for two weeks."

He smiled. "You've been there for over a year."

Lily's heart kicked hard. The words were referencing to his heart as well. She read the need in his voice and as always it consumed her.

"Get a room and get off the dance floor," Jason grunted with Minka in his arms. "I want to dance with my wife."

Minka gave her an apologetic look, then wrapped her arms around Jason's neck, and kissed her husband firm on the lips. Lily spotted her parents sharing a table with Adam's. Both husbands had their arms casually slung on the back of their wives' chairs. Keely was in Blake's arms against a corner wall, kissing. She looked at Adam. "I want what they have. I'm not jealous of their love, but I want a chance to have my own HEA."

The slightest frown touched his face.

She smiled. "Happily ever after. And part of that is to be able to shout to the world your love for them."

"You already know how I feel."

The dance floor was almost filled now. Lily took a step closer to Adam to make room and not get trampled. He caught her wrist and hauled her away from the crowd. In silence, she followed him outside the room, down the hall. She peeked at her table and met Rafa's gaze, disappointment in his eyes. Once alone, Adam gently pressed her against the wall, stepped into her, and cupped her face, tilting it up to his.

Lily's lips parted voluntarily, waiting. Their gazes met for a beat then Adam slanted his head and kissed her, rocking her world into total chaos. When he stepped back, her hand automatically went to her lips. "You're trying to break me down."

He smiled and took her hand in his. "Let's go home."

She closed her eyes, fighting back the temptation to throw it all to hell and go with Adam. "I can't."

Lily waited for him to push a little more, just a little bit more and she might give in. But he didn't.

"You know where I'll be, Liliana. Come to me if you want." He ran the pad of his thumb over her cheek then he was gone.

She wasn't sure how long she stayed with her back pinned against the wall, thoughts of everything she had with Adam racing through her head. Part of her wanted to go to him, that part was her heart. But common sense, the logical part, told her she'd never be happy if she settled.

Lily exhaled. She needed air—cool, crisp air to clear her mind. She peeled her body from the wall and opened the door to the garden and stopped. There in front of her, Claire walked up to Forrest and kissed him with so much passion that it even took Lily's breath away. Even in the coolness of the night, heat seared between them as Forrest enveloped Claire in his arms, deepening the kiss. The air between them filled with hunger and yearning.

Talk about passion.

"I'm all grown up now. I'm no longer the snot-nosed girl who followed you everywhere," Claire said once they finally stopped for air.

"I've noticed, Claire. I've always noticed."

"Then what's the problem?" Claire continued.

He released his hold of her and gently fingered a few strands of her hair. "You're temporary," he said in a husky voice. "I don't want temporary."

There was a long excruciating silence between them. Then Forrest stepped back and started toward the large door. He stopped when he spotted Lily and smiled at her. She smiled back, aching for him, for Claire.

"Are you all right?" he asked Lily, concern now replaced the dark mask of emotions on his face.

"Yes. I just needed some air."

"All right. I'll be inside." Then he disappeared without looking back at Claire.

Lily walked over to her friend. Claire gave her a wry smile.

"You're okay?"

Claire nodded, her gaze fixed ahead into the night. "You?"

"I'll be fine."

"You're still wearing his ring."

Lily glanced at the diamond around her finger, her heart burned with hurt. "I'll return it."

"He loves you, you know."

In her heart of hearts she knew that. "Just not enough."

29

"Sometimes I'm terrified of my heart; of its constant hunger for whatever it is it wants. The way it stops and starts."
Edgar Allen Poe

*H*eart pinched in her chest, Lily turned off the ignition of Rafa's Range Rover and wondered what the hell she was doing in the middle of the night in Adam's driveway. Oh, yeah, to return the ring. She looked at the screen of her phone. During the drive, she played the scene over and over in her head. She'd call him, actually text him and let him know the ring, secure in its little black box, was at his doorstep.

The night stretched before her like an endless black hole. Now she sat in the car, examining all the cracks in her perfectly laid plan.

What if he failed to read her text?

Adam was due to leave for Russia first thing in the morning. Which meant the ring, the very expensive ring, might get stolen if left outside.

Riiight. This was Martha's Vineyard and Adam lived in Chilmark for Pete's sake, a town with a population of less than a thousand people. People were known to sleep with their doors unlocked, and windows wide open. Chances of anyone stealing the ring were almost zilch, but nothing was a hundred percent. Prudent was always best practice. She peeked at the ring again, still on her finger. Just to be safe, she'd better hand it to him herself and then walk away.

She stepped out of the car, phone in hand, ready to announce her arrival. The door opened, Adam appeared in another one of his lounging around the house sweats, bare chest with a drink in hand. She froze in her track.

"I wondered how long you were going to stay in there."

His voice sounded husky, laced with whatever concoction he was drinking. It warmed her body. "What's in that glass?"

He lifted the glass to his mouth and took a sip. "Scotch."

She should have known. Scotch was his preferred poison.

One long finger crooked at her direction. "Come closer."

His voice was dangerously low and sexy as hell. Liliana had been in situations where Adam had been slightly drunk before and at times both had been tipsy. Those nights always ended with an all-nighter until her body ached. Just the thought made that delicate spot between her thighs tremble. And she so didn't want to go there. Well, maybe one more time. She shook the temptation out of her head. She needed to be strong and maintain a firm grip of her treacherous heart. She stepped closer.

"Are you drunk?"

He let out a low laugh. "No."

Lily had a feeling it wasn't for a lack of trying.

He looked at her, his eyes twinkled and his mouth smirked in this smile that made Lily know he was thinking something. And whatever it was probably meant trouble for her.

"Come inside, Liliana, it's a cool night."

"I shouldn't."

"Then why did you come to me?"

Good question. Oh yes, to return that beautiful engagement ring he'd given her. She almost forgot. She lowered her gaze to her finger then at Adam. "To return..." But she hesitated and he took note of that.

His free hand pushed the door wide. "Come inside."

"I shouldn't," she repeated, this time in a less convincing tone.

"Yeah, you should." His free hand pulled her gently inside the house. He kicked the door closed, and finished the last drop of his scotch before setting the cup on a nearby table. For a beat neither spoke, the air crackled with desire. A yearning that Lily knew no matter how hard she tried, she'd never get over.

"The ring," she breathed, but couldn't finish since her throat was tight with emotion.

He stepped closer and erased whatever space left between them, crowding her. Holding her gaze, Adam slid his hand around the nape of her neck and pulled her to him. Caught in the trance, her eyes stayed on his as he lowered his mouth to hers, oh so close but not quite touching. "The ring is yours, Liliana, forever."

Then he kissed her and the reason she found herself at Adam's doorstep slipped out of her mind. Things went out of control from there. His hands were on her, everywhere, blending them together.

Her clothes were removed quickly, her bra, then her panties, leaving her in a pair of wild copper ballet flats. She kicked them off and reached for Adam, desperately needing to feel his skin on hers. "I came here to say goodbye."

His gaze lowered to her breasts pressed against his chest. "Never goodbye, Liliana, we are forever linked." He smiled then sucked on her bottom lip. "Besides, this is much better."

With one quick motion, he swept her in his arms and carried her up the stairs into his bedroom. His lips leaving warm trail of kisses on her neck, her shoulder, and when his mouth found one of her breasts and ran his tongue over her hardened nipple, she cried out.

They tumbled on the bed, seeking each other out like wild creatures. Hands everywhere, their shadows shifted and she rolled over him, straddling him. She kissed him then, his face, mouth, and throat. Any piece of flesh she could find. It was a hungry kiss, restless and desperate. Her heart ached and wanted at the same time with an urgency she couldn't control even if she tried.

"Your pants," she panted against his lips, "off." Her fingers were already working on the waist of his sweats. His hands brushed hers aside as he worked off their last barrier until he kicked them off. She felt him grab his length and ran the tip of his erection against her entrance.

"Tell me this is where you want to be, Liliana."

Their eyes met, his looked wild, reflecting the hungry desire she felt inside. "Yes."

He rubbed against her again. "Tell me."

Dominated by the hunger inside her, she stubbornly tried to lower herself to his length but his hands clutched her hips and held her still, silently demanding she answer. "I want."

His head lifted and his mouth found one of her breasts. He sucked it between his teeth. "Me."

Oh, God yes. Forever. "You."

He let out a low laugh, satisfied with her answer. Then he was inside her. She cried out at the firm, smooth entry. In typical Adam form he took control then, holding her hips as he thrust up into her. "This is where you belong, Liliana, always."

He reared up, held her against him and rolled them over and pinned her under him. And then he was giving her what she craved. He pummeled inside her, expanding her walls with brutal strength and an urgency she knew wasn't his style.

Fast. God, yes. She wanted fast.

"You're so fucking delicious," he murmured and crushed his mouth to hers.

Madness took over then. Adam used his teeth, tongue and lips to pleasure her. Common sense tried to sneak back and reminded her she was here to officially break things off and say goodbye, but she quickly buried all logical thoughts and lost herself to Adam, to their wild animal sex, until her system exploded.

---

*E*yes closed, Adam reached over and pressed the snooze button on his cell phone's alarm. Ten more minutes with Lily before leaving for his flight. He rolled over, reached for her, and was greeted by emptiness. He opened his eyes and stared at the unoccupied space.

He listened for the water running in the shower, nothing. His gut tightened.

His immediate reaction was to shut down. His body didn't know how to react. Adam fell back on his side of the bed, scrubbed a hand over his face. For years he suffered with insomnia and the one night he shouldn't have slept, he managed to sleep so hard that he didn't even know when she walked out of his house. A bad feeling boiled in his stomach. *Shit.* He shifted his weight and when he was unable to get comfortable, he sat up.

Adam reached for his phone and his eyes landed on the engagement ring he'd slipped on her finger. Yeah, this was bad. Rubbing the back of his neck, he picked up the ring and rolled it between his fingers. He sat silently, a searing pain shot through his heart.

She wanted love, the whole idea of love. He should have known she would never settle for less. He was an idiot for thinking he'd won that battle.

A deep sense of numbness hit the pit of his stomach, catapulting him. Last night she came over with the intent to break things off, somehow he'd managed to sway her decision, at least delayed it. He'd thought he succeeded in convincing her. In the end, she still walked away. He'd overestimated their connection and underestimated her strength.

He was an idiot.

After a beat, he carefully placed the ring back on the nightstand, cracked his knuckles and rose to his feet. He had a commitment in Russia; sitting in his room wasn't going to take care of that. A nice warm shower would clear his mind. But halfway towards the bathroom, he stopped and hurtled to his phone. He tapped the name of the airline on his contact list and pressed the dial button. Minutes later, his flight was moved to the early afternoon, which meant he'd arrive in Russia with enough time to go straight to the track. The good news, now he had time to stop at Martha's Way for the brunch Jason and Minka were hosting before leaving for their honeymoon. He knew Lily would be there. She wasn't due to leave the island until later in the afternoon.

Two hours later, Adam walked into the rustic atmosphere of the smaller dining area of Martha's Way. Fresh grilled breakfast flatbread woke up his palate. He ignored the vibration of his empty stomach and scanned the room. He spotted Forrest and Charles Montgomery standing with a glass of bloody Mary in their hands, talking casually. Everyone was in attendance but one. Lily was nowhere to be seen.

Not too far of a distance away, Minka waved at him, said something to Jason then came to Adam.

"I thought you were leaving for Russia."

"I changed my flight." *Because I needed to see her and make things right.* "Where's Liliana?"

A sad smile touched Minka's lips. "She caught the first ferry out this morning." She reached into her purse and produced a fuchsia envelope with his name written on it. "She left this for you."

Adam took the envelope. "She knew I'd come after her."

Minka touched his shoulder. "I asked her to stay but she wouldn't." With another small smile, she walked back to her table and sat by Jason.

Envelope in hand, Adam slipped out of the room. He'd stop by later and make small talk. Right now he needed to read her note. He pushed the door and walked into the garden and carefully opened the envelope and read the handwritten note.

Adam,

I can't remember the last time I walked away from something or someone in my life. I wanted us to work so badly that I convinced myself I saw things that you don't feel. You see, my heart got the best of me for a while. In reality, the heart cannot, should not govern over logic. It's not the wisest tool, therefore, should not control every decision or everything we feel.

I hate to admit Rafa was partially right. You might have dealt with your past in order for us to have a future, but not enough for you to love me. Your birth parents relationship still weighs heavily on how you view love. The funny thing is you are surrounded by love. Your parents, your friends. Me.

Today, I say goodbye. It breaks my heart to do so because I love you and everything that you are. But I need for your feelings to mirror mine. Oh, you care, and love me even, but not enough.

. . . Always,

Liliana

P.S. You are right. We are forever linked. I'll let you know when our baby is born. Goodbye Adam. I love you.

Heart thudding in his chest, Adam carefully folded the note and buried it in his pants pocket. She thought he didn't love her enough. That's where she was wrong. He loved her too much, so much that it scared the shit out of him. Just thinking about it made him shudder from his feet to his head.

30

In all the world, there is no love for you, like mine."
Maya Angelou

Lily stood in her condo and waited for that wonderful feeling that always washed over her whenever she returned home after a long time away. Two days since she returned home, the feeling of home sweet home hadn't come. Instead, she ached. Her body and mind yearned for Adam. His face, smile, and touch haunted her. During the night she reached for him, only to find an empty space. Twice today in class, she slipped and called two little boys Adam. They looked at her as if she was crazy.

Absently, she placed her messenger bag on the living room sofa. She had papers to grade and assignments to prepare. Enough to occupy her mind for the next few hours. As she made her way to the kitchen, her phone buzzed. She reached in her bag and read Claire's message.

Adam's interview will be on tonight.
Check it out. Hugs.

She quickly responded to the text and went to the kitchen. It was also the night of his final race for the year. She'd set her DVR to record it, but she knew she'd be wide awake. The DVR was a just in case.

"Food. We need food," she said to her belly and ran a hand over her shirt. Officially nine weeks pregnant, and due for her next doctor visit tomorrow.

Aside from a sad, aching heart, she felt great. She couldn't blame her lack of energy on the pregnancy, nope. It was all due to a broken heart. She stared down at her naked finger, swallowed away the pain, and tried to focus her attention on her long list of to dos.

Hours later, she graded the last paper and was getting ready to start working on next week's class assignment when the sound of the doorbell startled her. She made her way down the stairs and looked through the peephole. Rafa. The two had not spoken much since the big fiasco at Martha's Way. Lily had told herself, they needed time. She opened the door.

"Hey," Rafa greeted and walked past her.

Lily closed the door and followed. In her living room, they stood facing each other. She'd hurt him by bringing up Lea and she hadn't meant to, but she was hurting, desperate.

"I'm sorry about Adam," he said. "I went too far, but something about him I didn't trust."

She walked over to the sofa and sat down. "You didn't trust me," she corrected. "You didn't trust me to make my own decision after Nate."

"I didn't want you to get hurt."

"You went about that the wrong way."

He let out a breath. "I know, and I'm sorry for that." He sat next to her. "Will you forgive me?"

It wasn't often big brothers apologized to their little sister. The best thing for her to do of course was to torture him, make him grovel, make him sweat. But a part of being the best little sister in the whole world was to know when to let go, forgive, and recognize, because of her brothers, she'd always have a friend. "I'm sorry I brought up Lea."

"It's okay."

But everything in the tone of his voice told Lily the Lea topic was still in the do-not-touch file. "You're leaving again," she noted. Her brother had been running away for the past year.

He nodded. "At the end of the week, I'm going to Haiti for a few months to help engineer their water supply. Four years after Sandy, the devastation is still grave."

She could have told her brother he didn't need to travel for months out of the year to help. Instead, she pulled up against him and put her head on his shoulder. "I love you."

He chuckled. "Yeah, I love you too."

After a comfortable silence passed between them, Lily reached for the remote and turned the channel to the major network Claire had mentioned Adam's interview would be aired.

"What's on TV?" Rafa asked.

She didn't need to answer, Adam's face appeared on the screen and her heart skipped at the sight of him. His face carved in stone and everything about his vibe was saying, *I'm pissed off.*

"When are you marrying him?"

"I'm not," she answered, eyes glued to the television screen.

Rafa reached for her left hand. "Did you throw that one in the ocean too?"

She pulled her hand away and managed a chuckle. See, that was why she loved her brothers. They always managed to make her laugh, broken heart and all. "I returned it."

"And he let you go?" he asked, surprise in his voice.

"Well, I snuck out while he was sleeping."

"Coward."

"No, it's knowing if I didn't do that I'd never be able to walk away."

He slid her a look. "He does love you."

She chuckled. "Oh, now you tell me." Rafa laughed. A rich sound of easy laughter that reminded them things were once again okay between them. A deep, masculine voice announced Adam Aquilani was here to set the record straight about his past and no questions were off the table.

"Sshh, Adam is getting ready to talk."

"He's not a bad guy, sis. He deserves you. I just don't like his arrogance."

"Because you should be the only arrogant alpha around."

He laughed again. "Something like that. How are you and my little niece or nephew doing?"

"Besides the obvious, great."

He kissed her temple, sat back and watched the interview with her. Nothing new was revealed, but Lily was glad to hear Adam openly talk about his past, the many organizations he and his friends have established on the island to help abused children and people with eating disorders.

Somewhere in the night, Lily opened her eyes, surprised to find herself nicely tucked in on the sofa. Rafa had stayed and kept her company well after the interview ended. They talked and laughed like old times. She must have drifted. She caught the red blinking light on her DVR indicating Adam's race was going on. She turned on the TV and caught Adam cross the finish line. He won the race, finishing the season as the top F1 driver. This time when he stepped out of the car with champagne splashing over him, he scrubbed his face and laughed as he accepted accolades from his teammates, but there was no scantily clad woman in his arms or kissing him.

"Adam," the pretty Russian reporter said with a smile. "Are you going by Cooper now?"

"No," he answered without a beat. "I love my parents. They invested in me. They gave me a home, their name and love." He smiled. "In a way they gave me life. It is because of them I am who I am today. I'll forever be an Aquilani."

So he was able to say the word, just not to her. Lily's heart sank.

The pretty woman beamed at him. "And who would you like to dedicate this thrilling win to? It was a close one."

Adam chuckled. "It definitely was. We have some great drivers on the scene. This win is for my parents, of course. And for Liliana and our baby."

Lily's heart stumbled.

"Who's Liliana?"

Adam chuckled and ran a hand through his wet silky hair. "My fiancée. I'm in love with her."

"Oh wow! Congratulations," she said smiling.

He said the words. She stared at the television screen but no longer listening. She missed him. She loved him. She wanted him to shout his love to the world and he gave that to her, leaving no room for doubts. Talk about a public service announcement. Her heart did that little dance only reserved for Adam as happiness washed over her. He'd officially given her everything she ever wanted from him.

Her heart pounded in her throat. She grabbed her cell phone on the coffee table and checked the time. Four a.m.. Damn, too early to call anyone for some distraction. She turned off the television, lay back on the sofa and pulled the blanket all the way up to her chin. In the dark, she stared at the ceiling, listening to her thundering heartbeat, wondering how quickly she could get back to the island. And sadly admitting sleep had eluded her once more, but this time for all the right reasons.

After jamming on Lily's doorbell several times, Adam dug in his pocket for his keys and opened the entrance door to Lily's condo. He rushed up the stairs, taking two at a time and nearly broke down the door when it swung open. He came face to face with Rafa.

Really, he wasn't in the mood.

"Out of my way," he growled, walking past Lily's brother.

"She's not here."

He whipped around to face Rafa. "What do you mean? She has a doctor's appointment."

"Exactly what I said, she's not here."

"Well!"

"Well what?"

Adam raked a hand through his hair. At this point, he was ready to pull off his entire head of hair. "Where the fuck is she? Jesus, you're an asshole."

Rafa shrugged. "Are you here to tell her you love her?"

"My relationship with Lily is not your business." He looked around the room, searching for some indication where she might be. He checked his watch. They still had one hour before her appointment.

"Actually, she'll always be my business. She's my baby sister."

He surveyed Rafa's chiseled face. He recalled the conversation between the siblings, the mention of Lea and how he had reacted to it. *Don't go there, Adam, sensitive topic.* Eventually they'd be family, so for now he took it easy on the big goof. Besides, everyone had a story. Who was he to judge? "Fine," he said in a reluctant tone. "I'm here to tell her."

Rafa smiled. A fucking smug one at that too.

"Good, because I was about to come back to that awful island of yours and kick your ass silly or until you were able to declare your undying love."

Somehow Adam believed Rafa. Well, at least the try to kick his ass part…actually succeeding at it that was another matter.

"Treat her well."

Adam smiled. "I intend to."

An awkward silence fell in the room. An accord reached. Neither moved. But the tension that had been thick around them since their first meet dissipated.

"What is going on here?" a male voice asked from the door.

Rafa and Adam turned to the lean, athletic, Ken-like man standing by the open door. Adam looked back at Rafa. Lily's brother shrugged.

"Who the fuck is that?"

"That's Ken, also known as Nate," Rafa answered with barely a glance in Nate's direction.

Adam made a mental note to share a beer with Rafa soon over the Ken comment. "You mean the cheating ex?"

Rafa nodded with a look *yep, that's the asshole* look on his face.

Adam walked up to Ken, AKA Nate. "What do you want?"

"Who the fuck are you?" Nate asked in a surprisingly brave tone.

"Liliana's fiancé. You should leave if you don't want your face rearranged."

Rafa chuckled. "I'd help, but I promised my sister I wouldn't touch him. I signed my name in blood."

"Well, I'm too smart to make such a stupid promise. Get out!"

Ken-Nate squared his shoulders. "I'm here to see Lily."

"She's not here," Rafa informed the cheating bastard. "You should leave or you can't say I didn't warn you."

"I'm not leaving. I want to speak to Lily."

Rafa snorted.

"Liliana is not here." Adam's eyes narrowed to crinkled slits on Nate. "Leave."

Nate walked past Adam into the living room. "Stop calling her that. Her name is Lily. Everyone calls her Lily."

Adam grabbed Nate's shoulder and spun him around to face him. "I'm not everyone. I'm the guy who can keep his dick in his pants when he makes a promise to a woman. Now get the fuck out." Nate tried to stare him down and failed. Adam crossed his arms over his chest. "I met her right after she found out you cheated on her. She put up this façade, but I also saw her broken down and sad. How could you do that to a woman you claimed to love?"

Nate shoved his hands in his pockets. "I want her back."

This time Rafa's deep laughter filled the room. "You're not getting her back. She's in love with him." He pointed at Adam. "I mean the crazy, passionate kind of love that only happens once in a lifetime."

Adam pulled his phone from his jacket. He scrolled to Lily's number and texted.

Where are you?

Her response flashed on his phone.

At the doctor. Why?

Adam shoved the phone back in his pocket and fixed his eyes on Nate. "She told you to let her go. I heard her. I was standing right next to her. You should. And I'm not saying that because I'm threatened by you. I'm saying it because you're her past, not her future." And just because he was a guy he added, "That's where I come in."

---

*L*ily flipped through the magazine appropriately titled *Pregnancy*. Hard to believe two weeks ago, she sat in the same room with her heart in her throat with angst. She looked at Adam's text again, and her bare finger where his ring once sheathed.

A soft knock came from the door. "Come in," she called to Paige and Dr. Mason.

Paige entered the room. "Dr. Mason will be here soon."

Lily studied the nurse. There was a slight tension behind her smile. "Is everything okay?" she asked with concern. She'd done the usual urine thing before her visit and wondered if something showed up.

Paige's eyes rested on her left hand for a second. "You're engaged. Where's your ring?"

"I'm not engaged." No point asking Paige how she got the scoop of her love life. She'd bet her savings where the nurse got her information and Lily would win. Her nosy, pain-in-the-ass brothers. "I mean, I am but I'm not."

Paige smiled. "Which one is it?"

She sighed. "I guess I am, but we're not together." At least not yet, he was still in Russia.

"Is his name Adam Aquilani?"

Puzzled, she met Paige's gaze. "How do you know his name?"

Paige smiled. "Beside the fact I'm a big Formula One fan." She grinned. "He's also in the waiting room demanding to be in here with you."

Lily's heart took a leap. "He's in Russia," she said in an effort to keep herself calm.

But the nurse shook her head. "He's here. Of course we have to protect our clients and refused to let him in until you approved it."

She recalled Adam's promise to not miss any of her appointments. He must be exhausted. The effort, the thought, the act, made her heart squeeze. "He can come in."

Paige squeezed her hand and headed for the door. "A little bird told me he met all three of your brothers."

Lily rolled her eyes. "It was a sight."

"Who gave him the hardest time?"

"Guess."

"I'd bet my savings on Rafa."

"You'd win."

Paige laughed. "I'll bring him in."

As soon as the door closed behind Paige, Lily jumped off the doctor bed, grabbed her compact powder and applied a stroke of lip gloss on her bare lips. She had bags under her eyes and truth be told, she looked tired, but she could blame that on the pregnancy, not the fact she hadn't slept much since she returned home because every night she reached for him.

And damn it, why had she already changed into that wretched gown?

They had to be the most unattractive thing ever created. She ran a hand through her hair, fluffed up her bangs and lightly patted her cheeks in hope for some color. It didn't work. So she sat back on the gurney with her socks down to her ankles, in the hideous, flimsy gown tied to her front, and tried to look as calm as possible when the soft knock came on the door again.

She cleared her throat, and edged some distance between her and the stirrups. The last thing she wanted Adam to think about was her spreading it wide for her obstetrician. "Come in," she called with her best I'm in control voice, only it cracked at the end.

The door pushed open. Paige appeared first, and then Lily's heart stammered as her eyes went straight to the tall, rugged man with a few days' old scruff and face set in a hard determined expression.

"You have ten minutes," Paige said, then left them alone.

He stood there for a minute. He scanned her from head to toe, his eyes stayed a moment too long on the pink and blue socks scrunched to her ankle then his gaze met hers, a soft smile curved his lips. "I came here straight from Russia," he said in a quiet voice.

"You must be tired," she said, heart pounding so hard she couldn't hear herself think. "You didn't have to come." But inside she was grinning like a ten-year-old with delight. Never mind the bags under his eyes were a dead giveaway he was tuckered out.

"I promised I would. But more importantly, Liliana, I want to be here."

She watched him walk across the room to the chair. He picked it up and brought it next to where she sat. He plopped his big body down and looked up to her.

"What are you doing, Adam?"

He took her hands in his and placed a kiss on the back of her hands. "I'm giving you my heart. If you still want it."

She was going to cry again, she could feel the tears burning the back of her eyes. She squeezed her eyes shut and shook her head. "I can't cry here."

He let out a low laugh. "Open your eyes, Liliana, and look at me."

Slowly, she did as he asked and saw all the emotions she knew he felt in his heart reflecting in his eyes. "I'm looking, Adam. I've been looking and I'm scared that what I see may not be what you feel."

"I'm in love with you, Liliana Serrano," he said quietly. "So much I fucking ache."

Her heart skipped. It had been surreal to hear him declare his love on television in front of millions of viewers. Still, it didn't compare to this private moment between them. Love, affection, and need rushed through her.

"That day I saw you walk by the Shanty with Minka, you took my breath away at that moment. Then the night at the beach, I lost myself in you, to you then." He smiled. "I'm forever yours."

With her heart in her throat, she let the tears flow.

"I can't tell if you're happy or if these are 'You're too late, Adam' tears."

Between the tears, she laughed at his words.

"I've been very careful not to say those words to a woman other than my mother and my extended family. But you've changed that. My mind is still fucked up somewhat, but the idea of losing you…" He shook his head. "I'd say it over and over for you."

"I love you. I tried to fight it. I was scared to love you, but my heart flipped on me and I fell really hard."

Adam rose to his feet, cupped her face in his hands and kissed her. "So I'm not too late."

She wrapped her arms around his neck and looked into his eyes. She saw all she ever wanted, hope, love, need and affection. "You can never be too late."

He kissed her then. His lips were firm and gentle as he pulled her in, burning her lips with his mouth until everything left her brain but this moment.

"Your ex stopped by your apartment," he said when they finally broke for air. "Are you sure that's over?"

Lily frowned. "I'll talk to him again."

"Are you sure that's over?"

She ran a finger over the scar on his brow. "I've learned from my relationship with Nate, but I let go of him a long time ago. It's about you. Us." She looked down at her belly. "And our baby."

Adam grinned. "I get to see him today."

"Or her."

He laughed. "It doesn't matter." He leaned down and kissed her, then ran the pad of his thumb over her temple, tucking a loose strand of hair behind her ear. "We should get married soon."

"Like how soon?"

He seemed to think about it for a beat then shrugged. "I don't care. Tomorrow if you want."

"We can't do that. Your parents would be so disappointed."

He chuckled. "Okay, how about this weekend? I can have them back in the States by tomorrow night."

She looked at him. "You're serious."

"Very serious."

"No regrets."

He looked her over. "I should ask you that."

Heart filled with joy and fluttering like a zoo, she tugged down the man she was going to marry on top of her and kissed him hard. "No regrets. And yes, I'll marry you whenever you want, Adam Aquilani. But you should ask me first. I don't even have an engagement ring."

After one more lingering kiss, Adam reached in his jeans pocket and produced the ring he once put on her finger. His expression turned serious, very serious. "Before I ask, I should tell you I am going to start going to counseling in Boston once a week for a couple of months. It will help me deal."

Her heart swelled. She touched his face, loving the feel of his skin. "What about prescriptions?"

He shook his head. "No meds. I sleep now, but I still need to accept some things."

She nodded, understanding the guilt he carried in his heart. "Anything else?" she asked after a beat.

"That's it."

Her brows went up. "I still don't have my ring."

He chuckled, then dropped to a knee. His expression once again grew very serious. "Liliana Serrano, will you marry me and give me forever?"

Her heart kicked hard. The emotions she felt on the beach when Adam first proposed washed over her once more. She leaned into him, slipped and nearly fell on top of Adam. His arms automatically circled her waist, holding her close.

"Don't fall."

She leaned into him and wrapped her arms around his neck. "Too late, I've already fallen."

He held her gaze. "Is that a yes?"

She smiled. "A big, loud yes."

"The ring stays on forever, Liliana, no matter what. Promise me you will never take it off."

"You have me, Adam." She leaned into him and lightly brushed her mouth on his. "For a lifetime."

His mouth captured hers, soothing every ache in her heart and soul. She wrapped her arms tight around his neck. And it felt good. It felt right.

The End

SNEAK PEEK OF TATTOOED HEARTS
BOOK 3 OF THE MARTHA'S WAY SERIES

Chapter One

Sneak Peek of Tattooed Hearts

> "One of the hardest things in life is having words in your heart that you can't utter."
> James Earl Jones

Vineyard Haven, Martha's Vineyard, thirteen years ago . . .

Claire ran her tongue over her lips, checking their current state. A soft, smooth, and slightly-moist mouth was ideal for kissing. Hers didn't feel chapped or dry, but to be on the safe side, she swiped the shea butter pomegranate chapstick over her lips, pressed them together then blew into her hands for a breath check.

Minty fresh.

Perfect.

The girls she knew were experts in the art of kissing. It embarrassed her to admit at fifteen, she hadn't kissed anyone. But they didn't pass judgment. Rather, her friends had given her pointers and informed her fresh breath was essential for a French kiss. For that reason, she managed to avoid garlic, onions, milk, and her favorite, corn. The tasty grain was on the *Cosmopolitan* list of "What Not to Eat" before a kiss. Last thing she wanted was Forrest pushing her away because of corn residue in her mouth.

Her gaze swept over Herring Creek Farm. The August sun shone on green everywhere. The edge of woodland sloped down gently to a bramble-filled ditch, overgrown with cow parsley. Beech trees lined the fence to the north. Their overhanging boughs provided dapple shade for the horses that stood idle, flicking away flies with their tails. Chirping birds and humming bees filled the air with the sounds of their daily duties.

Male laughter rose as Jason, Adam, and Blake tossed a football between them in the yard. They rarely let her wander away from their view, not that she had a wild streak or anything, but they were Alphas and they hovered. Always uncertain of what the band of brothers might throw at her, she didn't dare get too close to the boys. They loved to throw questions at her or worse, ask her to participate in their football tossing game, just so they could play the big brother role.

Sneak Peek of Tattooed Hearts

Big brothers tended to be overbearing.

Phooey! She wasn't even related to any of them.

Her gaze swiveled to Forrest. He stood not too far away in cargo Khakis and a fading Transformers T-shirt, throwing tennis balls to his father's two black Labs.

Warmth spread inside her chest, a sensation that was now synonymous with Forrest. The sight of him held an intriguing allure. Tall, athletic, with tousled dark brown hair that flopped over his eyes. Woven leather bracelets encircled his left wrist, drawing attention to the lean, hard muscles of his arms. All that football and skiing had done wonders for his amazing frame. His face wasn't too shabby either—sharp, angled jaw, full, firm lips that curved into a proud yet pleasant smile, and a nose that was just a little too big. The slight imperfection only made him more appealing.

Women often stopped in their tracks and stared at him. Claire noticed the admirers every time, but Forrest seemed oblivious to the sudden pauses and clandestine stares. When he did bestow them with a glance, his fans overcompensated with a weak smile or a blush, a dead giveaway of their admiration. He always took it in stride, never flaunted, and without a trace of arrogance. He was modest and unaware of the chaos he caused; this made the girls fall for him all the more.

According to the few conversations she overheard between Jason and the others, teenage boys were horny all the time. They thought about sex every second of the day. If the wind hit them just right, they would get excited.

Not Forrest.

He thought with the head on his shoulders, not the one south of his waist. He was different that way and stood apart from the others. Despite the opportunities that came his way, he dated very little. She once overheard him telling the other guys he was a one-woman man who prized genuineness and thoughtful conversation above lipstick and high heels.

He was handsome, breathtaking. Her racing pulse and breathlessness proved it. However, what she really loved about him was his inner beauty. From the way he cared for the animals on the farm, to his

Sneak Peek of Tattooed Hearts

warmth with everyone on the island, and his commitment to his family and friends. He was eighteen–if a day older–and he stole her heart without even knowing it was in his pocket.

For the last two years, these new and strange feelings often left her befuddled. They were too strong, too intense. Physically and mentally, she reacted to him in a way she never had with any boy. The slightest touch, whether it was tugging on her hair or fixing her backpack, sent her heart spiraling out of control. On days they weren't around each other, she missed him. When she saw him, heard his name, happiness filled her. At night, his face was always the last thing she'd see; her stomach would backflip and she'd tingle all over before drifting into a dream where they held hands and kissed.

Now in a few days he'd leave the island and head to Boston for college. Her heart screeched in anguish, its flesh lay bare in the raucous collision between reality and fantasy.

She had to kiss him. And for that she needed complete privacy.

She studied the stoned-faced, two story red barn with an old, worn-down tractor collecting dust next to it. She glanced at the boys, still lost in whatever they were talking about. Probably all the college girls they would be meeting when they arrived on campus. Which meant Forrest would be meeting college girls, too—knowledgeable, sophisticated girls living away from their parents, who no doubt would be on him as quick as lightning.

Panic set in. Fear. Her chance with Forrest was slipping through her fingers. She needed to kiss him and let him feel everything in her heart.

Here goes nothing.

Stealthily she moved around the farm and hauled open the unwieldy door, tired hinges creaking like a testy old man. She paused and waited for one of the boys to call after her. When they didn't, she rushed inside, closed the door behind her, and sucked in a deep breath, calming her nerves. A puff of the sweet, musty summer's straw odor pressed into her nose.

The barn had recently undergone extensive renovations by Luc and Marjorie, Forrest's parents. Old flooring was removed and replaced with a new tongue and groove floor. Claire walked passed the stalls

Sneak Peek of Tattooed Hearts

with rubber mats and hay racks to the corner away from the windows in case the boys peeked around. She dug inside her second-hand hobo bag for the ripe plum carefully picked from her mother's kitchen. Her friends had told her to find a nice piece of soft fruit that tasted good.

Tilting her head to one side, she bit a mouth-sized hole into the plum. The taut skin of the fruit was tangy, a complete contrast to the sweet juice that rolled down the side of her mouth. With a flick of her tongue at the corner of her lip, she licked away the sweet nectar.

It was delicious, just like how she'd imagined Forrest would taste.

She went in for another bite. Her eyes lulled shut as she drowned in the fantasy of kissing Forrest. She pushed her tongue into the flesh of the plum a little more and surrendered to the sheer pleasure of experimenting.

"Claire."

Startled, she jumped back and almost toppled over. The plum slipped from her hands onto the ground. *Oh. My. God.* Utter humiliation. Forrest saw her kissing a freakin' plum. She stood frozen, silently praying he'd turn and walk out of the barn, instead she listened to his steps closing in on her until they stood facing each other, barely inches apart.

He picked up the plum, brushed off the collected dirt, and examined it for a second or two. His eyebrows knitted close together. "Were you kissing a plum?"

"No." She tried to grab the fruit from him, but the big goof was already six feet tall and built like a quarterback compared to her small, five-feet-two-inch frame. He lifted his arm out of her reach.

"Then what were you doing?"

Pretending I'm kissing you. Pathetic. "Um…nothing."

His gaze searched her face. Claire's first reaction was to make a run for it, but then Jason would think one of his best buds did something to her. Mortified, she lowered her head and focused on the floor.

"Claire, look at me." His voice was low, with a trace of huskiness and authority.

There was no rescue from this embarrassment. Pure absolute torture. She coughed and pushed her hair back behind her ear, even though it was already there. He caught her chin and raised her face, forcing her to look at him. His eyes were gray, not a dull, unremarkable gray like that of concrete or stone, but a combination of misty gray and blue like the ocean at dusk. They were sensual, alluring, and warm. They beckoned her to reveal her deepest secrets, and to lose herself in their warmth.

"Who is the guy?"

A thick fog dampened her ability to think. "What?"

"The guy you want to kiss. Your crush." His eyes searched hers for answers. "Who is he?"

You. She wanted to scream. Instead her heart tripped and stalled.

"Claire, who's the guy?" His voice racked her brain as she scrambled for a name of any fifteen-year-old boy from her class. But they lived on an island where everyone knew everyone's business. If she was brave enough to lie—for the record she wasn't—the boy would have to live his life in fear with her four protectors breathing down his throat.

"I don't have a crush."

He smiled. "So I didn't just catch you making out with a plum?"

She turned hastily and tried to run off, but mortification followed. Forrest stepped in front of her, blocking her escape.

"Have you kissed your crush?"

"No." She tried to walk past him. He inched closer to the door. "I need to go," she said and hoped she sounded annoyed and angry. Unfazed, he made no attempt to move.

"Have you kissed anyone?"

Something in his voice grabbed her attention. It was low and gravelly as if he cared whether or not she'd been kissed before. Chin up, she stared into the eyes that had captured her heart, caught the twinkle of amusement, and her stomach flopped in disappointment.

Silly of her to think Forrest might actually look at her and see an actual girl with feelings instead of Jason's shadow. As if that wasn't bad enough, he was one of the Vineyard's elite. She was the half African-American, half-Japanese, flat-chested girl who lived in the same house with his best friend. Not that he was ever rude just…indif-

Sneak Peek of Tattooed Hearts

ferent. Unlike the others, he never went out of his way for her. Once or twice, she'd caught him looking her way, brows knitted, an annoyed look on his face. No, never rude. But his opinion of her was clear; she was the little girl who followed his best friend everywhere. A nuisance, plain and simple.

Humiliation quickly turned to anger. She planted her legs wide and crossed her arms over chest. "How did you know I was in here?"

He shrugged. "You weren't outside."

"I could have been by the lake."

The corners of his mouth lifted up, then his smile widened into a grin. "I saw you come in."

"You were watching me."

His eyes narrowed. "We all watch over you. That's what we do."

Not exactly what she'd hoped to hear. Realizing she stood no chance to win this banter, she quickly opted for plan B. The truth. What she wanted most in the world. To be kissed by him. She edged further into the room and leaned her elbows on the window sill, her denim shorts brushing against the dusty wall.

"Fine. You were right," she started in a low voice, her back to him. "I was practicing kissing because I've never been kissed."

"Go on."

"*Cosmopolitan* has a step-by-step guide on how to practice kissing and I was following the instructions." She paused and inspected her battered red Converse, building courage to spill everything. "But it also says the best practice is with another person." She turned to look at him. "Will you kiss me, Forrest?"

"No," he answered without a beat.

The swift blow of rejection knocked every wisp of air from her lungs. Claire struggled to inhale, to exhale, to do anything. Stunned and disoriented, she swiftly turned her attention back to the window. The sun stung her eyes, they watered. She quickly batted away escaped tears.

"Claire," he said, his voice a bit more soothing. "You're so young."

"I'm fifteen," she said in a desperate voice caught between frustration and crying.

Sneak Peek of Tattooed Hearts

"And I'm eighteen."

She whipped around and looked straight at him. "We're only three years apart."

He smiled. "Right now, it feels like ten."

They stood, staring at each other in a companionable silence, broken only when Forrest let out a deep breath.

"I'm leaving for college in a few days."

Although it was summer, the words chilled her spine. She needed to kiss him and let him see, feel everything she felt inside but could find no words to express. "What if I wasn't fifteen?"

"Still no."

The rejection, although gentler this time, still cut deep into her heart.

"Am I that unappealing to you?"

He dragged his fingers through his hair. "Claire."

She held up a hand. "It doesn't matter. Most of the boys here are trying to figure out what to make of me. An African-American-Asian girl. Is she pretty or just weird-looking?" She shrugged with indifference, but deep down the quick glances here and there bothered her.

"What do you care what others think? You're beautiful."

An equal mixture of pure ecstasy and excruciating pain made her heart go pit-a-pat. "You think I'm beautiful?"

He nodded. "Definitely."

"So why won't you kiss me?"

With quick strides, he came to stand next to her and gently stroked her cheek with the pad of his thumb. "You should be kissing boys your own age."

She looked into his eyes and her heart swelled from the emotion bottled inside. Feelings even she didn't understand, let alone try to express. He gave her a quick smile then walked back to the door. The bitter taste of regret stung her tongue like a rusty razor blade. The moment she had planned, spent so many sleepless nights imagining, had slipped from her hands.

He opened the door and turned to look at her once more. "When you do kiss your crush, I hope it's everything you imagined it to be."

Sneak Peek of Tattooed Hearts

He smiled—a sweet, sexy smile that got her all flustered—and then he walked out of the barn.

* * * *

Rain lashed down on Claire in cold, icy pellets bit into her skin. Wet grass and dirt mushed under her shoes, slashing up her legs and staining the skirt of her dress. Focusing on Forrest, she quickened her pace. She had fallen asleep watching her favorite soap opera.

Stupid. Stupid. Stupid.

She'd almost missed him.

"Forrest," she called after him, heart in her throat, fearful he would enter his parents' waiting pick-up truck and drive away forever. "Forrest," she screamed his name again, a dozen needles dancing in her stomach. She stopped, her breathing stuttered in her lungs, exhausted from fear.

Please look at me.

He slowed his steps and after a second or two he turned. "Claire," he said, squinting.

Her heart leaped with joy. She caught him just before his parents drove away to catch the ferry to Falmouth. Smiling, she ran forward, closing the distance between them, and said through ragged breaths, "You're leaving."

"I know." He looked over his shoulder at his parents' truck. "What are you doing? It's pouring."

She launched herself at him, strong arms clamped around her waist, shut her eyes, and whispered, "I love you."

For a minute neither moved. Time stopped. They stood still, holding on to each other, their bodies drenched from the downpour. She shivered, not from the coldness of the rain but the string of electricity shooting through her veins. Her heart, like a fly in a cobweb with nothing to do, waited for his laughter to confirm how ridiculous she sounded. But it didn't come. Sucking in a breath, she waited a little longer. Except for the huge raindrops splattering with charged energy, there was absolute silence.

Sneak Peek of Tattooed Hearts

Slowly, she opened her eyes and looked into the depth of his gray ones. A fluttery feeling took over her body. "Forrest."

He swept back her matted hair, and his lips cracked into a smile. "I'm your crush."

She shook her head. A crush was the lowest level of romance. Her feelings ran beyond that. "It's not a crush."

"Claire, you're fifteen."

The world around her began collapsing. "I'm in love with you," she said emphatically.

"It's an infatuation."

No. No. This was bigger than an intense, naïve, adolescent admiration. She searched his face for any hint that just maybe deep down he believed her, only to come up short. Empty. Nothing. Feeling weak and hopeless, her shoulders slumped. She was losing this battle. "You're going to have sex in college."

He let out a heavy sigh. "Claire."

"I know about sex."

"Jesus, Claire, if you're having sex with some douchebag."

"I'm not having sex," she cried, fighting back the tears threatening to spill. "But I know what it is. I don't want you doing it with girls in college." She grabbed his arms. "Please wait for me."

"What makes you think I haven't had sex?"

Raindrops, hard and thick, hit her face like bullets. With a quick brush of her hand, she swept a handful of hair away from her face. "I overheard you telling the guys you were waiting for that person." She was making a fool of herself but at this point what did it matter. "You want it to be special…your first time." She swallowed the panic choking her. "I want to be your first, Forrest, and you mine. I love you."

He looked at her for a long moment. His eyes became shadowed. Hope bubbled in her stomach. And then he sighed, took a step back and broke their connection. Her heart dropped all the way to her toes.

"This is a crush. It will pass," he said quietly.

"No." He owned her heart. Forever. It didn't matter she was only fifteen. Some things only happened once in a lifetime and had nothing to do with age. "Promise me, you'll at least try to wait for me."

"I have to go. I'm sorry, Claire." He touched her face and stared at her for a long beat. "One day you'll look back at this and laugh."

"No," she choked.

"Yes."

Their gazes locked. The pitiless rain continued thrashing her skin.

Forrest took her hand in his and brought it to his lips. "I have to go." He released his grip and walked to his parents' truck. For a brief moment, he hesitated and looked back. Hope stirred low in her belly, then he tossed his backpack in the truck and shut the door.

Nausea pained her stomach, heart and chest. She had waited for this moment to come forward with her deepest feelings and bring to life those three words she'd been harboring.

She fought and lost.

Her world collapsed.

Emotionally bankrupt, she stood in dazed isolation and took the onslaught of the chilled rain. Her wet dress hugged her, its weight heavy and oppressing. With blind eyes to the world, she stared at the shadow of the pick-up taillights until they faded. It was hard to tell when she started crying and even more difficult to discern between her tears and the rain as she turned her face to the sky above. Her eyelids fluttered to deflect the water, she wanted to move, to run, but her legs were weak and incapable of doing anything. So she stood in the pelting rain and let her body and mind drown in the cold, wet afternoon.

CLICK HERE to order Tattooed Hearts! My Book

NEED YOU NOW PLAYLIST

Need You Now Spotify Playlist

When I Get My Hands on You
The New Basement
It Was My Reason
Okkervil River
Need You Now
Lady Antebellum
Numb
Gary Clark Jr.
Let Her Go
Passenger
I Feel That Too
Jessie Baylin
Ain't No Sunshine
Bill Withers
TRansliterator
DeVotchKa
Just Give Me a Reason
P!nk & Nate Ruess

Need You Now Playlist

Not Ready to Make Nice
Dixie Chicks
Sleeping By Myself
Pearl Jam
You Do Something To Me
Paul Weller

ACKNOWLEDGMENTS

To my husband, thank you so much for all of your support and for taking over our happy chaos when I need to write. A toast to our lifetime of dating. You are my biggest fan and that makes you even sexier than you already are. Je t'aime.

My wonderful group of writers – WWLR and the ladies at Three Chicas and a Book. What can I say? You ROCK!

A big awesome hooray to my beta readers for your patience and your sage words. What can I say? We make a great team. You continue to push me and make me better.

Last but not least, to all the readers – without you this wouldn't be as much fun. Thank you so much for all you've helped me to accomplish.

ABOUT MIKA

Mika Jolie lives in New Jersey with her Happy Chaos—her husband and their energizer bunnies. She's a lover of words, wonder, an old-fashioned, and the whimsical delights of everyday living. When she's not writing swoon-worthy, sexy relatable romance, you can find her on a hiking adventure, beachin' it at the Jersey shore, apple, blueberry picking, or whatever her three men can conjure up.

Connect with Mika at . . .

BookBub
Mika Jolie's Wildflowers
Facebook
Amazon
Instagram
Bookandmainbites
Goodreads

ALSO BY MIKA
MARTHA'S WAY SERIES

Martha's Way Series
The Scale

Need You Now

Tattooed Hearts

Wrapped in Red

Need You Now

Platonically Complicated
The Boy Friend

Explicitly Yours

Rules of Engagement

Playing for Keeps
Intercepted Hearts

Defenseless Hearts

Standalone Novels
Somewhere to Begin

Layla's Chance

One Complicated Christmas

Freebie
Online Dating

HOT TODDY RECIPE

Hot Toddy Recipe from Need You Now—Book Two of Martha's Way

Adam prepared a hot toddy for Lilly the night she was fighting a cold. That was so sweet of the bad boy, wasn't it?

This salubrious drink is soothing and taste pretty good. The key to this drink is the way it balances sweet and sour elements while adding the complexities of spice and alcohol. Oh by the way, the alcohol inside the whiskey also helps fight off infection and the growth of microorganisms. Seriously, I'm not kidding.

Hot Toddy Recipe:
Ingredients
10 m 1 servings
1 teaspoon honey
2 fluid ounces boiling water
1 1/2 fluid ounces whiskey
3 whole cloves 1 cinnamon stick
1 slice lemon 1 pinch ground nutmeg
Directions
Pour the honey, boiling water, and whiskey into a mug. Spice it

Hot Toddy Recipe

with the cloves and cinnamon, and put in the slice of lemon. Let the mixture stand for 5 minutes so the flavors can mingle, then sprinkle with a pinch of nutmeg before serving.

Prep Time: 5 min
Ready In: 10 minutes

Made in the USA
Columbia, SC
06 July 2021